# "Watch the orb, Kane."

The tiny sphere suddenly turned scarlet, seeming to swell, ripping open the vast backdrop of the sky as if it were rotten old cloth. The translucent orb burst open from within, releasing a bloom of hellfire. A sheet of flame paled the sky, surging outward and upward. The waves of the sea divided and the orange-yellow incandescent flare poured into Kane and filled him to the backs of his eyeballs.

A coruscating wall of fire scorched the ocean, riding a booming shock wave, pushing the ocean ahead of it in an overlapping series of mile-high tsunamis. Kane tried to squeeze his eyes shut; he felt paralyzed, rooted to the spot like a statue. A wall of smoke swept over him, obscuring the shoreline and Fand, but he could still hear her.

"History will repeat itself if you do not heed me. And if you do not play your preordained role, this time there will be no survivors."

**Other titles in this series:**

# JAMES AXLER

# OUTLANDERS®

## HELL RISING

## A GOLD EAGLE BOOK FROM
# WORLDWIDE®

TORONTO • NEW YORK • LONDON
AMSTERDAM • PARIS • SYDNEY • HAMBURG
STOCKHOLM • ATHENS • TOKYO • MILAN
MADRID • WARSAW • BUDAPEST • AUCKLAND

First edition August 2000

ISBN 0-373-63827-2

HELL RISING

Special thanks to Mark Ellis for his contribution to the Outlanders concept, developed for Gold Eagle.

# HELL RISING

## The Road to Outlands—
## From Secret Government Files to the Future

Almost two hundred years after the global holocaust, Kane, a former Magistrate of Cobaltville, often thought the world had been lucky to survive at all after a nuclear device detonated in the Russian embassy in Washington, D.C. The aftermath—forever known as skydark—reshaped continents and turned civilization into ashes.

Nearly depopulated, America became the Deathlands—poisoned by radiation, home to chaos and mutated life forms. Feudal rule reappeared in the form of baronies, while remote outposts clung to a brutish existence.

What eventually helped shape this wasteland were the redoubts, the secret preholocaust military installations with stores of weapons, and the home of gateways, the locational matter-transfer facilities. Some of the redoubts hid clues that had once fed wild theories of government cover-ups and alien visitations.

Rearmed from redoubt stockpiles, the barons consolidated their power and reclaimed technology for the villes. Their power, supported by some invisible authority, extended beyond their fortified walls to what was now called the Outlands. It was here that the rootstock of humanity survived, living with hellzones and chemical storms, hounded by Magistrates.

In the villes, rigid laws were enforced—to atone for the sins of the past and prepare the way for a better future. That was the barons' public credo and their right-to-rule.

Kane, along with friend and fellow Magistrate Grant, had upheld that claim until a fateful Outlands expedition. A displaced piece of technology...a question to a keeper of the archives...a vague clue about alien masters—and their world shifted radically. Suddenly, Brigid Baptiste, the archivist, faced summary execution, and

Grant a quick termination. For Kane there was forgiveness if he pledged his unquestioning allegiance to Baron Cobalt and his unknown masters and abandoned his friends.

But that allegiance would make him support a mysterious and alien power and deny loyalty and friends. Then what else was there?

Kane had been brought up solely to serve the ville. Brigid's only link with her family was her mother's redgold hair, green eyes and supple form. Grant's clues to his lineage were his ebony skin and powerful physique. But Domi, she of the white hair, was an Outlander pressed into sexual servitude in Cobaltville. She at least knew her roots and was a reminder to the exiles that the outcasts belonged in the human family.

Parents, friends, community—the very rootedness of humanity was denied. With no continuity, there was no forward momentum to the future. And that was the crux—when Kane began to wonder if there *was* a future.

For Kane, it wouldn't do. So the only way was out—way, way out.

After their escape, they found shelter at the forgotten Cerberus redoubt headed by Lakesh, a scientist, Cobaltville's head archivist, and secret opponent of the barons.

With their past turned into a lie, their future threatened, only one thing was left to give meaning to the outcasts. The hunger for freedom, the will to resist the hostile influences. And perhaps, by opposing, end them.

# Chapter 1

*The North Atlantic*

The staccato rap of knuckles on wood barely roused Aubrey Quayle from his meditations. The study of Plato in the original Greek required such concentration he almost entered an altered state, especially since his comprehension of the language was completely self-taught. To absorb the text, Quayle practiced a form of autohypnosis, regulating his breathing and employing a relaxation technique he had learned as a private in the Imperial Dragoons.

The knock sounded again, but he continued to stare at the open book, pendulous lips unconsciously forming the words imprinted on the page, translating them into English: "O Solon, you Greeks are children. There have been and will be many destructions of mankind, of which the greatest are by fire and water."

Quayle couldn't argue with that bit of precognition, even had he cared to do so. The rap on his office door came a third time, louder and more insistent. Placing a blunt index finger on the sentence, he lifted his head. "Come."

The door opened and Corporal Jefferies stepped in, ducking his head both in deference and to keep his beret from being scraped off by the low frame. Snapping off a brisk salute, he announced, "It's time, Captain."

The corporal wore the dark red uniform of the dragoons, consisting of a hip-length leather jacket and beret canted at an angle on his close-cropped blond hair. The beret bore an insignia patch displaying a coiled, bat-winged serpent, bloodred, outlined against a black background. Mirrored sunglasses concealed his eyes. A Beretta M-92 autopistol hung in shoulder leather. The right side of his face bore a geometric design, a black rectangle superimposed over a small chevron.

"Thank you, Mr. Jefferies," Quayle replied. He poked around among the rolled charts and stacked volumes cluttering his desk and found a silver bookmark. Carefully, he closed the leather-bound book and levered himself upright by the arms of his chair. Wood creaked in protest.

Captain Aubrey Quayle towered a full head above the corporal. He wore a nearly identical uniform, except for shiny metal epaulets on the shoulders of the jacket. His massive belly strained the seams. He had always been a quartermaster's nightmare, even in his teens when the Imperium Britannia had first conscripted him into the dragoons.

His huge head, the size and shape of a pumpkin, rose between the broad yoke of his shoulders. It was completely hairless, both eyebrows and scalp a naked grotesquerie of dead white flesh and scar tracings. His left eye gleamed like a ruby, but his right was black, the iris a milky blue. A wealed, ridged mass of scar tissue surrounded the socket and creased across his heavy jowl, bisecting the two vertical bars tattooed into the flesh.

A pale slab of a hand removed his beret from a hook on the wall, and he took some time placing it just so on his bald pate. Jefferies respectfully stood aside in a parade-rest posture as Quayle swiftly inspected his reflection in a small mirror. Then he turned to squeeze his four-hundred-pound, six-foot-seven bulk through the doorway.

Followed by Jefferies, he lumbered down the passageway that connected the port and starboard quarters, the din of the four diesel engines filling his ears. The sealed hatch to the thyristor room vibrated with the deep hum of electric generators.

Quayle often felt that walking this stretch of corridor was akin to running a gauntlet of nerve-stinging noise. A stairwell pitched downward, the risers rust pitted and corroded in places to paper thinness. They squeaked and groaned beneath his booted feet.

The stairs ended at an open door, and Quayle pushed through it to the second-tier deck of the Northstar 40 drilling platform. He paused for a moment to inhale the sharp smell of the Atlantic Ocean, relishing the briny tang. Despite the sun blazing in the blue expanse of the sky, the temperature was still unseasonably cool. He didn't shiver from the chill wind gusting over the white-capped expanse of the sea, though he noticed Jefferies hunching his shoulders against its bite. Due to his mutagenically altered metabolism, he and his fellow dragoons were very sensitive to the cold. Then again, they didn't have Quayle's layers of fat to act as insulation.

He strode across the deck, glancing up at the flock of squawking gulls wheeling overhead. He briefly wondered how the carrion feeders knew in advance they would soon feast.

Seen from a distance, Northstar 40 rose from the
ocean surface like an iceberg made of steel. The platform was 280 feet long and 212 feet wide, with three
decks built around the skeletal drilling derrick, the top
of which climbed nearly ninety feet into the cloudless
sky.

The platform had been built as a floater, a dynam-
ically positioned semisubmersible rig. At the base of
each massive leg roared two-thousand-horsepower
thrusters that maintained the platform's position.

Tethered by heavy rope hawsers between the pair
of starboard legs was the *Cromwell*. A sleek, sharp-
prowed vessel painted a flat, sinister black, its streamlined, sharply faceted contours lent it a resemblance
to a gigantic knife blade.

Placed amidships, the snouts of three 40 mm Bofors
cannons jutted out from behind metal deck shielding.
The Limbo antisubmarine system, a quartet of three-
foot-long hollow pipes angled upward at forty-five-
degree angles was affixed near the bow. A pair of
tripod-mounted L7-A1 heavy-caliber machine guns
was bolted to the roof of the elevated bridge housing.

The *Cromwell* was a corvette, its regenerative gas
turbine engines capable of driving it at fifty knots max-
imum speed on smooth seas. She was a Stealth ship,
on the cutting edge of radar-baffling technology two
hundred years ago. But she was more than just a vessel
to Quayle. All his hopes and dreams were packaged
in her hundred-yard length. He was quarterdeck bred
to the bone, something his officers didn't understand
but respected nevertheless—or least all but one of
them did.

Lieutenant Richardson was already in place by the
guardrail, his ankles, wrists and arms tightly bound by

lengths of hemp. A number of fist-size lead balls were attached to the ropes. He stood directly beneath a thick I beam. Suspended from the beam was a squat, compact electric hoist. A length of chain tipped with a clip hook dangled from a movable boom arm at the end of the hoist.

Two dragoons held Richardson upright beneath the chain. The other twenty-two stood at stiff attention. A small figure wearing a hooded warm-up suit stood several feet away. Although Richardson still wore his uniform, his beret and sunglasses were missing and he squinted against the bright sunlight. His deeply socketed eyes were large and almond-shaped, with black vertical slits centered in golden irises. He had no eyebrows, only a faint interlocking pattern of scales that met at the bridge of his nose. When he caught sight of Quayle, he snarled, "You fat bastard—"

The dragoon on his right cut him off with a backhanded cuff to the mouth. Richardson reeled, spitting blood on the rust-streaked deck.

Quayle regarded the man dispassionately. "Let us proceed."

Richardson started to struggle. "Don't I even get a bloody blindfold? Not even any last words?"

"You said all you were going to say at your trial, Mr. Richardson," Quayle responded flatly. "The testimony was damning."

The man jerked his head violently toward the hooded figure. "*Her* testimony! She's a mutie and Irish to boot. Why take her word for anything?"

The figure moved forward with lithe, graceful steps, reaching up to tug down the hood, revealing a fair-skinned, heart-shaped face with a snub nose and full lips. She was beautiful despite her grave expression.

Her eyes were blue-white, with no irises or pupils visible. Hair the color of steel was intricately woven into round braids on either side of her head. Even the shapeless warm-up suit she wore did not completely conceal the voluptuous figure swelling underneath.

In a clear voice, touched with a brogue, she said, "You know who I am and my abilities. I am never wrong."

Richardson tried to sneer, but he couldn't quite bring it off due to his split lips. "If Lord Strongbow hadn't heeded your counsel, he would still be among us."

He forced a contemptuous laugh. "I was on the *Cromwell* when the selkies attacked, Morrigan. I saw you pulled overboard. Yet rather than be drowned or torn to pieces like so many of our brothers, a fortnight ago you returned to New London—safe and unhurt. How did you manage that, you mutie whore?"

Morrigan's face remained a blank, serene mask during the man's tirade. Quietly, she replied, "I explained all that to Captain Quayle's satisfaction. I do not justify myself to a thief."

Richardson strained against both his bonds and the hands of the dragoons holding him upright. "A *thief*?" he half screeched. "And what is Quayle here but a thief? He stole Strongbow's position and he wasn't even a member of the elite like me. Captain Evil-eye—"

Quayle took one step forward, his massive hand darting out and closing around the lower half of Richardson's face. His words became mumbles, then a muffled shriek as Quayle began to squeeze.

"You've had your say, Mr. Richardson," said Quayle in a low, rumbling half whisper. "Morrigan saw the treason in your corrupt little mind, an ambition to incite the crew to mutiny and take command of this mission.''

As he spoke, his white-skinned hand tightened around Richardson's face, his spatulate thumb digging into the soft flesh beneath the man's right ear. Richardson's eyes bugged out, and a keening wail escaped between Quayle's clenched fingers. ''You also stole, sir. I cannot and will not abide a thief. There can be only one penalty.''

Quayle released the lieutenant, shoving him away at the same time. The dragoons staggered as they tried to keep Richardson erect. Liquid scarlet shone bright and stark on the palm of Quayle's hand. ''Proceed,'' he snapped.

Jefferies maneuvered the boom arm around on its swivel mount and pulled down the chain. One of the dragoons attached the hook to the ropes encircling Richardson's ankles, and the others stepped away from him. The man tried to maintain his balance, wobbling this way and that.

A dragoon manning the winch controls gave the release lever a swift downward wrench. The hoist emitted an electric hum, and the chain snapped taut, yanking Richardson's feet out from under him. He crashed down on the deck plates with a grunt of pain, his legs stretched straight up as the clattering chain withdrew into the boom arm.

The winch raised Richardson clear of the deck. Jefferies swung the boom around so it overhung the ocean. Squirming and cursing, Richardson hung upside down fifty feet above the surface of the sea. The wind buffeted him, causing his body to sway gently.

Quayle turned to one of the bereted men. "The cutlass, Mr. Barret."

Ceremoniously, Barret thrust out a steel scabbard, held reverently in both hands. A small brass plate reading 1804 in swirling cursive script was affixed at the midway point of the sheath.

Fitting his right hand into the intricately molded brass-basket knuckle guard, Quayle drew the cutlass with a flourish, steel rasping loudly against steel. Longer than the traditional naval swords, it was a weapon of exquisite craftsmanship. The four-foot-long, mirror-bright blade reflected the sun, highlights chasing each other up and down its double-edged length. He hefted it for a moment, admiring its perfect balance. No matter how many times he held the ceremonial cutlass, he always felt a bit like King Arthur drawing Excalibur from the stone.

Quayle marched over to the rail and gazed steadily into Richardson's face. Blood had rushed to his head, giving it a ruddy hue. "You have been adjudged guilty in accordance with maritime and military laws. I give you one last chance to repent of your crime before the sentence is carried out."

Jefferies's crimson-coated lips writhed. His voice was a husky whisper. "You and every man jack who follows you are the ones who should repent. You're traitors to the Imperium. You've turned your back on it, and with my last breath, I curse all of you."

In a cracked, quavery tenor, Jefferies began to sing. "'Rule Britannia, Britannia rule the waves—'"

Quayle swung the cutlass in a flat half arc. The sun glinted blindingly from the blade so no one saw the instant of impact, but they all heard it. With a meaty chock, as of a butcher's cleaver chopping into a side of beef, Jefferies's head fell from his shoulders. It plummeted straight down into the ocean, followed by a vermilion rain. A gust of wind sprayed droplets in an artless pattern across Quayle's face.

The gulls cawed, wings beating the air as they dived toward the head bobbing among the whitecaps. Quayle turned away from the rail, presenting the cutlass to Barret hilt first. "Clean it thoroughly."

"Aye, aye, sir."

To Jefferies, he ordered, "Send Mr. Richardson to the locker."

"Aye, Captain." Jefferies stepped to the rail, leaned over and worked out the hook from between the rope strands. The man's headless body plunged down, entering the water with scarcely a splash. The lead weights almost immediately dragged it beneath the waves, leaving only a red stain to spread across the surface.

Not wiping the speckles of blood from his face, Quayle silently surveyed the assembled dragoons. None of their faces registered any emotion.

In a clipped, matter-of-fact voice, he said, "I regret what had to be done. But if we are to rescue the Imperium from chaos, discipline must be uppermost in all of our minds. I will not make allowances for violations of the law, no matter how trivial they might seem. Am I understood?"

In unison, the dragoons responded, "Understood, sir."

Quayle nodded. "Dismiss the men, Mr. Jefferies. Miss Morrigan, come with me."

He lumbered across the deck, carefully avoiding places where the welds had sprung. Morrigan followed him along the passageway, up the stairs and back into the day office. He closed and locked the door, then gazed levelly at the woman with his flesh-bagged right eye.

"I can ill afford to lose men," he said quietly. "Richardson was well liked, and I found him a decent bloke myself."

"Sometimes," the woman replied, "that kind is the most treacherous. The poison in the pudding, the knife in the hand patting you on the back."

Quayle took a handkerchief from a pocket and dabbed at the damp blood on his cheek. "You're positive he was the thief?"

Morrigan's full lips pursed in disapproval. "I thought you had faith in my abilities."

She unzipped the front of her warm-up suit. A silver chain hung from the delicate column of her throat to her waist, and from it dangled a small charm, a talisman fashioned in the shape of three circle-topped triangles, an isosceles bracketing a pair of two scalenes.

Quayle nodded toward the chain around her neck. "Lord Strongbow trusted them, but only because he wasn't aware of your true allegiance. You've admitted to me you were a spy dispatched by the Priory of Awen. You took a very big risk in doing that."

Morrigan shrugged negligently. "Not at all. You never shared Strongbow's vengeful agenda against Ireland."

With a mocking smile, she tapped her forehead with a finger. "You continue to underestimate the true depth of my gifts. I knew you were a pragmatist upon our first meeting...and also I felt your raging resentment against Strongbow for refusing to recognize your own gifts. He was a mad fool, blinded by ambition and hatred."

Quayle matched her mocking smile. "But as Richardson pointed out, he is gone and yet here you are."

"Strongbow ignored the counsel I provided," replied Morrigan coldly. "However, if my word isn't sufficient to damn Richardson as a traitor—"

She slid a hand into a pocket of her suit. "I found this in his quarters. So not only was he snooping through your charts, he was robbing me."

Between thumb and forefinger she held a small, perfect sphere. Though he had seen it before, Quayle could not help but stare at it. Appearing no more substantial than a translucent soap bubble, the little ball looked as if it were made of rolled moonbeams. Its surface was perfectly smooth, showing no signs of pitting or even the most minuscule of casting seams.

"The bead of orichalcum," Morrigan continued. "He didn't know what it was, of course. But he knew it was important to me, and that's why he took it. At least he didn't find the diskette."

"Important to *us*," Quayle corrected. "That's the real reason you wanted him dead, isn't it?" He gestured toward the litter of books and maps on his desk. "Not whether he went through this material."

"Richardson suspected I was running a game on you," she said. "Persuading you to undertake a mad quest so you would turn your back on Britain and allow the invaders to gain a secure foothold."

She paused and added dryly, "And the same notion has occurred to you, more than once."

"Several times," Quayle responded stolidly. "My country is in a state of anarchy, and New London itself is under siege by your people—and here I sit, with the Imperium's elite, out in the North Sea. I don't blame the crew for being suspicious, not only of you but of me.''

The woman's lips twitched in a smile. "Catch."

She tossed the little orb to Quayle, who snatched it one-handed out of the air, his flipperlike paw closing around it completely. He hefted it, his good eye narrowing to a slit. "Heavy. Deceptively heavy."

"Does it feel like metal, Captain? Like any kind of ore you're familiar with?''

Quayle opened his hand, caressing the sphere with his thumb. Almost hesitantly, he answered. "It does not. It feels almost…" He trailed off, groping for a description.

"Organic?" Morrigan supplied.

He considered the word for a moment, his lips creasing in a frown. "Yes. Organic. Like something alive."

She nodded toward the unshuttered window through which sunlight shafted. "Expose it to the sun, Captain."

Quayle eyed her quizzically, then did as she suggested, holding his hand in the sunbeam, the small sphere nestled in the hollow of his palm. Absently, he noted how the surface of the orb did not glint in the light. After a few seconds, he demanded harshly, "Now what?''

"Wait."

"Wait for how—"

The rest of Quayle's words blurred into a hoarse cry of pain and astonishment. A searing heat exploded in his hand, scorching its way up his forearm. He heard a sizzle, as of raw meat being thrown onto a red-hot grill.

He jerked, flinging the little ball away from him. It

struck the floor and rolled a few feet. Blinking back
the tears of pain, he saw how a faint shimmer surrounded the orb, like the haze produced by heat waves.
As the orb rolled, it left a thin black soot streak on the
floor, wisps of smoke rising in its wake.

Glancing down at his hand, he grimaced at the blis-
ter forming on the palm, an angry red welt bright
against the pale flesh.

"You Celtic bitch," he growled, but the insult
sounded distracted, like an afterthought. "So the
myths are true, then. The orichalcum is the firestone
of legend."

Morrigan nodded sagely. "A vast source of energy.
Imagine what you can do with a shipload of it. That's
worth a few lives, isn't it?"

Quayle tried to keep a smile from crossing his face.
Gruffly, he said, "Finding that shipload is the trick,
isn't it?"

Morrigan shrugged. "It isn't a trick, Captain. It's
an undertaking."

Quayle stepped toward the bead of orichalcum on
the floor, but he didn't bend down to touch it or even
nudge it with his foot. It no longer shimmered. Softly,
he said, "Everything turns out to be a trick in the end,
Miss Morrigan."

"Yes," she said unemotionally. "As the citizens of
Atlantis found out to their sorrow."

# Chapter 2

*New Schwabenland, Antarctica*

On the register of surprises, one of the most shocking was to have solid ground abruptly collapse from underfoot.

Grant had undergone many shocking experiences, but he couldn't repress a cry of fright as the crusted snow gave way beneath him. Bellowing, he fanned his arms as he plummeted downward, blinded by the miniavalanche surrounding his body. Turning in the air, he tried to grab the ice-coated walls of the crevasse. His gloved fingers failed to secure a hold.

He hit the bottom flat-footed, the twin impacts jacking both knees up into his lower belly. Over the explosion of violently expelled air, he heard the faint chime of metal beneath his boots.

Falling over onto his left side, Grant tried to drag the painfully cold air into his emptied lungs. Snow covered the lenses of his goggles so he saw nothing but gray-white. Over his own gasps and the sifting rustle of snow swirling down around him, he heard Kane's voice, calling his name.

Grant forced himself to his elbows, breath rasping in and out of his straining lungs, the subzero air abrading the moist tissues of his sinuses and throat. He gestured up and behind him, not sure if Kane, Brigid Bap-

tiste and Cotta could see him in the gloom at the
bottom of the hole. He realized he had strolled over a
crevasse bridged only by snow and hoarfrost, and he
cursed himself for not allowing Kane to take the point
as he usually did.

Clearing his goggles with a swipe of a mittened
hand, Grant craned his neck up and around and saw
the heads and shoulders of his companions outlined
against the blue sky. At least he assumed they were
his companions—it was hard to tell since they wore
woolen, face-concealing balaclavas, goggles and
hooded thermal suits as he did. He gauged the distance
to them at a little less than twenty feet.

In a strangulated wheeze, he called up, "I think I
found the front door."

"Good," Kane shouted down. "Guess you've
earned your bread for the week."

The vibration of his voice echoing back and forth
against the sides of the crevasse caused more snow to
break loose and shower down. Grant sputtered, averting his face.

He whispered fiercely, "Knock it off! You trying to
bury me alive?"

Grant's characteristic lionlike rumble couldn't easily be pitched to a whisper, and his voice triggered
more sifting rivulets.

"If that happens," Kane replied in a softer tone,
"at least you'd keep for a long time in this place."

Heaving himself to his feet, Grant silently endured
the twinge from his right leg. A few months previ-
ously, the tibia and talus bones had been fractured and
still gave him intermittent pain, particularly in cold
weather. And there couldn't be any colder weather
than on the vast ice continent at the bottom of the

world. He knew the South Polar region could support less life than even the most desolate of rad-scoured hellzones in what used to be America.

Brushing away crusts of snow clinging to his one-piece coverall, Grant swiftly examined his surroundings. Despite the garment's thick, quilted padding and battery-powered heat filaments in the lining, the sub-zero cold still penetrated. It bit at his nostrils, his lips, his eyes, anywhere it could find moisture.

He kicked at the snow underfoot and uncovered a patch of steel plate. "This is definitely the place."

Grant surveyed the crevasse walls and saw, half-embedded in the ice, horizontal strips of dark metal rising toward the opening. Moving closer, he saw the rungs of a steel ladder and he grunted in disgust.

"What have you found?" Brigid called down.

"A ladder," he replied sourly. "Wish I'd known."

"Our intel stated the installation was underground," she reminded him.

Grant didn't respond. Removing a small pickax from his backpack, he began chipping away at two centuries of Antarctic ice from the rungs, clearing just enough to provide toe and finger holds. The hollow space beneath the canopy of snow filled with a steady clang-clang. He climbed up as he worked. He wasn't too concerned about the vibrations causing the snow on the walls to collapse now that he knew it was only a covering for metal bulkheads.

After he hacked a narrow gouge between all the rungs and the wall to which they were bolted, Brigid, Cotta and Kane descended.

"A little warmer down here," Cotta observed.

"It just feels that way because we're out of the wind," replied Brigid. "It's still seventy below."

Lifting his goggles, Kane winced as the air stabbed his gray-blue eyes. "The sec door has got to be here somewhere."

From a zippered pocket in his coverall, he removed a Nighthawk microlight and clicked it on. He cast around the amber-hued, 5,000 candlepower minibeam, the halo of illumination sliding over the walls. He swept it back and forth. For an instant, something very small and a very dim green winked beneath the sheathing of ice. "There."

Taking the pickax from Grant, Brigid stepped to where Kane held the Nighthawk's beam steady. Carefully, she tapped and scraped away the frost, revealing a liquid crystal display panel glowing green above a keypad.

"Here we are," she announced.

"Why would the gateway be placed above the actual entrance to the installation?" Cotta's voice trembled slightly, either from fear or cold. He was still shaken by his recent trip through a mat-trans unit. Brigid, Grant and Kane sympathized with his reaction.

Cotta generally was quick-witted and fairly phlegmatic, but it was apparent he was scared half to death. Grant in particular couldn't criticize him for this. No human being, no matter how thoroughly briefed in advance, could be expected to remain unflappable on a hyperdimensional trip through the quantum interphase mat-trans inducer, colloquially known as a "gateway."

By stepping into the armaglass-enclosed chamber, one second a person was there, surrounded by glowing mist, and in the next second, the universe seemed to cave in. Perceptions changed, time jumped and for a heart-stopping instant, the cosmos seemed to stand still. Then the traveler was wherever the gateway had been programmed to materialize him or her. Whatever else, a trip through the gateway was unsettling to the mind, to the nerves and to the soul itself, as Grant had reasons to know.

By Cotta's view, less than an hour ago he had been in the Cerberus redoubt in Montana. Now he was inside the ass of the Earth itself, freezing and terrified and no doubt cursing himself for ever volunteering to be part of the jump team.

The gateway chamber into which the four of them had materialized didn't conform to the standard specs that Grant, Brigid and Kane had come to expect. It was very small, the walls not made of tinted armaglass shielding but rather of plates of sheet metal lined with lead foil. The door of the chamber was different, too, with a transparent panel set in its top half and a central wheel to open and seal it.

Once leaving the chamber, they saw that it was not placed on an elevated platform, and it opened directly into a small control center, barely ten feet across. There was no adjacent recovery anteroom beyond. A single, simplified master control console ran the length of one wall, and they recognized a few of the basic command panels from the Cerberus installation. Many of the indicator lights were dark. Beneath the concrete floor they heard the rhythmic throb of generators, beating with a nerve-scratching loudness. Within a few moments, the sound hummed down to silence.

They realized the little room was not part of a redoubt; it was the entire structure, a Quonset hut that was little more than a hutch standing between two bastions of rock. They were a little surprised and perplexed, but they didn't expend too much time trying to reason it out. Using the map provided by the Cerberus database, the four people had pushed out of the hut and onto the vast ice fields, trudging through the high snowdrifts and battered by the keening wind. It hadn't been dangerously cold at first, but the wind kept rising. All they saw through the veils of snow was a range of low mountains, rugged and bleak in the far distance.

In response to Cotta's question about the location of the gateway, Brigid said, "I can only speculate."

"We're listening," Kane prompted.

"If this was indeed a bioengineering facility, as Lakesh suspects, separating the means into and out of it is a sound security precaution. It prevents people from jumping directly into a potential biohazard or jumping out carrying contagions."

Grant nodded. "Yeah. But we don't know what kind of installation this really is. It's not part of the official Cerberus mat-trans network, so that means it's not a Totality Concept installation." He gestured in the general direction of the Quonset hut. "And that gateway unit looked like a prototype model."

Grant referred to the Cerberus Project, a subdivision of Overproject Whisper, which in turn had been a primary component of the Totality Concept. The Totality Concept was the umbrella designation for a long-range experimental program that explored arcane and esoteric scientific areas, from time travel to genetics. The researches dated back to World War II, when German scientists were laboring to build what turned out to be purely theoretical secret weapons for the Third Reich. The Allied powers adopted the researches, as well as many of the scientists, and constructed underground bases, primarily in the western United States, to further the experiments.

The Totality Concept was classified above top secret. It was known only to a few very high-ranking military officers and politicians. Few of the Presidents who held office during its existence were ever aware of the full ramifications.

"Whatever this place is," Brigid countered, "it has the same computerized lock as every other redoubt linked to the Totality Concept. Let's see what happens."

She punched in the access code on the keypad. The numbers 3-5-2 glowed in the LCD window. Kane and Grant tensed, making sure there was enough leeway between their right sleeves and heavy gloves to allow their Sin Eaters to jump into their hands if necessary. The Sin Eaters were big-bored automatic handblasters, less than fourteen inches in length at full extension, the magazines carrying twenty 9 mm rounds. When not in use, the stock folded over the top of the blaster, lying along the frame, reducing its holstered length to ten inches.

When the weapon was needed, the shooter tensed his wrist tendons, and sensitive actuators triggered flexible cables within the forearm holster, which snapped the pistol smoothly into his waiting hand, the butt unfolding in the same motion. Since the Sin Eaters had no trigger guards or safeties, the blasters fired immediately upon touching the shooter's crooked index finger.

They waited for what seemed like a very long time. Nothing happened. Grant stamped his feet impatiently as the cold penetrated his fleece-lined boots and three layers of socks.

Hugging himself, Cotta whispered, "What's going on?"

"Damn little, apparently," declared Kane. "All the works are probably frozen solid. Bet nobody's set foot in here since 2001 or before, so the barons couldn't be using it—"

A grinding rumble slowly built, overlaid by a series of squeaks, creaks and hisses. Long-disused gears, pulleys and hydraulics slowly moved. A huge oval of ice began to shake loose from the crevasse wall, quivering and acquiring a network of cracks that lengthened and widened. The four people recoiled as splinters of ice and clots of snow showered them. There was the prolonged hiss of seals releasing the door, and a thick metal disk swung ponderously out, like the door of a bank vault.

A surge of wonderfully warm air belled out through the round opening, forming a cloud of mist as it met the frigid atmosphere of the crevasse. Through the fog, they saw glowing lights as overhead neon tubes flickered and shed a yellow luminescence. The room beyond was small, more like a foyer than a chamber, but with a high, metal-ribbed ceiling. A vid spy-eye swiveled toward them, a power indicator light beneath the lenses shining steadily. Distantly, at the far edges of their hearing, they heard a low throb, a rhythmic tone as of machinery.

Cotta thrust his head forward cautiously and sniffed. "Smells sort of musty and stale."

Grant nodded. "Which is par for the course. I think Kane is right. The barons aren't using this place as a substitute for the Dulce facility. Nobody has been in here for a long, long time."

They weren't surprised by the functioning lights or

the vid camera. All Totality Concept and Continuity
of Government redoubts had been built with their own
nuke generators and most of them continued to provide power centuries after their designers had crum-
bled to dust.

Kane stepped through the open door and into the
foyer. The room narrowed down to another heavy
metal door, this one with a wheel lock centered in its
dark mass. It was covered by a thin patina of frost.

"Downright balmy in here," he said wryly. "Must
be at least ten above."

He stripped off the goggles and balaclava, running
a hand through his tousled hair. It was dark, a shade
between black and chestnut, but showed sun-touched
highlights.

An inch over six feet, Kane's lean, flat-muscled
body was completely concealed beneath the thermal
suit, but it was apparent most of his muscle mass was
contained in his upper body, lending his physique a
marked resemblance to a wolf. His high-planed face
held a watchful expression, as did his narrowed, gray-
blue eyes. A thin, hairline scar cut across his left
cheek.

Brigid removed her own mask, shaking loose an
unruly mane of long red-gold hair, tossing it back over
her shoulders. Despite the unflattering coverall garment, a discerning eye could see she held a woman's
willowy shape on long, athletic legs. Her hair framed
a smoothly sculpted face with a rosy complexion
dusted lightly with freckles across her nose and
cheeks. There was a softness in her features that be-
spoke a deep wellspring of compassion, yet a hint of
iron resolve was there, too. Even in the dim light, the

color of emeralds glittered in her big, feline-slanted eyes.

As they joined Brigid and Kane, Grant and Cotta peeled up their balaclavas. Grant stood six foot four, exceptionally broad across the shoulders and thick through the chest. His black hair was cut close to the scalp and peppered with a sprinkling of gray at his temples, but the down-sweeping mustache showed jet-black against his coffee-brown skin. His heavy-jawed face was set in a scowl.

Cotta was the shortest of the men, but built along stocky lines. His curly, dark brown hair and equally brown eyes gave him a boyish appearance. A flat case containing first-aid items and survival rations hung from his shoulder by a strap. Pitching his voice low to disguise a tremor of anxiety, he asked, "We're going to go in there?"

Kane lifted a quilted shoulder in a shrug. "That's why we're here."

"Yeah," Cotta agreed nervously. "But you said nobody's been in here for a long time."

Reassuringly, Brigid said, "That's probably true, but it might not be true in a few weeks, a few days or even a few hours. We have to learn if there's an installation the barons can press into service as a bioengineering facility other than the one in Dulce. It would be naive to assume there aren't more installations like that one to use as a contingency. At least we know the Anthill complex in South Dakota won't serve that purpose."

Not too long before, the vast genetic engineering and medical facility beneath the Archuleta Mesa in Dulce, New Mexico, had been, if not destroyed, then rendered virtually useless to the baronial oligarchy.

Built in the mid-twentieth century to house several divisions of the Totality Concept, it was later turned over almost entirely to Overproject Excalibur, which comprised the bioresearch programs.

Over the past thirty-odd years, the subterranean installation had become a combination of gestation, birthing and medical treatment center. The hybrids, the self-proclaimed new humans, were born there, the half-human spawn created to inherit the nuke-scoured Earth.

But there was a price to pay for the hybrids' inheritance. As intellectually brilliant as they were, particularly the nine barons who ruled the American continent, their bodies were fragile. Their metabolisms fell easy prey to disease, which was one reason they tended to sequester themselves from the ville-bred humans they ruled. Once a year, all the barons traveled to the Dulce facility to have their blood filtered and their immune systems boosted. In severe cases, even damaged organs were replaced from the storage banks of organic material stockpiled there.

Nor did the hybrids reproduce in conventional fashion. The males possessed underdeveloped genitals. Kane knew that from an eyewitness encounter with Baron Cobalt, but he had no idea if the female hybrids were similarly unformed. It wasn't something to which he cared to devote much thought.

That the hybrids reproduced by a form of cloning and gene-splicing wasn't open to question. However, it didn't seem reasonable they would put all of their eggs—biologically speaking—in the subterranean basket at Dulce.

Kane stepped over to the door, putting both hands on the wheel. Even through his gloves and mittens, he could feel the frigid metal. He turned it slowly and carefully. The wheel didn't spin easily; it caught and squeaked during the rotation, and he guessed it hadn't been used recently.

The lock completed its final turn, and he heard the metallic snapping of solenoids and latches letting go. Putting his shoulder against it, he pushed the door open slowly, a few inches at a time. Hinges squealed in protest.

Peering around the edge, Kane saw only a dimly lit passageway—and the swastika.

# Chapter 3

The large banner was stretched taut within a narrow metal framework, affixed to the fifteen-foot-high ceiling by wires and eyebolts. Bloodred, with a white disk in the center, the black symbol within it touched unpleasant chords of recognition within Kane, Grant and Brigid. All sharp corners and angles, the swastika seemed to float several inches above the encircling white disk. Rust red stains were barely discernible within the circle.

"The barons never used this place," Grant husked out.

"No," Brigid agreed in the same hushed tone. "Something a lot worse did."

Cotta's eyes flickered quizzically from the banner to the faces of his companions. "What's worse than the barons?"

Quietly, Brigid said, *"Nationalsozialistiche Deutsche Arbeiterpartei."*

Cotta grimaced at the conglomeration of consonants. "The what?"

"The Nazi Party," Kane muttered, not bothering to conceal the disgust in his tone. *"Sieg heil."*

Cotta's eyes widened, but he said nothing more. All four of them knew that the Totality Concept had originated with the Third Reich. But Grant, Brigid and Kane had a more personal familiarity with the Nazis.

During their journeys to the parallel casements, the so-called Lost Earths, the first alternate reality they visited was one where Germany had been the victor of World War II. Although their conscious memories of those places were now fragmented and vague, the sight of the swastika evoked a strong emotional reaction.

Dubiously, Grant asked, "You don't think this was a Nazi stronghold, do you?"

"At one time, probably," Brigid answered. "It's pretty much a historical given that a last battalion of high-ranking Nazi officers and scientists escaped to Antarctica in submarines during the last days of the war. It's apparent that once the Allies absorbed the Totality Concept researches and personnel, they absorbed this base, too."

"So this *is* a Concept-related redoubt after all," Kane declared.

Brigid shook her head. "If it was, it was an ancillary one, not the seat of any major division or subdivision. But somebody supplied them with the mattrans unit."

They moved down the corridor. It was about ten feet wide and concealed strip lighting flickered, casting gray, strobing shadows ahead of them. The temperature climbed the farther they walked. The walls and floor were not composed of softly gleaming vanadium alloy, as in most redoubts. They were constructed of dark, riveted metal that showed streaks of oxidization.

"Obviously, this place predates the Continuity of Government installation-building program," Brigid commented. "If this was a Nazi bolt-hole or an installation set up for them, they're long dead."

The corridor opened up into a huge room, and what

they saw caused them all to halt and stare in surprise. They found themselves in a huge office suite, furnished with fifty desks, stenography machines, metal file cabinets and typewriters. Tacked onto bulletin boards were dozens of memos, all of them in German and bearing either the swastika or a small symbol resembling two lightning bolts.

At the far end of the room was a glassed-in row of cubicles. In the cubicles they saw a number of computer terminals resting on desks, but none of them were even as recent as the old, remanufactured DDC models in use at Cobaltville. A box-shaped mainframe system spanned one wall. Behind the glass doors, big reels of tape were attached to spindles.

*Clunky* was the word that came to Kane's mind when he looked at it.

Brigid eyed the mainframe and said, "That looks like a version of the ENIAC model."

"What's that?" Cotta inquired.

"One of the first functional computers. It had about eighteen thousand vacuum tubes and when operating properly, it could make five thousand calculations per second. Trouble was, because of all its parts, it rarely functioned at all, much less properly."

"This place was cutting edge," Grant remarked dourly, "around 1960."

However, the place was as neat and tidy as if the people who worked there had simply gotten up to take a coffee break and would return in a few minutes. Items of a personal nature were scattered around the desks—framed black-and-white photographs of children wearing the neckerchief and shorts ensemble of the Hitler Youth, and "me, too" pictures, people wearing white lab coats shaking hands with men in uniform.

Brigid identified a few of the uniformed men. "Himmler, Goering...that one looks a lot like Mengele. A real gallery of human monsters."

Kane picked up and examined a small oil print that depicted Adolf Hitler on horseback wearing medieval knight's armor and waving a Nazi flag. He snorted disdainfully. The snort was followed instantly by what sounded like the snapping of a green stick of wood. A spark flared off a typewriter with a spray of metal flinders and a keening whine.

While the wailing echoes of the ricochet still chased themselves around the big room, Grant, Kane and Brigid dropped flat to the floor. Cotta continued to stand, blinking around in bafflement.

"Get down, asshole!" Kane barked.

Fearful realization suddenly shone in Cotta's eyes, and he joined the three people on the floor, behind the cover of a desk.

"What's with you?" snarled Kane. "You figure since the first shot missed, it's only polite to give the blasterman a second chance to plug you?"

"S-sorry," Cotta stammered. "Never been under fire before."

"When you go out on these field trips with us," Brigid said dryly, "you get used to it."

The Sin Eaters sprang into Kane and Grant's waiting hands. From a zippered pocket of her thermal suit, Brigid drew an Iver Johnson autoblaster. Cotta pulled an H&K VP-70 from a pocket of his own suit.

"Who the hell is shooting at us?" Grant demanded in a whisper.

"A squatter maybe," replied Kane.

More than once, they had come across redoubts that played host to interlopers, but he doubted his own words. Even before the nukecaust, Antarctica was the most desolate, uninhabited region on the face of the planet. It seemed very unlikely wanderers or looters had stumbled across this installation.

They heard a faint rustle of cloth, the clack of boot heels and wheezing, slightly labored respiration. A hoarse male voice called out in a foreign tongue.

Brigid lifted her head, eyes widening. ''He asked if we speak German.''

''Do you?'' asked Grant.

Her brow furrowed in momentary concentration. ''I've read the German-to-English dictionary in the database. I've never had the opportunity to speak it, but I can understand it.''

As the self-proclaimed possessor of an eidetic memory, she could say nothing else. Brigid Baptiste remembered everything she read or saw, which was how and why she ended up as an exile like Grant and Kane.

The man's voice demanded, *''Eich dort?''*

''He wants to know who we are,'' Brigid translated.

''Tell him,'' suggested Kane.

Brigid called out in German, and twice Kane caught the word *Amerikaner*. After a period of silence broken only by a muffled cough, the man responded. ''Americans? You come from where? Dulce? The Anthill?''

His English was heavily accented, and he sounded as if his tongue was unaccustomed to employing it. ''You have come for me?''

Rather than offering an answer, Brigid asked, ''Who are you?''

Once again there was a protracted period of silence. When the man spoke again, he sounded distracted.

"Skorzeny. Standartenführer Skorzeny of the Luft-waffe. You come for me, *nein?*"

Brigid's eyes slitted and she repeated the name be-neath her breath. "Skorzeny. *Otto* Skorzeny?"

"You take me back?" The man's voice held a plaintive, wheedling note.

"He sounds disoriented," Brigid whispered.

"Fused-out more like it," muttered Grant.

She rose to her knees, saying loudly, "We're going to stand up. We mean you no harm. Do you under-stand?"

"*Ja*—I mean, yes. I understand."

Very slowly, fisting her Iver Johnson but keeping it out of sight, Brigid half inched her way up behind the desk. When she reached eye level with its surface she paused. "Show yourself. *Bitte.*"

A figure stepped around a partition. A white beard spilled nearly to his stomach, covering the front of his black tunic like a fall of snow. His hair was equally white and very long, nearly the length of Brigid's. His face was deeply seamed and lined with a map of tiny furrows and blue veins. His white complexion was a deep, almost translucent pallor that came from not be-ing exposed to the sun for a very long time. His eyes glittered a hot, furious cobalt blue. They were in-tensely penetrating eyes, intelligent eyes, all-seeing eyes, the eyes of a visionary. Or a madman.

He wore a uniform, the black tunic, jodhpurs and knee boots Brigid recognized as belonging to the Shutzstaffel, the SS, the dreaded order of Black Knights who pledged their loyalty to Hitler, not to Germany. It was covered in gaudy emblems, including the twin lightning strokes and silver skull and cross-bones from another day and era. She noticed the cuffs of the tunic were frayed and the boot leather cracked. The Sam Browne belt crossing his chest and girding his lean waist showed greenish spots of mildew. Loose threads dangled from the shoulder seams. What captured her attention the most was the black Luger gripped in his right hand. It trembled ever so slightly, but she doubted it was due to fear or cold.

"Skorzeny," Brigid said, pitching her voice to a calm, reassuring timbre. "There are four of us. We're armed, too, but we have no intention of harming you. We'll all stand up. Understand?"

Skorzeny nodded, a quick, jerklike motion of his head. *"Ja."*

"First lower your blaster—your weapon."

The man glanced at the Luger in his fist with mild surprise, as if he had forgotten it was there. His arm dropped to his side, the barrel pointing toward the floor. His hand trembled even more, as if he were suffering from a nervous disorder.

Brigid rose to her full height, putting a friendly, inoffensive smile on her face. Skorzeny didn't return it, although it was hard to tell because of the whiskers draping the lower portion of his face. He tensed when, one by one, Kane, Cotta and Grant climbed to their feet. His eyes narrowed when he caught sight of Grant and he murmured a word in his own tongue. Brigid didn't understand, but she understood the tone of contempt.

Skorzeny demanded imperiously, "Who sent you?"

Brigid stated matter-of-factly, "You don't seem particularly interested in who we are."

"That is unimportant. Depending upon who sent you, that will tell me all I need to know about you."

Cotta hung back as his three companions approached the black-clad man. They moved cautiously, instinctively spreading out across the room as if to offer more difficult targets in case Skorzeny didn't like the answer to his question and started shooting again.

The man's eyes flicked apprehensively from one to the other, but he didn't raise his Luger. Impatiently, he asked, "Where are you from? To what unit are you attached?"

Kane decided Brigid had fielded enough of the old man's questions and he retorted, "Montana. Redoubt Bravo. Is that of any use to you?"

Skorzeny's bushy eyebrows knitted. "*Nein.* I've never heard of it."

"There's no reason why you should."

They halted in a loose semicircle around the man. Skorzeny was slightly under medium height and very lean.

"How long have you been here?" asked Brigid.

Skorzeny peered at her curiously. "You display many fine Aryan qualities, though you are not the ideal. Nevertheless, you are very attractive. You must take pride in your offspring."

His eyes darted toward Kane. "You must be the father. You are closer to a true Teutonic knight. Decision, authority, ruthlessness—I see those traits in your face. I trust you conceived your children in an SS cemetery."

"What?" Kane demanded in annoyed bewilderment. "A what cemetery?"

Skorzeny's gaze moved on to Grant, disdain glittering in his eyes. In a sneering tone, he said, "I had thought your kind would have been cleansed from the Earth by now. However, I suppose there is always a need for servants, even if they are *die Schwarze.*"

*"Die schwarzen?"* Grant echoed, stumbling a little over the pronunciation.

Quietly, Brigid said. "A racial epithet. Forget it."

The jaw muscles in Grant's face knotted. "What's it mean?"

Skorzeny's lips curled beneath his whiskers. "What is the English term, *nigger?*"

Grant lashed out with a big open hand at Skorzeny's face. The results were astonishing. There was a blur of motion, a chocking of metal against bone and Grant sat down heavily, eyelids fluttering. The bearded man had hammered him between the eyes with the butt of his Luger. The blow had come so swiftly Grant had not even glimpsed it.

"How dare you?" Skorzeny barked, eyes seething with utter hatred. "I'll have you castrated with piano wire!"

"Son of a bitch—" Kane lunged, clubbing at the man with the barrel of his Sin Eater.

Skorzeny ducked wildly aside and brought his Luger to bear. Brigid chopped at his hand with her Iver Johnson, crying out, "Stop this!"

She knocked the Luger aside, but not from Skorzeny's grasp. He pivoted on a heel and kicked out with a jackbooted foot. The toe took Kane in the groin. He folded in the middle, grunting in surprised pain. His grunt turned into a snarl of rage.

Grappling with Brigid, Skorzeny closed his left hand in the loose material at the front of her thermal suit and shoved her backward. She stumbled over Grant's legs and fell heavily against Kane, who was trying to straighten up.

The office suddenly quaked with sharp reports of blasterfire. A bullet passed so close to Kane it fanned cool air on his cheek. The glass wall of a cubicle shattered and showered down with a nerve-stinging jangle. A bulletin board split as two rounds clouted it.

Kane and Brigid joined Grant on the floor. Twisting around, Kane saw Cotta trying to draw a bead on Skorzeny, his H&K held in a two-fisted grip. The black-clad man backpedaled with astonishing speed and agility, the Luger in his hand spitting flame and noise. Cotta's blaster bucked as he returned the fire. Brigid, Grant and Kane hunkered down beneath the double fusillade, praying they wouldn't be caught in the cross fire.

Skorzeny danced and weaved among the desks. None of Cotta's rounds came near him, though they smashed through glass and flattened against the wall.

The thunder of blasterfire ceased. Flat planes of cordite smoke hung in the air like streamers of dingy chiffon. Cotta ran to the three people on the floor, gulping breathlessly. "I don't think I hit him, but I chased him off."

Grant heaved himself to his feet, hand on his forehead. "You stupe, trigger-happy bastard, you came closer to hitting *us* than him."

Kane and Brigid rose. Pain radiated out in waves from Kane's crotch, but the thick, quilted padding of his thermal suit had prevented the man's kick from incapacitating him.

Grant snatched the blaster away from Cotta. "Hey," the man protested. "What if I need that?"

"I'll be the one to make that determination," Grant rumbled. A welt swelled on his forehead, and he probed it gingerly. "Goddamn Nazi prick. Can't believe somebody that old is so fast."

With great effort, Kane managed to refrain from

massaging his testicles. He swallowed down bile and declared, "He can't be a real Nazi. He's some fused-out maniac who thinks he is."

Brigid's lips compressed. "He's fused-out definitely, but I think he *is* a real Nazi. A high-ranking one at that."

"What do you mean?" Grant asked.

"An Otto Skorzeny was the creator of an elite commando force, trained in foreign languages, sophisticated weapons, various forms of combat and assassination techniques. It was Skorzeny who had the responsibility for smuggling stolen Nazi art treasures out of Germany at the end of the war.

"He was never convicted as a war criminal. Instead, he made himself useful to American intelligence, even though he was a fanatic Nazi who kept the faith until his alleged death in the mid-1970s."

"Alleged death?" Kane echoed doubtfully. "If this guy is the same Skorzeny, he would be nearly three hundred years old, right?"

"Right," she countered crisply. "And Lakesh is nearly 250."

Comprehension shone in Kane's eyes. "You mean Skorzeny is a freezie like Lakesh, preserved here in cryostasis?"

She nodded. "That's the most likely explanation. And it's possible he's not the only one."

"A nest of freeze-dried goose-steppers," Grant commented darkly. "Just what the world needs at this point."

He ran a frustrated hand over his heavy jaw. "I've said this before and I'll say it again—why does this shit always happen to us?"

# Chapter 4

Before they left the office suite, Brigid slid open a file cabinet drawer and flipped through several sheaves of documents. Neither Kane, Grant nor Cotta lodged an objection to the delay. They were finally warming up and none of them was particularly anxious to pursue a deranged old German through the dark territory of the installation.

When she made a "hmm" sound of interest, Kane came to her side. "What have you found?"

"Information that basically confirms my initial assessment," she responded. "This place was built in 1944, the expansion of a smaller outpost established here in the late 1930s. It was overseen by die Spinne, the Spider, Skorzeny's own little branch of the SS."

Her finger moved down the dense columns of type, lips unconsciously moving as she read the language. "It was staffed primarily by Nazi scientists, most of them brought in after the war under the auspices of Operation Paper Clip."

"Paper Clip?" Grant repeated with a wry smile. "Not as dramatic sounding as the Spider."

"In some ways, it was worse," Brigid replied curtly. "It was a deceitful and sinister recruitment program organized by American intelligence. To keep Nazi scientists who had begun work on what became the Totality Concept from being tried as war criminals, they were given new identities and allowed to continue their work.''

She closed the file folder and tossed it contemptuously back into the drawer. ''This place was probably the last bastion of tried-and-true old-style Nazism left in the world before the nukecaust. The spider's web, so to speak.''

Kane's lips compressed in a tight white line. ''Then let's find the last old-style Nazi spider and squash his ass.''

Beyond an open door on the opposite side of the office was a metal spiral staircase, and they went up two complete windings before emerging onto another level. It was lit by naked bulbs in brackets bolted to the walls. Open doors led to various rooms and chambers. The four people entered a little galley with a gas stove and packed with concentrated foodstuffs, from powdered eggs to tea. Several of the shelves showed gaps, but still there appeared to be enough rations to last one man for many years.

All the furnishings were in remarkably clean order. A variety of mops, buckets and push brooms were kept in a closet. Kane couldn't help but smile at the incongruous image of Skorzeny in his SS uniform mopping floors and polishing furniture, humming *''Deutschland über Alles''* all the while.

Another chamber contained a huge collection of uniforms, weapons, division patches and medals dating back to the rise of the Third Reich. Grant examined a Mauser Kar 98K longblaster, working the bolt action. ''It's clean and oiled.''

Kane picked up a Walther P-38 pistol and squinted down its length. ''So is this one.''

''Not surprising,'' Brigid said. ''Skorzeny has a lot

of time on his hands to attend to this collection. I wouldn't be surprised to find out the Nazi flag we saw when we came in is the so-called Blood Banner.''

''What's that?'' asked Cotta.

''Hitler tried to take over Munich by force in 1923. A number of his followers were killed by the police, and Hitler kept the Nazi flag they carried, stained with the blood of his men who marched with him that day. Ever after, that banner was used to bless all other flags because it had been sanctified by the blood of Teutonic heroes.''

Cotta's face twisted in an indefinable expression. ''That's pretty crazy.''

''No shit,'' rumbled Grant, replacing the rifle in the rack. ''This kind of reminds me of Strongbow's military museum.''

''Strongbow?'' inquired Cotta. ''That maniac you met over in England?''

''The very one,'' Kane answered. ''Lord Strongbow, ruler of the Imperium Britannia. He and old Otto would have a lot in common.''

If the room storing the memorabilia was a combination of arsenal and quartermaster's depot, the next chamber was like a museum or a miser's hoard. They saw large open crates filled with jewelry, from pearl necklaces to silver bracelets. Open chests contained the cash and coinage of many nations. Under a glass case, winking in the light, were great, faceted diamonds, some of them the size of hen's eggs.

Magnificent oil paintings leaned against the walls, and gold ingots were stacked in two waist-high walls, each one four feet long. All the bars bore bas-relief stamps, depicting stylized eagles perched atop wreaths. Swastikas were centered within the wreaths.

Brigid ran a finger over the ingots, murmuring dryly, "The mystery of what happened to the Third Reich's gold reserves, solved at last."

There were many marble and granite statues, ranging from beautiful life-size nudes to small, gem-encrusted likenesses of animals. Kane picked up one resembling a falcon crafted from solid gold, studded with rubies and sapphires. The base bore an inscribed legend in English: The Stuff Dreams Are Made Of.

All four people gaped around the chamber in awed, astounded silence. They knew they were looking upon more wealth than even the most privileged predarker realized existed in one place. Kane couldn't even hazard a guess at the accumulated value of the hoard without growing dizzy.

Brigid broke the silence by saying, "Now we know how *die Spinne* financed this place…with the loot of conquered countries and plundered museums."

Grant gusted out a profanity. "Financed this place to do what? Not just as a hideout for war criminals."

"The Cerberus database had this facility footnoted as something of a consultation and research center for Overproject Excalibur." Brigid's voice was still pitched low. "Since Nazi scientists were the pioneers in eugenics, I suppose their findings and experiments were of some value to Excalibur, even if they didn't constitute an official subdivision."

They knew of at least three Excalibur subdivisions—the Genesis Project, Project Invictus and Scenario Joshua.

Kane replaced the falcon on a shelf. "Let's see what else we can find."

Back out in the corridor, they came across a pair of bunk rooms, each one containing a dozen narrow beds.

The footlockers chained to the frames held personal mementos and bric-a-brac. Several of them were jammed with cosmetics and women's hygiene products. A very large bathroom had five enclosed toilet stalls and five urinals, as well as a common shower area.

"Unisex facilities," Brigid noted. "I guess they already had experience quartering men and women together like cattle in the death camps."

"What happened to the men and women here?" Cotta asked. "If they're still around, shouldn't we have come across them by now?"

Brigid only shrugged.

They went back into the hall and entered a huge, luxuriously furnished bedroom. It would have done credit to a medieval king. The four-poster canopied bed was immense and could have easily held all four of them with room left over. An oaken high-backed chair looked like a throne. The floor was covered by an elaborately woven Persian carpet.

The walls were festooned with crossed battle-axes, swords and pikes. A full suit of knight's plate armor was mounted on a pedestal in a corner. There was even an en suite lavatory equipped with a sunken bath tub. Like the other chambers they had visited, the huge bedroom was in perfect, anal-retentive order.

On a mirrored dressing table, set in the center of a large lace doily, was a framed, hand-tinted photograph. It depicted two men posing stiffly in a sparsely decorated office. The taller of the pair wore the jet-black SS uniform, his clean-shaven, aquiline head held at an arrogant angle. His eyes were steel blue.

The smaller man wore a starched, pale brown uniform, very plain compared to the overdone garb of his companion. A lock of black hair curved in a comma over his forehead, and a small square mustache looked like a smudge of soot on his upper lip. The bottom of the picture bore handwritten words and a dated autograph. Brigid read it aloud. "'*Auf Wiedersehen,* Otto, Adolf Hitler, April 29, 1945.' This was signed and dated the day before Hitler's death."

Kane glanced around the bedroom, mentally comparing it to the cramped bunkroom. "Skorzeny really practiced the division between officer and enlisted men with a vengeance. A man after Baron Cobalt's heart."

Leaving the bedroom, they progressed down the corridor for only a dozen yards before it was blocked by a steel-sheathed and riveted door outfitted with a complicated-looking arrangement of levers and wheel locks. A transparent observation portal was set at eye level in the dark gray mass. A printed sign beside the metal-collared frame bore large words in red, and even a stylized human skull. The first word was very large and even Kane knew what it meant: *Verboten!*

Brigid translated the rest of the warning. "'Biohazard Beyond This Point. Authorized Ahnenrbe Institute Personnel Only.' That pretty much cinches the primary function of this place."

"What's the Ahnenrbe Institute?" Cotta wanted to know, managing to pronounce the word as Brigid had.

"The Third Reich's version of Overproject Excalibur," she answered flatly. "It oversaw the medical experiments on concentration-camp inmates and designed a breeding program for the German people. It was formed as a private scientific institution, then it was formally absorbed into the SS. The projects it was involved with earned its director, Wolfram Sievers, a hangman's noose."

The window revealed a wide, low-ceilinged room antiseptically white in color. A maze of sterile medical equipment glittered beneath the cold light shed by overhead fluorescent tubes. The big room appeared to be broodingly silent and lifeless.

Grant worked on the door. No high-tech or electronic locking systems were visible. He worked the levers, and there came the clacking sound of solenoids opening. As he spun the wheel, the door swung inward easily on oiled pivots.

Kane stepped in first, assuming the pointman's position, eyes and blaster barrel sweeping back and forth. He saw three closed doors set in the far wall. He, Brigid and Grant had visited similar laboratory setups before, so he wasn't mystified by the trestle tables bearing complicated glasswork, microscopes, fluoroscopes and oscilloscopes. He even recognized a hyperbaric pressure chamber.

"No surprises so far," he murmured.

"Except," Brigid said in the same subdued tone, "most of this equipment looks like it dates from the 1960s and 70s. Not like the stuff we saw in Dulce."

"What were they up to with it?" Cotta inquired.

She indicated a stainless-steel tank in a corner. The lid was open, revealing a honeycomb pattern of individual containers that had once held frozen human embryos. "What the Ahnenrbe Institute was always up to…trying to improve the breed."

Kane crossed the room swiftly, walking heel-to-toe as he always did in a potential killzone. At the first door, he tried the knob and it turned easily. When he opened it, a lighting system flashed on automatically. His hair lifted from the nape of his neck, and he felt his skin crawl. Although very clean and tidy, the big room beyond was a crypt. Ten complete wired-together skeletons hung from frameworks. On a long trestle table rested yellowed, grinning skulls, many of which bore deep cracks or were completely caved in.

He stepped into the room, followed by his companions. Cotta repressed a curse at the sight of all of the bones. Besides the skulls on the table, trays were laid out holding electronic components, odds and ends of small circuit boards, thread-thin antennae, and wires so small they were almost invisible.

Brigid poked at them, saying wryly, "I guess the microprocessor and silicon-chip revolution didn't reach as far as New Schwabenland."

Glancing down at a skull, Grant saw it was trephinated and inside the hole was a sleeve socket. "What the hell were they doing with this stuff?"

Brigid picked up a skull, revolving it between her hands, examining it with a critical eye. "Most of these skulls belong to an early type of *Homo sapiens*. Look at the supraorbital ridges."

Kane looked and saw the huge bar of brow bone and massive underslung jaw sporting chisel-like teeth. "Cavemen bones?"

"Earlier," she replied. "Protohumans, like *Australopithecus*."

Cotta was circling the room when he stopped and blurted, "Look at this!"

In a little niche was a pair of vertical, metal-framed vats. Within one, standing upright, was a very old corpse, a mummy. It floated in a dark amber fluid. The shriveled, gnarled limbs were covered in white, shaggy hair, and its dark eye sockets seemed to stare at them. It was very tall, the sagittal crest at the top of its skull topping nearly nine feet. Its withered facial features resembled those of an ape, but its hands and feet were more manlike than those of an simian.

In the other fluid-filled vat floated small, malformed figures, distorted imitations of the corpse. The sight awakened nausea in the stomachs of the four people. The figures were not so much malformed as half-formed. They bobbed in the preserving fluid like so many ghastly tadpoles. Most of them resembled hairless apes, but with tiny, vestigial limbs. Some of them had their intestines spreading around them from Y incisions cut into their small bodies.

Brigid, Kane and Grant had glimpsed similar horrors in the sublevel of the Dulce installation known as Nightmare Alley, so they weren't as filled with revulsion as they might have been.

Cotta, however, made a gagging sound and whirled away, covering his mouth with both hands.

"What the fuck is that thing?" Grant demanded, eyeing the mummified corpse. "Some kind of mutie they made here?"

"Maybe," Brigid said. "I don't think so. Maybe these skulls aren't fossils after all."

"What else could they be?" asked Kane.

A line of concentration appeared on Brigid's forehead. She glanced from the skull in her hands to the face of the mummy. "The Ahnenrbe had connections with certain religious orders in Tibet, like the Bonpo." She cast a questioning glance toward Kane. "Remember Gyatso?"

Kane's lips quirked in a mirthless half smile. "I'm not likely to forget that creepy little bastard."

They had encountered Gyatso at the same time their paths intersected with that of Grigori Zakat. Both men were fanatics, Zakat a Russian mystic, Gyastso a shaman of the old Bon-po religion that predated Buddhism in Tibet by nearly a thousand years. Spiritually, Gyatso and Zakat were the same—power mad and ruthless in their quest to harness the energies of the Chintamani Stone. Their shared quest had ended in their violent, richly deserved deaths.

"The Ahnenrbe undertook an expedition to Tibet in the late 1930s," Brigid continued, "supposedly to find proof that the Aryan race had conquered it in prehistory. The Bon-po religion and Nazi occultism had a lot of things in common, so the Germans were very well treated there."

"So?" asked Grant impatiently.

She gave him a slightly irritated look. "Rumor has it the Ahnenrbe was there to do a lot more than look at sacred writings and to examine artifacts. Maybe they were supplied with a yeti, or a family group of them."

"What's a yeti?" inquired Kane, interested in spite of himself. Brigid Baptiste wasn't quite the ambulatory encyclopedia she appeared to be, since most of her seemingly limitless supply of knowledge was due to her eidetic memory, but her apparent familiarity with an astounding variety of topics never failed to impress—and occasionally irritate—him.

"According to Tibetan legend, the yetis were subhuman throwbacks who haunted the Himalayas. They were known in the West as Abominable Snowmen. Though there were a lot of sightings of them, even supposedly a skeleton kept in a lamasery, their existence was usually dismissed as folklore."

"Why would the Nazis want to experiment on yetis?" Cotta asked, sounding completely at sea.

Grant scowled at the mummy, then at the collection

of electronic parts on the table. Comprehension suddenly shone in his eyes. "Mind-controlled warriors, bigger and stronger than humans."

Brigid nodded. "And worse than that perhaps. It's possible they bred human women with yetis to create a hybrid race, forging their own path to create a new human."

Kane repressed a shiver of loathing. "Is that possible?"

Brigid shrugged. "Who knows. If this is the corpse of a yeti, then it appears to be a bit more human than ape. Even the chromosomal makeup of a chimpanzee is less than one percent different from a human's." She gestured to the little bodies floating in the vat. "Those may be the failures of the undertaking, autopsied and tossed in there for further study."

"If that's what the Nazis were trying to accomplish here," Grant rumbled darkly, "it's no damn wonder they weren't an official part of the Totality Concept."

Cotta had managed to recover, so his steps were fairly steady when they moved on to the next room. It was even larger, a dispensary or sick bay. A row of hospital beds lay inside a curtained alcove. A glass-fronted cabinet contained a wide array of medical supplies, from wooden tongue depressors to pharmaceuticals to syringes.

Brigid gave them a cursory inspection and took out a pair of small vials. One was half-filled with a clear liquid and the other held white tablets.

"Methedrine and amphetamines," she announced, showing them to Kane. "And God only knows what else. If Skorzeny is self-medicating, it would go a long way to explain his nervous agitation and speeded-up reflexes."

"You mean he's wired up?" Kane asked.

"To the proverbial gills." She replaced the vials in the cabinet. "Maybe it's a form of hero worship, since Hitler was a drug addict himself."

At the opposite end of the dispensary, Cotta slid back an accordion-style partition on its floor and ceiling tracks. "What's all this?"

His companions joined him and saw, angled on a raised platform, two long white capsules, reminiscent of oversized porcelain coffins. Recessed farther into the wall on metal shelving behind the tubes were twelve small silver canisters.

"Cryo units," intoned Brigid. "Just like we suspected. Rip Van Standartenführer."

# Chapter 5

Coils of copper tubing festooned each of the small silver canisters, and the tops bore transparent convex ports. Brigid strode over to the shelves, stood on tiptoe and peered into one. She recoiled with a wordless utterance of disgust.

The others joined her and saw for themselves what triggered her reaction. Looking down into the port, they saw a face looking back up at them. The head of a man was nestled inside the container, but there was only a semblance left of his features. The lips were peeled like old leather over discolored teeth. Part of the scalp was completely bare of hair and skin, showing naked bone. The little flesh remaining on his face was rotted, liquescent tissue.

Moving down the line, Kane saw every canister held a human head in advanced stages of decomposition. Voice heavy with disgust, he demanded, "Why the hell is Skorzeny collecting heads?"

"He wasn't collecting them," replied Brigid. "He was preserving them...or at least that was the original idea. These are cryonic storage capsules."

"Just for heads?" Cotta's tone was incredulous.

"It wasn't unknown to deep-freeze heads in liquid nitrogen at a temperature of minus 196 degrees Celsius, back in the twentieth century. The process used to be known as neuro-suspension. If these are the heads of Nazi scientists, only their brains and the knowledge within them were important enough to preserve.''

"Why would they go along with that?'' growled Grant.

Brigid smiled wanly. "The Third Reich wasn't known for allowing people to make their own choices. Besides, it's possible they were told their heads could be transplanted onto new bodies. It certainly looks like some form of cloning was going on here.''

Gingerly, she touched the gleaming surface of a canister. "Apparently, there was a malfunction in the units.''

Kane's lips pursed. "Apparently. So why wasn't just Skorzeny's head frozen?''

Brigid stepped over to the pair of long cylinders. The exterior of both bore a small label: TransTime Technologies Inc., Los Angeles CA., Patent Pending. "He was probably the guardian, his unit programmed to revive him first so he could look after the others.''

Kane and Grant eyed the capsules, mentally comparing them to the suspended-animation systems they had seen in other places. "It's not like the other units we've seen,'' Grant pointed out.

Brigid nodded in agreement. "The ones we've come across before utilized Archon technology, stasis fields combined with cryogenics. These are strictly cryonic based. State-of-the-art for the time, but not up to the advances later developed.''

She turned to face her companions. "The Germans here didn't have access to that tech. Maybe it was withheld from them, or maybe they were already in suspension by the time it became available. My guess is that by the time the Totality Concept researches achieved a certain level, the project overseers saw no reason to keep this installation supplied. It and the people here were swept under the rug.''

''With the connection between the Archons and the Nazis,'' Kane said thoughtfully, ''you'd think this place would have favored-nation status.''

According to what Kane, Brigid and Grant had been told upon their arrival at the Cerberus redoubt more than a year ago, the entirety of human history was intertwined with the activities of entities called Archons, although they had been referred to by many names over many centuries—angels, demons, visitors, ETs, saucer people, grays.

Archons traditionally allied themselves with conquerors and despots from Genghis Khan to Adolf Hitler, conspiring with willing human pawns to control mankind through political chaos, staged wars, famines, plagues and natural disasters.

But despite their superior technology and intellects, the Archons were not omniscient, as Hitler discovered. World War II was not just a defeat of the Third Reich, but a defeat of the Archons, as well. After the war, they took measures to insure that they would not be beaten again, and one of those measures was the development of the Totality Concept. A pact was formed between elements in the United States government and the Archon Directive, essentially an exchange with the Archons for high-tech knowledge. Part of the trade agreement allowed the Archons use of underground military bases. The elite who knew of the Archon Directive believed that the Archons were benevolent, that their primary interest in sharing the Totality Concept technology with humanity was to make nuclear war obsolete. That faith proved worthless with the nuclear holocaust of January 2001.

Kane had accepted all of that, the hidden history of humanity. Despite how insane it seemed to him at first, he grew comfortable with having a focus for his hatred. For months, he woke up hating Archons and he went to bed hating Archons. It was easy, it was simple and he saw no reason to change his mind, despite the fact he came across discrepancies, facts at variance with the Cerberus doctrine as put forth by Mohandas Lakesh Singh.

In the past few months, he had learned his hatred was not only pointless, but pretty much without merit. The Archon Directorate, which supplanted the Archon Directive, did not exist except as a cover story created two centuries before and expanded with each succeeding generation. It was all a ruse, a skein of outrageous fiction interwoven with threads of truth. Only a single so-called Archon existed on Earth and that was Balam, who had been the Cerberus redoubt's resident prisoner for more than three and a half years.

Balam claimed the Archon Directorate was an appellation created by the predark governments. Lakesh referred to it as the Oz Effect, wherein a single vulnerable entity created the illusion of being the representative of an all-powerful body.

Even more shocking than that revelation was Balam's assertion he and his folk were humans, not alien but alienated. Kane still didn't know how much to believe. But if nothing else, he no longer subscribed to the fatalistic belief that the human race had had its day and only extinction lay ahead. Balam had indicated that was not true, only another control mechanism.

Kane in particular was still skeptical of Balam's version of the facts, but so far he had encountered nothing to prove them false. Besides, Balam was gone and with him the threat of the Archon Directorate, though the myth remained. Only the half-human hybrids spawned from Balam's DNA were left to contend with. Or so all of them fervently hoped.

Rapping one of the cryo-cylinders with her knuckles, Brigid went on. "It's possible Skorzeny was frozen as far back as the 1970s or 80s. When he revived, let's say fifteen or so years ago, he found that the other storage units had malfunctioned. He's been trapped in here ever since, wandering around alone, probably thinking he's the last human being on Earth."

Cotta winced at the notion. "That's long enough to fuse him out permanently."

"He was probably well on his way before he was frozen," Grant gruffly observed. "Why didn't Skorzeny use the gateway to jump out of here?"

Brigid frowned slightly. "A lot of reasons. Maybe it was installed after he was frozen. The fact that it's outside the facility instead of inside gives that theory some weight. He might not even know it's there. And if so, he might not know how to operate it or he's afraid to."

"I don't think that old racist is afraid of much," Grant said darkly. "Who was in the other unit?"

Brigid shrugged. "It could have been Josef Mengele himself for all we know. Both men supposedly died at roughly the same time. But whoever it was is probably long dead."

Kane released his breath in a long sigh. "There's nothing here for the barons."

"We don't know that for sure," Brigid replied.

"There may be a nuclear stockpile somewhere in here."

"Or just more memorabilia from the good old days of the Third Reich," Kane responded. "I think we should take as much of the valuable stuff as we can haul, jump back to Cerberus and come back with a larger team. This place doesn't represent a threat."

After a thoughtful moment, Brigid said, "That might have been true until we showed up…and gave Skorzeny the idea there are other people in the world."

"So?" asked Cotta.

Grant picked up on Brigid's thread. "So if there are other people, Skorzeny may figure it's past time to go out and conquer them."

Kane snorted. "One crazy old Nazi?"

"One crazy old Nazi who might be sitting on rockets with atomic warheads. That's something the barons would be interested in."

They moved out of the dispensary and through the last door. It opened onto a narrow, dimly lit passageway. Cotta's nostrils flared. "What's that smell?"

All of them sniffed the air experimentally, even though it was a wasted effort for Grant. His nose had suffered several breaks over the years and had always been poorly reset. As a result, his sense of smell was severely impaired. Kane caught a gamy whiff, redolent with the stench of excrement and a cloying odor reminiscent of a wet dog. His point man's sixth sense rang an alarm, and his finger hovered over the trigger stud of his Sin Eater.

The corridor passed beneath a stone arch and led into a chamber shaped like a perfect cube. Glowing torches were set in sconces on the high, vaulted walls and cast a flickering illumination. The four people stood in a cramped aisle between a guardrail and a triple row of theater-type seats.

The aisle overlooked a square pit, a smaller cube within the larger. The walls plunging downward were sheer. Kane guessed it was about a fifteen-foot drop to the flagstone floor below, which showed dark stains. Two heavy metal doors faced each other at opposite ends of the pit. The objectionable odor seemed to waft up from below, a miasma of stink.

"This is like a theater," Brigid observed, looking around.

"More like a stadium," suggested Cotta.

"Or an arena," said Kane grimly, leaning on the rail.

Grant grunted disinterestedly. "Let's move on."

As Kane started to turn away, a small sound at the periphery of his hearing reached him. It was a metallic scrape-click. That sound was almost immediately overwhelmed by a flat, hand-clapping bang. A spark jumped from the guardrail barely three inches from his right hand. Wiry slivers of lead struck his sleeve.

As he recoiled, he caught a blurred glimpse of a black-clad, white-bearded figure hastily drawing back behind the nearest door in the pit below. Skorzeny moved so swiftly out of sight Kane had no opportunity to return fire.

"The bastard is down there," he barked, vaulting the rail.

"Wait—" Brigid called.

Landing on the balls of his feet and instantly throwing his body forward, Kane caught himself with his left hand and went into a roll. Coming to his feet within a yard of the door, he took up position on one side of it, double-fisting his Sin Eater.

Grant, Cotta and Brigid followed him down, hanging on to the bottom cross bar of the rail before dropping to the floor. When they joined him, Kane whispered to Grant, "I'll go high, you go low."

The man nodded, crouching down. "On three."

Grasping the handle, Kane mouthed, "One… two…*three!*"

He yanked the door handle with all his strength. It refused to budge, and he nearly staggered backward. In angry frustration, he pulled on the handle again and heard the clink of steel on the other side.

"Drop bar," he grated, glaring at the sheet metal covering the door. "No shooting our way in."

Brigid glanced anxiously toward the door on the opposite wall. "I have a feeling that one isn't locked."

Apprehensively, Cotta asked, "Why do you say that?"

"Skorzeny is playing us," she replied. "He may be insane, but he's still cunning."

Kane threw her a dour glance. "It'll take longer to climb up out of here than to check that door."

"Yeah," Grant rumbled sarcastically. "And that's probably what Skorzeny expects us to do."

He withdrew the H&K VP-70 from the pocket of his thermal suit and handed it butt first to Cotta. "You can have this back, on the understanding you don't shoot until either I or Kane tells you to."

Cotta nodded, swallowing hard.

Kane moved toward the door. "Let's not disappoint the son of a bitch."

He took only a few steps before his pointman's sense began screaming an alert. He continued to cross the pit, but he angled slightly away from the door. He tried to ignore the icy fingers of mounting fear at the base of his spine. The closer he got to the door, the more insistent became his mental alarm. He received the distinct impression of being watched and he sensed the pressure of unseen eyes. The three people behind him didn't speak or stir.

When he was within ten feet of the door, he came to a halt. He tensed, then slowly took a long step back.

At the same time the pit filled with a clanking, ratcheting racket. The door rose upward between deep channels in the frame. A woolly, musky odor clogged Kane's nostrils, and he heard a hoarse, rasping grunt.

In the darkness behind the door, something heavy and huge moved, shifting on padded feet. Before the portal had risen completely, a great, shaggy shape emerged from the gloom as if flung from a catapult. With a throaty growl, it rocked to a clumsy halt on two bowed legs, leaning forward to support itself on knuckles the size of doorknobs.

# Chapter 6

The dim light showed a giant humanoid body, but greater in girth and height than any man. The body was covered in a coat of dark gray hair, shot through with threads of white. The creature's forearms appeared to be as thick as Kane's thighs. Its large, long head, sunk between lumps of shoulder muscle, was topped by a sagittal crest for the attachment of the massive jaw muscles.

The face was a distorted imitation of a human's. The heavy supraorbital ridges above the eyes, the flat nose with flared nostrils, the protruding jaw and long yellow canines behind the writhing lips put Kane in mind of a gorilla. He had seen pics of the extinct great apes and even a stuffed exhibit on display in the ruins of the Museum of Natural History, so he immediately saw the similarities, as well as the differences.

The skin tones were a pale brownish hue. Like the mummy they had seen earlier, its broad, splayed feet didn't possess the near-opposable big toe of the ape. Kane noted that a small bare spot had been shaved in the roach of hair at the top of the creature's skull. Several splinters of metal gleamed there.

The creature sniffed around, deep brown eyes darting back and forth. Kane eyed the massive, protruding swag belly, the huge muscular pectorals swelling in giant arches over the chest. Although his finger still hovered over the trigger of his Sin Eater, he didn't fire. Unless his first shot was exceptionally lucky, the dense muscle tissue would slow down the round before it penetrated the clavicle bones and struck the heart.

Behind him he heard Grant demand breathlessly, "What the fuck is it? Some kind of ape?"

Skorzeny's voice floated to them from the gloom beyond the raised door panel. He sounded genuinely amused. "Yes and no. His name is Jacko, and he is a fairly accurate reconstruction of *Paranthropus,* the giant hominoid who lived in East Africa half a million or so years ago. He is the living basis of many folktales, including what Americans called the Bigfoot, or Sasquatch."

Kane did not take his eyes off the creature, who, even stooped, still towered nearly a foot above the crown of Kane's head. Erect, Kane figured Jacko would be close to nine feet tall. He estimated the creature weighed in at a minimum of nine hundred pounds. At the moment, he didn't seem hostile, only mildly curious.

"In a Tibetan lamasery," Skorzeny continued, "we found the preserved remains of one of his kind. There they were known as yetis. The creatures were almost extinct and the chances of bagging a live specimen extremely remote, so we appropriated the corpse for our researches."

"So you could grow your own at home?" Brigid asked, her voice surprisingly calm.

"Yes," came Skorzeny's reply. "But Jacko was our only success. He went into cryo freeze with me and has been my only companion since I awakened. I'm sure by now he is the last of his kind, unless I can find a way to propagate his seed.''

Skorzeny paused, chuckled wheezingly and continued. ''You, *liebchen*, will be able to assist in that. You might find the process emotionally repugnant, but you would not be physically endangered. Despite his truly impressive size, Jacko's erect Johnson is only two inches long.''

''His what?'' mumbled Cotta.

Still sounding unruffled, Brigid replied, ''You'll understand if I decline.''

''It makes no difference whether you decline or agree,'' Skorzeny replied. ''Once your companions are in Jacko's belly, you'll have very little to say about it.''

''In Jacko's belly?'' Grant repeated in a challenging tone.

''His kind were popularly supposed by anthropologists to be vegetarians, but he had no choice but to develop a taste for meat.''

''What kind of meat?'' Kane asked, already guessing the answer in advance.

Skorzeny spit contemptuously, ''What do you think, *schwein?* Human meat. I wasn't about to keep the bodies of our staff in cold storage forever.''

His voice broke, as if he were biting back a sob. ''The scientists who created him died, but Jacko survived. There's some kind of joke in there.''

''You brought him up well,'' Kane said blandly. ''He seems very well behaved for an ape-man.''

Skorzeny laughed, a high, scornful tittering. ''You can thank Dr. Kurt Plotner of the Ahnenrbe for that— or rather you can thank his head. He developed the electronic devices to control the brain functions by remote control. Watch.''

Kane heard a faint click, as of a plastic switch snapping over, and Jacko suddenly quivered, then lay down on the floor in a fetal position. He appeared to go to sleep. There was another click and suddenly the ponderous creature was on his feet, bellowing and roaring, eyes wide and wild.

Kane centered the Sin Eater's sights on Jacko's head, but with another click, all the tension went out of the creature's body and he slumped over on his knuckles again. He blinked at Kane drowsily. There was something primordially beautiful about the man-ape, but the beauty was lost on Kane. There was fat under that shaggy hide, but there were also massive bones and muscles holding the strength of ten men Grant's size.

"Do you understand now?" Skorzeny asked. "Tiny circuits are connected to his brain through holes drilled in his skull. The electrodes were implanted in the areas of the brain controlling specific behavior. I can control him by flicking switches and turning dials. He can be driven to attack by electrically stimulating the part of the brain that controls aggression.''

Skorzeny heaved a sad sigh. "Poor Kurt. He envisioned devices of this nature implanted in the brains of every human being at the end of the war. It never came to pass. Still, it is quite the invention, is it not?''

Kane didn't respond. Another wisp of a memory of his journey to the Reich-ruled parallel casement ghosted through his mind. Although he couldn't recall solid details, he remembered how a mind-controlled warrior race was being bred there.

"I asked you a question, *schwein!*" Skorzeny half-shrieked.

"Very impressive," Kane said, stepping back from Jacko. "I hope you two will continue to be very happy here. Now we really must be going."

With a chilling calm, Skorzeny announced. "That is very true." A click reached Kane's ears. "*Auf wiedersehen.*"

Jacko uttered a thunderous roar and bulled toward Kane, swinging wide his hairy arms.

KANE'S FINGER DEPRESSED the trigger stud of his Sin Eater just as one of Jacko's keg-size hands closed over the barrel. He glimpsed blood and shreds of flesh explode from the heel of the massive paw. Jacko's grip didn't loosen. He wrenched at the blaster as if he were trying to pry a nail from a piece of lumber.

White-hot agony exploded the length of Kane's arm, a nova of pain flaring in his shoulder socket. He had no time to cry out as Jacko, with a whipping motion, yanked the Sin Eater and its holster from his forearm. Leather ripped, cables parted with twangs, seams split and metal buckles popped. The blaster came free, peeling away some sleeve and skin.

The force exerted on Kane's arm pulled him off his feet and slammed him facefirst into the pit wall. He rebounded like a handball, mouth filling with blood from a laceration in his lip, his right arm feeling as if it had been torn from the socket.

He managed to keep his footing even though he staggered the width of the pit to the opposite wall, arms windmilling. Through the amoeba-shaped floaters clouding his vision, he saw Jacko toss the blaster and holster aside.

The man-ape charged him in a swift, lumbering lunge, fangs bared, bowed legs hurtling him forward. Kane heard Brigid cry out and Grant yell. They had no time to fire their blasters before Jacko swept Kane up in a crushing embrace.

Kane planted a blow to Jacko's swag belly with all the power of his left arm. His fist bounced away from the steel-hard sheathing of muscle. Although his right arm burned with pain, he lifted his hand, wrist locked, fingers curled, and smashed a leopard's-paw strike into Jacko's nose.

Instead of crushing the cartilage and driving bone splinters into the brain, the heel of his hand skidded up Jacko's flat, flaring nose and was deflected by the heavy brow ridge. Still, Jacko's head jerked back a trifle and his long arms loosened around Kane's body for a fraction of a second.

That was enough time for Kane to drop and wriggle out of the hug. A swinging backhand caught him between the shoulder blades and propelled him into a clumsy half cartwheel. His lungs had emptied with a whoof at the strike, and he landed on his side, gasping and wincing, trying to drag in enough air to remain conscious.

Grant brought Jacko into target acquisition and squeezed off a tri-burst. The 9 mm rounds struck the creature low in the chest, impacting at 335 pounds of pressure per square inch. The trio of slugs knocked Jacko backward, but his bowed legs did not fold.

Voicing a hoarse, gobbling cry, Jacko bounded at Grant so swiftly that he was only a dark, shaggy blur to Brigid and Cotta. Grant sprang to one side, but not swiftly enough to escape completely untouched. Long, beveled nails tipping a great paw raked over Grant's forehead, tearing two crimson furrows in the flesh. Blood gushed out, momentarily blinding him.

Kane hiked himself up to one knee, still snapping at air. He reached down to his right boot, his hand finding the quick-release button of his combat knife and snatching it free of its scabbard. He scrambled to his feet as Jacko closed in on Grant again. He frantically tried to clear his vision with swipes of his forearm.

Brigid drew a careful bead on the creature's head with her Iver Johnson handblaster, as if she were aiming at the tiny electrode planted in the shaved section of scalp.

Cotta shouldered Brigid aside to put himself between Grant and Jacko. He fired his VP-70 twice, flame and thunder leaping from the short barrel. The man-ape shot out one arm and grabbed Cotta by the right wrist.

Bellowing, Jacko twisted and jerked, flipping Cotta off his feet, then upside down. He screamed shrilly as his legs kicked like those of a disjointed puppet. All of them heard the mushy tearing sound, as of wet cloth being ripped in half. When Cotta hit the floor, he stopped screaming. His right arm was clenched in Jacko's fist. Bright arterial blood gushed in a torrent from Cotta's shoulder socket.

Brigid cried out in wordless horror, and Jacko whirled toward her. He wielded the dismembered arm like a club, slapping her across the side of the head with the scarlet-squirting stump. She staggered sideways, face coated with blood, and fell to all fours.

Kane launched himself from the floor as Jacko struck at Brigid with Cotta's arm. He landed full on the creature's back, at the same time driving the fourteen-inch tungsten-steel blade to half its length into a lumped shoulder muscle.

Jacko screamed horribly and wheeled around and around like a dog chasing its tail. Kane locked his legs around the man-ape's torso while he stabbed again and again with his combat knife. Jacko rose to his full height and reached up and around, clawing for Kane's hair.

Yelling at the top of his lungs, Grant charged the huge creature. Jacko and Kane were too close together, a whirl of thrashing limbs, for him to risk shooting. Jacko batted at him with Cotta's arm. He dodged and kicked at the giant's hair-covered paunch. His boot impacted solidly, and Jacko bellowed so loudly he half deafened Kane.

Jacko stumbled backward toward the pit wall, apparently intending to crush the man on his back. Kane almost managed to kick free, but Jacko slammed him hard against the concrete with a bone-jarring force. Little multicolored pinwheels spiraled behind Kane's eyes, but he forced himself to keep his legs clamped around Jacko's body.

Grant leaped forward again, battering at Jacko's face with his left fist and clubbing him with the barrel of his Sin Eater. Scarlet rivulets sprang from the creature's nostrils, and he struck at Grant again and again with his flesh-and-bone bludgeon.

Weaving and ducking, Grant avoided the blows, but he slipped in the blood spilling from Cotta's maimed shoulder socket. He fell almost directly beneath the man-ape. Jacko could have dropped to all fours and smashed Grant against the floor, but instead he lifted one monstrously huge foot and stamped it down against Grant's right wrist.

Grant cried out in pain, and he definitely heard something give within the frame of his Sin Eater.

Jacko returned his attention to Kane. Dropping Cotta's arm, he reached up and behind him, his talon-tipped fingers securing grips in Kane's thermal suit, ripping through the tough fabric and padding beneath. Inexorably, he began dragging the man around in front of him, within reach of his fangs.

Kane resisted the pull of the creature's arms, tightening his legs around Jacko's barrel-shaped body, his knife sinking over and over into hair-covered flesh. He knew if his blade didn't quickly pierce a vital spot, Jacko's inhuman strength and energy would keep him alive and on the attack.

He stabbed Jacko in the lower back and kept the blade there, working and goring. He relaxed the tension in his legs and allowed the man-ape to drag him up and forward. The razor-keen edge of the blade sheared a path through hair, hide and layers of muscle.

Screaming in agony, Jacko convulsed, bouncing up and down on his short legs, but he didn't relinquish his grasp on Kane. Neither did Kane loosen his grip on the knife as he slashed a scarlet-lipped gash all the way up the giant creature's back. The man-ape stank with a strong, vile smell as human as it was animal.

Maddened by the pain, Jacko clawed at him, and for an instant Kane felt as if he were caught in the teeth of an earthquake. His thermal suit shredded beneath the creature's flaying nails.

Then with a volcanic burst of strength, Jacko wrenched him loose, hurling him against Grant, who had just risen to a crouch. Both men sprawled, rolling, on the floor, but Kane kept his knife in his fist.

Grant was up first, Sin Eater leveled at the end of

his arm. He fired at point-blank range, sewing three red-rimmed holes in the huge belly. Then metal ground against metal within the blaster and the trigger froze, refusing to move. Jacko fell against the wall and lurched forward, knees bending, catching himself on his knuckles. He trembled violently, his massive paunch heaving, head hanging between his enormous shoulders.

The brief respite gave Grant and Kane time to scramble to their feet and stumble to the opposite side of the pit. Kane staggered dizzily, blood streaming down his right hand and dripping from the blade. Sidling over to them, Brigid made a move to support Kane but he shook her off impatiently.

"The direct approach isn't working," he husked out. His joints felt as if they had been dislocated, and blood trickled from scratches where Jacko's fingernails had torn through all the layers of his clothing to the skin beneath.

Jade eyes preternaturally bright behind the layer of Cotta's blood glistening on her face, Brigid said tensely, "As long as Skorzeny holds the controls, Jacko won't stop. He's flooding the poor beast's system with adrenaline."

Very faintly, from the gloom on the other side of the open door came a series of clicks.

With a gasping roar, Jacko heaved himself up to his full height like a gray whale breaking the surface of the sea.

"Poor beast, my ass," Grant growled.

The shaggy giant charged them, clumsily and more slowly than before. They spread out, ducking wild long-armed blows and splashing through the puddle of blood spreading around Cotta's body. Kane sprang to one side just before Jacko was on him. The man-ape rammed head-on into the wall with a crash that made the floor tremble under the feet of the three people.

Jacko recovered swiftly, whirled and was after Grant, who had leaped into a corner. Using the two walls as a brace, Grant levered up his body and shot his legs out. The heavy treads of his boot soles collided with the creature's face.

Grant fell down but rolled and was up and out of the reach of Jacko's arms while the man-ape shook his head, snorting blood from his nostrils. He launched himself at Kane.

The long nails snagged in the back of Kane's thermal suit and ripped a wide rent in the fabric. Putting his feet against the wall behind him, Grant used it as a springboard to dive under the creature, between his legs.

Jacko was completely taken by surprise by this maneuver. He spun around, but Grant bounced to his feet and was on his back. He applied a full nelson, curving his arms up and under Jacko's shoulders, locking his hands at the back of the creature's bull neck.

Grant was an exceptionally strong man, but he realized immediately that Jacko's neck muscles were as hard as wood. But he hung on, veins on his temples bulging, the muscles in his arms quivering in tortured knots.

Kane dived in just as Jacko's head was forced onto his breast, slashing with his knife at the tendons behind the man-ape's right knee.

The blade didn't cut deeply enough to hamstring Jacko, but he toppled over on his side. The fall broke Grant's hold, and he tried to get away. Jacko, snarling, elbowed himself to all fours. He clawed at Grant, hands closing around his leg and twisting. Grant spun clumsily in the direction of the twist, yelling in pain and fear, visualizing the man-ape doing to his leg what had been done to Cotta's arm.

Brigid rushed forward, jumped in the air and came down with both feet on the back of Jacko's massive neck. It was like jumping on a hair-covered boulder, and she fell off. Still the impact of her feet caused the creature to relax his grip on Grant's leg long enough for him to tear himself loose. He rolled away, then came to his feet, drawing his own blade from its boot scabbard.

The three people backed into a corner, all of them wincing, grimacing and panting. They watched as Jacko, coughing from deep in his lungs, slowly got to his feet. Crimson rivered from the multitude of wounds on his body. He stood for a few moments, looking at them. Favoring his knife-slashed leg, he shambled to the side, tottering away from them.

Brigid looked past Jacko toward the open door and whispered tensely, "Try to get his attention."

Grant and Kane gave her incredulous stares. "I think we've already got it," Kane snapped.

"Do as I say," she bit out.

Kane exchanged a swift glance with Grant, then bounded forward, kicking Jacko in the rear with his right foot. Jacko became a roaring maniac again. He whirled so swiftly that Kane couldn't completely avoid the openhanded blow directed at his face. He ducked, but the tip of a fingernail caught his chin and opened a small cut.

He glimpsed Brigid darting quickly, trying to circle around the man-ape. Instead of trying to put as much distance between him and Jacko as the confines of the pit would allow, he yelled wordlessly and waved his arms.

Jacko's eyes caught Brigid's furtive movement, and he spun toward her. With nimble grace, she leaped sideways. His big hand lashed out and gripped her left ankle. She fell, catching herself on the flats of her hands and tried to struggle loose. Grunting, Jacko dragged her toward him.

Lifting her right leg, Brigid thrust out her foot, the heel catching Jacko on the side of the jaw. Had it been a man's jaw, the bone would have shattered, but the hairy giant only squinted. She slammed the sole of her boot into his nose with a crunching of cartilage.

Jacko continued to haul her to him, as if her leg were a rope. She kicked again, her right foot sinking into the shaggy juncture of his thighs with a sound as of an ax hitting soft wood. He screamed with surprised agony and released her, hands clutching at his testicles.

As Brigid rolled away, Kane rushed Jacko, panting under his breath, "At least that part of him is human."

Kane stab-kicked him on his wounded leg. The creature staggered. Before Kane could backpedal, Jacko grabbed him with both enormous hands, snatching him clear of the floor.

The great arms shook him violently, and his knife fell from his hand. Jacko put his arms around him, tightening them across his spine. He felt his vertebrae compress. Rather than trying to fight his way out of the hug, he rammed the crown of his head forward, hearing and feeling teeth give way.

Cupping both hands, he slapped them against the giant's ears with all of his strength. Jacko howled, tossing his head as the double shock waves drove nails

of pain through his eardrums. Reflexively, he released
his grip so he could cradle the sides of his head.

Kane fell and back-somersaulted away from Jacko,
plucking his knife from the floor in the same motion.
As he rolled to his feet, he tried to catch a glimpse of
Brigid, but Jacko blocked his view.

Voicing an animalistic bellow himself, Grant
launched himself in a feetfirst dive, his body almost
parallel with the pit floor. The soles of his boots
slammed into Jacko's lower belly, all of his 230
pounds powering the dropkick.

The creature uttered a strangulated cry and jack-
knifed at the waist. On his back in front of him, Grant
whipped up his right leg. The steel-reinforced toe of
his boot impacted against Jacko's receding chin with
a crack like metal striking flint. He sat down unceremoniously on the flagstones, deep-set eyes acquiring
a glassy sheen.

Without hesitation, Kane and Grant flung themselves on Jacko. All three of them went down in a
grappling thrash of limbs, a whirlwind of blows and
the dim flash of razored steel. They barely heard the
gunshots.

# Chapter 7

As Grant's boot impacted against Jacko's chin, Brigid reached the door, her blaster in hand. Throwing herself to one side of the recessed frame, she fired blindly into the gloom beyond, the thunder of the shots echoing hollowly.

She heard a choked outcry in surprised German, followed by the cracking report of the Luger. Skorzeny squeezed off three rounds, the slugs ripping through the open portal nowhere near her position. She heard a warbling shriek from Jacko and glanced behind her.

Jacko rolled and writhed, slapping at himself. His hands bloody, he shoved Grant and Kane away from him, tumbling them in a head-over-heels tangle.

Skorzeny cursed loudly when he realized his wild return fire had struck his mind-controlled assassin. While he was still swearing, Brigid dived through the door, going low, her Iver Johnson spitting flame.

The muzzle-flash limned a narrow stone-walled interior. Skorzeny stood at the midway point, his pistol in one hand and a bulky leather-encased box hanging by a strap from his neck. She glimpsed an antenna projecting from its face a shaved sliver of a second before a spark flared from it.

Skorzeny staggered from the impact, which was deflected by the metal and leather of the control unit. He didn't return the fire. His stagger became a shambling, backward run down the passage, and he ducked out of sight around a corner.

Rising to her feet, Brigid shouted over her shoulder, "I nailed Jacko's controls. I'm going after Skorzeny."

Kane's alarmed, breathless "Wait" reached her, but she sprinted forward anyway. Before she reached the end of the narrow corridor, she heard the clang of metal on metal.

The passageway opened into a cramped chamber. She went to the door, which was no more than a slab of steel set tightly in the stone-block wall, with a handle curving out from its rust-pimpled surface.

Brigid waited at the door for a moment, listening, but she heard nothing from the other side. Taking the handle, she lifted it carefully, hearing the click of a latch. She tugged the steel square open, flattening against the wall.

A wash of very cold air poured in. Quickly, she peered around the frame. Semidarkness met her eyes. A long, low tunnel stretched away before her, timbers and beams shoring up the sides and ceiling. A dim, firefly halo of light glimmered in the distance. The ground was earthen, muddy and damp and showed both the prints of Skorzeny's boots and the enormous tracks of Jacko. She moved swiftly, shivering from the frosty air fanning down the shaft.

Brigid hugged the left-hand wall as she trotted. She hadn't gone far when she came across the control box, noting the pair of bullet holes perforating the carrying case. Faintly, she heard Kane call, "Baptiste! Wait!"

Brigid hesitated, on the verge of replying, then went on. Within a few seconds the trans-comm unit in her pocket shrilled. Uttering a sound of irritation, she unzipped the pocket and withdrew the palm-size radiophone. Thumbing up the plastic cover, she pressed the key that opened the frequency and Kane's angry voice blasted out. "What the hell do you think you're doing?"

She touched the volume-control knob and whispered into the transceiver, "Running this sick bastard down. What are you doing?"

"Trying to keep you from strolling into another of that sick bastard's traps. Wait for us. Your poor beast is about on his last legs. He'll drop in a minute and we can get out of here."

"No time," she bit back. "I'll keep my channel open so you can trace me."

"Dammit, Baptiste, what are you trying to prove?"

Brigid closed the cover and returned the comm unit to her pocket. She crept along the passageway, walking heel to toe. Doubts began to assail her, and she wondered briefly if she was indeed trying to prove something. If so, she wasn't sure if it was to Kane or herself.

Brigid Baptiste was not impulsive or reckless by nature. Having spent almost half of her twenty-eight years as an archivist in Cobaltville's Historical Division, she had been trained to be methodical and analytical, reason always winning out over emotion.

Kane was almost the exact opposite, yang to her yin. Not too long before, in the heat of anger, she had accused him of contaminating her with his darker side, his propensity to always take violent action before weighing other options.

Perhaps he had contaminated her, she reflected, in ways too subtle for her to consciously notice. Before her exile, before the life she'd been leading for the past year, she would have no more pursued a madman on his home turf than she would have tried to walk to the moon.

Actions of that nature were the purview of Kane and Grant. Even after all this time, it was difficult to keep in mind that the two men had spent their entire adult lives as killers—superbly trained and conditioned Magistrates, bearing not only the legal license to deal indiscriminate death in the service of Baron Cobalt but also the spiritual sanction.

As she moved stealthily along the tunnel, she realized bleakly she was engaging in an action that was pure Kane, and that if their positions were reversed she would even now be upbraiding him.

Up ahead, the wedge of light widened, dissolving the darkness. The air current increased in volume, and Brigid guessed she was approaching a ventilation and air-recycling center. A steady stream of cold air whipped against her face, ruffling her hair. The roar of turbines pressed against her eardrums as she approached the end of the shaft. The earth floor became a concrete slab.

Before her lay a vista of great machines, every piece of which seemed to rattle, clank and roar, with giant flywheels spinning and gears turning. Ventilators stretched toward the ceiling. Motor-driven fans pulled fresh air out of the shafts reaching to the surface. The armatures of pumps clattered up and down.

The close air was overlaid with the thick odors of grease and hot metal. A network of platforms and catwalks crisscrossed above and between the turbines and generators.

On the concrete floor, she saw puddles of oil and diesel fuel. In one of them she saw boot prints, and smeared tracks leading away from it. Little speckles of blood shone between the footprints—so one of her shots had found a flesh-and-blood target.

Brigid paused, every sense alert, eyes scanning from side to side, up and down. She saw no movement other than that of the machinery, but she suspected Skorzeny of deliberately leading her to this place, planting a trail for her to follow.

Carefully, she scaled a short ladder that led up to a catwalk forming a narrow, elevated bridge between whirring turbines. The casings looked old, some of them showing splits that had been poorly welded. She saw no sign of the type of nuke generators that powered Totality Concept and Continuity of Government redoubts.

Because of the eardrum-slamming racket, Brigid didn't hear the shot; she felt a jarring shock against the meat of her left shoulder. She went with the impact, flinging herself backward to the guardrail. She vaulted over it, clinging to the bottom crossbar with her left hand. It still had feeling, so the bullet hadn't done severe damage either to the nerves or the muscles. As she hung there, she saw a bullet strike sparks from the grilled catwalk floor.

Her shoulder burned and throbbed, and she felt wet warmth sliding down her ribs. The slug had gouged a furrow through layers of epidermis.

She dangled one-handed above a spinning flywheel and tried to remember how many shots Skorzeny had fired and how many rounds a Luger contained. Although she couldn't be sure, she guessed eight. Kane had often rebuked her for what he perceived as a stubborn indifference to firearms, and now she reprimanded herself.

Teeth clenched, Brigid chinned herself up so her

eyes were level with the floor of the catwalk. At the far end, she caught a shifting of movement. Skorzeny appeared, crouching behind the rocking armature of an air pump. Arm trembling with the strain of supporting her entire weight, Brigid watched him stand up, eyes flicking back and forth. Then, very cautiously, he stepped onto the catwalk, the slender barrel of the Luger sweeping in short arcs. If not for the dim light, he would have seen her. As it was, from her position, only his tangled hair and beard were clearly visible.

Propping the Iver Johnson on the lip of the catwalk, Brigid squeezed the trigger. She barely heard the report. Skorzeny clapped a hand to his right hip and spun around in a clumsy pirouette. He dropped out of her range of vision.

Ignoring the pain in her shoulder and the ticklish sensation of oozing blood, Brigid laboriously hauled herself up and climbed the railing. Skorzeny lay near the end of the walkway, as she had seen many corpses lie—arms and legs bent unnaturally, head to one side.

Cautiously, she approached the fallen man, squinting, trying to detect the rise and fall of respiration. She began to nudge his right ankle with a foot, thought better of it and started to step back.

With an eye-blurring burst of speed, Skorzeny uncoiled from the walkway, a leg lashing up and around in a semicircle. The toe of his boot caught the barrel of her blaster and ripped it from her grasp.

Brigid threw herself backward, faintly hearing the pistol banging against metal beneath the catwalk. The man bounded to his feet, Luger in hand, but she saw that the breech-lock toggle at the rear of the blaster was open. Meaning, she knew, he had expended all the rounds in the clip. She also saw two damp stains spreading across his black uniform—over his left rib cage and his right hip.

Lips working beneath his whiskers, Skorzeny swiftly reversed his hold on the Luger, gripping it by the barrel, and leaped at her, clubbing with the butt.

Brigid dived headlong over the guardrail, hooking the top bar with her elbow, letting her momentum swing her out, over and around. She landed behind Skorzeny as he pivoted at the waist, lashing out with the pistol in a backhand swing.

She ducked, feeling the gun butt graze the top of her head. Simultaneously, she drove the heel of her left foot into the back of Skorzeny's knee. His leg buckled, but he managed to twist himself around even as he sagged. Bracing herself on the handrails on either side of the catwalk, Brigid levered her body up, driving the soles of her boots directly into the man's beard.

He went down heavily on his back, blood squirting from his flattened nose and mashed lips. Almost immediately, Skorzeny struggled back to his feet, eyes blazing with unregenerate, cobalt-blue madness. Brigid froze for a microinstant, amazed and unnerved by the man's superhuman vitality.

He lunged for her, swinging the Luger in an overhead, skull-fracturing arc. She skipped away and he stumbled, off balance from the force of his wild swing. In the second it took him to regain his equilibrium, Brigid turned and raced to the end of the catwalk, plunging into the maze of clanking, whirring machinery that kept the installation alive—heat, light, water tanks, air and cooling systems.

Brigid couldn't help but be reminded of her visit to the Manufacturing Division of Cobaltville, a man-made hell of iron, steam, noise and sparks. She wheeled around a turbine and skirted a chute that led downward. At its lower end, she could make out the red glare of flames. Pushing on beyond the chute, she found a metal ladder that led to another catwalk above. Rather than climb it, she ducked into an aisle between a row of rattling heat exchangers and crouched in a wedge of shadow to catch her breath.

A touch of panic brushed her mind, but she fought herself to calmness. Tentatively, she probed her shoulder, inserting her finger into the rip torn by the Luger's bullet. Though the fingers of her glove came away shining with blood, her first assessment that the wound was superficial seemed correct. She had gotten off lucky, far luckier than poor Cotta.

Brigid repressed a shudder as she touched the man's blood drying on her face. She hadn't known Cotta very well, but over the past year or so she had taken his presence in Cerberus for granted; she had grown accustomed to seeing him in the redoubt's control room, as much of a fixture as the enviro-ops console he usually manned.

Cotta had been among Lakesh's first batch of exiles, and for some irrational reason she had never seriously considered his mortality. She, Grant, Kane and even Domi were the personnel who undertook the missions, walked the hellfire trail as a matter of course. She always went out into the field armed with the inner knowledge one or all of them could die. Why it hadn't occurred to her that the same fate could befall someone like Cotta was a mystery.

With a conscious effort, Brigid pushed back the thoughts of the man and peered out into the aisle, looking in both directions. She saw no movement except that of machinery. The air between the heat exchangers had grown intolerably hot, and she felt sweat cutting runnels through the blood crusted on her forehead.

As carefully as she could manage, she moved out into the aisle. Briefly, she contemplated the wisdom of backtracking so she could rejoin Grant and Kane. They could discuss the option of returning to Cerberus with Cotta's body and coming back at a later time for Skorzeny. But she knew Kane would insist on searching for the old madman. Vengeance demanded a reckoning.

Brigid's foot touched something hard but yielding, and she just managed to catch the long metal rod before it fell from its place against a machine. It was a three-foot-long extension wrench of some kind, made of heavy, cold-rolled iron with the larger end bearing thick, sharp-cornered flanges. She hefted it experimentally, gauging its weight at around fifteen pounds.

She took a few forward, sideways steps so she could see the catwalk. Skorzeny wasn't anywhere to be seen, and she hoped he had skulked away to tend his wounds. Regardless of his pumped-up strength and reflexes, he was still an elderly man. The punishment he had received so far would have incapacitated a man half his age.

Holding the iron rod in both hands like a quarterstaff, she edged out toward the catwalk. She caught a blurred flicker of movement from a dark space between a pair of machines. Brigid spun on her heel, swinging the wrench blindly. A nerve-stinging shock of impact traveled up her arm, accompanied by a loud clang of metal striking metal.

Despite the gloom, she saw Skorzeny bounding for

her, a mate to the wrench she held gripped in both of his hands. Fresh blood stained his whiskers, like red paint spilled on snow.

Skorzeny swung his wrench as if it were a sledge-hammer. Brigid desperately parried the blow. Sparks showered at the point of impact, and the force nearly tore the iron rod from her hands.

The man rushed viciously to the attack, driving Brigid backward. Even over the clatter produced by the machines, the ringing of iron against iron was nearly deafening.

As Brigid parried each of the blows, she saw the gleam of demented determination in the man's eyes. It was the determination to kill her, by any means possible.

# Chapter 8

Skorzeny swatted out with a spinning crescent kick. His foot glanced off Brigid's wrench, and she hooked the black-clad man's heel with the rod and gave it an upward jerk.

Skorzeny started to fall, but in a lightninglike explosion of reflexes and sinews, he turned the fall into a gymnastic back flip. He landed gracefully in a crouch. At the same time, he launched a blow with his wrench toward Brigid's unguarded midriff.

With animal quickness, Brigid sprang away from the flanged head of the weapon, but she wasn't quite quick enough. The sharp corners scraped her, slicing through the fabric of her thermal suit but not cutting the skin beneath. Still, the force was sufficient to make her swallow a grunt of pain.

Skorzeny rose to his full height, his red-filmed teeth flashing beneath his beard, clenched in a snarl of anger or a grin of pleasure. He spun the wrench by the handle in his right hand.

Brigid watched him with narrowed eyes, and by degrees, anger replaced her fear. Men like Skorzeny had laid the foundations for the tyranny of the barons, had set in motion the events that led to the nukecaust, the near extinction of humanity and the enslavement of the survivors.

She blocked another blow, then executed a lightning-fast riposte. The corners of the flanges brushed the backs of Skorzeny's hands and drew a continuous thread of blood across both of them. His eyes widened in surprise, then his lips creased in a scornful smile beneath his scarlet-stained whiskers. He paused for an instant, regarding her curiously, head slightly cocked to one side.

"Bastard," Brigid hissed, though she knew he couldn't hear her. She eyed the wet spots on his uniform. "Why don't you just die?"

Skorzeny tossed his head contemptuously, then fell into the classic fencer's position, knees bent, right foot forward and left hand on his hip. He raised the wrench to the height of his shoulder, flanges pointed straight at her face. He said a few words, but Brigid caught only one of them. It sounded like "Heidelburg."

Then he sprang, slashing savagely. Brigid ducked the first swipe and stepped inside the backswing. She rammed the butt of her wrench into the pit of his stomach and rocked Skorzeny back on his heels. Blood sprayed from his pulped lips.

He lunged again and her parry was barely in time to keep the flanges from whacking her across the side of the head. With surprising grace, Skorzeny turned his lunge into a sideways dive and he vanished into a slit of shadow between the humped casings of two turbines.

Brigid impulsively started to plunge after him, then caught herself. She turned and crept back in the direction of the catwalk-bridge, knowing Skorzeny would reappear to cut her off.

She walked only a few yards before she spotted an opening between two ventilation shafts. It was small, but she thought she could just squeeze her body into it.

Brigid wriggled her way into the cleft and smiled without mirth. The fit was so tight it would take Skorzeny's wrench to pry her free. She waited for more than a minute, then felt slight, jouncing vibrations in the grilled flooring underfoot. They stopped for a handful of seconds, then began again. The vibrations were caused by nearby footfalls.

Tensing, Brigid gripped the wrench tightly in her right hand, bracing with her left against the sheet metal to thrust her out of the opening. She waited, not even daring to breathe.

Exactly opposite her hiding place, Skorzeny appeared. She gathered her muscles, preparing to leap out after he passed and brain him with her iron bludgeon.

Suddenly, he halted, and drawn by some sixth sense, the one Kane always referred to as pointman's sense, Skorzeny turned his head and stared directly into Brigid's eyes. His bloody lips parted, and he stood stock-still in surprise for a fraction of a second, feet still separated in midstride, his own wrench at his side.

Brigid's arm flashed up and out. She hurled her extension wrench with a downward sweep. The heavy rod didn't fly true like a javelin, but the butt end struck Skorzeny on the breastbone. The man careened backward, face screwed up in pain.

Brigid struggled to free herself from the metal-walled alley. Before she was out and clear, Skorzeny bounded to meet her, wrench held in a two-fisted grip. She flung herself bodily on the black-clad man, striking with a fist as they collided.

Skorzeny dipped aside, her blow missed and she

spilled to the floor. She rolled, fingers finding and closing around the shaft of the fallen rod. She lifted it just
in time to catch a poleax blow from Skorzeny. She
countered by slapping him on the left leg with the
flanged end, just above the knee.

The wrench didn't land solidly, but the man still
cried out and hopped backward, out of reach. She
heaved herself up and as she took a pair of retreating
steps, Skorzeny pressed his attack.

He made a series of swift feints that Brigid blocked.
As her wrench came up and over to parry, Skorzeny
slipped his weapon under hers and lunged, apparently
trying to gouge out her unprotected eyes.

She skipped backward, fetching up hard against the
casing of a roaring machine. The corner of a flange
touched her cheek beneath her right eye, slitting the
skin and bringing a line of crimson.

Skorzeny laughed, snorting crimson droplets, and
came boring in. Brigid weaved, spun and stepped
back, letting the wrench go over her head or whip past
her belly. She thrust, parried and hammered. Above
the ringing, scraping slither of iron, she heard another
sound, at the far limits of her hearing. It was Kane,
calling her name—rather bellowing it at the top of his
lungs; otherwise she never would have heard.

She and Skorzeny were out of Kane's field of vision
and even if he managed to hear their wrench duel, he
would attribute the clamor to the machinery.

If Skorzeny heard Kane's call, he gave no sign. He
continued striking at Brigid with his makeshift saber.
Her hands stung sharply from the repeated impacts,
and the muscles in her arms felt as if they were full
of half-frozen mud. Her shoulder wound burned as if
acid had been poured into it. Her breath whistled in

her throat as they danced around the machinery. Skorzeny's pallid face darkened as he called on all his reserves of strength. He left no killer's tricks untried, but the wrench sank lower and lower, threatening Brigid's thighs and knees instead of her head and trunk.

His chest rising and falling spasmodically, Skorzeny breathed in snapping gasps, his knees wobbling. The man's reflexes and speed were little short of superhuman, but he didn't possess the stamina for a prolonged conflict.

"Give it up," Brigid said, hoping he could read her lips. "Give it up."

Skorzeny snarled out a laugh and lunged forward, swinging the wrench in a deadly half circle. Brigid easily dodged and he half stumbled. Before he could regain his footing, she smashed the blunt end of her wrench into Skorzeny's right side. He would have fallen if not for catching himself on an air pump.

Gasping for air, Skorzeny pushed himself erect, probing his rib cage for fractures. Brigid bounded to him before he could recover his wind. He managed to block a blow, but he had do so using both hands. Now he was on the defensive, and judging by the fearful glint in his eyes, he didn't like it one bit.

Skorzeny, lips writhing, tried to mount a counterattack. Brigid sidestepped a vicious roundhouse with the iron rod. The force of his unconnected blow turned Skorzeny around completely, and Brigid swept the blunt butt end of her wrench against the side of his head, then slapped him lengthwise with it across his mouth.

He reeled to one side, flailing with his left arm as he tried to maintain both his balance and consciousness. Skorzeny's groping hand plunged between the big square teeth of a pair of massive gear wheels, each one the diameter of a wag tire.

The teeth closed and meshed on Skorzeny's forearm, with a crunching snap, just below the elbow. The bearded man threw back his head and shrieked, trying frantically to yank his arm free. Hopping up and down, screaming wildly, he jammed the end of his wrench between the gear teeth.

Brigid watched, paralyzed by horror for a long tick of time. Then, moving purely on instinct, she shoved the handle of her own wrench between the gears, heaving up on it with all her strength, trying to slow their inexorable rotation. The iron rod bent, the wheels groaned but continued to turn. Skorzeny struggled, throwing himself backward, twisting from side to side, convulsing like a pain-mad animal with a limb caught between the jaws of a trap. He shouldered into Brigid and sent her stumbling sideways a few paces.

Planting his feet against the bottom of the machine, Skorzeny shrieked and strained. Then he staggered backward, leaving his uniformed arm from the elbow down to be crushed between the gear teeth. Powered by his over-stressed heart, bright blood jetted in a long stream from the ragged stump. It splashed over the surface of a heat exchanger, almost instantly drying and smoldering. The dense odor of hot copper clogged Brigid's nostrils.

Still screaming, Skorzeny spun around in a dervishlike whirl, completely maddened by agony. He led with the wrench still in his right hand. Brigid didn't see it coming, not even with the thick flanges smashed against the left side of her head.

Intolerably bright white pinwheels spiraled behind her eyes. Distantly, as if her body belonged to someone else, she was aware of staggering sideways. Her memory replayed the wet sound of iron tearing flesh and grating against bone. She was blinded by a fiery wetness.

Her entire body clenched against the cascade of pain. Slapping a hand to her head, all she could feel was fresh hot blood pumping out between her fingers. Agony was a clawed beast trying to rip its way out of her skull, but even dazed, sickened and blinded, she knew if she fell Skorzeny would batter her to death as his final act.

Brigid lashed out with both hands, fingers hooking into stiff cloth and a leather strap. With desperate effort, she kicked herself off the floor, muscling Skorzeny backward, hearing him scream through a ruin of splintered teeth, blowing bloody froth from his pulped lips.

He toppled against the vermilion-splashed gear wheels. The man was dying on his feet, but Brigid didn't give him the opportunity to simply pass on through loss of blood or shock. She punched him as hard as she could on his whisker- and gore-covered chin. His head snapped back, his long hair tangling in the gears.

His scalp stretched toward the clashing teeth and though he had no more breath with which to scream, he kicked out at her. She barely felt it although she careened backward into an air pump.

She clung to it and watched as, pulled by his hair, Skorzeny's head was drawn in short, fitful jerks between the chiseled teeth of the rotating wheels. They closed on the top of his skull with a prolonged, mushy pop. Mangled tissue, crushed bone, hair, blood and brain matter spewed into the internal mechanisms of the machine and the wheels ground to a shuddering halt.

Skorzeny continued to kick and wave his one hand feebly as if his black spirit refused to acknowledge the death of his body.

By the time Brigid saw Kane and Grant, the man's kicks had become intermittent twitches. The ragged, blood-spattered men spared the body of Skorzeny swift, wrathful glares. Kane put an arm around Brigid's waist, and she sagged into him gratefully.

"Are you all right?" Kane asked.

Brigid sluiced streaming scarlet away from her eyes, realizing distantly that, in the semidarkness, Kane couldn't distinguish Cotta's blood on her face from her own. "I don't know," she murmured. She doubted if he heard her at all.

Staring at Skorzeny's maimed body, Grant intoned, "That settles the Third Reich."

In an aspirated whisper, Brigid said into Kane's ear, "Like the mikado said, 'Let the punishment fit the crime.'"

Then she pitched forward as limp as a corpse into his arms.

# Chapter 9

Grant and Kane carried the motionless Brigid across the catwalk and down to the concrete pad where not only was the light stronger but also they could talk without shouting. Her scalp wound still oozed blood, crimson flooding her face and neck and clotting her mane of hair.

She didn't stir, not even a flicker of an eyelid when Kane unzipped the front of her thermal suit and opened the khaki shirt beneath, heedless of the buttons. He examined her bullet wound and found it to be little more than a deep graze. It was more unsightly than critical.

The same diagnosis couldn't be applied to her head injury. Grant's big fingers probed with a surprising delicacy of touch. He parted her scarlet-soaked hair on the side of her head, wincing away at the sight of the raw flesh laid open to the bone.

Kane noticed him flinching. "Bad?"

"Bad enough," rumbled Grant. "Blunt trauma to the skull. She's in deep shock."

He pulled the balaclava from his pocket and, folding it in two, pressed it to her temple, applying as much pressure as he dared. Kane placed a forefinger at the base of her throat, timing the pulse that beat there. Lowering his head to her mouth, he listened to the faint, panting respiration.

"She may have a skull fracture," Grant stated, trying to sound matter-of-fact. "She's definitely concussed."

Both he and Kane knew basic field medicine and first aid—it was part of their training as Magistrates. Both also knew head injuries were extremely unpredictable.

Refusing to acknowledge the cold fist of fear squeezing tight around his heart, Kane said, "We've got to get her back to Cerberus as soon as possible."

Grant's brow furrowed in consternation. "It's a long way back to the gateway. We'll have to drag her through the installation and up the ladder and then into the cold. Not a good idea."

Kane's thoughts raced ahead, considering Grant's words, coming up with and discarding half a dozen alternate plans before saying, "The only other option is for one of us to get to the gateway, jump back to Cerberus and come back with DeFore."

DeFore served as the redoubt's resident medical specialist. She wasn't really a doctor, but she was the closest thing to one that ville training provided.

"And all she can do here," Kane continued, "is first aid. Maybe stabilize Brigid enough to be moved. As it is, we'll still have to move her to the gateway anyway, right? Why stretch this out, making three jumps instead of one before she receives full treatment?"

Grant gnawed at his lower lip. "We'll have to leave Cotta."

"He's dead," Kane declared flatly. "Brigid is still alive, at least for the time being. We'll send a detail back for his body."

With narrowed eyes, Grant gazed levelly at Kane

and said, "We'll have to rig some kind of harness and stretcher to get her out of here and up the ladder. If she does have a skull fracture, the slightest bump could chill her."

"We'd have to do that even if DeFore was here," Kane argued, rising to his feet. "I'll go fetch the medical kit from where Cotta dropped it. There may be something in there to counteract the shock. At the very least, we can get the bleeding under control. Then I'll scrounge up materials to jury-rig a stretcher."

"You sure you don't want me to do it?" Grant's tone held no particular inflection. It was as level as his gaze, but Kane understood the true meaning behind the question.

"No," he said. "Call me gutless, but I don't want to be the one who watches her die."

His voice almost, but not quite, caught in his throat. He didn't wait to hear Grant's response, if there was one. Kane turned and ran flat-out, ignoring the flares of agony igniting all over his body. His clothes hung in tatters, and Jacko's horny-taloned fingers had left deep, painful scratches across his back. His muscles and tendons felt as if each one had been individually pummeled.

He dashed into the dimly lit passageway, battling the tentacles of dread and panic that threatened to engulf his reason. Most of the time, he shied away from scrutinizing his feelings for Brigid Baptiste. They were as deep as they were complicated, and the unspoken bond between them was an issue neither one discussed.

From the very first time he met her, he was affected by the energy Brigid radiated, an intangible force, yet one that triggered a melancholy longing in his soul.

That strange, sad longing only deepened after a bout of jump sickness both of them suffered during a mat-trans jump to Russia when they had shared the same hallucination. But both knew on a visceral, primal level it hadn't been gateway-triggered delirium, but a revelation that they were joined by chains of fate, their destinies linked. Kane often wondered if that spiritual bond was the primary reason he had sacrificed everything he had attained as a Magistrate to save her from execution. The possibility confused him, made him feel defensive and insecure. That insecurity was one reason he always addressed her as "Baptiste," almost never by her first name, so as to maintain a certain distance between them. But that distance shrank every day.

Nearly six months before, during the op to the British Isles, when Kane had protested to Morrigan that there was nothing between him and Brigid, the Irish telepath had laughed at him and said, "Oh, yes, there is. Between you two, there is much to forgive, much to understand. Much to live through. Always together…she is your *anam-chara*."

In ancient Gaelic, Kane learned, *anam-chara* meant "soul friend."

He wasn't sure what that meant, but he knew he always felt comfortable with Brigid Baptiste on a spiritual level, despite their many quarrels.

Kane found the thought of losing his *anam-chara* too horrifying to contemplate, not just because of the vacuum she would leave in the Cerberus personnel, but because of the void her absence would leave in his soul. The memory of the kiss he'd given her when they'd taken the jump back in time to the eve of the nukecaust drifted across his mind. It was no surprise that he should remember the kiss, but the intensity of emotion associated with it shook him.

He also recalled with startling clarity what Sister Fand of the third parallel casement had whispered to him about Brigid Baptiste: "The lady is your saving grace. Trust the bond that belongs between you. The gift of the *anam-chara* is strong. She protects you from damnation—she is your credential."

Although most, if not all, of the details of his visits to the three parallel planes of reality were now misty fragments, he remembered those words as if they'd been imprinted in his mind.

Kane shook his head furiously to drive out the recollections of the past so he could focus on the present. He had seen Brigid injured before, he argued with himself. She had always recovered, sometimes so quickly it seemed almost miraculous.

Panting, he loped along the corridor, lungs laboring, wincing at the pain of a stitch lancing up and down his side. His pounding footfalls sounded like a primitive funeral dirge beaten out on a drum. He tripped over Skorzeny's discarded control box and stumbled for nearly a score of feet before managing to regain his balance.

By the time Kane reached the open door that led to the pit, he was sweating profusely despite the cool air. He constantly had to blink the stinging salt from his eyes. Skidding to a clumsy halt, he went through the door, down the narrow corridor and into the cube-shaped chamber. It reeked of cordite, and was so drenched in blood and stinking body wastes, it looked and smelled like an abattoir. His stomach lurched in a jolt of nausea.

Kane skirted the maimed corpses of Cotta and Jacko

as he crossed the pit. He found the survival kit on the far side, surrounded by a pool of Cotta's blood. His dismembered arm lay nearby, like the limb of a doll torn off and tossed away by a petulant child.

Cotta himself lay on his back, bled almost white, his sightless, glassy eyes staring at the ceiling. His face was contorted in a rictus that looked more like astonishment than pain. Kane tried but failed to suppress a shudder. Bending over him, with thumb and forefinger he gently closed his eyes.

"This was no way to die," he said hoarsely. "I'm sorry."

*"Sahh-ree."*

The grumbling, gasping voice raised Kane's nape hairs and caused him to whip his head around so fast his neck tendons twinged. To his amazement, he saw Jacko stirring fitfully on the floor, hands clenching and unclenching.

"Sahh-ree...ah'm sahh-ree..."

Kane gaped at him incredulously, refusing to believe that any creature, no matter how big and powerful, could have survived his multitude of wounds long enough to mock him.

In a sudden fury, he glanced around, found Cotta's VP-70 and picked it up. He marched over to the fallen giant. Jacko appeared to be floating in a lake of liquid vermilion. Kane aimed the pistol at the little electrode on the monster's forehead.

Bitterly, he growled, "Monkey-man see, monkey-man do. Monkey-man fucking well dies."

As his index finger constricted on the trigger, Jacko coughed up blood and words. "Sah-ree. Couldn't he'p mysel'. Din't mean—din't *want* to hurt."

Kane's finger froze. Jacko's pronunciation was

slurred due to the structure of his mouth, but he understood what he said nevertheless. The hairy giant's eyes peered up from his massive brow bones. In their dark depths swirled the light of intelligence, far more human than bestial.

"Free now," Jacko grunted softly. "Free."

His body quivered and became rigid. Kane side-stepped away, cold sickness leapfrogging in his belly as he realized the man-ape wasn't a mindless animal, but a sentient being. He had seen a number of abhorrent genetic hellspawn over the past year, from the hybrids in Dulce to the Martian transadapts, but unlike them, Jacko was far more victim than mutant.

Tucking the VP-70 into a pocket, he retrieved his Sin Eater in its ruined holster and left the pit. As soon as he was out in the passageway, he started running again.

Reeling and light-headed, he didn't slow his pace until he came in sight of Grant, still applying steady pressure to Brigid's head.

"The bleeding has tapered off some," Grant said, taking the medical case from him, "but there's no sign of her coming around yet."

Wheezing, Kane bent over, hands on his knees, watching as Grant unlatched the lid and opened the kit. Methodically, he began removing items from it— a vial of sulfa, antiseptic, coagulant powder, pressure bandages, a roll of gauze and a small hypodermic of stimulant. Kane didn't offer any suggestions on procedure since Grant was as proficient in field medicine as he was.

After his lungs stopped aching, Kane went in search of materials to make a stretcher. In a small storage room adjacent to the generator area, he found squares of canvas, lengths of rope, leather straps and lumber, no doubt used to shore up the walls and ceiling of the passageway.

Working with a feverish haste, he constructed a makeshift stretcher out of a pair of long boards, holding them together by knotted turnings of the rope. By the time he dragged everything back to Grant, Brigid's head was bandaged like a mummy's and her face cleaned of some of the blood, but by no means most of it.

Holding her wrist, timing her pulse by his wrist chron, Grant announced, "The stimulant has regulated her heart rate. Respiration is improving. I think I've gotten her stabilized for the moment. This is the best time to get her out of here."

Kane spread out the canvas over the stretcher and, taking Brigid by the ankles, he and Grant carefully lifted her onto it. They wrapped her up in the canvas, swathing her in its folds like a cocoon. Kane secured her to the boards by the leather straps. Gripping the ends of the boards, the two men picked her up and carried her into the passageway.

"Once we navigate our way out of here," Grant said, grunting, "our real problem is going to be getting her topside."

Kane nodded toward the leather straps cinched tight around Brigid. "We can make a sling out of those and the tarp and lift her out."

"That won't be as easy as you make it sound," said Grant skeptically.

"Hell," snapped Kane, "what is?"

They shuffled sideways down the corridor, straining under the weight, the exertion exacerbating the pain of their injuries. Both men knew there wasn't a way up to the higher level through the door that led to the pit, so they moved on past it. They didn't go far before they saw the old-fashioned caged-in elevator. Neither of them repressed sighs and exclamations of relief as they squeezed into it.

Grant pulled the lever projecting from the wall, and with creaks and clanks, the elevator ascended. It brought them to a little anteroom just outside the office suite. It was on the opposite side from where they had entered and was concealed from view by partitions covered with framed photographs of the Berlin skyline.

Laying Brigid on a desk, they adjusted what was left of their protective clothing, snugging their mittens, lowering their goggles and drawing close their hoods. They made sure Brigid was completely covered by the canvas. Kane steadfastly refused to look at her face, a shocking pale beneath its layer of drying blood. Grant checked her pulse one more time and found it satisfactory.

The two men lifted her up and carried her out through the office and to the entrance foyer. As they passed under the Nazi banner, Kane wrestled with the mad urge to shoot holes in it. But his Sin Eater was probably damaged, and Cotta's VP-70 was zippered in a pocket. Besides, his hands were full and it seemed a fairly futile gesture at this point.

The temperature at the bottom of the crevasse seemed to have dropped and the cold struck at them like bludgeons of ice. It felt shockingly cold after the relative warmth of the installation.

Teeth chattering, Grant eyed the rungs of the ladder doubtfully. "Who goes first?"

Looping the slack of the rope and passing it under

and over Brigid's canvas-shrouded body, Kane said curtly. "You're the strongest, so you'll have to do the hauling. I'll push and keep her steady."

Grant's dark eyes clouded with worry. "Once we get up there, we'll have to move bastard fast. She could contract hypothermia in minutes. All of us could."

"I wasn't intending to sightsee." Kane threaded the ropes through the straps around Brigid's shoulders, knotting them expertly. He tugged them experimentally, then entwined two lengths of rope together and tossed it to Grant. "Let's get it done."

The men lifted the board-bound woman upright. Her head lolled loosely as Kane raised the fur-lined hood of her thermal suit and snugged it tight around her face by its drawstrings.

Rope in one hand, Grant scaled the ladder to the top rung. Kneeling at the opening, he began hauling Brigid up, hand over hand. Kane stabilized her ascent, preventing her from bumping against the icy wall or revolving at the end of the rope. It was strenuous, muscle-pulling work. Kane followed Brigid rung by rung. Twice he nearly lost his grip on the frost-rimed rungs.

Finally, after what seemed like a chain of interlocking eternities, all three of them reached the surface. Kane and Grant shivered violently as a gust of subzero wind buffeted them. Their footprints leading from the hutch were almost obliterated by the drifting snow, but they moved in that direction, each man dragging the stretcher-bound Brigid by strands of rope.

Within a minute, the wind moaning over the ice field turned into a shrieking wail that seemed to fill the entire world, tearing at Grant and Kane with a clawing fury. They were blinded by a white, stinging curtain. Breathing in the gale was difficult as snow-flakes and ice particles seared the moist, soft tissues of their mouths and sinus passages. The wind cut through the rents in Kane's thermal suit like razor-edged blades.

The two men put their heads down and trudged forward, dragging Brigid behind them as if they were dogs hauling a sled. She lay only a few feet behind them, but she was almost invisible in the shifting veils of wind-whipped white.

Their faces, hands and legs grew numb, and ears and teeth ached fiercely. Blind, freezing and aching, they fought their way onward, tiny splinters of ice scouring the exposed portions of their faces like hundreds of insect stings.

Although they could no longer see their tracks, both men possessed an ingrained sense of direction, partially due to their Magistrate training but primarily derived from instinct. Neither Kane nor Grant feared becoming lost so much as succumbing to the soul-killing cold, falling and freezing solid within minutes.

Breasting the wind, Kane shambled and shuffled until he struck something hard and unyielding. He stumbled and nearly fell. Pawing at the frost on the lens of his goggles, he was just able to make out, through a part in the whirling streamers of snow, a dark mass.

He had bumped into one of the two rock outcroppings that bracketed the Quonset hut. Had he been only a couple of feet to the right, he would have bypassed it without knowing it was there. Grant continued trudging onward, unaware of Kane's collision.

"Here!" he shouted, but his voice was swallowed by the roar of the wind. Kane reached out, and after a few groping swipes, grabbed Grant by the shoulder, pulling him to a halt.

By feel, the two men edged around the rock until they found the front of the little structure and finally the door. Already a snowdrift was heaped halfway to the top.

Fumbling with the latch, Kane tried to open it, but for a heart-stopping, despairing half second, it appeared to be frozen shut. Fueled by fear and anger, he hurled his whole weight against it and it swung open, breaking loose the ice that had formed on the hinges and jamb.

They dragged Brigid's stretcher inside. It took Grant two attempts to push the door shut against the battering ram of the wind. When it was closed, he leaned against it, breath rasping in and out, pluming before his face. His lungs sounded like a pair of ruptured fireplace bellows. Pulling down his hood, he fingered the ice clinging to his mustache.

Breathing just as heavily and painfully, Kane knelt to inspect Brigid, pulling away the folds of canvas from her face. She was still unconscious, although the blood that had seeped through the bandage was frozen as hard as a sheathing of metal. Neither man could do anything other than pant for a minute, their eyes dulled by a marrow-deep fatigue.

"What do you know?" croaked Grant at length. "We made it."

Kane didn't bother with a response. He stumbled to his feet and started dragging Brigid across the floor toward the mat-trans unit. Pushing himself away from the door, Grant swayed on rubbery legs. "Don't you want to take her off that thing before we make the jump?"

Kane shook his head. "Once we're back, we can carry her straight to the dispensary without waiting for a gurney."

Grant shuffled toward him. "If the transponder signal is getting through, DeFore will already be waiting."

Everyone in the Cerberus redoubt had been injected with a subcutaneous transponder that transmitted not just their general locations but heart rate, respiration, blood count and brain-wave patterns. Based on organic nanotechnology, the biolink transponder was a nonharmful radioactive chemical that bound itself to an individual's glucose and the middle layers of the epidermis. The signal was relayed to the redoubt by the Comsat, one of the two satellites to which the installation was uplinked.

"With the weather conditions, we can't be sure they're receiving the signal," replied Kane. "Only a couple of weeks ago, the entire system was down, remember?"

Grant took a length of rope. "I'm glad one of us is thinking ahead."

"If one of us had thought ahead, we wouldn't even be in this goddamn place." Kane half snarled the words.

Grant didn't take offense. He knew the anger wasn't truly directed at him.

They maneuvered Brigid into the jump chamber and laid her on the floor. Grant closed the heavy armaglass door, and it locked with a click and a hiss. Immediately, the hexagonal disks in the floor and ceiling exuded a glow, and a low, almost subsonic hum began, quickly rising in pitch to a whine. The noise changed, sounding like the distant howling of a cyclone.

The glow brightened. A mist formed below the ceiling disks and rose from the floor. Tiny crackling static discharges flared in the vapor. The insubstantial tendrils thickened to a fog, curling around to engulf them.

Someone who had never traveled the hyperdimensional pathways opened by the mat-trans units might wonder if the fog really existed or if it was an illusion, a figment of the imagination produced by a mind already in the process of being deconstructed and digitized. Kane knew it wasn't an illusion, but it wasn't really mist, either; it was plasma bleed-off, wave forms that only resembled vapor.

Regardless of what it really was, Kane felt grateful for the fog as it billowed over Brigid, obscuring her bloody, bandaged face.

Kane closed his eyes.

# Chapter 10

Ka'in opened his eyes—and swayed in the saddle, grabbing the pommel and nearly dropping Gae Bolg, his war spear, in the process. Dibhirceach snorted, scolding him in equine to keep alert.

The morning sky was starkly blue. On either side of horse and man, tall stones inscribed with ogham runes marked the boundaries of the counties traversed by the Boyne road. It was little more than a dirt track, winding down and around leading to the council hall near the banks of the river.

Ka'in peered through the road's border of copper beeches and heard a dim uproar of voices and laughter from beyond. He saw the great hall that would play host to the chieftains of all the clans this summer day. He glimpsed them milling about, their moods unusually festive for such a grim council.

He straightened in the high-canted saddle and glanced down at himself, feeling a faint shock of disorientation but not knowing why.

From hip to throat, supple molded leather encased him. The overlapping scales of polished steel on the breastplate caught the sun, sparkling and glinting. A crimson cloak fastened to his shoulders with golden torques given to him by King Conor flowed out behind him. In his right hand, he gripped the long, slender shaft of his war spear. From a leather scabbard at his hip swung a broadsword, the hilt and pommel worked in gold and precious stones.

The stallion beneath him uttered a challenging snort, turning his head to look at him. Then he broke wind explosively. Distractedly, Ka'in muttered, "Mind your manners, Dibhirceach. We're not particularly welcome down there as it is."

The name was taken from the Gaelic tongue and meant "vigilant." At the sound of his name, the stallion pricked his ears and nickered, pawing at the ground impatiently. The horse stood eighteen hands tall or more, very broad through the chest and hindquarters. Long muscles roped his long-legged frame, giving light to the truth that he was bred for war and battle, able to carry his master without fear.

His glossy coat was a pure cinnamon color, with ginger tints in his flowing mane and tail. His hooves were black as coal, matching the wide-set eyes. Scars crisscrossed his body, testifying to the battles the horse had already seen.

Ka'in looked toward the heavy-timbered, thatch-roofed hall again, squinting at the people clustered around it, searching not just for familiar faces but friendly ones. He glimpsed Balor in the throng, and his hand tightened reflexively on the wooden haft of Gae Bolg.

Although aging, Balor was still a mighty chieftain, gigantic of height, massive of breadth. He wore his gray beard plaited into two thick braids upon his chest. A scar marred the right side of his pale face, which cut down over a raw, empty eye socket like a fault in snowy terrain.

He derived his name from that red-rimmed hollow, which meant "evil eyed." Sunlight glinted from the silver wire wrapping the pommel of the five-foot broadsword strapped to his back. Whereas Ka'in invested Gae Bolg with an almost mystical power to slay, Balor did the same with his sword, which he called Riastradh. The huge man claimed direct descent from the Formorian king of the same name.

Even if that were not true, Balor's behavior couldn't be any more offensive than if he was of Formorian blood. Whispers in taverns painted the man as a rapist, a treacherous, red-handed reaver.

Strangely, Balor appeared deep in conversation with Padraic, the monk who preached a strange gospel called Christianity and swore fealty to the White Christ. He was a slender, handsome man with a florid complexion and russet hair.

Balor could have been talking to Padraic simply to be polite, since even the Druid mummers respected the man. Ka'in knew Padraic well, and the monk had presented no conflicting view to his own principles. In fact, many clansmen frequently sought out Padraic for advice, since the Gaels regarded him as a learned man. He had taught many of the chieftains how to read and write in several languages, Ka'in included.

But despite the high degree of respect in which he held him, Ka'in still had no intention of putting aside his spear and sword to take up the cross. Especially not now, with the Firbolgs invading from the south. Obviously, the Firbolg ambassador hadn't arrived yet, else the general mood would not have been so lighthearted. The Tuatha De Danaan were dispatching an emissary of their own to act as mediator for the negotiations.

Ka'in heeled Dibhirceach forward. He never used spurs. First and foremost, the huge horse's pride would have never tolerated it, and second, there was no need for them. Man and steed shared a bond of understanding that was almost supernatural.

Dibhirceach thundered down the road, Ka'in's red cloak belling out from his shoulders. He was dressed in all of his warrior's finery for the occasion and he presented a striking picture.

As the people caught sight of him, they shouted his name: "Cuchulainn, the Hound of Ulster, Terrible Champion of Eire, Cuchulainn, Ka'in—"

He reined Dibhirceach to a halt right outside the entrance to the hall and vaulted from the saddle. He strode through the laughing crowd, clapping shoulders and shaking hands. When he reached Balor, he thrust out a hand. The chieftain's scarred face was set in a scowl, silently telling him he was not entertained by his dramatic entrance.

Padraic, on the other hand, smiled in genuine amusement and took Ka'in's proffered hand instead. "Ka'in, my son. It gives my heart joy to see you taking such pleasure in such a simple matter as keeping an appointment. Particularly when peace is at stake."

"Peace, Father Pat?" Ka'in inquired, smiling crookedly. "That's rather a premature judgment, isn't it?"

Ka'in extended his hand to Balor again. The man hesitated just an instant before taking it. His huge, callused paw nearly engulfed Ka'in's hand. Bleakly, he said, "There are some of us who favor coming to terms with the Firbolgs. They have much to offer from their homeland."

A flush of anger sent hot prickles to the back of Ka'in's neck. "What could ugly little goblins from a sea-drowned kingdom offer Eire?"

Balor's grip tightened around Ka'in's hand. "Things of a more substantial nature than was ever given to us by the Danaan. They're naught but invaders themselves."

Ka'in didn't allow the pain of Balor's crushing grip to register on his face. He braced his feet and began squeezing the chieftain's hand in return. Between clenched teeth, he growled, "They were here long before your clan left the trees."

Tendons and muscles swelled along Balor's massive forearm as he resisted the pressure of Ka'in's hand. "It's no secret why you favor them, Cuchulainn. You're in love with a Danaan princess. You left your own devoted wife so you can lie with an inhuman sorceress—"

Ka'in's anger instantly blossomed into rage. Padraic saw it flaring in his blue-gray eyes and stepped up, inserting his body between the two men, placing his hands on their wrists.

"My sons, brave warriors," he said admonishingly. "This is not the time or the circumstances for a quarrel among ourselves. We must not appear to be divided when the Firbolgs arrive."

Neither Balor nor Ka'in appeared to hear him. They continued to try to crush each other's hand. Then ram's-horn trumpets blared from the edge of the clearing. Men shouted, "He comes! Lord Eochy mac Erc comes!"

Balor and Ka'in ceased trying to cripple each other. They relaxed their grips and turned their attention to the chariot clattering up the road. It was drawn by four roan steeds, froth flecking their muzzles, their coats damp and dark with sweat.

Eochy mac Erc seemed determined to make as dra-

matic an entrance as Ka'in, but it was not one to evoke
much admiration. He lashed the horses mercilessly
with a long black whip, oblivious to their squeals of
pain. Dibhirceach blew through his nostrils and laid
his ears back. Ka'in ran his hand absently up and down
the shaft of Gae Bolg and wondered if he could make
an accurate cast into the Firbolg chief's chest. He saw
three bodyguards cantering behind the chariot at a dis-
creet distance and quashed the homicidal impulse.

As the chariot drew closer, he made out more details
of the fearsome warrior's appearance. He was not tall
in fact, he was at least a head and half shorter than
Ka'in, but his squat, barrel-shaped body looked very
powerful.

In contrast, Erc's face was gaunt, with a short,
hooked nose reminiscent of a falcon's beak. The lips
formed a thin, cruel line above a stone jaw. Heavy
black eyebrows framed the man's most disquieting
feature—his deep-set eyes possessed irises like burning coals. Dark, silky hair hung in a single braid from
beneath a tight-fitting leather skullcap. It was a drab
brown, like the rest of his attire. He appeared to wear
crudely cross-stitched leather bags of mismatched
shapes and sizes. A scabbarded broadsword nearly as
long as he was stretched sideways across his chest.

Eochy mac Erc sawed at the reins, wrenching the
frothing horses to violent, rearing halts, slewing the
chariot around in a semicircle so that gravel sprayed
from beneath the wheels and rattled against the wall
of the council hall.

Springing from the chariot, Erc tossed the reins to
a nearby clansman. He strutted over to Balor, grinning
crookedly in greeting, showing what appeared to be a
set of discolored fangs.

"You look well, old Evil-eye." He clasped Balor's extended forearm tightly.

"As do you," Balor replied.

With cold sarcasm, Ka'in said, "It pleases me to see old friends reunited."

Balor did not acknowledge the remark but said to Erc, "The Danaan ambassador is late. You cannot trust them to be punctual since they do not have a human sense of time."

Ka'in understood Balor's antipathy for the Tuatha De Danaan, but he had no patience and certainly no sympathy with it. If Balor was indeed descended from the Formorian king, then he viewed the Danaan as the conquerors of his people, routing them completely from the shores of Eire. But if that actually happened, it was so long ago there was no living memory of it, only legends and fables.

The Firbolgs were a different matter altogether. According to the tales told around the hearths in Ulster and Tara, the Firbolgs claimed to be the survivors of a cataclysm that sank their island homeland. They were, however, not the lords of that mysterious land but a slave race created to till the fields and fish the seas.

When some of the survivors reached Eire, they did constant battle with the Formorians who had established a stronghold on the north coast. When the Tuatha De Danaan appeared and claimed a large portion of the country, the Firbolgs and the Formorians struck a pact, an alliance of convenience to drive away the new invaders. Instead, both the Firbolgs and the Formorians were defeated by the Danaans' superior weaponry and skill.

The Firbolgs left Eire in despair, joining a handful

of other survivors in Greece, where because of their appearance they were shunned, oppressed and finally enslaved as in their sunken homeland. But Eochy mac Erc's own grandfather staged a revolt and the Firbolgs returned to Eire in three groups.

The Formorians were long gone and so the Firebolgs claimed their empty fortresses and exacted a crushing tribute from the surrounding lands. The war with the Firbolgs had been going on sporadically for two generations.

In a studiedly neutral tone, Padraic said, "We can at least begin the preliminaries."

Despite his growing anger, Ka'in could not repress a smile at the man's practiced diplomacy, a habit that had no doubt kept his head attached to his shoulders during his long imprisonment by Miliue of Antrim.

Horns blasted again, and the people began pushing their way into the great assembly hall. All the warriors were required to stack their weapons outside, in the care of attendants. Fires burned in the trough that bisected the vast room. Columns of blue smoke curled upward among the heavy support beams and escaped through holes in the roof.

Shields and banners, emblazoned with the emblem of noted clans, hung in rows from the overhead beams. Along each side of the hall stood tiers of benches that quickly filled with spectators and clansmen. At the center of the big room, on a raised dais, was a throne intricately carved of dark wood.

The chair was occupied by a heavyset, bearded man wrapped in colored silks with a bleached doeskin mantle thrown over his shoulders. A golden circlet confined his mass of curly red hair. This was Conor, a man of vast lands, wisdom and much respect, a fact that led him to be chosen king of Eire.

Ka'in ducked his head to him deferentially as he entered, inasmuch as the man was his liege and lord. But since he was a drinking companion, too, he also flashed him a sly smile.

Conor's lips twitched ever so slightly beneath his beard in acknowledgment.

When the hall was filled, King Conor raised his hand, bringing the assembly to order. He then sang, in a beautiful tenor, a prayer of his own composition asking the guidance of the gods. His prayer was followed by a lengthy one from Padraic, who beseeched only one deity and the White Christ to lead them all down the proper path. He crossed himself repeatedly.

Ka'in noted how Eochy mac Erc glared at the monk impatiently.

A Druid priestess entered, carrying a large pot from which colored smoke billowed. As she made a purifying circuit of the hall, she sang words Ka'in could not understand, but he knew them to be the words of sorcery.

With the opening ceremonies completed, Conor stood and addressed the assembly. "I am gratified to learn that there have been no active hostilities among the clans in more then a year. All of Eire can take pride in this fact. Let us keep this in mind during the talks."

He gestured toward Erc. "You may present the case of your people."

The Firbolg stood and came forward, swaggering a little as he swept the crowd with his eyes. "I am Eochy mac Erc of the Firbolgs. You know who my people are."

"You are well-known to us," Conor said smoothly. "The stories of your raids on the Britons have long been an entertainment to us. None would deny we hold great respect for your bravery."

Erc's thin lips creased in a preening, prideful smile.

"However," continued Conor, in the same smooth tone, "you call down the wrath of the Britons, not just against your folk but all of us here. You jeopardize trade agreements and court war. No longer can we permit your people's raiders to launch their attacks from our shores. Do you understand?"

The Firbolg bristled. "I am not an idiot, Your Majesty."

"Perhaps not," Conor replied calmly. "Just greedy. But if your people and mine are to reach terms, the first thing you must do is to put aside your weapons and cease the raids."

Eochy mac Erc, in mounting outrage, muttered something inaudible.

"Speak up, man," demanded one of the watching clansmen.

"I said I would think on it," the Firbolg half shouted.

"Unacceptable," Conor said dispassionately. "We must have your agreement now or the talks will go no further."

Erc fairly trembled in rage, a crimson flush spreading over his weathered face. In a guttural voice, more of an animal's growl than a language, he demanded, "If I give you my word, swear an oath, then will you allow my people to retain their lands on the coast?"

Ka'in rose to his feet in a rush. "Those lands were stolen from their rightful owners. Shall we allow thieves to hold on to the spoils of robbery?"

Conor favored him with a disapproving glance. "You forget our procedure, Cuchulainn. The time to hear your words regarding an agreement will come."

Ka'in did not take his seat. "We can reach no agreement until the Danaan emissary arrives."

"And when will that be?" Eochy mac Erc snapped, fuming with anger and impatience. "The Tuatha De Danaan are not even human, so therefore their meddling in our affairs is arrogant assumption."

"Not even human?" Ka'in echoed, taking a long stride to the center area. "Look who's talking."

Erc spun around toward him, hand reaching for the pommel of a sword that was no longer there. For an instant, he looked so baffled Ka'in couldn't help but laugh derisively.

With a full-throated bellow of wrath, Erc lunged toward him, arms swinging wide. Easily evading the man's lunge, Ka'in hit him as hard as he could in the middle of his belly. At the moment of impact, his fist sank into flab like a finger jabbed into wet peat.

The Firbolg doubled over, gagging, clutching at his midsection, but he managed to stay on his feet.

Conor rose from his chair angrily. "Cuchulainn! Enough!"

Before guards could reach him, Ka'in snatched the leather skullcap from Erc's head. "Who is human and who is not, Your Majesty?"

A disconcerted murmuring broke out among the assembly. Eochy mac Erc's head was bald; the long braid of hair was attached to the inside of his cap. Sprouting from his naked scalp were small, cartilaginous masses, like claws with spongy surfaces—or horns.

Throwing the skullcap to the ground, Ka'in locked

eyes with Conor. "The Firbolgs are no more human than the Danaan—less, because they were spawned as a race of slaves to serve their Atlantean overlords. They are mixtures, more beast than man, the spawn of Belial. They were driven from our shores once by the Danaan, who were sickened by their depredations against our people. Would we now welcome them back to live and intermarry among us?"

He gestured toward Balor, a contemptuous wave of a hand. "Some of us here don't find that necessarily repugnant. I can't help but wonder why."

Balor rose from his bench, rising to his full, formidable height. His one eye pierced Ka'in with an invisible lance of hatred. He lifted his voice in a bellow. "The Danaan are relics of our past. Most of them are long, long gone. It is the future with which we must concern ourselves, not ancient enmities and wars that occurred when our grandfathers were mere babes."

He stabbed an accusatory finger at Ka'in. "Cuchulainn has been bewitched, he is under a *geas* placed upon him by that lying temptress, that whore Fand. He is her puppet, and his words are meaningless."

A roaring red rage filled Ka'in's mind, sweeping aside all caution, all concern for the due process of the council of the clans. He felt himself gripped in his infamous berserker fury, the battle madness that had earned him the title of Terrible Champion of Eire. Hands outstretched for Balor's thick throat, he leaped—

AND STUMBLED to a halt on a rugged shoreline.

The surf boomed against the great black boulders thrusting up from the pebble-strewed beach. The sky was leaden and cast its pewter hue on the restless ocean. Tendrils of mist floated at ankle level in the small sheltered cove in which he stood. Kane glanced down at himself and saw without much surprise he was naked. He knew he should have been cold, but he was not. He felt nothing at all.

He saw the long scar along his left rib cage where the jolt-walker had stabbed him during a sweep of the Cobaltville pits, and a smaller pucker on the outside of his right biceps, a memento of the time a Roamer scored a lucky, if superficial shot with an old musket. There were many more marks of violence scattered over his body—Kane's body, he told himself fiercely, not Cuchulainn's.

"Ka'in."

He knew the voice instantly, that throaty, melodious rustle. "Time is a river that twists on itself. Past, present and future are its waters. The fluid of time is life. When life, the spirit, ceases to exist, time becomes meaningless. I am overjoyed your spirit lives still, Ka'in. There is still meaning."

Wearily, he said, "You didn't go to all this trouble to contact me just to repeat yourself, Fand. Show yourself."

The sea began to boil, bubbles roiling and ripples spreading. Fand did not so much rise to the surface as seem to be lifted from the depths. She was tall, nearly as tall as he was and sleek and beautiful, with the look of a lioness about her. Her narrow face was finely chiseled, with prominent cheekbones, and her full lips held a secret, faintly amused smile.

Her skin had the blue-white hue of skim milk, and her golden, unbound hair tumbled down past her thighs like a flaxen waterfall. She was as naked as he

was, her high, firm breasts like opals, her body slender
with a catlike grace. Great physical strength showed
in the arching rim of her rib cage and her flat, tautly
muscled belly. The fine hair at the junction of her
smoothly contoured thighs was like threads of spun
gold. She held a long wooden staff in her right hand,
enwrapped with vines and many turnings of silver
wire. An ivory knob, like an oversize egg, topped it.

Fand seemed to glow, to sparkle like a creature of
sunshine and meadows and deep forests. Her huge, tip-
tilted eyes, golden with vertical slit pupils, never left
his.

Her full lips parted and in a liquid voice, in a language he had never spoken but understood, she said,
"Do you know where you are, my darling Ka'in?"

Stolidly, he replied, "I'm in gateway transit, suffering from a jump dream. I've had them before."

Fand moved lithely toward him, her delicate feet not
touching the sea or even the rocks. "How can you be
so sure?"

"For one thing," he retorted gruffly, "I'm naked."

She laughed, the sound a musical trilling. "Naked
is the best disguise, my darling Ka'in."

"I told you the first time we met," he growled, "the
name is *Kane,* not Ka'in, not Cuchulainn or any var-
iation thereof."

She continued walking to him. "This is Skatha, the
Land of Shadows, where the spirit of Ka'in resides."

Fand pressed up against him, and with a faraway
shock he realized he could feel the hard nipples of her
breasts pressing against his chest, feel her heartbeat,
the heat of her body. With a sense of dismay and not
a little embarrassment, he found himself aroused, his
throat and other parts of his body tightening.

"This is not a dream," she said breathily, her molten gaze locked on his. "It is a summons, a call for help. Our destinies are ever intertwined, even if we are not meant to be together in these incarnations."

Her words struck a chord of memory. "Yes," he said. "So you've told me. Something about our transplanted souls."

He paused and though his throat felt constricted, he added coldly, "What makes you think I give a shit about any of that?"

Fand did not seem to be offended or even to have heard him. Her fingers lightly caressed the hairline scar on his left cheek, inflicted there only a few months before. "Some things have changed since we last saw each other."

He caught her arm, noting how his hand easily encircled the long, narrow wrist. "Not everything. You still think you can invade my mind and screw with my perceptions whenever you feel the urge."

She surprised him by laughing in genuine amusement. The Fand he had met before, more than half a year ago, would have been enraged by his grim observation. That Fand was tempestuous to the point of madness, flipping from loving passion to homicidal fury in between eye blinks.

"I felt the urge to contact you many, many times, Kane," she said quietly. "But I restrained myself. I respected your wishes."

He realized she had spoken his name without the annoying insertion of the glottal stop. "You call invading my mind without my permission respecting my wishes, Fand?"

"I would never have done so unless the matter was urgent." The golden light in her inhumanly huge, inhumanly beautiful eyes dimmed. "More than urgent. You saved Eire once, Kane. You saved *me*. Now the stakes are far higher and can affect every corner of the globe."

He frowned at her, knowing she wasn't being deliberately melodramatic. "What do you mean?"

Her full lips turned down at the corners. "This was a wild land, with terrible feuds raging among the clans. Blood of my people was spilled here, which is a tie that forever binds my soul to this island. Your blood was spilled here, too—and that of Balor."

Before he realized it, Kane blurted, "Old Evil-eye?"

She nodded. "I stirred your spirit so you would remember him."

"Why?"

"Because his spirit stirs again, drawing you to him to settle the feud that was not resolved more than fifteen hundred years ago."

Kane said nothing. He had heard Fand's doctrine of soul transmigration and reincarnation before. It was part and parcel of her religion.

Lifting her slender left arm, she extended it straight out, so the hand was parallel with the horizon. A small, fragile-looking orb nestled in her palm. It looked like a tiny globe of spun glass, though it was not transparent.

Fand lowered her arm, and the sphere remained in place, floating in midair, balanced on the faint line of demarcation between the ocean and the sky. She stated, "Out there lies England, the Imperium Britannia."

"Strongbow's empire."

Fand shook her head. "Strongbow's no longer. But

his absence has not improved the relations between our two nations. It has worsened. My people openly war against the Imperium, but the war goes badly for both parties.''

"What's that got to do with me?" Kane demanded.

"Look at the orb of orichalcum."

"The orb of what?"

"Watch, Kane."

He did as she said, fixing his gaze on the little ball. From the sea beneath it, thrusting up like a finger, rose a great stone pillar, a greenish monolith dripping with seaweed. He could make out the bas-reliefs carved into it. It lifted from the ocean until its tip seemed to touch the bottom of the sphere.

"What is that?" Kane asked.

"A city, an outpost of the Atlantean Empire. It was known to my people by many names—Poseidia, Lyonesse, Lethosow. After aeons incalculable, it has risen again, torn loose by the cataclysms birthed by the holocaust of two centuries ago. Within its deep vaults is the means to finish what the nuclear apocalypse started. Watch the orb, Kane."

The tiny sphere suddenly turned scarlet, seeming to swell, ripping open the vast backdrop of the sky as if it were rotten, old cloth. The translucent orb burst open from within, releasing a bloom of hellfire. A sheet of flame paled the sky, surging outward and upward. The waves of the sea divided, and the orange-yellow flare poured into Kane and filled him to the backs of his eyeballs.

A coruscating wall of fire scorched across the ocean, riding a booming shock wave, pushing the ocean ahead of it in an overlapping series of mile-high tsunamis.

Kane tried to squeeze his eyes shut, but he felt paralyzed, rooted to the spot like a statue. A vast mush-
room cloud towered from the horizon, shot through
with arcing skeins of blinding, destructive energy. A
wall of smoke swept over him, obscuring the shoreline
and Fand, but he could still hear her.

"Hell is rising anew from an ancient tomb beneath
the waters. History will be repeated if you do not heed
me. And if you do not play your preordained role, this
time there will be no survivors. Anywhere."

The wall of sooty smoke enveloped him, blinded
him, and he saw nothing more. For an eternity, he felt
suspended in a pocket of infinity, of nothingness, of
nonexistence.

Then, very faintly, he heard the hurricane howl.

# Chapter 11

Judging by the flashing icons on the monitor screen, Lakesh realized he should steel himself to accept the loss of another Cerberus recruit.

Banks touched the screen and said tensely, "Cotta flat-lined half an hour ago. No change." He was a youthful, trim black man with an earnest manner.

The telemetry transmitted from Kane's, Brigid's and Grant's transponders scrolled upward. The computer systems recorded every byte of data sent to the Comsat and directed it down to the redoubt's hidden antenna array. Sophisticated scanning filters combed through the telemetric signals using special human biological encoding.

The digital data stream was then routed to the console on Banks's right, through the locational program, to precisely isolate the team's present position in time and space. The program considered and discarded thousands of possibilities within milliseconds.

Lakesh didn't respond. The icons representing Brigid Baptiste's bio-signs flashed and jumped in a manner neither he nor Banks had ever seen.

"Perhaps it's just a glitch in the system," Banks said uneasily, as though he didn't quite believe his own words. "Like the kind we had a couple of weeks ago."

Lakesh nodded as if he were seriously considering

the suggestion. Actually, he was thinking about sitting down. As a man who was chronologically a shade under 250 years old, he felt he was justified. Although he didn't look his age, he looked old enough. A long-nosed, wizened cadaver of a man, he wore thick-lensed glasses with a hearing aid attached to the right earpiece. His hair was the color and texture of ash.

Upon his revival from cryogenic sleep, Lakesh had undergone several operations in order to prolong his life and his usefulness to the Program of Unification. His brown, glaucoma-afflicted eyes were replaced with new blue ones, his leaky old heart and lungs were exchanged for sound new ones. The joints in his knees were not the same as those he had been born with, either. Though his wrinkled, liver-spotted skin made him look exceptionally old, his physiology was that of a fifty-year-old man.

"It's not that," Bry said from the main ops console of the Cerberus redoubt. He had short, curly copper hair and was a round-shouldered man of small stature. "What happened then was solar flares, completely interrupting the satellite signals. We have solid transmissions now."

Lakesh glanced around the central control complex of the trilevel, thirty-acre facility. The room was long, with a high, vaulted ceiling. Consoles of dials, switches, buttons and lights flickering red, green and amber ran the length of the walls. Circuits hummed, needles twitched and monitor screens displayed changing columns of numbers.

A huge Mercator relief map of the world spanned the far wall. Spots of light glowed in almost every continent, and thin glowing lines networked across the countries, like a web spun by a radioactive spider.

They delineated locations of all functioning gateway units in the Cerberus mat-trans network. At present, none of the lights flickered, which would register activity in the network.

Exhaling wearily, Lakesh pressed an intercom key on a desk. "DeFore," he called. "Are you there?"

Her crisp voice responded quickly. "I am. What's up?"

"Please bring a med kit and a gurney to the ops center."

"Who's hurt?"

"I just need you to stand by." He cut off further questions by releasing the key. He cast a worried glance through the open door of the ready room to the jump platform. The six-sided chamber was enclosed by slabs of brown-tinted armaglass to confine quantum energy overspills. All of the official Cerberus gateway units of the mat-trans network were color-coded so authorized jumpers could tell at a glance into which redoubt they had materialized.

Despite the fact it seemed an inefficient method of differentiating one installation from another, only personnel holding color-coded security clearances were allowed to make use of the system. Inasmuch as their use was restricted to a select few of the units, it was fairly easy for them to memorize which color designated what redoubt.

Lakesh usually felt a small flush of pride whenever he looked at this particular gateway unit since it was the first fully debugged matter-transfer inducer built after the prototypes. It served as the basic template for all the others that followed. But today he eyed the jump chamber with trepidation, even a touch of fear.

He was afraid of what might materialize in it at any moment.

DeFore entered, followed by her aide, Auerbach, who was pushing a wheeled gurney ahead of him. Stocky and buxom with deep bronze skin that contrasted starkly with her intricately braided ash-blond hair, DeFore's brown eyes cut over to the medical monitor. They widened when she saw the icons and data scrolling across it. Instantly, she stood over Banks.

"How sure are you of these readings?" she snapped.

With a touch of asperity, Bry said, "Ninety-six percent probability they're accurate."

DeFore's full lips pursed contemplatively. "Cotta's totally flat-lined. Maybe the transponder itself was damaged."

Without waiting for anyone to agree or disagree, she went on curtly, "Baptiste's blood pressure is well below normal systolic levels. Her heart rate is irregular. All the symptoms of deep shock."

She cast a hard glance in Lakesh's direction. "Where did you send them this time?"

Lakesh quashed his sudden flash of angry resentment. Tapping his narrow chest, he declared, "*I* didn't send them anywhere. I no longer have the authority to do that, as you know. The decision to make the jump to the Antarctica unit was reached among Kane, Brigid and Grant."

DeFore swung her around, scrutinizing the webwork of light crisscrossing the Mercator map. "I don't see a gateway there."

"Because it's unindexed," Lakesh retorted, irritated by how defensive he sounded. "It wasn't part of the official Cerberus program. It's apparently one of the mass-produced modular units. Brigid found the codes by searching the database."

He hooked a thumb over his shoulder toward the jump chamber. "It obviously was functional. Otherwise, they wouldn't have been able to achieve a destination lock."

Auerbach spoke for the first time, in a slow, faltering voice. He was a tall, burly man with a red buzz cut. "But because the unit isn't indexed, you won't know when they'll be returning?"

Lakesh inclined his head toward the map. "That's right. If it was indexed, the mat and demat process would be registered there."

Crossing her arms over her ample chest, DeFore said irritably, "So you just want me to stand by in here for God only knows how long? They might not return for hours, for days. It makes more sense for me to put together a comprehensive med kit and jump there myself."

Lakesh self-consciously cleared his throat. "I considered making that proposal to you, but after your recent sufferings in Louisiana—"

She cut him off with a short, sharp gesture. "My injuries weren't serious. And if it's my emotional state you're concerned about, you can just go and—"

Suddenly, lights flashed and needles wavered on the consoles. All of them spun as a humming tone vibrated from the gateway chamber.

"Incoming jumpers," Bry announced.

DeFore ran through the anteroom, past Lakesh and Auerbach and came to a stop facing the armaglass door. Bright flares, like bursts of distant heat lightning, arced on the other side. The droning hum climbed rapidly in pitch to a hurricane wail, then dropped down to inaudibility as the device cycled through the materialization process.

Grabbing the handle, she wrenched up on it. She was nearly bowled off her feet by the door flying open on counterbalanced hinges, pushed by Kane's shoulder. He leaned against it for a moment, eyes glassy and unfocused. Both DeFore and Lakesh winced when they saw him. His thermal suit hung in tatters, his face blood-streaked and bruised, hair in disarray.

Hoarsely, he barked, "Get her out of there!"

IT WAS BARELY controlled chaos for a moment as Kane stumbled from the platform, catching himself on the edge of the table. Grant followed, equally unsteady and bloody.

DeFore and Auerbach pushed their way into the jump chamber, fanning away the dissipating tendrils of vapor.

"Where's Cotta?" Lakesh demanded.

Hanging his head, respiration labored, Kane said, "We had to leave him behind."

"What happened to him?"

Before either Kane or Grant could answer, Auerbach and DeFore emerged from the chamber, carrying Brigid on the makeshift stretcher. As they laid her gently down on the gurney, Lakesh caught sight of the bloody bandages wrapped around her head. He blurted something in a language no one understood and rushed to her side.

Peeling back one of Brigid's eyelids, DeFore asked, "Who bandaged her up like this?"

"I did," Grant replied a trifle gruffly.

"You did a good job," she stated. "Her pupils

aren't contracting. Can you and Kane make it to the dispensary under your own steam?"

Both men nodded.

"Let's go then. Banks, I'm going to need you on this."

Banks was not brought into Cerberus to act as a medic. For the past couple of months, he worked under the tutelage of DeFore while Auerbach languished in a detention cell on the bottom level of the installation. He had been confined there when his participation in a scheme to murder Kane, Brigid and Grant was uncovered. Because he had been duped, Auerbach had only recently been released and returned to his duties on a form of parole.

As Auerbach wheeled the gurney out of the center, DeFore worked on untying the knots that bound Brigid to the boards. She subsided when Kane stepped forward and cut through the ropes with his red-stained combat knife. Lakesh followed, barely able to refrain from wringing his liver-spotted hands in agitation.

"What happened down there?" he asked in his reedy voice. "What did you find?"

Grant and Kane were too enervated, too wrung out by fatigue and pain to answer him. Grant just shook his head. "Later, Lakesh." He looked around, as if suddenly recalling something he'd forgotten. "Where's Domi?"

"Out," Lakesh answered impatiently. "Taking a walk, I don't know. Please, tell me what you found."

Kane shot him an icy, blue-gray glare that glittered with anger. "Works of art, gems, gold bars. Nothing of any value to us."

Lakesh's eyes widened behind the thick lenses of

his spectacles, which made them look as big as saucers. "Gold bars?"

"Yeah," Grant muttered. "All of them marked with the cutest little swastikas you've ever seen."

The two men refused to answer any more questions, even though Lakesh followed them down the wide corridor and into the dispensary. DeFore said, "Kane, Grant—strip. Banks, Auerbach, look after them. Lakesh, stay the hell out of our way."

Grant and Kane did as she said, removing their ragged thermal suits and sitting on examination tables, wearing only their khaki trousers. DeFore wheeled Brigid into a curtained-off alcove. Lakesh hovered at the door, trying to contain his curiosity but doing a very poor job of it.

DeFore's two aides efficiently and methodically attended to Kane's and Grant's contusions, abrasions and lacerations. At one point, swabbing a scratch on Kane's back, Auerbach murmured, "You guys really got the shit kicked out of you." He didn't sound sympathetic.

After the wounds were disinfected, liquid bandage was sprayed on them from aerosol cans. The film that formed over the wounds contained nutrients and antibiotics that would be absorbed into the body as the injuries healed.

As the scratches on Grant's forehead were being sterilized, DeFore thrust aside the curtain, expression grave, holding a handful of crimson-crusted gauze. Kane caught a glimpse of Brigid lying on a bed, an IV shunt attached to her right arm, respirator hose leading away from her nose and mouth. Her face, cleaned of blood, looked paper pale.

"She's suffering from a violent concussion," DeFore announced. "What was she hit with?"

Kane shrugged. "Some kind of tool. A wrench, I think."

"I haven't found any signs of a break in the cranial casing. Her hair must have acted as a cushion."

Kane tried to heave a sigh of relief, but his ribs hurt too much. He contented himself by saying, "That's good."

DeFore shook her head and dumped the bandages in a waste can. "Not necessarily. She still has trauma to the brain. I'm going to induce a coma in the hopes of relieving it. If—when—she comes around, the aftereffects of the blow may linger for a long time. Her vision and autonomic reflexes may be severely impaired. She might not have enough coordination to spit. There is some good news, though."

Grant eyed her skeptically. "There is?"

"The bullet wound on her shoulder is little more than a scrape. The laceration in her scalp is clean. I can suture it up without shaving her head, and what little scarring she'll have will be hidden by her hair."

Kane pushed out a disgusted breath. "So she'll be a good-looking vegetable. Is that your prognosis?"

DeFore locked angry eyes with him. The medic had never disguised her antipathy toward him—or rather, what he represented. In her eyes, as a former Magistrate he was the embodiment of the totalitarianism of the villes, glorying in his baron-sanctioned powers to dispense justice and death. At one time, she had believed that due to his Mag conditioning he was psychologically conflicted and therefore couldn't be trusted.

Although her attitude toward him had softened

somewhat over the past couple of months, the earlier resentment now flashed in her dark eyes.

"Muzzle it, Kane," she snapped. "Something like this was inevitable, with the risks each of you take when you go out into the field. Like you said to me, every day you're alive is just another spin of the wheel. Winning is just breaking even. When your number is up, it's up and you're dead."

Kane couldn't think of anything to say, so he opted to remain silent.

DeFore turned her attention to Grant. "Cotta's dead?"

He nodded bleakly. "Thoroughly."

"Is it safe to send someone back to recover his body?"

"We chilled what chilled him, if that's what you're asking."

Lakesh stepped away from the door, entering the dispensary. "We should make some arrangements to return there."

DeFore waved away the suggestion. "Later. You two need some downtime, some bed rest. I'll prescribe painkillers so you can get some sleep."

"What about Baptiste?" Kane asked.

"I'll suture her up, like I said. But other than that, all we can do is wait."

Grant and Kane accepted the pills offered to them by Banks and climbed down from the examination tables. DeFore returned to the curtained alcove. Kane lingered, absently rattling the pills in his hand, reluctant to leave.

Quietly, Grant said, "You won't do yourself or her any good loitering around here."

Lakesh nodded in agreement, head bobbing on his

wattled neck. "Follow the good doctor's orders, Kane. If dearest Brigid's condition changes, you'll be one of the first to know."

They went out into the corridor and when they reached the T junction that separated the operations section from the personal-quarters wing, Lakesh inquired, "When will you feel like sharing with me what happened in Antarctica?"

As Grant slitted his eyes, Lakesh added hastily, "Just a broad overview. We can save the details for a full debrief at some later date."

"Fine," Kane said harshly, and in curt, unadorned language, told Lakesh what they had encountered— and suffered—in the installation at the South Pole.

When Kane was finished, Lakesh's seamed, yellowish-brown face had paled by several shades. "Dear God," he muttered mournfully. "Poor, unfortunate Cotta."

"Yeah," drawled Kane snidely. "Poor unfortunate Cotta. Good thing you rescued him from his life of unendurable hardship in—where was it, Mandeville?—and brought him here."

Lakesh's thin lips compressed, and he cast a swift, guilty glance over his shoulder.

"Nobody's around," Kane said in a mocking stage whisper. "Your secret is still safe—for the time being."

All three men knew the meaning behind the oblique reference. Overproject Excalibur's subdivision Scenario Joshua had sprung from the twentieth century's Genome Project. The goal of this undertaking was to map human genomes to specific chromosomal functions and locations in order to have on hand in vitro genetic samples of the best of the best, the purest of the pure.

Everyone who enjoyed full ville citizenship was a descendant of the Genome Project. Sometimes a particular gene carrying a desirable trait was grafted to an unrelated egg, or an undesirable gene removed. Despite many failures, when there was a success, it was replicated over and over, occasionally with variations.

Some forty years before, when Lakesh resolved to build a resistance movement against the united baronies, he rifled Scenario Joshua's genetic records to find the qualifications he deemed the most desirable. He used the barons' own fixation with purity control against them. By his own confession, he was a physicist cast in the role of an archivist, pretending to be a geneticist, manipulating a political system that was still in a state of flux.

Lakesh had admitted that Kane was one such example of his covert manipulation, but he hadn't stopped there—and that was the crux of the current tension between the two men. Using the genetic records, Lakesh selected candidates for his rebellion, but finding them and recruiting them were not the same things. With his authority and influence, he set up prospective candidates, framing them for crimes against their respective villes.

It was a cruel, heartless plan with a barely acceptable risk factor, but Lakesh believed it was the only way to spirit them out of their villes, turn them against the barons and make them feel indebted to him.

Only recently had Lakesh's practice been exposed. Grant, Kane and Brigid had staged something of a minimutiny over the issue, but nothing had been settled. However, Lakesh was on notice his titular position as the redoubt's administrator was extremely weak.

Peering at Kane intently over the rims of his spectacles, Lakesh said flatly, "Brigid was right when she accused you of being a cruel man."

Kane crooked challenging eyebrows. "Said the master of the art to the novice."

Grant heaved a profanity-seasoned sigh. "I've heard enough of this shit."

Turning smartly on his heel, he stalked toward his quarters. His standard procedure upon returning from a field op was to take what weapons they'd carried back to the armory. But since his Sin Eater wasn't working anyway, he didn't feel like backtracking. Nor did he feel like listening to a continuation of the feud that had begun on the very first day Kane and Lakesh exchanged words.

Grant hesitated at the door to his apartment, then strode farther down the corridor. He turned a corner and stopped at the first door on his right. He rapped on it, listened, then knocked louder. From within, he heard a high female voice chirp, "C'mon in."

Turning the chrome knob, he opened the door, stepped into Domi's two-room suite and froze in midstride. Domi glanced up at him curiously from her place on the floor. "Hi."

Large, overlapping sections of paper covered a large portion of the carpet. Three skinned rabbit carcasses lay in a neat row on one sheet of paper. Piled on another was a heap of blue-sheened intestines and fur. Splotches of blood soaked into the paper, and Domi's arms were scarlet-stained up to the elbows.

She continued gutting the fourth rabbit with a long, serrated blade. Grant recognized the knife—it was the same one Domi had used to slit Guana Teague's throat when the Cobaltville Pit Boss was strangling the life out of him.

As he closed the door behind him, Domi regarded him speculatively from beneath her ragged shock of bone-white hair. An albino, she had skin the color and fine-pored texture of a pearl. Her eyes on either side of a thin-bridged nose were the color of the fresh blood splashed over her naked body. She was waiflike, almost childish with her firm, pert breasts and petite build.

An outlander by birth, she was always at ease being nude in the company of others and if those others didn't share that comfort zone, she couldn't care less.

Grant had seen her naked many times but never with her exquisitely molded little body gleaming wetly with blood. The sight sent a spasm of nausea through him. Before he could stop himself, he demanded, "What the fuck are you up to?"

She frowned at his harsh, peremptory tone. "Thought we could use some fresh meat so I went hunting." She gestured casually with the knife. "Used that instead of a longblaster. Kind of fun."

Grant's eyes followed the wave of the blade and rested on the small crossbow he had brought back from the mission in Louisiana. The swamp muties who dwelt down there preferred them even to home-forged muzzle loaders.

"Made my own arrows," she explained. "Only missed once."

Grant knew Domi had lived an almost feral existence before being smuggled into Cobaltville by Teague to be his sex slave. Still, he had difficulty visualizing her creeping among the deep, forested ravines that surrounded the mountain plateau, armed with only a crude crossbow.

Hunting was unnecessary. The food lockers and meat freezers of the redoubt were exceptionally well stocked. Lakesh had taken a lot of time and trouble to insure that one item the personnel wouldn't be deprived of upon their exile was food.

So for Domi to go out stalking game struck Grant as more than a little disquieting—it almost seemed as if she were indulging an urge to kill.

As she returned her attention to slitting open the rabbit, she asked, "When did you get back?"

"Not quite an hour ago." He paused to take a breath. "Cotta didn't make it back."

The expert movement of her knife faltered for just an instant. She nodded brusquely. "Chilled?"

"Yeah."

"Good death?"

"No. A very hard one."

She nodded again. "Didn't know him very well. He used to look at me when he thought I didn't know. He'd get all hard. He almost never said anything. Figure he was afraid."

Grant understood her apparent indifference to the news of the man's death. In her worldview, death was a constant companion, always trailing along with a rattle of bones. There was little point in his upbraiding her for her callous attitude. After all, he barely knew Cotta himself.

She swung her head toward him, squinting. "You hurt? Kane? Brigid?"

"All of us to one degree or another. Brigid is the worst. She's in the dispensary right now, in a coma."

He licked his lips. "DeFore isn't sure if she'll ever wake up."

Domi finally showed some reaction. She bounded to her feet, teeth bared, fisting the knife as though she was prepared to stab someone. "Who did it?" she demanded between bared teeth.

She was less distressed by news of Brigid's injury than the notion the perpetrator might have gone unpunished. In her simple Outland way, she wanted to kill the person who hurt her friend.

"A fused-out old slagger did it," Grant answered. "He's dead."

None of the bestial tension went out of Domi's posture. Her ruby eyes glittered. "He die hard?"

"Exceptionally hard."

Domi lowered the knife, looking up and down Grant's body. "He hurt you, too?"

"He saw to it, but like I said, he paid the price."

The albino girl nodded in savage satisfaction. "Bastard."

"Yeah," Grant half whispered. "Bastard. Just the latest in a long line. And God knows how many more are left."

He turned toward the door, but Domi plucked at his arm. "Stay with me."

He recoiled from the touch of her scarlet-coated fingers and he wasn't sure why. Domi claimed to be in love with him, viewing him as a gallant knight who rescued her from the shackles of Guana Teague's slavery. In reality, quite the reverse was true. Teague was crushing the life out of him beneath his three-hundred-plus pounds of flab when Domi sliced his throat.

Regardless of the facts, Domi had attached herself to him, and though her attempts at outright seduction were less frequent, she still made it fiercely clear that Grant was hers and hers alone.

She had more than once evinced jealousy of De-Fore, suspecting the woman of having designs on Grant. He had no idea if the medic had such an intent. She was a mature woman, certainly attractive and closer to his own age than Domi, but there was nothing between them but a guarded friendship.

Of course, he reflected, he had fought hard to make sure there was nothing but friendship between him and Domi, too, but he feared it was a fight he would eventually lose. He had no idea of Domi's true age and neither did she. She could be as young as sixteen or as old as twenty-six, but either way, he was pushing forty and felt twice as old. He couldn't deny he was attracted to her youthfulness, her high spirits and her uninhibited sexuality. But now the idea of being caressed by bloody fingers repulsed him.

Domi caught the disgust momentarily reflected in his eyes and expression and she stared at him in hurt wonder. "What wrong?" Under emotional stress, her abbreviated mode of outlander speech became pronounced. "What I do, make you look at me like that?"

Grant shook his head, feeling a bone-deep weariness settle over him like a heavy cloak. "Nothing. You're just being yourself. But right now I'm sick of everything and of everyone. Even myself."

He closed his eyes for an instant, leaning his head against the door. "I'm sick of blood," he intoned, as if to himself. "Sick of the sight of it, of spilling it and shedding it."

He pulled open the door and stepped out into the

corridor. He closed it quietly behind him, blocking his view of Domi standing there, naked, knife in hand, blood-spattered and confused.

"Welcome to the club," he muttered.

# Chapter 12

Quayle hummed to himself as he strode across the gangway from the berthing dock of the drilling platform to the deck of the *Cromwell*. Morrigan followed him, hands on the rail, surprisingly surefooted for one deprived of sight.

The chill wind had dropped, and Quayle's mood had risen in direct proportion with it. Even Morrigan had shed her unflattering warm-up suit and was dressed in a simple belted jerkin and short, pleated skirt that showed off her finely molded legs to full advantage.

In the two hours since the demonstration of the orichalcum bead, Quayle barely felt the burn in the palm of his hand. As he crossed the deck to the staircase leading to the elevated bridge housing, he looked pridefully around at the *Cromwell*.

Just as he had more or less appropriated Lord Strongbow's position, he also laid claim to the man's most important possession. The black vessel was truly a masterpiece of late-twentieth-century British engineering. The Stealth technology incorporated into the corvette wasn't designed merely to hide from an enemy, but to confuse him, too. The beveled contours of the hull and superstructures produced dual-path radar reflections; the vessel also possessed the capability of changing the size and shape of its radar signature by raising and lowering a set of retractable reflectors in the aft communications pyramid.

The *Cromwell* possessed another novel form of camouflage, the ability to generate an artificial fog made by heating seawater, which also helped to blank out enemy radar. Of course, the vessel had never been brushed by hostile radar. Ocean warfare had played no significant part in the final conflagration of nearly two centuries before.

As he ducked beneath an antiship missile emplacement, he called cheerily over his shoulder, "Mind your step, Miss Morrigan."

"Mind yours, Captain," she retorted with a dazzling smile.

Once again Quayle was impressed by the woman's beauty, despite her blank white eyes. He climbed the stairs and, because of his height, he had to enter the door to the bridge hunched over and with a shambling sideways gait. Even the inconvenience couldn't dampen his enthusiasm. In his hand, he held a slip-sleeved computer diskette.

The bridge room was empty, the consoles and instrument panels unlighted. He took a seat before the navigation computer terminal and booted it up. He inserted the disk into the drive port and waited. Morrigan stood over him, a hand resting on his shoulder.

"You're sure it's not encrypted or copy protected?" he asked.

She shook her head. "We of the Priory don't believe in such precautions. Knowledge should be free for all."

Quayle stopped himself from snorting in derision. He had always been a cautious man, always concealing his superior traits from his comrades and particu-

larly from Lord Strongbow. It was the main reason he
had not risen very fast or high in the Imperial Dragoons. There were other reasons, of course, one of
them being his unusual size. The other was a bit more
basic and bitter. The one time he had displayed his
superiority had ended in personal disaster.

After losing his right eye in an engagement against
Celtic smugglers and being decorated for his valor in
battle, he had applied for membership in an elite unit
of dragoons who were answerable only to Strongbow.

Those men selected for the duty were required to
undergo a prolonged medical treatment, a series of in-
jections and transfusions that would mutagenically al-
ter their DNA. If the process was successful, the sub-
jects would find their reflexes enhanced, their physical
strength augmented and their capacity to recover from
injuries and illnesses improved. The trade-off was a
permanent change in the eyes to allow for expanded
optic abilities—not to mention a growth of reptilian
scales that replaced eyebrows.

A doctor had provided Quayle with a broad, non-
scientific overview of the process. According to him,
Lord Strongbow had created a nontraditional method
of gene-splicing. Through the use of a certain type of
biological material, Strongbow concocted a viral mixture to synthesize a small protein molecule that fit cellular receptors in human tissues. The virus replicated,
infected and transformed the cellular structure, rewrit-
ing the genetic code.

Although he didn't understand it, particularly the
source of the "certain type of biological material,"
Quayle volunteered anyway. The treatment's only effect was an illness that caused him to hover in a deep
coma between life and death for nearly a month.

When he finally awakened, he found he had lost all of his hair, skin and eye pigmentation. He returned to his unit, not necessarily shunned by his comrades but certainly viewed as a reject. He was told he should consider himself fortunate despite his disfigurement, inasmuch as other men on whom the process failed were dead.

So Quayle pretended to consider himself fortunate. He kept his place and found another subject to occupy his intellect. He found that subject in an old book, *Timaeus,* by the Greek philosopher Plato. That book served only as a jumping-off point for a search that had consumed him for the past three years.

It had ceased to be a mere intellectual exercise when Morrigan came to him. He glanced up at her as she toyed with the silver emblem around her neck, the insignia of the Priory of Awen.

Quayle knew about the existence of the Priory long before he met Morrigan. The society was the bane of Lord Strongbow's life for reasons he'd never explained.

Allegedly founded by Saint Patrick in the fourth century, it was formed as an enclave of scholar-priests to safeguard the secrets of pre-Christian Ireland, secrets that flew in the face of accepted religious doctrines. In the Gaelic tongue, *awen* meant "inspiration," and the practitioners, the *awenyddion,* solved problems or looked for hidden information.

Quayle sometimes wished Strongbow were still around, at least long enough to see his face when he learned his trusted telepathic adviser, Morrigan, had been a Priory priestess, a spy all along. Upon her return to New London, when she revealed her association with the Priory to Quayle, his initial reaction had been to laugh uproariously at the irony. His second impulse was to have her drawn and quartered, but then she spoke one word to him: "Atlantis."

That one whispered word did more than send chills up his spine—it encapsulated all of his covert labors and humiliations over the past five years.

The nav comp uttered an electronic beep. The monitor screen displayed a color aerial map of the North Atlantic, overlaid with a longitude and latitude grid. The British Isles and the northern European coastlines were depicted as they had been before the nukecaust.

As he moved the cursor over the image, data scrolled in a separate window to the right of the screen. The information detailed the ocean depth and distance from any given reference point along the North Atlantic seaboard. A tiny red dot, shining like a pinhead of blood, glowed in the Irish Sea. Judging by the map coordinates, it was surrounded by thousands of square miles of empty ocean.

Quayle's eyes narrowed. On-site inspection of the area in question would have to be implemented, but the data thus far seemed very promising. It correlated closely with his own calculations. So closely, in fact, he felt a quiver of suspicion.

"So," he said slowly. "The Priory believes this is the true location of Atlantis?"

"No," said Morrigan. "The location of the actual continent is still unknown, even to the Priory of Awen. More than likely, it is where Plato, Solon and the Egyptians said it was—beneath the mid-Atlantic in the vicinity of the Azores. But the Atlantean League explored and colonized, establishing outposts. That small island is one of them."

Quayle propped his chin on his big fist. "How long has it been on the surface?"

She shrugged negligently, as if the matter was of little importance. "Perhaps since the sea quakes caused by the nuclear holocaust. Who can say?"

Aubrey Quayle had researched the subject for years, painstakingly gathering information from many sources. He alone had put together all the pieces of the puzzle, broken the codes embedded in the old texts. It took a brilliant mind to unravel the tangled threads and understand the mistranslated documents.

He knew the nukecaust had radically resculpted the face of the globe, and the coastlines of England were greatly changed. Most of old London itself was underwater and New London had been built on the ruins of Liverpool.

The same nuke-triggered seismic activity that altered sea levels and tectonic plates had caused long-submerged landmasses to reappear, bursting forth from ocean floors all over the world. These sudden reappearances were, for the most part, ignored or unknown, simply because the population of the world no longer had the resources or technology to rechart and explore the seas.

The sketchy reports Quayle had put together maintained that a landmass had once been situated off the west coast of Ireland, thousands of years ago. Before the nukecaust, the closest western land to Ireland was Iceland, then Greenland, and beyond that, the northern area of what had been North America. This new island was less than one hundred miles off the coast of County Clare. Even his own people had a similar myth, that of the isle of Lyonesse.

If this isle was the same one destroyed by a global

catastrophe, then it wasn't surprising that all accounts of the place were garbled nonsense. Those who survived the cataclysm, sometime around 10,000 BC, might have fled to the nearest shore, which would have been ancient Eire.

To Quayle, the pieces of information he had collected and assembled over a period of years pointed to Ireland, which might hold the final clue. But the island of Eire was perpetually surrounded by a fog bank that sometimes extended far, far out into the Irish Sea. Sailors trying to navigate those waters found themselves wandering in circles.

Radar and sonar still worked to navigate in the dense pall, but the people interpreting instrument data couldn't focus their eyes upon it. Mental disorientation led to many ships running aground. Strongbow always referred to it angrily as an Irish trick, and even now Quayle couldn't help but suspect Morrigan was playing another one on him.

He favored her with a slit-eyed stare. "If your people knew about its reemergence, why haven't they looted it long before now?"

"Your question is its own answer, Captain. If by 'your people' you mean the Irish as a whole, they don't know about it except as one more unsubstantiated legend among thousands in our collective history. If you mean the Priory of Awen—"

"I do," he broke in irritably.

She nodded, a patronizing smile creasing her lips. "We are scholars, preservers and protectors of knowledge, not plunderers. We have a few Atlantean artifacts in our archives, like the bead of orichalcum, but that is all. The continent and the entire Atlantean

League was destroyed. To root among their remains would be a violation of the natural order of things."

"Then why are you violating that order?"

Her smile widened. "There are ways, Captain, to do things that are in tune with the natural order. And there are just as many ways not to do things. Lord Strongbow found that out with his so-called Singularity."

More than once Morrigan had referred to Strongbow's Singularity, the device he created by which he could invade Ireland from within instead of without. All Quayle knew was that Strongbow had enlisted the aid of four Yanks, two men and two women, to help him achieve this objective.

They and Morrigan had set sail aboard the *Cromwell* one dawn six months before. The ship returned without them, carrying a boatload of casualties. After that, events unfolded with chaotic rapidity.

Lord Strongbow vanished without a trace. During the confusion in the aftermath of his disappearance, the Celts invaded in force. They joined a contingent of Irish already insinuated within the Imperium's territories, and within days, bloody war erupted on two fronts. Inside of a month, the active combat had become a stalemate, broken by sporadic forays either by the Britons or the Celts.

Without Strongbow as a rallying point, the Imperium fought a primarily defensive action. The man always claimed complete credit for organizing fragmented England into an empire, and without him, the Imperium appeared to unravel.

Quayle was never quite certain of the veracity of Strongbow's oft-repeated assertions. As long as he could remember, Lord Strongbow had been a presence in Britain. More than a presence—a totally pervasive influence. Morrigan hinted darkly there was far more to Strongbow's history than he ever revealed, but Quayle wasn't particularly interested. The mystifying and disturbing items he found in the subterranean foundations of the Ministry of Defense building certainly lent heavy credence to Morrigan's inferences.

When New London itself came under siege and the harbor was bottled up, he took command of the dwindling military forces. As the siege inexorably tightened, he decided to flee rather than surrender. Three midnights ago, he, Morrigan and a unit of dragoons commandeered the *Cromwell* and, with its artificial fog generator, managed to slip past the blockade. They sailed directly to the Northstar 40 drilling platform, more than one hundred miles offshore. Years before, Strongbow had seen to its refurbishing as a supply depot for the imperial navy, but now, as far as Quayle was concerned, it served as the supreme headquarters of the Imperium Britannia and he was the supreme commander. He bore Lord Nelson's cutlass to prove it.

Quayle forced his mind back to the present. "Who else among the Priory scholars has this information?"

"No one," Morrigan answered. "I calculated and triangulated the isle's position myself, based on old documents and the few eyewitness accounts that came to us."

He slitted his one eye in sudden alarm. "Eyewitness accounts? Who?"

She chuckled. "The selkies. You know who they are."

Quayle's lips curled as if he tasted something very

sour. "I do. According to the Priory's documents, there is a stockpile of orichalcum on the isle?"

"The firestones were the primary source of energy for all of the Atlantean League. If there is anything at all from that era on the island, we should find orichalcum."

He grunted disapprovingly.

Morrigan ran a hand over his shoulders. "I thought you trusted me, my captain. Serendipity brought us together, intertwined our two paths."

In a musing tone, Quayle said, "'My captain'...I like the sound of that."

He turned in his chair, the gimbel squealing, and reached for her hand. "My lovely blind scholar-spy."

Morrigan stiffened, but she said nothing as his huge paw enfolded her delicate hand. In a crooning whisper, he said, "It was more than serendipity that led you to me, sweet Morrigan."

She remained silent, standing stock-still as he clumsily caressed the palm of her hand. "It is destiny."

Her breath caught in her throat. "Destiny?"

"Indeed. You do not realize it, but my physical appearance is abhorrent to the eyes of most women—except for the whores I've paid from time to time. Yet you who are sightless can see beyond the physical and to the spirit that is trapped within this grotesque shell."

Morrigan still didn't respond, not cracking so much as a smile at his flowery eloquence.

Quayle peered into her face and asked, with a trace of uncertainty, "You do, don't you?"

"That I do, Captain," she retorted confidently. "That I do."

If Quayle noticed the cold timbre of her voice, he

showed no sign. "You fled your country and betrayed your order, all for me. Words cannot begin to describe how deeply those actions touch me, how profoundly moved I am."

Morrigan carefully tried to disengage from his grasp without appearing repulsed. "I'm gratified to hear that, Captain."

He chuckled in wonderment. "And to think I was suspicious of your motives when you first sought me out. I had resigned myself to just being Captain Evil-eye, never knowing true power or true love. You've brought me both."

"Captain—"

"Aubrey," he corrected gently. "You must call me Aubrey now."

"Captain," Morrigan repeated firmly. "My motives are the same as they always were—to end this sense-less war between Eire and the Imperium so we may accept each other and recognize each other's right to exist."

His brow furrowed. "But you brought the data and the orichalcum to me."

"Because the Priory is content to allow matters to run their own course, regardless of how many lives may be lost. And even if they intervened, I doubt my people would heed their counsel of peace. Anger and hatred toward the Imperium has festered for too long.

"I have given you the means to prove to my people the Imperium can destroy them unless they lay down their arms. You will be able to force them to petition for peace."

As she spoke, Morrigan managed to work her hand free of his sweaty grasp. "The orichalcum is but a tool, a means to an end, Captain. That end is peace between our two nations."

Quayle sat in his chair, head bowed. In a softer, conciliatory tone, Morrigan continued. "You are correct about one thing—my abilities enabled me to glimpse your spirit, to know that you alone have the desire and influence to bring peace. All you need is a fulcrum to achieve that. That is what you will find on that isle."

The big man ran a hand over his face, fingers tracing the scar on his cheek. He heaved a sigh. It sounded like the compression of huge fireplace bellows. "I see."

"Do you?"

"Yes," he replied dolefully.

"I didn't intend to wound your feelings, Captain."

He sighed again, less heavily. "So many women have said much the same thing to me."

Morrigan's white eyes suddenly flew wide, and she took a swift backstep. The braids in her hair slid apart, unraveling as the separate tresses stretched out. "Captain, you don't want to do that—"

Quayle rose from the chair and struck her in the same furious, fluid motion. The flat of his hand impacted against the right side of her face with the meaty report of a whip crack.

Morrigan reeled across the bridge and fetched up against an instrument panel. She tasted the warmth of salty blood in her mouth, where her teeth had cut into the tender lining of her cheek.

Her senses staggered under the force of the blow, even though she had glimpsed his intention a few seconds in advance. She heard his ponderous footfalls and felt one of his hands close tightly around the back of her neck, nearly encircling it. His index finger and spatulate thumb met at her windpipe.

Morrigan gagged for air immediately, too consumed with the desperate need to pry open his steely fingers to stop his other hand from ripping the clothes from her body. Within seconds she was naked, as helpless in his grip as a kitten in the hands of a sadistic child. His hot breath scalded the side of her face, and over the pounding of blood in her ears she heard him grunt, "Destiny, you arrogant mutie bitch. This is yours."

Quayle devoted only a moment to roughly squeezing her breasts and probing between her legs before undoing the snap on his trousers. He forced her to her knees. "Pull them down."

Morrigan tugged at his pants, sliding them down the hairless pillars of his legs. His turgid member sprang out, the bulbous tip brushing her cheek. She tried to lean backward and away, but Quayle's clasp was inexorable.

"Aubrey—" she said in an aspirated whisper.

"Captain!" he half shouted. "Captain Quayle, Captain Evil-eye. You'll obey my commands, every one of them, as soon as I give them. Understand?"

Morrigan didn't reply, and his huge hand tightened around the slim column of her throat again. "Do you understand, damn you?"

"Yes," she managed to gasp.

He cuffed her across the top of her head. "Yes what?"

"Sir. Yes, sir."

Quayle grunted in satisfaction and relaxed his grip a trifle. With his free hand, he began stroking himself. "Right. Now take it. No, not in your hand. If you perform that assignment properly, I'll only bugger you. Now snap to it."

# Chapter 13

Kane lay on his bunk and tried to think of anything
but the pain. It had not abated in the hours since his
return to Cerberus. Instead, it had slowly built into
what could only be described as a crescendo of agony.

It came in waves. Some of the surges were bearable;
others were so intense he felt as if the walls of his
skull would fly apart. The pills given to him by DeFore
had done very little to control it, and if the pain increased, he intended to go to the dispensary and get
something stronger—whether DeFore liked it or not.

As a Magistrate, Kane had been taught a technique
to manage pain, but he wasn't a Mag anymore. He
realized bleakly he had experienced more periods of
pain in the year since his exile than during his entire
sixteen years as a hard-contact Magistrate.

Swinging his legs over the side of his bed, he sat
there and cradled his throbbing head in his hands. He
hadn't felt such agony since the time he jumped from
Tibet with the three pieces of the Chintamani Stone in
his coat. As he recalled that incident and those that
followed, he felt a frown tugging at his lips. Lakesh
had postulated the so-called jump dreams might not
be hallucinations at all but inchoate glimpses into
other lives and other realities.

It was possible his vision of ancient Ireland was one
of those glimpses into a past life he couldn't con-

sciously remember. Fand had always maintained that
was the truth. At the time, he'd sneered at the possibility, but now he wasn't so sure.

As a new needle of pain stabbed through his temples, Kane pounded his fist into his pillow, then lay
back down, closing his eyes and breathing deeply and
regularly.

Although sleep didn't come, the dreams did. A mist
rolled over him, thickening and swirling like a maelstrom. In the center of it curled a black staircase, spiraling off into infinity. He fell down the stairs, tumbled
through a kaleidoscope filled with a shifting pattern of
colors. A small part of him panicked, but another part
of his mind said confidently, "It's all right. We've
done this before."

Out of the darkness, a glowing nebula formed and
acquired a definite shape. It spoke to him, a voice he
recognized. The underscoring vibrations sent a thrill
to the core of his soul.

Fand's eyes were a pair of blazing suns, her words
a cascade of gold and silver that caressed his every
nerve ending. "Ka'in, my darling."

For an instant, he forgot everything in his life, including the pain. The beautiful Danaan princess with
eyes burning like stars filled his world. "Ka'in, I knew
if I called, you would hear me. Come to me. Time is
growing short."

Her inhumanly beautiful eyes flickered, like a candle flame caught by a draft. He felt her urgency, shivered from her own terror. "What you experienced before was not a dream, nor is this. I need you. The
vision you saw was a true one."

Her shimmering image retreated toward black eternity. It swallowed her up and, as she vanished, pain lanced through his temples. Faintly, her voice a gossamer wisp of music, she said, "See what comes soon, Ka'in. Time grows short."

The universe seemed to unfold as a vast blossoming explosion tinted in the colors of hell. Sheets of flame roared across skies, burning, scorching, obliterating—

Kane shoved himself upright in the bunk, eyes squeezed shut, feeling sweat flow down from the roots of his hair. Then the pain in his head gave a great surge and vanished—just like the image of Fand.

Still, he felt weak and slightly sick to his stomach. He heard repeated knocking at his door. "What?" he called hoarsely.

"Kane, are you all right?" demanded DeFore.

"Yeah," he replied, managing to stand up on numbed legs.

"Let me in."

He glanced at the chron on the bedside table and saw, with a sense of astonishment, it was nearly 8:00 a.m. He had been sleeping for almost ten hours. DeFore's coming to him at this time of the morning didn't portend good news. Wrapping a sheet around himself, he stumbled to the door, turned the lock and opened it.

The medic stood there, fist poised to rap again. "It's about time. When you didn't respond to the transcomm, I thought you might have—"

"How's Baptiste?" he broke in.

"No change in her condition. She's stable." She eyed him curiously. "How about you?"

Kane shrugged, swaying a little.

"Go ahead," DeFore said curtly. "Sit down before you fall down."

Kane walked over to the bed and half collapsed on

it. DeFore eyed him critically. Slipping a pen flash from a pouch on her bodysuit, she shone it into Kane's eyes.

"Knock it off!" he snapped, jerking his head away. "I'm okay. I just got groggy from those pills you gave me."

DeFore gazed at him stonily. "How many did you take?"

His brow knitted thoughtfully. "All of them."

"All of them?" she echoed incredulously. "One of them should have been sufficient to make you sleep. No damn wonder you dozed through comm calls."

"Why were you trying to raise me?"

"Just checking on you." Her lips twitched in a mirthless smile. "That's what doctors are supposed to do with their patients."

Kane nodded, running a hand through his hair. "Has there been any discussion about retrieving Cotta's body?"

"A little. As you can imagine, nobody's anxious to do it without either you or Grant. Domi has volunteered."

He nodded again, then haltingly asked, "Will you know when Brigid is waking up?"

DeFore shook her head. "It could be a gradual process, over a period of hours or days. Or she could just snap back to consciousness like she was waking from a nap. There's no way to tell."

"Then there's nothing you can do for her?" A hint of a challenge lurked in Kane's tone.

DeFore sunk her teeth momentarily into her underlip and replied with frustration, "I'm not really a doctor, Kane, not by the predark definition of the word. My training was superficial, down and dirty."

Kane gazed at her steadily, not allowing the surprise he felt at her admission to show on his face.

"I'm not a specialist in any one field of medicine," she went on sadly. "In the twentieth century, people like me were called general practitioners. A century before that we were called sawbones because the answer to every injury was to amputate.

"There are some things I know how to do well, and there are a lot more I know next to nothing about. Catatonia and injuries involving the brain are two of those."

She inhaled a deep breath. "So to answer your question, there's absolutely nothing I can do for her without the proper training. I'm sorry."

"I'm not blaming you, DeFore. Everyone here has suffered from the deliberately limited ville educational system. It's one way the barons control the herd so the pigs, geese and cattle won't realize they're owned and start questioning it."

DeFore forced a humorless smile to her face. "I don't know if I'm comfortable with that analogy."

She turned toward the door. "Sorry to have disturbed you. Go back to sleep if you can."

"I'll try...Doctor."

DeFore threw him a fleeting, appreciative smile over her shoulder. As soon as she closed the door behind her, Kane strode to the closet and pulled out a one-piece, formfitting bodysuit, the standard duty uniform of the Cerberus personnel. Quickly, he slipped it on, zipping up the front and fastening the Velcro tabs on the boot socks.

*See what comes soon, Ka'in. Time grows short.*

The Fand he remembered might have been mad, but she wasn't a liar. Cautiously, Kane opened the door and peered both up and down the corridor. Stealthily, on almost soundless feet, he padded down the hall, around the corner and to Brigid's door.

He wasn't surprised that it was unlocked. Back in the villes, doors to the residential flats didn't come equipped with locks. Since every possession was considered more or less on loan from the baron, theft among the citizens was virtually unknown.

Pushing the door open, the overhead track lighting system flashed on automatically, tripped when the floor-mounted photoelectric sensor was triggered. He swept his eyes over the interior, realizing he had never visited Brigid's quarters before.

There wasn't much to see, since what few personal items all of them possessed had been left behind when they escaped Cobaltville. On the built-in bookshelves, he saw big photographic reference books she'd taken from a storage room. She had told them they were once known as "coffee table" books. On the bedside table, he saw a pair of eyeglasses, wire-framed with rectangular lenses. They were her former badge of office as an archivist in the Historical Division of Cobaltville, even though she claimed she needed them to do up-close work. The sight of them sent a jolt of pain through him, but not in his head.

He turned and took a seat at the comp-equipped desk against one wall. The small machine was another item Brigid had found in storage. She had hooked up a direct feed to the main database in the ops center.

Kane was only moderately familiar with computers. To him, they were simply sometimes useful machines, and their more arcane workings held little interest for him. Besides, there were other people in the redoubt to perform the comp work for him. But this time, he didn't want to share his investigation with anyone.

He switched the comp on, the screen juiced with an electric pop and the menu layout appeared. He manipulated the mouse to access the historical files. He browsed the selections, found what he was looking for and carefully, using two fingers, he typed a single word.

"Atlantis."

# Chapter 14

The precipice plunged straight down a thousand feet or more. Lakesh could see very little by gazing over the edge except the blue-and-white ribbon of the rushing stream, now almost a river due to the meltwater from the higher peaks.

Although summer had yet to give way to autumn, the mornings were still chilly at such a high altitude. Lakesh seemed particularly susceptible to cold temperatures and he wasn't sure if it was due to his advanced age or was a metabolic legacy from the century and a half he'd spent in cryostasis.

He gazed down at the foaming torrent of water. The rusted-out carcasses of several old vehicles were completely submerged. They had lain in the streambed since at least the days of the nukecaust. Also down there, completely invisible among the rocks bordering the stream, lay the three pieces of the Chintamani Stone, the Shining Trapezohedron.

In an act of impulsive self-righteousness, an act Lakesh still bitterly resented, Kane had dumped them down there like so much garbage. More than once, Lakesh had contemplated climbing down the cliff face to search for them. Not only would the effort be exceptionally hazardous, but it would also be futile. Even if he managed to retrieve the three black stones, he would never be permitted to put their dimensional-rifting properties to use again.

With a sigh, he backed away from the brink of the precipice and glanced around. The late-morning sun flooded the broad plateau with a golden radiance, striking highlights from the scraps of the chain link enclosing the perimeter. The air smelled fresh, rich with the hint of verdant growth wafting up from the foothills far below. He had spent most of his adult life laboring in installations like the Cerberus redoubt, and the natural world had held very little appeal. There was a dismal irony in the fact that it was only after the Earth had become a rad-scorched hellscape that he had come to appreciate the small things about nature.

Lakesh had singlemindedly devoted his life to science, to dispelling the unknown, reasoning that was the only way to save the half-insane world from itself. Thus he had studied most of his life, learned twelve languages and left the country of his birth to work for what he truly believed was the only endeavor that would restore sanity on Earth. Though his devotion and belief had been utterly and thoroughly betrayed by the fact of the nukecaust, he still labored to arrest the tide of extinction that threatened to engulf the human race.

He crossed the tarmac toward the partially open sec door. When Lakesh had reactivated the Cerberus installation some thirty years before, the repairs he made had been minor, primarily cosmetic in nature. Over a period of time, he had added an elaborate system of heat-sensor warning devices, night-vision vid cameras and motion-trigger alarms to the surrounding plateau. He had been forced to work in secret and completely alone, so the upgrades had taken several years to complete.

Still, with its vanadium radiation shielding still intact, and powered by nuclear generators, Cerberus could survive for at least another five hundred years. Lakesh had taken great pains to make sure the installation was listed as abandoned and unsalvageable on all ville records.

As he entered and passed the luridly colored illustration of Cerberus, he gave the second of the hound's three heads an affectionate pat. Proceeding on down the wide corridor, he met Farrell at the T junction. The middle-aged man's goateed face was drawn and haggard, his eyes netted with red as if he had been weeping.

Farrell had taken the news of Cotta's death very hard. Both men were from the same ville and had arrived at the redoubt within days of each other. Without preamble, he said, "I'm ready to go and recover Cotta's body."

Quietly, Lakesh replied, "We can put together a detail once I speak to friends Grant and Kane—"

Farrell made a scornful spitting noise and waved away Lakesh's words. "To hell with them. We don't need to discuss it with either one of them, particularly Kane. Auerbach and I can do it."

Lakesh blinked in mild surprise, a bit taken aback by the edge of hostility in the man's voice and bearing. "I think either he or Grant should accompany you. They know their way around."

"Yeah," Farrell snapped. "Kane knows it so well mebbe he can get the rest of us chilled, too."

"What happened wasn't Kane's fault," Lakesh retorted, feeling odd to be speaking in Kane's defense. "Deaths are bound to happen in this line of work."

Farrell squinted at him. "In the two and a half years I've been here, we didn't have a single fatality—until Kane and Grant arrived."

He ticked off the names on the fingers of one hand. "Adrian, Davis, Beth-Li, Cotta and now maybe even Brigid."

Lakesh didn't bother correcting him on the details of Beth-Li Rouch's demise. She had been killed by Domi when the outlander girl uncovered her plot to murder Brigid, Kane and Grant.

"Besides," Farrell went on, voice rising in anger, "I thought the whole fucking point of bringing those fucking Mags here was so they could take the fucking risks—not the technical-support staff."

What Farrell said contained more than a nugget of truth. The people Lakesh had recruited to staff Cerberus were primarily academics, technicians and specialists in a variety of fields. Farrell, like Cotta and Bry, received his training in cybernetics, and Wegmann was an engineer. All of them had led structured, sheltered lives in their respective villes. Until the arrival of Grant, Brigid, Domi and Kane, the Cerberus resistance movement had consisted of little more than intelligence gathering.

Kane and Grant acted on that intel, performing as the enforcement arm of Cerberus. In that capacity, they had not only scored a number of victories against the barons, but contended with other threats, as well.

As resentful as he felt toward Kane at the moment, Lakesh knew Farrell's assessment was unjust.

Sternly, he said, "Friend Farrell, I understand your grief, but your anger is misplaced. I remind you Cotta volunteered for the mission. I definitely recall Grant trying to talk him out of accompanying them. Cotta was not drafted or pressed into service."

Farrell opened his mouth to lodge an objection, but Lakesh rushed on, "Friends Grant and Kane have, in their time here, shouldered the lion's share of the risks and never expected any of the staff to join them on their missions. Although I appreciate your distress over losing a friend, I can't help but wonder if the primary source of your anger isn't derived from an incident among you, friend Cotta and Kane."

Farrell didn't display surprise or any sign he had to ransack his memory to recall the incident. He knew instantly to what Lakesh referred. Vehemently, he retorted, "Kane violated our sec protocols. Cotta and I were only following established procedure."

A humorless smile stretched Lakesh's lips. "You laid hands on Kane, and he humiliated you for your trouble." He shook his head ruefully. "As you said, you're technical support, not a Magistrate. You should've known better."

Farrell glanced away, averting his eyes. He exhaled noisily, in resignation. "Point taken. I guess I'm still pissed off about it, even after all this time."

"Under the circumstances, with you and friend Cotta putting guns on him, Kane's reaction was restrained. He could have easily crippled you. Cotta managed to find the strength within himself to forgive Kane. It's way past time for you to do the same."

Farrell passed a hand over his shaved head. "I suppose you're right. But I still want to be on the retrieval detail. It's the least I can do."

Lakesh's humorless smile became one of reassurance. "I'm sure that can be arranged."

He stepped around the man and went on down the passageway to the dispensary. He was not overly surprised to see Kane seated in a chair at Brigid's bedside, one hand atop hers. What did surprise him was the sheaf of paper-clipped printouts on his lap. When Kane caught sight of him, he withdrew his hand.

Lakesh stopped at the foot of the bed and repressed a shudder. Brigid's eyes were closed, and her chest rose and fell in a spasmodic, uneven rate of respiration. She was almost as starkly white as the sheets. Only her red-gold tresses, spread out over the pillow, lent her any color. An IV bag hung upside down to the left of the bed, dripping slowly into a shunt on her arm. Diagnostic scanners hummed purposefully, monitoring her heartbeat.

"No change?" Lakesh inquired softly.

Kane shook his head, expression inscrutable.

Shuffling his feet uncertainly, Lakesh ventured, "I understand that some catatonic people are actually aware of their surroundings. It's possible Brigid knows you're here with her."

Kane didn't respond.

Clasping his gnarled hands behind his back, Lakesh cleared his throat. "You're not to blame, Kane. You aren't responsible."

Kane finally cast his gaze in his direction, blue-gray eyes glinting gimlet hard. "I could've put a thumbs-down on the mission."

"As could friend Grant or dearest Brigid. You all agreed it was important. Now you understand the two-edged sword of a populist democracy. One person, one vote. If everyone is responsible, no one is responsible."

Kane's eyes narrowed. "Mebbe it's time to go back

to the way it was here. One person in charge, in command and ultimately the responsible party.''

Lakesh experienced a quiver of dread. He realized he wasn't certain if he wanted to assume the role of authority again.

Kane stood up, tucking the printout under an arm. Lakesh nodded to it. ''What have you got there?''

''A briefing jacket I compiled.''

Lakesh's trepidation gave way to startlement. ''That *you* compiled? From the database?''

''Where the hell else?''

''Briefing jacket for what?''

''An op that I'm going on. I'll give everyone who's interested the full details and ask for volunteers. Even if I don't get any, I intend to go anyway.''

Lakesh's eyes darted from Brigid's wan, marble-white face and back to Kane's. ''At a time like this?''

''Time is the whole crux of the matter, Lakesh. We don't have a lot of it.''

He stepped away from the bed. ''I'll be in the cafeteria in fifteen minutes.''

THE CERBERUS REDOUBT had an officially designated briefing room on the third level. Big and blue-walled, it featured ten rows of the theater-type chairs facing a raised speaking dais and a rear projection screen. It was built to accommodate the majority of the installation's personnel, back before the nukecaust, when military and scientific advisers visited.

Now, because the briefings rarely involved more than a handful of people, they were always convened in the more intimate dining hall. Lakesh, Grant, Domi and Kane sat around a table, sharing a pot of coffee. Access to genuine coffee was one of the inarguable benefits of living as an exile in the redoubt. Real coffee had virtually vanished after skydark, since all of the plantations in South and Central America had been destroyed.

An unsatisfactory, synthetic gruel known as "sub" replaced it. Cerberus literally had tons of freeze-dried packages of the authentic article in storage, as well as sugar and powdered milk.

"Is this everyone who's going to show up?" Kane asked, taking a sip from his cup. He noted how Grant sat across the table from Domi and didn't meet the reproachful gaze she cast toward him. Unlike the rest of them, Domi wasn't wearing a white bodysuit. Her petite but firm figure was encased in a very tight, exceptionally short red dress that barely kept her modest. Nor was she wearing shoes.

Grant shrugged. "It appears so. Once they heard you were looking for volunteers for an op, they decided to stand down. After what happened yesterday, I can't say as I blame them."

Kane nodded shortly and, without a preface, stated, "During the quantum transit from Antarctica, I experienced a psi communication from Fand."

Grant's eyebrows lifted toward his hairline, then lowered. "That fused-out three-way mutie in Ireland?"

"Three-way hybrid," Kane corrected. "Human, Annunaki and Danaan."

Predecessors of the Archons, the Danaan and Annunaki were also extraterrestrial races intent on hybridization programs that would secure their control of humanity.

"Whatever. She thought you were the incarnation of—what's his name, Cuchulainn?"

Grant mangled the pronunciation and Kane said patronizingly, "It's 'Koo-kull-ayn.'"

Scowling, Grant said, "Whatever. How do you know it wasn't just a jump dream?"

"Did you have one?" Kane asked.

"No, but that doesn't mean anything."

"In this case, I think it does. I experienced another telepathic communication from her while I was asleep. The message was the same."

Lakesh interjected quietly, "DeFore mentioned you took all of the pain relievers she gave you. Don't you think it's possible they may have had some effect on your mind?"

"It's possible," countered Kane. "But not probable."

"Why isn't it?" Domi challenged.

"First of all, remember what we learned about Fand?" He turned his attention to Grant. "As I recall, you made the connection first, even before her own mother."

Grant nodded reluctantly. "Yeah, Strongbow conducted a gene-splicing program on himself and his dragoons, with genetic material harvested from Enlil to give him Annunaki characteristics, including a hive-mind tendency. That's how he exerted such control over his dragoons."

Kane said, "And Fand, because her mother was impregnated by Enlil, had those same characteristics. That's one reason Strongbow and Fand were so obsessed with each other, on an unconscious level seeking to achieve some kind of fusion but always failing. That's why she was mad."

"What did Fand impart—or what do you believe

she imparted in this telepathic communication?'' Lakesh asked.

Quickly, Kane related what he had seen and been told. Tapping the printout sheaf, he declared, ''I went into the historical database and found keyword correlations to almost everything she mentioned. *Atlantis, Lyonesse* and *orichalcum* are all in there.''

He touched the side of his head, smiling wryly. ''They weren't up here until *after* my dreams or communications.''

Domi ran an impatient hand through her unruly hair. ''What are those places? Villes, countries, what?''

''Nobody's sure,'' Grant muttered.

Folding his arms over his chest, Lakesh commented musingly, ''A very pertinent point, friend Kane. Assuming you underwent a true psionic contact, how can you trust anything Fand says. You just said she was mad.''

Kane's eyes flashed in annoyance. ''And she was. If her dementia was due to the psychic link she had with Strongbow, it stands to reason she recovered when he died.''

''We don't know what happened to the snake-eyed son of a bitch,'' Grant pointed out. ''You threw him into the Singularity.''

Kane nodded contemplatively, an image of his last sight of Strongbow flashing into his mind. Impaled by a spear, Strongbow had dropped from the bronze spearhead and somersaulted into the center of the Singularity.

Kane remembered hearing a slight pop of air rushing to fill a sudden vacuum, and then the man was gone. He brought his mind back to the present. ''Regardless of what happened to him, the material about

Atlantis checks out. You can read it over or I can give you an overview.''

Domi eyed the dense, single-spaced copy on the printout and said positively, "Overview."

# Chapter 15

No one commented on the incongruity of Kane delivering a briefing on such an esoteric subject as a lost continent, complete with a background comp printout.

Linking his hands atop the table, he said tersely, "Nearly every culture in the world has myths and legends of an ancient world before recorded history, and the cataclysm that destroyed it. Dim memories of the great civilization of Atlantis have been hypothesized to be responsible for the myths of the Garden of Eden, the Elysian Fields and others. According to Plato in two of his dialogues, *Timaeus* and *Kritias,* Atlantis was a vast island lying beyond the Pillars of Hercules."

The corners of Grant's lips turned down. "The what of Hercules?"

"The Strait of Gibraltar. Plato claimed the text was taken from ancient Egyptian records. Some nine thousand years before he was born, Atlantis had been a powerful kingdom with a high civilization, which dominated the Mediterranean and much of the Atlantic. They established a number of colonies and outposts all over the world. What Fand called Lyonesse was one of them. The Atlantean science was very advanced, even to the point where they supposedly bioengineered slave labor and cloned dinosaurs."

Domi wrinkled her nose in bewilderment. "What for?"

Impatiently, Kane shot back, "How the hell do I know? The computer never said. In the *Kritias,* Plato talks about the strange metal orichalcum which was mined and refined in Atlantis. This was used as a power source, like some kind of solar-energy semiconductor chips. They were called firestones and allowed the Atlanteans to attain the neutralization of gravity for their zeppelin-type airships.

"Though I'm not clear on this, there was a connection between material inventions and spiritual force. The deterioration of Atlantean spiritual beliefs made its final destruction all the more certain. There was civil unrest, the institution of slavery and the creations of 'mixtures,' the offspring of human and animal interbreeding. According to other scholars, there was a long conflict between the so-called Sons of the Law of One and the Sons of Belial, who practiced human sacrifice and the misuse of the forces of nature, particularly the orichalcum."

"Those other scholars," Lakesh said severely, "based their opinions on very specious sources. Like treatises written by nineteenth-century crackpots such as Ignatius Donnely and Madame Helena Blavatsky."

Kane ignored the observation. "Supposedly, a natural catastrophe triggered a thermonuclear chain reaction with the orichalcum and blew Atlantis off the map. It caused a worldwide change in the sea levels, and many civilizations were drowned."

"No Atlantean survivors?" inquired Grant.

"As a matter of fact, yes. Some scholars thought that a few Atlanteans had foreseen the coming catastrophe and escaped to other countries where they founded all the world's subsequent civilizations: Egypt, Sumer, Akkad, the Mayans, the Aztecs and so on. Apparently, there were a lot of similarities between pre-Columbian culture and the ancient Middle Eastern civilizations.''

''Yes, there were,'' Lakesh said. ''In my day, archaeologists and anthropologists were still unconvinced the similarities were evidence of a vanished 'mother' civilization.''

Kane sighed wearily. ''When you scrape away the myths, there's still some hard evidence, such as twentieth-century undersea explorers finding roads and ruins on the seabed, not to mention a lot of odd artifacts.''

''Like what?'' Domi wanted to know.

Kane thumbed through the printout. ''Like electric batteries found buried in Iraq and jewelry that showed signs of being electroplated. These things were so old they couldn't be accurately dated.''

Lakesh removed his eyeglasses, breathed onto the lenses and cleaned them on his sleeve. ''A fascinating account, but the reality of Atlantis was never conclusively proved.''

''It was never conclusively disproved, either,'' Kane replied.

Lakesh shrugged. ''True. Instead, it was dragged into occult lore and pretty much discredited.''

A bit raggedly, Kane stated, ''You've said many times that for every myth and legend, there's a foundation of reality.''

''Yes, not only have I said it, I believe it, too. However, the foundation, the roots of the myths must be closely examined and subjected to the scientific method before they can be accepted. For example, you're postulating that some remnant of Atlantis has surfaced off the coast of Ireland?''

Kane nodded. ''I found a reference to the Firbolgs in the database, too. Irish tradition states they were the pre-Gaelic people of Ireland, 'mixtures' who came from Atlantis or a colony. That fits exactly with the dream I had. So what else could Fand have been trying to tell me with those images?''

Grant knuckled his jaw thoughtfully. ''Bait, mebbe, trying to lure you back to her.''

''I thought of that.''

''And?''

''I discounted it. The Fand I met in Ireland was crazy, but she wasn't deceptive.''

''But you claim she's changed,'' Domi said. ''You said she was different in your dream.''

''She said she changed,'' Lakesh argued. ''You can't trust your perceptions during phase transit, Kane. You should know that by now.''

Kane didn't respond to that, knowing Lakesh was just getting started.

''Furthermore,'' the old man continued, ''most legitimate scholars felt Plato's tale of Atlantis to be only a parable, an allegory based loosely on the Theran civilization that flourished around five thousand years ago. It was destroyed by a volcanic eruption in 1520 B.C.''

Kane nodded impatiently throughout Lakesh's dissertation. ''Yeah, yeah. I found references to that, too. But Thera as Atlantis was only an archaeological hypothesis, put forth in the mid-twentieth century. It doesn't cover the corresponding Egyptian legends or the isle of Lyonesse. Even Balam mentioned several global catastrophes.''

Lakesh waved away Kane's words with a dismissive gesture. "I'm not arguing against worldwide cataclysms. They happened, that's a given. But the island of Lyonesse is an even more elusive legend than Atlantis. Over the course of centuries, the Britons and the Welsh Celtic people tied it in with the tales of King Arthur."

Kane rolled his eyes ceilingward in exasperation. "If I'd known you were familiar with all this stuff, I wouldn't have wasted three hours on the computer. Anyway, are you denying the quakes caused by the nukecaust couldn't have uprooted landmasses from the seabed? Our trip to Ambika's pirate empire proved otherwise."

He shot a challenging glare at Grant. "Right?"

Grant nodded brusquely. "Right."

"Even if dozens of islands popped up," Lakesh stated, "that doesn't make them colonies of Atlantis and worth our investigation. Just because Fand may think so doesn't make it true. In my opinion, it's a rather tenuous line on which to anchor a transatlantic jump."

"Especially," Grant rumbled, "since to check out Fand's story you'd have to jump to England first…to that tree-place controlled by the Imperial Dragoons. And they weren't particularly happy to see us the first time."

"I didn't say it wouldn't be risky," Kane retorted.

"And you didn't say it wouldn't be suicidal, either," Grant argued. "I think the whole deal is ridiculous. I vote no."

"Me, too," Domi piped up.

Lakesh pinched the bridge of his nose and made a studied show of being deep in thought. At length he said, "Reluctantly, I must my cast my vote with them, friend Kane."

The corner of Kane's mouth quirked in a hard, stitched-on smile. "I don't recall putting the matter to a vote."

KANE'S MATTER-OF-FACT pronouncement stopped conversation for a handful of seconds. Finally, almost idly, Grant remarked, "None of us go on solo jump missions."

"Where is that written?" Kane inquired, as casually as if he were only feigning interest to be polite.

The big black man shook his head. "It doesn't need to be. Sure, we've gone off on our own before, but always it was part of the overall op. This is a personal path you're going down."

"I don't believe it is. Something nasty is brewing that could affect all of us." Kane added, as an afterthought, "This is my pointman's instinct talking."

Grant's lips compressed, but he didn't speak. He had always had the utmost faith in Kane's instincts, what he referred to as his pointman's sense. During their Mag days, because of his uncanny ability to sniff danger in the offing, he was always chosen to act as the advance scout. Kane had never led a contact team into an ambush and, in fact, had prevented an entire squad from being ambushed during a Pit sweep two years before.

"Everything you said comes from a very untrustworthy source," Grant said. "A fused-out hybrid who thinks you're the reincarnation of a dead Celtic warrior."

"I felt what Fand felt," explained Kane, striving to sound logical. "She communicated her fears."

"*Her* fears," Grant repeated harshly. "Just because she's scared doesn't mean there's anything for us to be scared of."

He leaned back in his chair, face a grim teak mask. "No way, Kane. A big neg on this."

Kane's jaw muscles knotted. "I," he said in a very measured tone, "am going. I thought I made that clear. You can either come with me or stay out of my way."

"Third option," Grant growled menacingly. "Your ass is thrown into a detention cell until you come to your senses."

Kane scoffed, a sneer twisting his lips and turning his features into something ugly.

Domi and Lakesh watched and listened to the threatening exchange apprehensively. Both of them had witnessed Grant and Kane's disagreements before, but never with such a cutting edge. The two men glared at each other, eyes locked and unblinking, tension crackling between them like static electricity before a thunderstorm.

Lakesh rapped sharply on the tabletop with his knuckles, like a teacher trying to get the attention of unruly students. He raised his reedy voice. "Enough! I want to drink my coffee with cream, not testosterone. You two gentlemen will come to order."

Kane and Grant swung their heads toward him. Anger still glinted in their eyes, but a bit of the dangerous energy in the room ebbed. Lakesh's choice of the word *gentlemen* hadn't been arbitrary. It struck a responsive chord with them, reminding both men of Magistrate Division briefing sessions. Years of conditioning died hard. Though neither man replied, Lakesh knew the kind of thoughts spinning through their minds.

Magistrates were a highly conservative, duty-bound

group. The customs of enforcing the law and obeying orders were ingrained almost from birth. The Magistrates submitted themselves to a grim and unyielding discipline because they believed it was necessary to reverse the floodtide of chaos and restore order to postholocaust America.

Magistrates were proud that each of them accepted the discipline voluntarily, so by nature their rigid self-control won out over raw emotions, at least temporarily.

"Now then, friend Kane," said Lakesh, his tone reasonable, soothing. "Perhaps there is another motive at work here, one that you're not consciously aware of."

"Which is?"

"I submit—with all due respect—you're looking for an avenue of escape."

"Escape from what?" demanded Kane.

"Guilt over what happened to Brigid and to Cotta. It's possible you're in so much emotional pain, particularly due to Brigid's present condition, you're unconsciously looking for any reason to get away from it. Concocting a life-or-death mission is just the sort of ploy a man of action like you would take."

In a low, dangerous tone Kane asked, "Are you implying I manufactured everything I told you?"

"Not at all. I accept on your word that you experienced the visions you told us about. Subjectively, you are utterly convinced of their veracity. However, your subjective faith doesn't necessarily translate to the objective."

Grant gusted out a heavy, prolonged sigh. "Well, as we've said before, there's only one way to find out."

Lakesh's head swiftly swiveled around on his wattled pipe stem of a neck. "You're in favor of this?"

"Absolutely not. But I'm less in favor of trying to lock Kane up. He'd just escape and go anyway."

Kane grinned, but Lakesh continued to gape at Grant incredulously. "You said it was a personal path Kane was walking!"

"Yeah," Grant grunted. "And not too long ago you insisted on walking one yourself. Remember that little trip you took to South Dakota to visit an old girlfriend?"

Spots of red appeared on Lakesh's cheeks. For a moment his lips worked as if he were thinking about spitting at Grant. Then, in an unsteady voice he said, "That is a terribly hurtful thing to say to me."

Grant inclined his head in a nod. "I didn't say it to hurt you, Lakesh. If I did, I apologize. I was making a point. A blunt one, but I think you get my drift."

He focused his dark, shadowed eyes on Kane. "Against my better judgment, I'll go with you. But only for a recce. At the first sign of a dragoon, we haul ass out of there. I don't think they'll be as cordial this time around. Understand?"

Kane presented the image of somberly pondering Grant's words. "Understood."

"I'll go, too," Domi put in.

Both Grant and Kane snapped in unison, "No."

Her ruby eyes flared in sudden anger, and Grant said firmly, "You need to oversee the retrieval of Cotta's body. With us gone, you're the only one in the redoubt with combat training."

A little sullenly, the albino woman said, "You said the place was pacified."

"We're fairly sure it is," replied Kane. "But that

doesn't mean you shouldn't go in there expecting the worst. If I had, Cotta might still be alive and Baptiste might be up and around.''

''What about Brigid?'' Lakesh asked, barely able to control the tremor at the back of his throat. ''What if she regains consciousness while you're gone?''

''If what Fand imparted to me is true,'' snapped Kane, ''it might not matter if she wakes up or not.''

Kane ground his teeth together, tamping down on his frustration-fueled rage. ''I can't do a goddamn thing for her. The decision of whether she lives or dies or sleeps or wakes up is out of my hands. Like it or not, it's up to her, not to me.''

He stood up swiftly, the legs of his chair screeching loudly on the linoleum floor. Peeling back the cuff of his sleeve, he consulted his wrist chron. To Grant, he said, ''Let's make the jump time to arrive over there around daybreak. We can ask Bry to pull up the destination codes for the English gateway.''

Grant arose. ''Do you want to go in hard?''

Kane's brow wrinkled in momentary concentration. ''I don't think so. We managed the last time without our armor. But we need to pick up some odds and ends from the armory to make up for it.''

''Not to mention new side arms.''

The two men strode purposefully out of the cafeteria. Lakesh and Domi remained at the table, sharing an uncomfortable silence. Domi broke it by saying lowly, ''Got a bad feeling about this.''

Lakesh didn't know how he felt so he opted to stay quiet and finish his cup of coffee.

Propping her chin up on a hand, Domi said musingly, ''Thought for a minute there they'd go at it bigtime.'' She sounded almost disappointed.

"Stress has deleterious effects on the strongest men," Lakesh commented inanely.

She shook her head in disagreement. "Seen the same thing before, out in the wild. Two male wolves fight to be king of the pack, to give the orders, to fuck all the females."

Lakesh frowned at her crudity but he didn't rebuke her. Domi's rough, outspoken manner was due to her upbringing in the Outlands. He said, "Friends Grant and Kane are men, not animals. Even the best of friends have serious disagreements from time to time."

She smiled at him condescendingly. "If you say so."

A flush of irritation prickled the back of his neck. "Assuming for the sake of argument that what you say has some validity, would you want to be part of either man's harem?"

Domi pursed her lips thoughtfully for a long moment, then grinned broadly. "At this point, I could live with it."

# Chapter 16

Grant slapped the flat toggle switch on the door frame, and the overhead fluorescent fixtures blazed on, flooding the armory with a white, sterile light.

The big square room was stacked nearly to the ceiling with wooden crates and boxes. Many of the crates were stenciled with the legend Property U.S. Army, and others bore words in Russian Cyrillic script.

He and Kane moved along the aisles, past glass-fronted cases holding M-16 A-1 assault rifles, SA-80 subguns, and Heckler & Koch VP-70 semiautomatic pistols complete with holsters and belts. Lining the walls were bazookas, tripod-mounted M-249 machine guns, and several crates of grenades. Mounted on frameworks in a corner were two full suits of Magistrate body armor, standing there like black, silent sentinels. Every piece of ordnance and hardware, from the smallest-caliber handblaster to the biggest-bore M-79 grenade launcher, was in perfect condition.

All of the ordnance was of predark manufacture and had been laid down in hermetically sealed Continuity of Government installations before the nukecaust. Protected from the ravages of the environment, nearly every piece of munitions and hardware was as pristine as the day it rolled off the assembly line. Over a period of years, Lakesh had smuggled out all of the weaponry from the largest COG facility, the Anthill.

Most of the exiles had never so much as touched a blaster until they arrived at Cerberus. All of them were expected to become reasonably proficient with guns, and they had spent some time on the indoor and outdoor firing ranges under Grant's tutelage. The lessons were restricted to the use of the SA-80 subguns, lightweight "point and shoot" autoblasters even the most firearm-challenged person could learn to handle.

Kane and Grant stopped at an open gun case where nearly a dozen Sin Eaters in their forearm holsters hung from pegs. They had appropriated the spares a short time before from a squad of hard-contact Mags dispatched from Cobaltville.

After choosing a pair of Sin Eaters, they took them over to a table, testing the tension actuators and the spring cables inside the holsters. Swiftly, expertly, the two men field-stripped the blasters with practiced hands. The Sin Eater was a Mag's assigned weapon, almost a badge of office. They knew it more intimately than anything else in the world.

As they took apart the weapons, Kane said quietly, "I appreciate it, you know."

Grant didn't look at him, laying the blaster's parts neatly on the tabletop. "Appreciate what?"

"Believing me."

Grant snorted. "I believe *in* you, Kane, not what you claimed Fand said to you. That's not quite the same thing."

Kane opened the cleaning kit. "I appreciate the vote of confidence, then."

Grant laughed, but it had little mirth in it. "Has it occurred to you if I had *real* confidence in you, I'd let you go on this sortie on your own?"

Kane angled an eyebrow at him. "I don't get you."

"I'm going with you on this jump because it so happens we're partners. It's a matter of policy, not a matter of my utmost faith in everything that comes out of your mouth."

"I'd do the same for you," Kane said, an edge in his tone.

"Yeah, I know. That's why I'm doing it."

"I think I'd do it with a little more grace than you're showing."

Grant vigorously oiled his Sin Eater's barrel with a square of cloth. His terse, gruff "How the hell do you know?" ended the conversation.

Kane devoted his attention to cleaning the parts of the weapon in earnest. The Sin Eater didn't make the jump with him to the other casements, but it occupied his attention now.

After a thorough oiling and cleaning, the two men put the Sin Eaters back together, working in silence. They strapped the holsters to their right forearms, adjusting the straps and buckles.

When they were satisfied the Sin Eaters worked properly, they went through the crates and the cases, picking and choosing from their lethal contents. Both of them took four grens apiece—two high-explosive, and two ovoid concussion grens of the Alsatex series, developed by the military two centuries ago for crowd control.

They attached the grenades to the combat harnesses they would wear beneath their Kevlar-weave coats, then clipped three 20-round magazines for their Sin Eaters to the harnesses, as well.

Kane went to a gun case, sliding back the glass door. From it, he selected their close-assault weapons. Chopped down subguns, the Copperheads were barely two feet in length. The magazines held fifteen rounds of 4.85 mm steel-jacketed rounds, which could be fired at a rate of 700 per minute. Even with their optical-image intensifiers and laser autotarget scopes, the Copperheads weighed less than eight pounds.

From a notched wooden rack at the rear of the case, Grant took a pair of black, six-inch-long cylinders. He handed one to Kane and screwed the other carefully into the Copperhead's bore. The two-stage sound and muzzle-flash arrester suppressed even full-auto reports to no more than rustling whispers.

Slinging the subgun over a shoulder by its strap and holding his combat harness in his right hand, Grant faced Kane. "We primed?"

"Appears so."

"Then I'll meet you at midnight at the jump chamber." With that, he turned on his heel and strode from the armory.

Kane followed him out, walking down the corridor in the opposite direction, not able to repress a shiver when he passed the electronically locked door that had once opened into Balam's prison habitat. Despite the fact he had learned Balam was less an inhuman, conniving monster than the tragic sole survivor of a lost race, he still didn't miss his presence in the redoubt.

Entering the dispensary, he walked to Brigid's bedside. DeFore was there, checking her patient's pulse rate. Her dark eyes flicked toward him, then looked him up and down in mild curiosity. "Where are you going?"

"England."

"Lucky you," she replied dryly. "I hear it's nice this time of year."

Kane ignored the observation. He moved around to

the opposite side of the bed and studied Brigid's blank, pale face. Her hair, spread out over the pillow, resembled a captured stream of sunset.

"No change," DeFore told him. "If her condition persists for another twelve hours, I'll hook her up to the EEG and see what kind of brain-wave activity I can monitor."

"Why haven't you done that before?" Kane asked.

"I don't want to irritate the sutures. I've got to be sure there's no latent infection."

Kane nodded. "Do you think she's dreaming?"

DeFore lifted an eyebrow. "She very well could be."

"Don't people usually wake up from dreams?"

She chuckled. "Eventually. But maybe she's in such a pleasant dreamworld she doesn't want to wake up. Maybe where she is there's no violence, no barons, no killing. A world where she's found her heart's desire."

"Wouldn't that be nice," Kane murmured wistfully.

"So nice she doesn't want to leave it." DeFore turned and walked away.

Kane continued to gaze down into Brigid's face, noting the angry red line on her right temple, extending and disappearing into her hair. He thought he detected the barest hint, the merest ghost of a smile at the corners of Brigid's lips.

"What's so pleasant, Baptiste?" he whispered in a voice so faint he barely heard it himself. "Wherever you are, I hope you're without pain and happy. Nobody deserves it more than you."

He glanced around, making sure neither DeFore nor Auerbach was in sight as he bent down. Gently, he kissed her cold, dry lips and breathed into her ear, "Come back to us, Brigid. Come back to me, *anamchara.*"

WEARING ONLY his undershorts, Grant sat down cross-legged and stared at the white wall in his room. He focused his gaze on an ink print of his thumb that he had impressed there some time back. He relaxed his neck and shoulders first, then worked all the way down to his toes. He concentrated on regulating his respiration, putting himself into a quasi-hypnotic state.

He was trying to achieve the "Mag mind," a technique that emptied his consciousness of all nonessentials and allowed his instincts to rise to the fore. He'd been trained to do it while a Cobaltville Magistrate and used it for handling pain when he'd been wounded or dealing with physical exhaustion.

After memorizing the thumbprint on the wall, he closed his eyes, visualizing it in his mind. He struggled to superimpose a mental image that matched the actual print, but he couldn't do it. His concentration was scattered.

Grant wasn't sure if it was due to the nagging pains of the injuries inflicted by the man-ape, or whether he was simply emotionally and spiritually drained. Rather than seeing the thumbprint when he closed his eyes, he kept seeing Cotta's arm being ripped from his body, like a vid tape on continuous replay.

He had witnessed many violent deaths, and even been responsible for dozens of them during his Mag days and after. Why Cotta's death should disturb him so profoundly wasn't that much of a mystery. He feared the most obvious answer: he was getting old.

His last five years as a Magistrate had been fairly

routine. He could count on the fingers of one hand how often he had fired his service weapon. His transfer to an administrative position was pending, and had he not opted to join Kane in exile, he would now be sitting at a desk reading requisition reports. The prospect of hanging up his blaster and putting his armor in storage hadn't disquieted him at all.

A knock sounded at his door, a familiar three-sequence rap, and he repressed a groan. He knew he'd hurt Domi's feelings earlier, but he had no desire to spend time apologizing to her. The rapping repeated, this time impatient and demanding.

With a curse, Grant heaved himself up from the floor and crossed the room. As soon as he opened the door, Domi slipped in, a little white wraith in the semidarkness of his quarters.

As he closed the door behind her, she pivoted to face him, hands on her flaring hips, head tilted at a challenging angle. "Why did you act that way to me before?"

Grant ran a weary hand over the liquid-bandage film on his forehead. "I don't know, Domi. I'm sorry. It wasn't you. I guess I was shook up. I'm still shook up."

Domi wasn't appeased. "Cotta knew the risks. If he didn't, he was stupe. And Brigid is strong. She'll get better. But I don't want to talk about them. I want to talk about us."

Grant forced a smile to his face. "We've talked about 'us' before. I've tried to make it plain how different we are—"

Domi interrupted, blurting angrily, "Something wrong. Is it me? Something about me? I disgust you, make you sick?"

Grant tried to laugh. "Of course not."

Domi slitted her ruby eyes, regarding him suspiciously. Always before he had tried to make the gap in their ages the reason he didn't want to get sexually involved with her. He knew how lame the excuse was, since Domi was certainly no stranger to sex, not after spending six months servicing the gross lusts of Guana Teague.

In truth, she represented a simple kind of innocence, a waiflike winsomeness he didn't want to complicate. And hovering always at the back of his mind and emotions was the memory of Olivia, the only woman who'd truly claimed his heart.

Domi had been patient and understanding over the past year, but now, he realized with a sinking sensation in the pit of his stomach, she was tired of waiting. She wanted to quench the sexual appetite that had long been building.

"What is it, then?" she asked sharply.

Grant sighed. "I'm sorry, Domi. It isn't your fault."

Domi didn't even try to mask her scorn. "If you can't do it, if you're impotent, then let me know right now so I can make plans."

Fury surged through Grant, and he was barely able to restrain himself from striking her. Not a slap to the cheek to punish her for her insolence, but a closed-fisted blow of rage. "I'm not impotent," he growled.

"Then it *is* me, you lying sack of shit."

Either Domi didn't guess how near she was to harm or she didn't care. "So if you don't want me, you wouldn't care if I went down the hall to Kane's room, or Farrell's or even Wegmann's?"

"Why stop there?" Grant retorted. "Why not Lakesh, too?"

Domi's lips curled. She flicked her gaze up and down his near naked body. "Big man, big chest, big shoulders, legs like trees. Guess they don't tell the story, huh?"

She pushed past him, yanked open the door and stalked out. She tried to slam the door shut behind her, but Grant caught it by the edge. He found himself on the verge of calling out to her, but the words stuck in his throat. He watched her stride away with a furious, hip-swinging gait, the personification of wounded female pride.

It wasn't until he returned to his place on the floor and resumed his cross-legged position that he realized he was in a high, hard state of arousal. At first he was surprised, then pleased, and finally annoyed by yet another distraction.

RACING ACROSS the emerald-green hills, rider and horse blended into one powerful creature galloping toward the cliffs. Below them, waves crashed against the craggy boulders on the shore. Brigid was truly thankful to be alive on this beautiful spring day. The countryside of Le Havre had worked its usual magic on her mood, and the rhythm of the huge beast beneath her soothed and excited her at the same time. Scarcely minutes before, she had been melancholy, even sad, but no sooner had she mounted Trillium than her mood lightened.

In the sheltered cove that was her special retreat, Brigid dismounted. The wildflowers, bluebells and fuchsias in the surrounding fields filled the air with a heady perfume that mixed with the smell of the sea to produce a wildly exhilarating scent. What a glorious day, if only there was someone by her side with which to share it all.

Brigid began to feel the smallest bit melancholy again. Sometimes it seemed she was always alone, always yearning to fill the emptiness. When would her opportunity for love ever arise? She was almost eighteen, and had not as yet had even one serious prospect since her debut last year. She understood that the rumblings of discontent with the reign of Louis XVI and his queen, Marie Antoinette, had spread out from Versailles and were now directed against the rural well-to-do, like her family. The Great Fear, as it was coming to be known in Paris, was a significant worry, particularly among eligible bachelors.

As it was, she had met only one man recently who had actually attracted her, an American merchant seaman whom she knew only as Captain Kane. He had seemed not only dashing and dangerous, but also strangely familiar. He was handsome in a rather cruel way, deeply tanned from the suns of many climes, his eyes faded to a pale blue-gray, like the color of high sky at sunset.

Her father, though not averse to doing business with him, had dismissed him contemptuously as an adventurer, a soldier of fortune. Brigid led Trillium along the shoreline, not trying to avoid the breakers that threatened to soak her shoes. With a smile, she recalled how Captain Kane had surreptitiously given her a book, essays by Edmund Burke, a British scholar, brought all the way from London, as if he knew in advance she was bookish and would appreciate such a volume far more than a bauble.

It was true she had read almost every volume in her father's library by the time she was sixteen, and perhaps that was the problem, after all. Brigid knew a lot of pointless facts, but she never could seem to apply them to situations in the real world. What in heaven's name was the use of knowing Greek philosophy if you couldn't apply it to getting yourself a good match?

The sunlight glinted from a glassy substance right at the shoreline. Halting, she squinted at it, realizing it was a corked bottle. Holding Trillium's reins in one hand, she knelt in the wet sand and dug it out. Within she saw a sheet of paper. For some reason, her heart pounded. She knew, without knowing just how she knew, that the message was meant for her.

After she wrested out the cork, it took several attempts to remove the paper. She unrolled it and read the swirling, cursive script, obviously inscribed with a crow-quill pen. "Come back to us, Brigid. Come back to me, *anam-chara.*"

Brigid smiled and slipped the note inside the bodice of her dress, next to her heart. She whispered, "Not just yet, Kane. Not just yet."

# Chapter 17

The two men stood in the cold and bleak dawn, among ankle-high grasses glistening with dew. Grant tucked his hands into the pockets of his coat and remarked unnecessarily, "Things have changed."

Both Kane and Grant wore the Mag-issue black, ankle-length Kevlar-weave overcoats. The right sleeve was just a bit larger than the left, to accommodate the Sin Eaters holstered to their forearms. Fingerless black gloves encased their right hands and their eyes were masked by dark-lensed glasses. Their ensembles weren't for show. The lenses of the glasses allowed them to see clearly in deep shadow, and the overcoats were insulated against all weathers, including acid rain showers. Trans-comm circuitry was sewn inside the lapels, terminating in tiny pin-mikes connected to a thin wire pulley. If they were searched, the transceivers would pass a cursory inspection. Long combat knives, the razor-keen blades forged of dark blued steel, hung from sheaths at their hips. The gloves allowed secure grips on the butts of the Sin Eaters.

Under their coats, they wore high-collared sweaters, combat harnesses, tough whipcord trousers and high-laced, heavy-treaded boots. A flat case containing survival stores like bottled water and concentrated rations hung from Kane's shoulder. A motion detector, not much larger than a chron with an oversized LCD window, was strapped around Grant's left wrist.

They stood midway on a gentle grade that slanted down toward a narrow stream. Behind them yawned the mouth of a tunnel that stretched back to a tree of mind-staggering proportions. The trunk was more than massive, more than huge—it was a pillar fifty yards around at its narrowest point. Interwoven limbs and branches joined nearly two hundred feet up in the air, roofing the entire area with its leafy canopy.

Even the smallest boughs were three times the breadth of Grant's body, the twigs thicker than his thigh. The tree butted up against the base of a gray mountain, looming high above them, the new sun blocked by the peak. The mountainside showed no vegetation whatsoever, stripped of turf and topsoil, showing only the dull gleam of dew-damp rock. The gigantic tree was all that remained of the community of Wildroot.

Scarcely twenty minutes before, the two men had materialized in the same gateway chamber to which they'd jumped a little more than half a year before. The unit was not part of the official Cerberus network, nor was the tree-fortress directly related to any Totality Concept project.

The details about the community were sketchy, derived mainly from the *Wyeth Codex*, purported to be the journal of a woman scientist by the name of Mildred Wyeth. Allegedly, Wyeth had been in suspended animation during the nukecaust, and she'd survived skydark and the long winters. Revived a century later, she had traveled the Deathlands with Ryan Cawdor.

Sometime during her wanderings, she'd found a working computer and recorded her thoughts, observations and speculations regarding the postnukecaust world, the redoubts and the wonders they contained.

Three decades before, Lakesh had discovered the journal and seen to its dissemination throughout the Historical Divisions of the villes.

According to Wyeth's narrative, a century or more before, the community of Wildroot had been established by combining the ancient Druidic principles of nature worship with bioengineering sciences, applied to flora rather than fauna. A gigantic tree had been developed to act as both a symbol and a home for a new society where plant life was the dominant species.

The community's leader, the self-styled Lord Boldt, intended to release a plague bacteria into the underground water system of Britain to kill most, if not all of its human inhabitants. A revolt among his Celtic followers and an assault by a militia based in New London ended the scheme—not to mention the intervention of Cawdor and his band of survivalist warriors.

But the enormous tree was still a marvel, a wonder of the world. Kane and Grant retraced their steps through it, Sin Eaters unleathered, combat senses at high alert. They crept stealthily through the circular resin-smelling passageways; the root-tunnels did not bend, they curved gently to the left and to the right, then back again. The floors, walls and ceilings resembled fibrous wood bark that had been sanded, polished and overlaid with lacquer. Even the staircases were formed from a continuous growth of the fibrous wood, showing no seams or mortise joints.

When the two men reached the point where they had been set upon before by a contingent of Imperial Dragoons, they came to a halt, straining their ears for even the most distant of sounds. They heard nothing, which in one way alarmed them more than if they had heard small noises.

During their previous visit, they had learned how thermal-imaging scanners broadcast the change of interior temperature to a nearby guard post. So they waited, fingers hovering over the trigger studs of their blasters. When three full minutes passed with no sound or registration of movement on Grant's motion detector, they descended the staircase, went through a root tunnel and out of the tree.

They strode down the slope to the narrow stream and crossed the wooden footbridge spanning it. The high fence surrounding the cube-shaped blockhouse still stood, as did the stone building itself, but the garrison of dragoons was nowhere to be seen.

"This makes no damn sense at all," Grant said, unconsciously lowering his voice. "Where are those slaggers? I thought this was a permanent outpost. Strongbow was afraid the Celts would use Wildroot as a rallying point."

"Fand said the Imperium was no longer Strongbow's," Kane murmured, making a careful visual circuit of the vicinity.

"So his soldiers just abandoned their posts once he disappeared? They seemed a lot more disciplined than that."

Kane's shoulders lifted in a shrug beneath his coat, and he stepped through the open gate into the compound. As they drew close to the blockhouse, they saw the marks of many feet in the soil, and where twigs had been stepped on and broken. The concrete facade of the building bore hundreds of bullet pocks.

Grant bent and picked up a small brass object, revolving it between thumb and forefinger. "A cartridge case from a 7.62 mm assault rifle. A hell of a firefight went on here. But between the dragoons and who?"

The steel-reinforced door to the blockhouse hung slightly ajar, and by the feeble sunlight peeping through the high, barred windows they saw a wide aisle cutting between a double row of consoles and comp stations. Chairs and desks were smashed, and the walls were smeared with blackened scorch marks and perforated with bullet holes.

All the consoles had been blasted into twisted masses of metal, plastic and broken glass. The interior looked as if grens had been lobbed into it. Everything had been shot, smashed and torn, and there was nowhere for anyone to hide. There didn't appear to be a square foot of floor not covered by debris.

"Like you said," commented Kane darkly. "A hell of a firefight."

The door on the opposite side of the blockhouse hung askew on one hinge. Outside on the concrete parking apron, they saw more scattered shell casings, as well as rust-red stains of dried blood.

A broad-axled Hummer lay on its side a few yards away, completely burned out. As they strode past it, Grant stooped to peer through the cracked and soot-black windshield. The charred skeleton of a man lay crumpled within, the exposure to searing heat contorting him into a fetal position. Clasped between the corpse's fleshless hands, he saw an H&K MP-5 subgun, the standard-issue blaster of the dragoons.

At the far end of the fenced-in compound stood an open-sided vehicle depot. The concrete floor showed oil drippings and tire tread marks, but no wags were to be found.

"Shit," Grant swore. "Don't expect me to hoof it all the way to New London and the coast."

Kane didn't respond to Grant's declaration. He stepped around the corner of the structure and found, half-hidden by fuel drums, a motorcycle leaning against the wall. Heaving it up by the handlebars, he used his hip to push a fuel canister out of the way. Drawn by the noise, Grant came around the side of the depot.

"What's that?" he demanded, eyeing the two-wheeled vehicle suspiciously.

"A way to spare your delicate hooves," answered Kane, inspecting the machine.

A peeling decal on the gas tank showed the winged-serpent insignia of the Imperial Dragoons. The bike proved to be a BSA Lightning, a heavy brute of a machine. The rear fender was bent, but the motorcycle appeared to be in good condition.

"I'm not riding on that goddamn thing," said Grant flatly. "I'd rather have a mule. Besides, it's probably more than two hundred years old."

Kane nudged down the kickstand and tested the throttle controls. "So are Deathbirds, but I never heard you complain about them."

Deathbirds were modified AH-64 Apache attack gunships, dating back to the tail end of the twentieth century. Most of the Deathbirds in the Mag Division fleets had been reengineered and retrofitted dozens of times.

"At least I know how to jockey a Bird," Grant countered gruffly.

Although motorcycles weren't a completely unknown mode of transportation in the outlands, they weren't commonly used, either. Even the best roads were in a serious state of disrepair and lone cyclists were too exposed, too vulnerable to the weather or sniping coldhearts.

A few motorcycles had been in use by outriders of Chapman's ore caravan in Utah, but they were wired-together rattletraps.

Kane rocked the bike on its stand and heard gasoline sloshing in the tank. He checked the oil sump and found it full, though slightly dirty. There was still the ignition. He switched it on, mounted the torn leather saddle, closed the choke lever and gave the start pedal a kick. Nothing happened except that he lost his balance and nearly tipped the machine over.

Grant smirked. "You really think you can get that piece of shit running?"

"Why not? It hasn't lain here all that long. No rust on it anywhere."

"If you do get it started, it'll make the devil's own noise, advertising us to any dragoons for miles around."

"I don't think there are any dragoons between here and New London."

"Yeah," Grant said dourly, "but the people who overran this place might be."

"What's that phrase Lakesh likes to use—'the enemy of my enemy is my friend'?"

"Providing they let us live long enough to tell them we're the enemies of their enemies. Somebody with a half-assed sniper rifle could pick us off on that thing at half a klick and we wouldn't know what hit us."

Kane decided to drop his end of the discussion. Grant's foul humor was easing into one of his periods of intractable stubbornness, and he knew from long experience arguing with the man was a waste of time.

It took four kicks to get the BSA Lightning lit off, but once it was running, the big 700 cc engine sounded smooth and well maintained. When it was purring nicely between Kane's legs, he pushed the choke lever all the way open, squeezed the brake and clutched it into bottom gear.

The Lightning jerked forward a bit. Kane heeled up the stand, brought up the revs and popped the clutch. The bike leaped forward in a wheelstand. Grant sprang aside, yelling something profane over the engine roar.

The torque came on like rocket thrusters as Kane struggled to hold the wheelie, dirt and gravel spewing from beneath the rear tire, lashing Grant's coattails. When Kane eased up on the throttle, the front wheel dropped with such force he jounced with a spine-compressing jolt in the saddle.

The bike slewed around in an S slide, and with muscle-straining effort, Kane barely managed to keep from laying it down. He rode around the perimeter, getting the feel of the big machine, sorting out the gears. He changed through from bottom to top, then back down again. The Lightning possessed more power than he imagined, but was smooth, totally responsive.

Kane carefully gave the steel steed a workout, cutting a few doughnuts and figure eights. Downshifting, he wheeled back to Grant. "Nothing to it. A hell of a lot better than your mule."

Grant brushed dirt from his black coat and said tonelessly, "Hee-haw."

THE CLOUDS WERE white wisps, resembling cotton threads against the clear azure of the morning sky. With the sun shining down, the English countryside was the epitome of bucolic beauty. However, the blacktop road winding through the hedgerows and meadows was anything but. It went from bad to worse, and very occasionally back to bad. Kane and Grant were pummeled, jolted, jounced and bounced.

With the engine thrumming purposefully, the BSA Lightning took every obstacle in stride, lofting around potholes and ruts. Even Grant's weight on the seat behind Kane didn't slow it or affect its performance.

Kane found himself enjoying the ride immensely, feet planted firmly on the pegs, leaning and swinging his body like a pendulum to control the vibrating metal horse beneath him.

Grant leaned with him, as Kane shouted over his shoulder to do so, but he refused to put his arms around his waist. More than once, when they were swerving around a split in the pavement, Grant nearly took a nasty spill.

The terrain on either side of the motorway alternated from woodland to open fields, with gently rolling hills. When they followed the road on their first visit, they had been chained in the back of a Land Rover and unable to see much of their surroundings. They recollected the drive from the Wildroot garrison to New London had taken more than an hour.

The road climbed up a steep grade, and the faint odor of brine tickled Kane's nostrils. As the bike topped the incline, they saw to their right a large body of water glimmering through breaks in the trees. Both men recalled how Brigid guessed it was Cardigan Bay.

At the foot of the slope, the motorway abruptly forked to the east and to the west. Kane downshifted to neutral, the engine idling. He dredged his memory for the direction the Land Rover had taken more than half a year ago.

"East, I believe," Grant said loudly into his ear.

Kane thought it over for a few seconds and nodded in agreement, guiding the Lightning along the eastward fork. The roadbed became progressively smoother, obviously repaved within the past few years.

As the two men swerved around a wide curve, smoke blossomed from a wall of shrubbery to their left. An AT rocket scorched overhead, a quick darting streak that bloomed into a yellow flame flower in the tree line on their right. The crumping explosion compressed their ears, and the bike shuddered from the jar of the concussive shock wave.

Grant yelled, "I fucking told you so!"

Kane screwed the BSA's throttle down and leaned forward, belly tight against the gas tank. The big machine roared ahead at full revs. As they swung around a lazy curve, they saw two armored cars, like the Land Rovers they remembered, turned broadside to block the motorway. They saw no one around the wags at first, then within seconds, six figures darted around from behind them, moving with fumbling, panicked haste.

They didn't see the red hip jackets or berets of the Imperial Dragoons, but they did recognize the type of subguns all of the men held.

# Chapter 18

From behind the barricading vehicles about two hundred feet ahead, the men began firing their H&K MP-5s immediately.

Kane jerked the handlebars toward the left side because he saw more room on the ground between the rear of the Land Rover and a shallow culvert. There were also only two blastermen covering that side, even if the weapons were semiautomatic.

Crouched as low as he could and still see, with Grant pressed tight against his back, Kane ran at the left-hand wag with the bike's wheels in the claylike mire on the shoulder of the road.

Kane caught only blurred glimpses of the blastermen, but he could see they wore quilted vests of bright red over coarse homespun shirts of green. Red half boots of dyed, crudely stitched deerskin shod their feet. Most of them were bearded, unlike the clean-shaved dragoons.

The stutter of autofire was easily audible over the engine roar, and chunks of asphalt jumped from the road ahead and behind them. Bullets thudded through the air over their heads. Kane felt a jarring shock against his right forearm as a round just touched the dense fabric of his coat sleeve and was deflected.

The two men with the MP-5s scattered when they realized Kane wasn't going to stop and allow them to shoot him and Grant at their leisure. If they had just stood their ground, they could have riddled bike and men at point-blank range. The fact that they flinched showed Kane they had little practical experience as coldhearts. Although a rough-looking crew, they were disorganized.

The Lightning shot through the mud, the front wheel spinning on the lip of the culvert. Kane straightened out and slid close to the roadbed for the tires to gain solid purchase. Grant detached and unpinned a gren from his harness as they sped past the rear of the Land Rover, tossing the lethal egg directly beneath the vehicle.

The two men didn't see the maneuver. The high-ex gren detonated with a brutal concussion, rupturing the gas tank. The fuel ignited instantly, and the explosion lifted the back of the wag, engulfing the pair of blastermen in flames.

The shock wave caused the bike to wobble dangerously, but Kane quickly brought it back under control. He glanced back to see the men rolling frantically over the road, wreathed in fire. Their companions beat at the flames with their red vests, trying to smother them.

When the BSA rounded another curve, skirting close to a flat-stoned wall, Kane downshifted. Over his shoulder he asked, "You all right?"

"Yeah," Grant retorted, "but only because we were lucky and they were amateurs. Who were those slaggers?"

"Not dragoons, that's for sure," replied Kane. "They acted surprised as all hell to see us."

"Especially coming from the direction of Wildroot. It was more like they were blocking the way *from* New London, not to it."

Kane nodded, a cold realization creeping to the forefront of his mind. ''Mebbe we should have talked to them.''

''They started shooting first,'' Grant declared flatly. ''With a rocket launcher no less.''

''That kind of overkill really paints them as amateurs...trigger-happy stupes playing guard, looking for any excuse to show off with their new toys.''

Gloomily, Grant said, ''One of their new toys may be a radio. I think we can pretty much expect another welcoming committee. Guess there's no way now to turn around and get back to the gateway.''

''You said we wouldn't do that except at the first sign of a dragoon,'' Kane reminded him.

''Yeah,'' Grant snapped with cold sarcasm. ''I guess there's no way these stupes can lay an ambush and catch us in a cross fire like those snake-eyes. We're perfectly safe.'' He paused, then added harshly, ''Hell, for all we know, the road is mined up ahead.''

Kane pondered Grant's snide remarks for a few seconds, looked to the left and right, saw a narrow break in the stone wall and cut the motorcycle's wheels toward it.

They bounced over fallen slabs of stone, over logs, splashed across a shallow stream and then hit a thicket that slowed them down. Grant didn't question Kane, not even when thorns and briars tore at their clothes and scratched their faces and hands.

The motorcycle burst out of the thicket onto a gently rolling grassy sward. A herd of sheep, unnerved by the racket of the machine, scattered across the fields, bleating and bawling in dismay.

Turning the Lightning in the general direction of New London, Kane steered along the edge of the tree line, paralleling the road. The strategy certainly wasn't foolproof since even if more blasterman lay in wait along the motorway, they could still hear their approach and rush through the thicket to intercept them. At the very least, this route reduced their chances of riding into a cross fire. Also, it was very unlikely the meadows had been mined since grazing sheep could set them off.

Kane couldn't pilot the BSA at a high speed because of the many dips and ruts in the terrain, but he managed to maintain a fairly steady pace. The sun climbed higher in the sky, fleecy clouds thickening around it. The day promised to be comfortably warm.

A very distant thunderclap rumbled over the hills. Startled, Grant tilted his head back, looking at the sky. "I don't see any storm clouds."

Another boom followed the first. Kane eased up on the throttle, bringing the motorcycle to a full stop, letting the engine idle at low revs. Both men strained their ears. Within seconds, they heard a third echoing thump, overlaid by a flurry of cracks.

"Not a storm," Kane announced grimly. "Artillery fire."

From the far side of the range of hills a smudge of gray-white smoke arose. Kane put the machine back in motion, wrestling it across a drainage ditch then up the face of the slope.

At the crest he braked so sharply to a halt, the motorcycle stalled out. He didn't try to kick it back to life. He stood straddling the bike and gazing at the panorama of violence spread out across the valley field below.

The ground quivered with explosions, the staccato stuttering of autofire. The meadow floor blossomed with flame and smoke. Although the distance was at least three hundred yards, both Grant and Kane easily picked out the bright red jackets of the Imperial Dragoons.

Three armored vehicles formed a loose crescent in the center of the valley, and from between and behind them, the scarlet-jacketed troopers ran to and fro. Spearpoints of fire flickered in a rippling sequence from the H&K subguns in their hands. Kane guessed there were around twenty of them, although more could be inside the heavy-metal walls of the wags. Something about the way the dragoons moved suggested exhaustion, as if they were a squadron worn out by long days and nights of fighting.

They saw a two-wheeled L-6 WOMBAT recoilless cannon hooked to the bumper hitch of the middle wag. A dragoon manned the cannon, yanking the lanyard. Smoke and thunder gouted from the long barrel.

The shell screamed across the length of the field and impacted at the mouth of an overgrown draw between two bluffs.

"What the hell are they shooting at?" Grant grated, swinging off the motorcycle. He squinted to see through the rising umbrella of dust.

From behind the brush came a sequence of little puffballs of white smoke and thudding reports. Mortar rounds burst among the huddle of dragoons and wags. An explosion lifted the center vehicle into the air and dumped it on its side, taking the WOMBAT artillery piece with it. The split gas tank vomited a torrent of orange flame.

The men who had used the wag for shelter dashed behind the remaining pair. The dragoons had placed their vehicles far enough apart so the explosion of the fuel tank didn't start a chain reaction. Still, their firing tapered off to sporadic crackles as they regrouped.

In that handful of seconds, the tangle of shrubbery between the two bluffs drew apart and a light assault car lunged out onto the floor of the valley. An erect figure wearing a brass helmet and a red vest over a green shirt stood behind a roll bar–mounted box-fed machine gun. A crest of feathers waved from the top of his headpiece. On his left arm he carried a round, brass-embossed shield. Grant and Kane realized they had seen a similar shield before.

Behind the wag trailed a column of similarly attired men. All of them were heavily armed with swords, assault rifles and subguns. The canopy of drifting smoke obscured their numbers, but Kane lost count at thirty anyway.

"The Celts," he said. "They've risen up against the Imperium."

Grant intoned, "The enemy of my enemy is my friend. You hope."

A line of explosions from the concealed mortar emplacements in the draw ripped open the earth in front of the wags, making it impossible for them to fire their own weapons with any degree of accuracy.

The assault car emerged from the pall of smoke, and the helmeted man gave intricate arm signals to the column running behind him. They instantly spread out in a horseshoe formation, forming an ever-widening circle. The discipline displayed by the green-and-red-garbed men was impressive. They paid no attention to the mortar rounds arcing over their heads. A blinding barrier of fire, smoke and pulverized turf arose around the dragoons' wags.

The valley filled with the hammer of raking autofire,

as well as screams and yells, both of pain and battle fever. A brief but concerted volley from the dragoons dropped half a dozen Celts but didn't slow the overall advance.

The helmeted man in the assault car took hold of the pistol grip of the mounted machine gun and held down the trigger. He swung it on its pintle in short left-to-right arcs, a tongue of fire lipping from the long, perforated barrel.

The rounds struck the heavy metal chassis of the wags with semimusical clangs and little flaring sparks. Puffs of dust mushroomed up around the wags. Tires blew and two dragoons were slapped off their feet in tumbling, limb-twisting tangles. Other dragoons returned the fire.

The driver of the car clutched at his chest and slumped behind the wheel, but miraculously maintained a straight and steady course. He drove the vehicle toward the opening between the burning wag and the one on the far left. The gunner on the roll bar continued with his jackhammer drumming, the machine gun's cartridge belt writhing like a brass serpent, spent shell casings spewing from the ejector port in a glittering rain.

A dragoon sprang from cover, putting himself directly in the path of the onrushing car, the butt of his MP-5 jammed tight against his hip. Rounds from the heavy machine gun clawed open his torso from sternum to groin. The nose of the assault car smashed into him broadside, tossing him into the flames billowing from the undercarriage of the tipped-over wag.

The force of Celts swirled around the dragoons, the arms of the horseshoe meeting and closing in a circle. The wags and the crimson jackets disappeared behind a green-and-red wall of flesh and blood. The blasterfire built to a frenzied crescendo.

"That pretty much writes *fini* to that," Grant observed sagely.

Before Kane could reply, Grant suddenly uttered a gargling cry, half grunt of pain, half bellow of outrage. Flinging his arms out wide, back arched, he catapulted forward and nearly off the crest of the hill. He fell heavily, catching himself on his elbows.

Kane twisted swiftly on the Lightning's seat, looking behind him and down. Four men in green and red raced across the grassy sward toward the base of the slope. One of them shouldered a longblaster outfitted with a telescopic sight. As he ran, he clumsily worked the bolt action, cycling a fresh round into the chamber.

Snarling wordlessly, Kane flexed his wrist tendons and the Sin Eater filled his hand. A triburst roared from the barrel instantly. The range was too great for a handblaster so the rounds didn't find targets, but they came close enough. The men scattered, two of them dropping full-length to the ground.

Grant struggled to his knees, gasping for air. His hand probed the center of his back. Kane didn't see a hole in the coat. The tough fabric had deflected the rifle bullet, but the kinetic shock had knocked the wind from Grant's lungs.

Kane started to get off the bike to help him up, but Grant managed to struggle to his feet, lips writhing over his teeth, face locked in a grimace of pain. His night-vision glasses had been flung off by the impact of the round, but he didn't waste any time looking for them.

With a groaning curse, he mounted the motorcycle's saddle. "Get us moving."

Kane shoved the Sin Eater back into its holster and kicked the engine over. "Those are the assholes from the roadblock. I guess we really pissed them off for them to chase after us on foot."

Between clenched teeth, Grant hissed, "Pissed *them* off?"

The motorcycle lurched down the face of the slope, Kane angling away from the mass of shouting, shooting men surrounding the ATVs. Although the frequency of blasterfire was ebbing, it still made enough of a racket to cover the bike's engine noise. The planes of smoke and dust floating about the battlefield were both a blessing and a curse. They concealed them but also limited their visibility to only a few yards.

Once they were rolling across the valley, the astringent stink of spent powder and cordite stung their nostrils and set their eyes to watering. Kane was trying to clear his vision by blinking repeatedly, when a long-haired man with a double-barreled shotgun suddenly appeared out of the fog. His beard was soaked in blood, and scarlet rivered down his face. His left eye had either been swollen shut or shot out. The one visible eye was blue and glinted with cobalt fury.

With a fierce cry, he grasped the shotgun by the barrel and clubbed at them with the wooden stock. Kane swerved away from him, but Grant thrust out an arm and clotheslined the man as they sped past. He went down heavily, the back of his head striking the ground first.

A few seconds later, Kane found himself wending the motorcycle among a squad of red-and-green-garbed troopers as they double-timed it across the field. They gaped at them, astonished by how the two men and the big machine seemed to materialize mag-ically out of the fog. By the time they recovered their senses enough to bring their blasters to bear, the swirling vapor had swallowed Kane and Grant up again.

A hoarse male voice began rapping orders in a tongue neither man understood but recognized nonetheless. It was Gaelic.

A gust of wind tore a tattered hole in the swirling curtain of smoke. Kane saw they were less than twenty yards from the camouflaged draw from which the Celtic soldiers had emerged. Twisting the handlebars, he turned the BSA away from it. He heard a man shout raspingly, in alarm and anger.

The thump of a mortar launcher pressed painfully against his ears. A shaved sliver of a second later, the fog and the ground split in a blaze of light less than three feet ahead of the bike's front tire.

The BSA reared up like a stricken horse, and a bucketful of hot grit scoured Kane's face. If not for his night-vision glasses, he would have been blinded. Something struck him on the shoulder and flipped him head over heels off the bike's saddle. He hit the ground on his back with breath-robbing force. Instantly, he threw himself into a roll, trying to avoid being crushed by the big machine as it tumbled end over end. He glimpsed Grant flying overhead, his arms and legs outspread, coattails flapping like the wings of an ungainly bird.

The motorcycle crashed down barely a foot from Kane's head, and he struggled to one knee. His shoulder and right arm were more than numb; they felt as if they had been amputated. He couldn't tense his wrist tendons so as to unleather his Sin Eater. He realized a chunk of shrapnel had struck his shoulder, and though the coat prevented the sharp metal from piercing him, the shock of impact had paralyzed his side. He blinked around for his Copperhead but didn't see it anywhere.

As he started to rise, a fist rocked the side of Kane's head, knocking him onto his left side. He caught himself with his left hand. A young, rangy Celt with spirals tattooed on his bare, muscular chest came boring in with fists and feet. Balancing himself on his left arm, Kane used it as an axis and spun, slamming a reverse heel-kick into the back of the warrior's ankles.

As he went down, Kane sprang to his feet and delivered the steel-reinforced toe of his right boot to the underside of the young man's jaw. The crack of bone was loud and ugly.

Kane pivoted and saw Grant lying facedown on the ground, not stirring or even appearing to breathe. Kneeling beside him, he shook the big man, but he didn't react. He inserted his fingers between Grant's head and the ground and discovered the medium-size rock protruding from the turf. The man's skull had crashed against it, but there was no sign of blood.

Kane stood up, clumsily unsheathing his combat knife left-handed. His right arm hung useless and numb at his side, like a sack of bird shot. He took up a spraddle-legged position over Grant as half a dozen men crept out of the dissipating vapor.

They gazed at Kane with wild eyes, still in the grip of battle madness. Although it was apparent neither he nor his fallen companion was an Imperial Dragoon, they weren't of their own number, either. Blaster barrels snapped up, and fingers curled around triggers.

A voice shouted stridently, *"Sin e!"*

The warriors shifted, casting startled, uneasy glances over their shoulders. A tall figure strode swiftly from the direction of the draw, shouldering between a pair of men. *"Sin e!"*

As gun barrels began drooping, Kane saw the figure wore a polished, plumed helmet with a visor and grilled face guard. The leather leggings and bulky flak vest couldn't completely disguise the female form swelling beneath. Instead of a weapon, the figure wielded a long staff, wrapped with vines and many turnings of silver wire. An ivory knob, like an oversize egg, topped it.

A gloved hand came up and removed the helmet. Kane's heart jumped into his throat at the sight of the huge eyes and full lips. Though her blue-white complexion was smudged by dust and soot, her eyes burned hot and bright, like droplets of molten gold. She tossed her head, freeing her long braid of flaxen hair.

"Hello, Fand," he said matter-of-factly. "I thought you'd be expecting me."

# Chapter 19

Grant chose that moment to regain consciousness. Still glassy-eyed, he allowed two of the Celtic soldiers to pull him to his feet, but they backed away when he favored them with a threatening scowl. His greeting to Fand was in the form of a hostile glower.

She affected not to notice and said to Kane, "I wasn't so much expecting you as hoping. You received my communications, after all. That pleases me."

Although her eyes glittered, they did not possess the gleam of madness he had half expected. She noticed Kane's searching stare and laughed, a melodic trilling. "Rest easy, Kane. I'm not the deranged woman you first met."

"I was hoping you'd say that," replied Kane with a studied nonchalance. He noticed she had pronounced his name without the insertion of the glottal stop.

"Score one for your instincts," Grant sidemouthed to Kane.

Fand cocked her head quizzically. "What's that mean?"

"I had some trouble convincing him that you'd contacted me telepathically," answered Kane.

Fand's full lips pursed. "Indeed? The bond of trust I sense between you is very strong."

"If you go along with everything he wants to do

without question," Grant said sourly, "you'll just spoil him."

Fand laughed again, and the musical sound caressed Kane's nerve endings. Before she said anything more, the assault car rolled across the field toward them. The helmeted man who had operated the roll bar–mounted machine gun sat behind the wheel. The man who had driven the wag during the charge lay slumped in the passenger's seat. Despite the fact his eyes were open and a smile creased his lips, he was very dead, shot several times through the upper chest.

The vehicle braked to a halt, and the driver climbed out. Grant and Kane recognized him immediately as Phin mac Cumhal mac Trenmor, chieftain of a forest-dwelling clan of Celts they had met in Ireland.

The helmet perched on his head made the big, burly man appear even taller. He was muscular without a spare ounce of flesh anywhere on his rangy body. A three-inch brass ring perforated his right earlobe. A red spade beard clothed his hard, bony face. The shield strapped to his arm bore dents, dings and deep depressions.

"The Yanks," he said laconically, his words slightly blurred by his brogue. "Where are the others who were with you before—the girl as white as the swans of Lir and the green-eyed woman with the name of our patron saint of wisdom?"

Fand narrowed her eyes, casting a surreptitious but expectant glance at Kane. Choosing his words carefully, he answered, "We thought it best to send in a minimum recon party until we learned the lay of the land."

Phin nodded. "Sound tactic. But 'tis all over now but the shouting."

"Now that you bring it up," Grant drawled, "what's all over?"

"The fall of the Imperium Britannia," Phin stated. "The casting off of the shackles of tyranny. New London is ours."

He turned to the red-and-green-garbed troopers, raised his shield over his head and roared at the top of his lungs, *"Erin go bragh!"*

The soldiers bellowed the same phrase back at him, shaking rifles, pistols and knives over their heads. *"Erin go bragh!"*

In short, clipped sentences, as if she found the entire matter distasteful, Fand explained how New London had been under siege for the past month. The Celtic forces had breached the walls the day before, and after nearly eighteen hours of vicious street-by-street fighting, the city had finally surrendered.

The skirmish Grant and Kane witnessed was actually more of a pursuit, a chase of a small group of Imperial Dragoons who had broken through the pickets and escaped the city.

Fand turned to Phin. "How many did we lose this time?"

Phin gestured toward the corpse in the car. "Liam, for one. I haven't had time to compile a body count. The serpents are dead, though."

Responding to an order in Gaelic, two warriors pulled Liam from the vehicle and carried him away.

"That's the end of the story," commented Grant. "Mebbe you can let us in on the beginning."

"The beginning was nearly a thousand years ago," Phin snapped bitterly, "when the first snakeheart to bear the name Strongbow invaded Eire and waged a genocidal war against us."

"Let's not go that far back," suggested Kane.

At that moment, the four men from the roadblock came pounding up, red-faced and short of breath. The faces of two of them bore blisters and second-degree burns. When they saw the two interlopers casually chatting with Fand and Phin, they snarled in anger, bringing their blasters to bear. Fand snapped a stream of invective in hard-edged Gaelic, and they backed off, muttering peevishly.

Her lips creased in a slight smile. "They said you set them afire."

"They didn't give us much choice," Kane countered, trying to flex the fingers of his right hand.

Fand noticed how his arm dangled limply at his side and how Grant rubbed the rising lump on his head. "You two need attention." She opened her vest and patted a large doeskin pouch attached to her belt. "When we reach New London, I'll treat you."

Grant's and Kane's Copperheads were retrieved and returned to them. Fand, Phin, Grant and Kane climbed aboard the assault car. Phin drove with Grant in the blood-wet passenger's seat. Phin steered through the opening between the two bluffs, honking the horn. Men scuttled out of the way, dragging mortars with them.

The vehicle bounced along a narrow path, the grasses flattened and worn away by the passage of many sheep over a period of years. Kane slid a hand under his coat and kneaded his shoulder. The numbness was ebbing, but he took no pleasure in that, since the returning sensation was one of intense pain. With the terrific strain Jacko had put on his arm, combined with the shrapnel strike, he wouldn't be surprised to learn the socket had been seriously damaged.

Fand, sitting across from him, put a hand on his knee. "I'll take care of you."

The way she said it made her words sound less than a sympathetic assurance than a promise of something else entirely. He found himself not particularly dismayed by the prospect.

They passed a number of warriors, both men and women in the red-and-green ensemble of the Celtic forces. They called out jubilantly to Phin and Fand as they drove by, but their faces were haggard and their eyes weary. The car drove along a trail hacked through the thicket, between a break in the stone wall, then out onto the paved motorway.

Grant said, "You didn't seem too surprised to see us."

Phin jerked a thumb over his shoulder. "Our lady foresaw your return."

"Too bad you didn't let your soldiers in on that. It would've saved them—and us—a lot of time, trouble and ammo."

Phin grinned, a flashing of strong white teeth. "We couldn't be one hundred percent certain now, could we? Sometimes the ancient magic ways work, sometimes they don't."

"Yeah," muttered Grant darkly, massaging the side of his head. "And some days you eat the bear and some days the bear eats you."

Phin nodded sagely. "Very well put, Yank."

"How did all of this happen? When did Ireland invade?" Kane asked.

Fand smiled wanly. "We didn't, not in the sense you're thinking. We didn't stage a mass landing. Hundreds of our people were already here, assimilated into

Imperium society, concentrated in New London. They worked primarily as laborers and servants.''

Remembering how Morrigan had been a plant in Strongbow's Ministry of Defense, Kane inquired, ''Did the Priory of Awen mastermind this?''

Phin turned his head, hawked up from deep in his throat and spit scornfully onto the road. ''The bloody Priory couldn't mastermind a *houlie*. Only Morrigan was of any use to us.''

Kane wasn't certain what a *houlie* was supposed to be, and he declined to ask for clarification. From his previous visit, he knew bad blood existed between the Priory of Awen and the clan mac Trenmor.

Fand said, ''Once we passed along the word of Lord Strongbow's disappearance—''

Grant turned around in his seat, breaking in. ''Just what did happen to that scaly son of a bitch?''

''Yeah,'' Kane interposed. ''I dumped him into his Singularity and I figured he went through the quantum conduit to Newgrange where you, Phin and your mother would take care of him.''

Fand lifted her shoulders in an expressive shrug. ''He never arrived. The vortex collapsed in on itself before he came through.''

Lowering her voice, staring directly into Kane's eyes, Fand said, ''But I no longer feel him.'' She tapped her forehead. ''Wherever he is, his mind is gone from here. That's the important thing.''

Kane felt a twinge of disappointment. He had fervently hoped the madman who called himself Strongbow was dead. He recalled how, when the Singularity imploded after Lakesh's interphaser device was thrown through it, Brigid speculated that a quantum shift occurred, sending him down a hyperdimensional side artery.

"At any rate," Phin declared, picking up the narrative thread, "word was passed along. It didn't take too much time before cracks started showing up in the Imperium's foundation. More of our people arrived from Eire, landing upon the coast, setting up bases on the Shetland Isle. Our Scots allies slipped us ashore under the cover of night. Inside of a couple of months, we were fifty thousand strong, spread out all over Britain."

"No one stepped into the power vacuum left by Strongbow?" inquired Grant.

Fand's huge eyes reflected in an inner anxiety. "One man tried."

Phin brayed out a scornful laugh. "A buggering fat bastard, a one-eyed albino by the name of Quayle. Our people call him Balor."

"Evil-eye," Kane murmured, feeling cold fingers of dread knot in his chest.

"Evil-eye," Fand confirmed quietly. Her aureate gaze fixed on his face. Kane nodded once in understanding.

The car rolled between a double column of warriors marching in the same direction, shouldering assault rifles. Hoarse cries of *"Erin go bragh!"* arose from their throats when they caught sight of Phin and Fand. Phin shouted the same phrase in return.

"Our warriors overran the dragoons' weapons and munitions depots," he explained, pointing to the wide variety of firearms carried by the soldiers. "We managed to appropriate enough ordnance to adequately arm our people. During later engagements, we gained heavier weapons and vehicles."

"So you fought a guerrilla war?" Grant asked.

Phin nodded. "At first, anyway. Aye, we drove all of the dragoons out of the countryside, forced them to retreat to New London. We bottled up the harbor so their navy was virtually immobilized." He paused to grin again. "A few ships made it past us, sailing to Ireland in the hopes of cutting off the invasion at the source. They never made it."

"The selkies were a great help," said Fand. "I'm sure you remember them."

Both Grant and Kane did a poor job of repressing their distaste. The bloody battle aboard the *Cromwell* between human and aquatic semihuman wasn't an event they would ever forget. Kane easily visualized the selkies, with their streamlined, torpedo-shaped bodies, seallike pelts and bestial, fanged faces. The memory of their huge, dark eyes alive with human intelligence and savage animal cunning was still fresh.

"The selkies planted limpet mines on the ship hulls below the waterlines," Phin went on, as if he found the story vastly amusing. "After a few boats sank to the bottom of the Irish Sea with all hands, the navy stayed where it was."

"The cream of the Imperium's military was aboard those troopships," Fand said. "After those losses, the resistance against us lost momentum. We offered terms of surrender several times, but Quayle always refused them."

Grant grunted. "Seems like your strategy really paid off, though."

Phin didn't smile at the compliment. His hands tightened on the steering wheel, knuckles distended. "We've had our own losses. Every night in the camps all you hear is the keening of the banshee, mourning our dead.''

"That's war," commented Kane.

"Aye," Phin agreed glumly. "So it is."

The wag followed the road around another bend, and Phin let up on the accelerator, slowing it down. He gestured beyond the hood of the car. "And there lies the prize. Doesn't look worth all this bother, now does it?"

"No," replied Grant in a flat monotone. "It doesn't."

Grant and Kane easily recalled their first sight of New London, six months before, and how impressed they had been by it. Worked stone buildings, a few of them half as tall as the three-hundred-foot-high Administrative Monolith in Cobaltville, rose from behind a twenty-foot stone wall that stretched away from a pair of gateposts. Glinting strands of razor-wire curled along the top of the wall. The gateposts were capped by gun turrets, the bores of 20 mm cannons protruding from them.

A steel latticework formed a barrier at the gate, with a checkpoint cupola standing just outside and to the left of it.

Now the skyline was nearly invisible in rolling plumes of dark smoke. The steel gate lay twisted and broken. The walls themselves showed huge breaches in some places, and in others they had collapsed altogether. Light artillery pieces, pack howitzers and a number of Aden 30 mm automatic cannons were deployed in the fields outside the battered walls.

As Phin steered the wag along the road leading to the gate, they passed a multitude of bodies sprawled on both sides. Some were motionless, while others still stirred. A young boy with curly red hair and a freckled face sat on the edge of the pavement, hands clasped over his spilled guts. Phin slowed when they came abreast of him and called him by name, Aidan.

The boy gave him a courageous grin with red-filmed teeth, croaked *"Erin go bragh,"* vomited blood and fell over on his back.

Phin drove on, teeth bared and growling gutturally in Gaelic. No one spoke as they rolled toward the downed gate, threading a gauntlet of slaughter. The car jounced roughly over the scraps of the gate.

When they entered the walls of New London, Kane had to blink, not just because of the eye-stinging smoke, but in an attempt to reconcile the panorama of devastation with his memories of the city.

Although they hadn't done a complete tour of New London, Kane and Grant had received the distinct impression of a remarkably clean and well-ordered community. Now the narrow cobblestoned lanes bore smoldering craters, the shopfronts with their quaint awnings were shattered and belching flames and smoke. Overturned vehicles seemed to mark every corner, and all the walls were marred by bullet-pocks.

They drove down a street between the gutted, flaming shells of buildings. The pavement was completely covered by rubble where it wasn't gone altogether. The sky was hidden by a dense pall of black, choking smoke. The heat was so oppressive all of them began perspiring.

Bodies lay everywhere, in scattered profusion. Corpses were shoved into gutters, stacked against walls like cordwood, and lying half in and half out of doorways. The heaps of the dead showed the battle's progression, with bodies in green and red, then scarlet jackets and berets, then more green and red making a top layer over the dragoons.

The stench of death was as thick as the smoke. The gutters that weren't jammed by the dead were flooded with blood.

There was no sound other than the crackle of flames and the thrumming of the wag's engine. A shared aura of nightmarish unreality numbed them. The farther they drove away from the main gate, the less frequent became the sight of fatalities. Kane guessed that upon the news of the walls being breached, defenders were pulled from all over the city and concentrated in the main thoroughfares.

Throughout it all, picking their glaze-eyed way among the rubble and shattered masonry, were the civilian citizens of New London. Although some wept bitterly at the carnage, most were blank-faced with shock.

"What are you going to do about the citizens?" Kane asked.

"The war is over," Phin declared confidently. "We'll help them rebuild. They can have any form of government they want as long as the Irish are part of it."

"Part of it?" Grant queried. "Or approve of it?"

Phin waved a diffident hand through the air. "A bit of both, most likely."

"Have you captured Quayle?" Kane asked.

Fand shook her head. "Not yet. He may still be in hiding in the ministry compound. The place is a labyrinth."

"Yeah, I know," replied Kane, thinking of the network of underground tunnels and chambers Strongbow had constructed.

"I doubt Quayle is still in New London," Phin said. "The *Cromwell* set sail three nights ago. As yet, there have been no sightings of her."

Fand's face tightened, but she said nothing.

Phin took a sharp corner with the left tires on the sidewalk to avoid an overturned, burned-out shell of a van; then the stone facade of a sprawling building came into view. The Ministry of Defense stood tall and austere, rising three stories above a small, velvet-green park. A square stone-block tower extended straight up from the roof, concealing a gun emplacement.

Phin keyed off the engine and all of them disembarked and climbed a set of wide stone steps. Two dragoons sprawled on the stairs. Kane cast a glance into their lifeless faces, a bit surprised to see they lacked the scaly brow ridges. A banner lay on the stairs, shot full of holes. It depicted in red on a black background the coiled, winged dragon motif. The pole to which it had been attached projected nakedly overhead.

"Why haven't you hoisted your own flag?" Grant asked.

"Haven't got one," Phin replied brusquely, kicking the wadded-up cloth out of his way. "Besides, the point isn't to conquer England, but to end their ability to conquer us."

They reached a heavy brassbound door set inside a deeply recessed, bevel-edged frame. Phin pushed it open and stepped into a dim, shadowy entrance hall. "That's been accomplished. They can make war no more."

As if on cue, the staccato drumming of subguns on full auto reverberated hollowly from deep in the bowels of the building.

# Chapter 20

Phin blurted in angry surprise, "Fuckin' hell! They told me this bloody place was secure!"

He lunged forward a few paces, clawing a Beretta from beneath his vest, then he paused uncertainly, head cocked as if he were listening.

"Have you ever been here before?" Kane asked.

"No," Fand answered. "The ministry was the last pocket of resistance. We waited to come here until we received the report it was pacified. Have you been here?"

"We know our way around." Kane exchanged a quick glance with Grant, then the two men strode swiftly down the hall, taking point positions. Grant's Sin Eater slapped into his palm. Kane gingerly tensed his tendons. When his blaster sprang into his hand, needles of pain shot up and down the length of his arm. He bit back a cry of pain.

Grant took the right side of the oak-paneled passageway, and Kane sidled along the left. They stalked stealthily, automatically dropping into crouches, placing their feet heel-to-toe. Fand and Phin trailed close behind, imitating their stances and gait. Although Phin's shield might offer some protection, the hard leather wrapping Fand's legs wouldn't turn a bullet.

The rattle of blasterfire sounded again. Grant looked over at Kane and pointed down. Kane nodded in understanding. The subterranean foundation of the ministry building was at least as large as that visible aboveground, reinforced with vanadium alloy. Although Strongbow had never said as much, it was apparent the underground compound was built to serve as a crisis shelter.

The two men crept around a corner, and Grant opened the first door they saw. The drumming of subguns floated up the stairwell, much louder now. They heard angry, frightened shouts in Gaelic interwoven into the blasterfire.

The four people went down the wide steps that led directly to Strongbow's council room. As the nerve center for the Imperium, the room was huge, seeming to occupy at least half of the building's underground foundation.

The overhead lights struck highlights from the upright glass cases holding mementos of human warfare over the centuries. Reverently mounted in spotlit displays were broadswords, maces, suits of medieval armor, halberds, shields and battle standards from thousand-year-old military campaigns. At the far end of the aisle rested a conference table, a highly polished, ten-foot-diameter disk of teak.

Kane strode directly to a small alcove hidden between a pair of display cases. The concealed portal of vanadium alloy he remembered was partially open, and the edges showed the marks of tools.

Fand said tightly, "Our people didn't do that. They wouldn't have had the time or even known it was there."

"Dragoons are probably responsible," Kane said, ducking his head beneath the panel as he entered the opening. Pry bars and sledgehammers lay scattered on the floor. He held up his right hand.

Lights glowed overhead, a geodesic pattern in precisely regular channels. Grant and Kane walked through the narrow passageway and into a chamber. They knew what they would see next, but Phin and Fand came to a clumsy halt and uttered awed exclamations in their own language.

As in the council room, the light reflected from many upright glass cases. Unlike the collection in the council room, the artifacts on display were not military mementos. One case contained what appeared to be a thick column of dark stone, rounded on both ends. Very faint spiral designs were cut into the pitted surface.

"The Stone of Destiny," murmured Fand. "Also known as the Stone of Scone...imbued with the dreams of the Danaan."

Mounted beside it, hanging in a network of silver wires, was a leaf-shaped spearhead, the dark metal free of rust, the edges notched. Phin husked out, "Can it be? The Spear of Destiny, forged by Lugh, the Danaan king?"

On a pedestal rested an innocuous-looking hollow cylinder, barely three feet tall and a foot in diameter. As on the Stone of Destiny, spiraling, labyrinthine symbols crawled over the exterior.

"The grailstone or Cauldron of Dagda," said Fand in a faint, trembling voice. "The relic that became confused with the Holy Grail."

Strongbow had admitted that by laying claim to the sacred objects of Celtic belief, he'd denied them access to their own spirituality. Possessing the Stone of

Destiny in particular made him, at least by his own twisted logic, the rightful monarch of Ireland.

"My mother told me how Strongbow stole our holy relics," Fand whispered in a quavery contralto. "He took them from a Priory vault on Great Skellig Island. I always sensed their presence here, but to actually see them, to know that we have finally reclaimed them—"

Blasterfire stuttered again, from the open door on the opposite side of the room.

"You can ooh and aah later," Grant snapped. "Let's move on."

They entered a long corridor. The sounds of battle were much louder, emanating from around a right jog in the passageway. Quickening their pace, Kane and Grant passed an open doorway from which light gleamed feebly. The two men knew the room was a combination of laboratory and mausoleum, holding the preserved remains of Enlil, the last of the so-called Serpent Kings. Although neither man expressed it, they were relieved not to have to look upon the reptilian corpse floating in its gel-filled vat a second time.

Kane was particularly glad because of his feelings for Fand. She was no doubt aware of her paternity, but viewing the inhuman carcass of her father might send her mind skittering back over the brink of insanity.

They rounded the corner, proceeding into an unfamiliar part of the subterranean facility. The crash of blasters echoed hollowly, and from a high, arched doorway floated scraps of cordite smoke. A pair of Celtic warriors reeled out into the corridor. Both men were youthful, and one supported the other, who held a hand to stanch the flow of blood sliding from a scalp wound.

Phin rushed forward. "Oisin, what the fuck is going on here? You reported you secured this shite-hole!"

Oisin met Phin's angry gaze with one of his own. "Aye, and we thought we had, didn't we? Until we came downstairs, through that door in the museum, and ran into a buggerin' nest of the vipers."

He jerked his head toward the doorway. "Chased 'em up there, up some steps. I think it's some kind of emergency exit, but they can't get the door open. Now they hold the high ground and we can't get to 'em unless we want to be riddled. I'd just as soon let the bastards escape. They won't surrender."

Phin, Grant and Kane edged close and peered around the door frame. A wide set of metal stairs curved up and out of sight. A dozen green-and-red-garbed men hunkered down along it, using the risers as cover, snapping off shots with handblasters. Return fire from above had stitched the walls and floor with little black dots.

Oisin said tensely, "Not sure how many there are, maybe only a baker's dozen, but like I said, they hold the high ground."

Kane crept closer, reaching the foot of the steps and gazing up the stairwell. On a terracelike landing, he glimpsed scarlet jackets shifting in the smoke behind a barricade of office furniture. The flight of stairs was very steep and offered an attacker no shelter. A handful of determined defenders could hold out for a very long time.

"Get your bloody head down!" barked a Celt.

A fusillade of shots burst from above, spattering against the wall behind Kane, smashing away the plaster, coating his hair with dust. The Celts returned the fire as Kane swiftly backed out into the corridor.

"They're dug in as tight as a stickie's fingers on a virgin," he said flatly. "You can maybe take them in a rush, but you'll incur heavy losses, probably seventy percent."

Phin's face contorted in frustrated fury, blue eyes blazing. He snatched the shield off his arm and hurled it against the wall where it struck with a gonging chime.

"Fuck!" Because of his brogue, it came out as *fook*. "After all we've gone through, to be stymied like this—"

Calmly, Fand said, "You're not thinking, Phin. The stairs obviously go somewhere, probably topside. Send some of our people to search the outside of the building and find a door. Perhaps the dragoons can't open it from the inside, but our people might be able to get it open."

Grant nodded approvingly. "If they can, we'll catch the snake-eyes in a double bind, a squeeze play."

Phin's face brightened. To Oisin, he ordered, "Make your way back to the street. Round up as many of our warriors as you can find, have them circle the ministry. Go over it centimeter by centimeter, on your hands and knees if you must. Find that bloody door."

Oisin took off at a sprint. Fand examined his wounded companion, Bran by name, and found only a nick in his hairline. Kane nudged Phin's shield with a toe, frowning at it thoughtfully. "If your assault team had these, your casualties might not be as high. The dragoons aren't using AP rounds."

"AP rounds?" Fand repeated, puzzled.

"Armor piercing."

A grin split Phin's red beard. He called a man away from the stairwell, then sent him and Bran to Strongbow's military museum, commanding them to bring back as many shields as they could reasonably carry.

The exchange of blasterfire ceased, and Phin called up the stairs, "Hey, you pommie idjits—this is your last chance to give up."

A taunting voice wafted down from the landing, sounding as if it belonged to a teenager. "Shove it up your arse and let it roll around, Paddy!"

Phin didn't seem to be offended. "Is old Evil-eye up there with you?"

There wasn't an immediate response. When it finally came, the tone dripped with contempt and barely repressed anger. "The fat bastard done cut and run with the black ship."

"Why didn't you go with him?" asked Phin, hands cupped around his mouth.

"Because we're loyal to the empire. That one-eyed piece of sheep shit ordered us to go with him because we were in his unit, but we come back 'ere. The bastard thinks he can defend the Imperium from a bloody oil platform—"

Another man's voice hissed sharply, and the young dragoon who had been venting fell silent.

"Look, ye," called Phin, doing his best to sound reasonable and friendly. "There's no point in this. New London has fallen. There's no place for you to go. We can starve you out if we've a mind to, but we've got better things to do."

A subgun chattered, sending a burst of lead pouring down the stairwell. The men on the steps cursed and flattened as bullets chipped notches and struck sparks from the risers. Phin ducked back, though no rounds came near him. "Fuckards!"

Kane smiled wryly. "They've got balls, you've got to say that."

"Not for much longer, if God grants," Phin spit.

The gunfire didn't resume, and the Celts and Brits contented themselves with exchanging insults instead of shots. Grant and Kane found them interesting but mystifying.

"What's a shaggin' scouse git?" Grant wanted to know.

Before either Phin or Fand could elaborate, Bran and his companion returned, bearing a stack of shields between them. Some were triangular, others round and even a couple of rectangular *sectum* from the era of the Roman legions. Most were made of hammered brass, reinforced with iron plates and bronze bosses.

Kane hefted a big Norman shield, ovate in shape, narrowing down to a sharp point at its base. It was nearly five feet long and three feet wide at its broadest point. He inserted his left arm through the handles and hefted it, gauging its weight at around fifty pounds.

"Are you planning to lead the charge?" Fand asked, a line of consternation furrowing her smooth brow.

Kane didn't answer. He asked, "Do any of your people have grens?"

Phin looked puzzled for a second, then comprehension showed on his face. "Grenades? No, we found very few of those in the depots. The ones we did appropriate were used weeks ago."

Grant picked up a round shield bearing an embossed boar's head. "You have rocket launchers. One of those or a bazooka would clear those stubborn assholes out in a hurry."

"True," replied Phin. "But all of our long-range

missile throwers are out in the field. It would take some time to have one brought here, and by then the bastards could figure out a way to open the door and escape.''

"Besides," interjected Kane, "I want at least one of them alive for questioning.''

"Questioning about what?'' Grant demanded.

"The whereabouts of Quayle.''

Phin's and Grant's eyebrows lowered at the same time. Phin asked, "Why do you care about Evil-eye?''

Fand stated quietly, "There are reasons.''

Oisin suddenly pounded up, red-faced and breathless. He gestured upward excitedly. "We found the door. It's got a heavy lock bar—that's why the dragoons couldn't get it open.''

"How many of our men did you find?'' inquired Phin.

"Six.''

Phin sighed in exasperation and Oisin snapped defensively, "All I could round up. They're well armed, though. I told them to wait ten minutes before they opened the door and went through. That was—'' his brow furrowed in concentration "—six minutes ago.''

Phin ordered his men back from the stairs and distributed shields among them. Kane detached an Alsatex concussion gren from his harness and moved to the doorway. Grant moved to his side. In a low tone, Kane addressed the warriors. "When I hear your people come through the door, I'll throw this. Then I'm heading up as fast as I can. Everybody understand?''

There were nods and murmurs all around. Everyone fell silent, waiting tensely, straining their hearing. A bit of the tension reached the dragoons on the landing.

The young man who had spoken before called down, "What are you Paddies up to now?"

Before the echoes of the question died in the stairwell, they heard the slamming crash of metal, the rapid scuttle of many feet, and cries of surprise from the dragoons.

# Chapter 21

Kane moved swiftly to the foot of the stairs, unpinned the gren and hurled it with a looping overhand, seeing it bounce on a riser just below the terrace. He ducked down behind the shield a second before a stunning, painfully loud thunderclap battered at it. Simultaneous with the bone-knocking concussion of compressed air, a nova of white light of dazzling intensity erupted.

While the air still shivered with the echoes of the explosion, Kane bounded forward, racing up the first ten feet of stairway, taking two at a time. He heard howls of pain, then blasters crashed and flamed from above. The shots were sharp reports on Kane's ears, the impacts of the bullets clanging heavily against his shield. A hailstorm of bullets struck the shields of the men following him, making a racket like a gang of blacksmiths hammering repeatedly on anvils. He heard Grant mumbling breathlessly behind him. "Oh, I love this, I really get a fucking big kick out of this—"

Then Oisin bulled past him, shouldering Grant out of his way. He fired his Beretta in a frenzy, the pistol bucking and flaming in his fist. His cry of *"Erin go bragh!"* blurred to a shrill scream as a spray of auto-fire knocked his shield sideways. Chest spurting banners of blood, he cartwheeled down the steps, taking down Grant and two other men with him in a thrashing tumble.

Kane squeezed off six rounds, holding the blaster around the rivet-studded rim of the shield. The men behind him hammered up a ragged volley. The bullets sliced past Kane's ears, and he lowered his head quickly, not slowing his pace up the steps.

Handblasters cracked sharply from above, and men screamed in pain and defiance. Kane was forced to throw himself to one side to avoid being bowled off his feet by a red-jacketed corpse somersaulting down the flight of stairs. He glimpsed the vermilion-rimmed cavity of an exit wound in the rear of the man's skull. Skull shards and brain matter slopped onto the back of his neck.

Another dragoon pitched down, and Kane used the shield to slam him aside, jumped over the body and shot a bereted man who tried to wrestle past him in a screaming panic.

The dragoons' autofire, which a second before had verged on the overwhelming, now tapered off, replaced by the grunts and thuds of hand-to-hand combat. Kane scrambled up the last few risers onto the landing. It was a miniature slaughter yard of smoking, broken furniture, blood and mangled flesh.

At least eight Imperial Dragoons lay in a heap. Only two of the soldiers were still on their feet, and they were being brutally pistol-whipped by the Celts. He didn't see any injuries among the Irish. The concussion gren had blinded and deafened the dragoons long enough for the warriors to swarm all over them.

As Grant, Phin and the others crowded onto the landing, Kane yelled, "Enough! That's it!"

The Celts paid him no heed, battering the pair of dragoons to their knees, kicking and clubbing them. Phin roared, "Stop, you murderous bastards!"

Getting in among the men who wanted to avenge a near humiliation, Phin shoved them back, swearing and snarling. He hauled a dazed dragoon to his feet. Despite the blood masking his face, Kane saw he didn't possess the scaled brows or slit-pupiled eyes. He also looked very young.

Phin dragged him over to Kane. "You wanted to ask him something?"

Kane demanded, "Where's Quayle?"

The youth fingered a lacerated lip and spit a jet of scarlet on the floor. "You're a Yank," he mumbled. "Why do you care?"

"You should care that I care," retorted Kane grimly. "It's all that's keeping you alive right now."

The young dragoon swayed on unsteady legs. "All I know is that the captain sailed for an oil platform in the North Sea."

"I don't suppose you have the map coordinates?"

The man shook his head. "I've got shit, Yank. Thanks to you."

"One more thing—you said you served under Quayle?"

The dragoon nodded. "For the past four months."

"Does he know you by sight?"

He blinked at him in confusion. "No reason why he shouldn't. My name is Harper. I was his orderly."

Kane turned and descended the stairs. Grant said, "We got off lucky. Only one casualty. Oisin."

Kane smiled wryly. "The last defenders of the Imperium have had their collective asses kicked. England and Ireland are united just like in the old days—at the point of a blaster."

Though Grant chuckled, Fand stared up at them solemnly as they approached. In a voice so low it was almost a whisper, she said, "Until we find Quayle and Morrigan, both of our nations may very well be united in death."

"Morrigan?" Grant echoed in annoyance. "What's she got to do with this?"

"Yeah," said Kane, eyes narrowing to suspicious slits. "I was under the impression she was in still in Ireland, with the Priory of Awen."

Fand's lips parted as if she were groping for a response. Phin and his warriors chose that moment to clump down the stairs, pushing the wounded dragoons ahead of them. Clapping hard hands on Kane's and Grant's shoulders, he exclaimed happily, "Brilliant strategy! It was desperate enough to work."

The Celts crowded around the two Americans, shouting their congratulations and voicing ribald jokes. The reality was finally sinking in—the Imperium Britannia was inarguably and undeniably overthrown. Thirty years of tyranny ended in an underground stairwell. Kane figured by the end of the day some self-styled bard would compose a ballad, "The Battle of the Stair," wherein he and Grant obliterated an entire platoon of dragoons by breaking wind in their direction.

He looked around for Fand and, when he didn't see her, he pushed through the mill of men. He instantly knew where she had gotten herself to, and his nape hairs prickled with a preternatural chill.

Kane went down the corridor in a fast, long-legged stride, turning the corner. He saw lights shining brightly from an open doorway, and he set his teeth on a groan of dismay. He went in fast, passing the pieces of medical and surgical equipment, pushing a wheeled dissecting table out of his way.

Fand stood motionless before a long, deep transparent-walled vat. "Don't," he said urgently. "Don't look at that thing, Fand."

She cast a puzzled glance over her shoulder. "What thing?"

Kane rocked to a halt, staring wide-eyed. The vat was empty, drained even of the preserving gel. The horribly distorted form of Enlil no longer floated within it.

Fand's huge eyes glinted with sudden comprehension. "Enlil isn't here. Did you believe I wasn't aware of his contribution to my life? After I regained my mind, my mother told me how Strongbow—then called Laurence James Karabatos—arranged for her abduction and rape by the last of the Serpent Kings of old. And therefore broke the pact struck by the Tuatha De Danaan millennia ago."

Fand moved close to him, saying quietly, "Your concern touches my heart, but I am no longer the wretched, mad creature who forced you to relive your incarnation as Cuchulainn. When Strongbow vanished, my sanity, my sense of self, returned."

She stroked his face with soft fingers, gently tracing the hairline scar on his cheek, as she had done in his jump dream. "But one thing remains the same...my soul's desire for you."

Fand suddenly threw her arms around him and kissed him with a passionate possessiveness. He felt her heart thudding fast, even through her combat vest. "How you fought," she husked out. "How you fought, beloved!"

Kane's own heart pounded, and he felt his body respond to her wild ardor. She felt it, too, and smiled with a wicked innocence into his face, her golden eyes seething, seeming to pour molten heat through his skull and down into his groin.

Carefully, he disengaged himself, stepping back half a pace. "In my dream, you showed me a vision of imminent destruction. You said time was short. Were you speaking the truth?"

The corners of her lips turned down in disappointment, but she said, "I was. And time is exceptionally short. Let us fetch Phin and Mr. Grant, and I'll tell you what I know."

THE BABBLE OF RIOTOUS revelry wafted in through the open study windows. The conquerors of New London celebrated with an unrestrained joy, singing, piping tunes on their tin-whistle flutes and beating drums.

Phin, Fand, Kane and Grant occupied Strongbow's former office, a wide room with aggressively masculine furnishings: a wide oaken desk, intricately carved; four leather armchairs and high bookshelves of dark, brooding wood. A large oil portrait of Oliver Cromwell occupied one wall. The study also contained a liquor cabinet, the contents of which Phin sampled enthusiastically.

In a little adjacent room, not much larger than a closet, Grant found several file drawers built into the wall. While Phin slugged down a bottle of wine, Fand, Grant and Kane brought the folders to the desk and went through them. Most of them appeared to be personnel records and the only entry under *Q* was Quayle, Philip Aubrey.

Kane skimmed it quickly, noting how unremarkable it was. The man's service record was undistinguished, except for a notation recording a wound received in the line of duty. Quayle had been promoted to the rank of captain a little more than a year before and placed in command of a small group of regulars, a patrol unit.

The only entry that he found impressive was the man's height and weight. Quayle was truly a human leviathan, a man who dwarfed Grant in height and outweighed the late, unlamented Guana Teague by more than a hundred pounds.

A medical transcript detailing a serious illness was almost unreadable due to the words Unfit and Rejected stamped across it in bright red letters.

Phin leaned out the window, guzzling the wine, laughing and occasionally exhorting the people to "Dance, you bastards!" He was a happy man. When Kane tossed aside Quayle's file, Phin turned toward him.

"Let Evil-eye float around in the North Sea," he said, his voice slightly slurred by drink. "He's a fuckin' exile now. Got nowhere to go and nothin' to do."

"He has the black ship," Fand reminded him severely. "That makes him far more dangerous than a bushelful of frightened soldiers trapped in a stairwell. You thought they were worth your time."

Phin snorted and took another pull from the bottle.

"Found it," announced Grant, holding up a folder. "Northstar 40."

Fand and Kane moved to his side. Grant's finger moved over the copy typed on a sheet of paper. "According to this, it was built in 1980 by British Petroleum and cost forty-five million dollars." His eyes darted over the specs. "Goddamn, the thing is huge. Predarkers really went in for size."

He detached a grainy black-and-white picture from a paper clip. A long view of the Northstar 40 platform gave an impression of a skeletal iceberg, its six gigantic legs seeming to be the mere tips of shafts extending all the way to the bottom of the sea.

Kane, reading over Grant's shoulder, saw that, on the contrary, the bulk of the rig floated above the ocean surface. Voluminous ballast tanks were filled and emptied with seawater to raise and lower the platform and, more importantly, to keep it balanced. He made a mental note of that.

Another square of paper displayed an aerial map, containing longitude and latitude coordinates, distance in miles from New London and pinpointing Northstar 40's location by concentric circles.

"So we know where it is now," Grant declared, fixing an unblinking gaze on Fand. "You need to tell us why it's important. I agree with Phin—Quayle can't do much harm sitting out there on it, even if he has a Stealth ship."

"True," admitted Fand. "Presuming he stays there. But he won't."

Phin voiced a raucous, scornful laugh. "Let him take the black ship to Ireland. Let him try. The selkies will settle with him like they did the last time the dragoons tried."

"He won't be sailing to Ireland," she retorted. "He'll set his course for Lyonesse."

Phin's liquor-glazed eyes slitted, widened, then slitted again. "The place is nothing but a legend, lass. And if it wasn't, it sank thousands of years ago."

"The sea eventually gives up its secrets," Fand replied. "Lyonesse rose again, or at least a portion of it did. The selkies reported it to the Priory and the Priory to me. The place is there, make no mistake."

"And if it is?" Phin challenged. "How is another ruddy rock important?"

Fand folded her arms over her combat vest, leaning an ample hip against the corner of the desk. "Haven't you wondered where Morrigan has been this past fortnight? She was deeply involved in the initial planning for the invasion because of her inside knowledge of the Imperium's workings."

Phin acknowledged the comment with a nod. "Aye, without her we wouldn't have known what parts of the coast and countryside were underpatrolled." He shrugged. "I just assumed she was still in Ireland, waiting for news."

Fand shook her head. "She's with Captain Quayle aboard Northstar 40."

Phin glared at her in angry incredulity. Then a torrent of outraged Gaelic burst from his mouth. He shook the wine bottle accusingly in Fand's direction. Turning, he hurled it across the room where it shattered on the gilt-edged frame of the Cromwell portrait.

Grant and Kane eyed each other, not knowing what Phin shouted at Fand but gleaning the meaning nonetheless. He was enraged that plans were made without his input or consent and, as commander of the invasion forces, he felt he'd been deliberately omitted from the loop.

Fand let him rant for nearly a minute, then interposed sharply, "It was all of Morrigan's doing, Phin. It wasn't approved."

Reverting to English, Phin half snarled, "*What* wasn't approved? Another one of her spyin' missions?"

"No. She meant to trick Quayle, to insinuate herself

back into the Imperium's inner circle, to gain his trust and bring about England's utter destruction.''

"For Christ's sake," Phin cried in angry frustration, "isn't that what we've just accomplished?''

Kane cleared his throat and caught the red-bearded man's attention. "You've brought about England's defeat. I think Morrigan wants it completely decimated, laid waste forever. A permanent scorched-earth policy with a vengeance.''

Phin's lips curled skeptically. "How can a mere slip of a blind girl manage that?''

"Remember the old legends of our land's history?" Fand asked. "Where the Firbolgs came from?''

Phin thought for a moment. "They came from an isle that sank during a cataclysm. They were supposed to be half-breeds, mixtures of animal and human, created as a slave race. Some scholars think the selkies were mixtures, too, and they came from the same place as the Firbolgs. Atlantis.''

Fand nodded curtly. "They may have come from an Atlantean colony, what we know as Lyonesse. Like Atlantis, Lyonesse used an element known in ancient texts as orichalcum as an energy source...the power of the sun harnessed inside tiny balls.''

"The fire stones?''

"Exactly. The selkies explored the risen isle and described a dark vault filled with thousands of small spheres. They brought one back to the Priory for examination. Morrigan made the connection that they were the firestones that supposedly brought about the destruction of Atlantis.''

"And if they are?" snapped Phin. "So bloody what? Can we use them?''

Fand shook her head. "Without the machines the

Atlanteans built to properly harness the energy, they are like miniature thermonuclear warheads, awaiting only detonation.''

She took a very deep breath and said in a rush, ''If they are detonated, the atmosphere in this part of the world will heat, right up to the stratosphere. Not quite hot enough to cook everything, but the temperature will rise to the point where every organic thing will perish, every bit of metal will heat to melting, all sea life boiled alive, the soil scorched through till nothing can grow again. That is what Morrigan has planned for Britain.''

While Phin struggled to digest Fand's declaration, Grant rumbled, ''How can she be so sure the same thing won't happen to Ireland?''

''She can't be, nor can she be certain that all of Europe won't be affected, either, regardless of the precautions she takes. I'm not privy to all the details of her plans. Once she took me into her confidence and I lodged an objection, she refused to speak further of the matter. I'd hoped she changed her mind. But when she vanished from the Priory citadel, I knew where she had gone and why.''

''Her hatred of the Imperium is that strong?'' asked Grant.

''Aye,'' Fand answered sadly. ''Like me, she is the issue of a rape. In her instance, a dragoon upon her mother. During her years as a Priory spy, she was forced to stand idly by while atrocities were perpetrated upon the Irish. She pretended to approve of them. Her guilt, like her hatred, is deep.

''Morrigan will not find satisfaction in the mere defeat of the Imperium. By her way of thinking, as long as one Briton survives, the empire could rise again.''

She paused and added, "This is far worse. This is hell rising to consume the entire world."

Kane ran a hand through his hair. "The firestones react to solar energy?"

"That's what the old texts say."

"Morrigan probably persuaded Quayle they would be a decisive weapon against your people. Mebbe she's hoping to have him return here to England, then somehow arrange for their detonation."

"That's what I fear, as well," Fand agreed. "We must stop them, either before they set sail from Northstar 40 or during the voyage to Lyonesse."

Phin released his breath in an explosive sigh, crossing himself. "Sweet Jesus, Mary and Joseph. Why can't even a damn war be simple?"

Grant chuckled, but there was little humor in it. "I ask the same question all the time."

After a few minutes of discussion, some of it heated, the four people developed a plan. A number of boats were still anchored in New London's harbor, and Phin stated he would round up as many volunteers with maritime experience as he could find. They agreed to set sail no later than midnight, which should put them in visual range of Northstar 40 shortly before daybreak.

"One other thing," put in Kane. "The dragoon prisoner you took today, the kid, Harper?"

Phin cocked his head. "What about him?"

"Clean him up and bring him along. Make sure he's got an entire uniform on him."

"What good will he do?" asked Phin.

"Mebbe none at all. Mebbe all the good in the world."

# Chapter 22

It was midafternoon when Grant, Fand and Kane left the study and entered a big, high-ceilinged common room decorated in Victorian style with overstuffed furniture, polished tables and even a hearth. Grant and Kane had been there before, and knew four bedrooms faced off from the sitting room.

"Let me fetch some materials," Fand told them, "and I'll see to your injuries."

After she left, Grant shrugged out of his Mag coat and dropped into a chair with a sigh of relief. Kane did likewise, although removing the coat sent pain lancing through his shoulder socket. "I hope you're glad I don't like saying 'I told you so.'"

Grant gave him a glare. "The hell you're not. You're just more sneaky about the way you say it."

Kane smiled mockingly. "I told you so."

Rolling his eyes ceilingward, Grant said, "I'll concede that so far what you said in Cerberus is panning out."

"So far?"

Grant cast a look over his shoulder and lowered his voice. "There's more to this than Fand has let on. I can't figure out what she needs us—or you—for. Everything would have played out exactly as it happened whether we were here or not."

"What are you implying?" Kane asked, an edge in his voice.

"Whether Fand is sane now or not, that doesn't make her normal or her motives above question. You can't tell me you haven't noticed the way she looks at you."

Kane shrugged, not wanting to discuss Fand with Grant, especially since he had raised a disturbing point. He dragged over a small table and propped his feet up on it. "Enlil's body is missing."

Grant grunted in surprise. "Who would've taken that butt-ugly thing? One of the Irish?"

"They didn't have the time, even if they wanted to touch it."

"Quayle?"

"Mebbe," Kane admitted. "But why? There's no reason for him to want the body. What use is it to him?"

Grant waved a dismissive hand through the air. "Mebbe he plans to tour Europe with it and charge two tuppence a head to take a look."

A sudden thought caused him to eye Kane reproachfully. "I hope you're not suggesting the goddamn thing was really alive all along, woke up after Strongbow vanished and just strolled away?"

Kane started to chuckle at the concept, then realized even the possibility wasn't very funny.

Fand returned, bearing a tray with a jug and two cups. She had shed the bulky combat vest and the leather leggings. A thin shift of loosely woven cloth covered her from shoulder to midthigh, but it was apparent she was naked beneath it. Her braided hair fell below her waist, to the backs of her knees. The little golden balls Kane remembered so well were tied onto the ends and they clicked as she walked.

From the pouch belted at her narrow waist, she removed a little packet and emptied its contents into the jug. It looked like chopped-up leaves, diced so fine they were almost a powder. After sloshing the liquid around in the jug, Fand dipped a soft cloth into it and gently swabbed at the lump on Grant's head.

"You were injured before you came here," she said sympathetically.

"Yeah," Grant replied brusquely, refusing to elaborate.

She poured the liquid from the jug into one of the cups and handed it to him. "This is a herbal mixture, a natural analgesic and relaxant. Take three swallows."

Sniffing at the thin brownish fluid in the cup, Grant asked, "Is this the stuff your mother gave me in Ireland?"

"If you were injured, then yes, more than likely. Did it work?"

"Guess so." He brought the cup to his lips, sipped, grimaced and took three deep swallows, drinking it off. He shuddered. "Yeah, it's the same stuff."

He handed the cup back to her, then carefully probed the side of his head. "Doesn't hurt as much."

"Soon you won't feel any pain. You should go and lie down now. You won't receive the full healing effects unless you sleep."

Grant heaved himself to his feet and passed a hand over his eyes. "The first stuff I drank didn't make me sleepy."

Fand didn't respond, busying herself shaking more ground-up herbs into the jug. When a reply wasn't forthcoming, Grant walked into a bedroom, smothering a yawn.

Fand faced Kane. "Take off your shirt."

He did as he was bid, pulling off his sweater and the shirt beneath. She winced when she saw the great blue-black bruise spreading from his shoulder and streaking down his upper arm to blend in with the splotches of discoloration caused by Jacko's violent removal of his Sin Eater.

She touched him gently. "Are you in much pain?"

"I can tolerate it."

Fand passed the damp cloth over the bruised flesh. "And your inner pain," she said softly, "can you tolerate that?"

"What do you mean?" he asked irritably.

"Where is the woman who was with you before? The one Morrigan called your *anam-chara?* I sense you fear you have lost her, yet I do not sense grief as if she were dead."

Kane's skin prickled as Fand's fingers caressed him. "She's not dead. She was seriously injured a couple of days ago."

Fand's eyes glimmered strangely. "Yet you came when I called?"

"There's nothing I can do for her." His voice sounded harsher than he intended. He forced a smile. "Besides, if I allowed the Western Hemisphere to blow up so I could sit at her bedside, she'd never let me hear the end of it."

His smile vanished. "Presuming she ever wakes up."

"But you feel guilty about not staying with her." Fand didn't ask a question; she made a statement.

Kane groped for a response, even an unsatisfactory one. "Yes. No. Hell, I don't know."

"Something happened between you, didn't it? The bond of the *anam-chara* was strained to near breaking."

He sighed. "Yes. She blamed me for—" He broke off, shaking his head. He remembered her cutting words, as painful at this moment as they were when she'd first uttered them a couple of months before: "You're a cruel man, Kane, and the more I'm in your company, the more your cruelty contaminates me."

He directed a level stare into Fand's face. "I don't want to talk about it. I'm here now and I'll help you, then be out of your life again."

Fand's lips curved in a patronizing smile. "We'll never be out of each other's lives, Kane, not completely. No matter how many of them we live."

"Please don't start that shit again," he said wearily.

Her back stiffened. "As you wish." She handed him a cup. "Three swallows."

Kane raised it to his lips and drank the bitter mixture. To his surprise, he felt the intense pain seeping away, as if it flowed down his body and out through the soles of his feet, to be absorbed by the carpeted floor. "Good stuff," he commented inanely.

Fand picked up her staff and touched Kane's shoulder with the egg-shaped knob. He flinched away, remembering all too well the painful shock it had administered upon his first meeting with her.

Sternly, she said, "I channel my bioelectric energy through this, drawing upon the electromagnetic field of the Earth. It is not an unknown process, harnessing the Gaia power. I'll focus it on your injury to increase blood circulation."

Kane gazed with trepidation at the staff, then at her, searching for any signs of duplicity. He nodded his assent.

The knob grazed him and Kane experienced a flush of warmth, accompanied by a pleasant pins-and-needles sensation that spread through his shoulder. Fand withdrew the staff, a faint dew of perspiration filming her forehead.

"There," she announced. "My bioenergy complements your own. Now you must sleep."

A wave of drowsiness crept over Kane, and he swallowed a yawn. "Who'll wake me up?"

"When it's time, I will. Have no fear of that."

Kane arose from the chair and walked to a bedroom, the same one he had occupied as a guest of Lord Strongbow. Fand followed him, carrying his shirt, sweater and coat. As he stretched out on the canopied bed, she lit a small flare-topped oil lantern, suffusing the room with a soft, yellow-orange glow.

The mattress was as hard as he remembered, but at the moment it felt like the consistency of a cloud. He closed his eyes. Right as he glided away into sleep, he heard Fand's faraway, loving whisper, "Sleep, Ka'in, my beloved Cuchulainn. Sleep...dream...and *remember.*"

AT FIRST, KANE WAS aware he dreamed. Images were formless and vague, but he sensed they were all connected in some mysterious way. Chaotic scenes and landscapes shifted and tilted around him, like clouds rolling and tumbling before a gale. Slowly, these settled into one distinct landscape, strange yet familiar. He received a dim impression of a greater strangeness than mere difference of distance—a hint of misty abysses and vast gulfs of aeons, of a time long forgotten.

Kane watched as Cuchulainn arrived at the trysting place, the Strand of the Yew Tree. The quarter moon gleamed at its apex and the surface of the Boyne danced with reflected highlights. The long reeds and marsh grass undulated in the breeze. Here and there rose gaunt and gray monoliths, menhirs reared by non-human hands.

Cuchulainn tugged the long cloak tighter about his body and adjusted the hood to cast his face into deep shadow, as if he were trying to conceal his identity from unseen observers. Only the long spear, Gae Bolg, marked him as the notorious Ka'in, Hound of Ulster.

As though he floated high above the banks of the river, Kane aloofly watched Cuchulainn stride impatiently back and forth, twice circling the yew tree, ducking his head beneath the low spread of branches. He seemed agitated and Kane wondered why.

Then, with the suddenness of thought, he felt himself drawn toward the man like a sliver of iron pulled by a magnet. He sped headlong down and into him, melding seamlessly with his perceptions. In a micro-instant, he was Ka'in, and he knew what he knew and felt what he felt.

He was consumed with anxiety, anger and even a touch of fear. The sound of a stealthy footstep was almost inaudible, but to the wilderness-honed ears of the Gael, it was as loud as a trumpet call. Pivoting on a heel, leading with Gae Bolg, he saw a slender figure part the reeds bordering the riverbank, appearing to be disgorged by the shadows. Like him, the figure was draped head to toe in a hooded cloak.

Lowering the spear, he strode forward aggressively,

demanding, "Where were you today, Fand? I was censured by Conor himself—"

Long, delicate fingers reached up and gently pressed themselves against his lips. "Hush, beloved. You did well on your own. You exposed the Firbolgs for what they are and Balor's complicity. You did not need my counsel."

Ka'in pulled down the woman's hood to reveal a beautiful face that wasn't completely human. She had huge, slanted eyes, as big in proportion to her high-boned face as those of a cat. They were the sparkling blue of mountain meltwater, and he had always found them beautiful despite, or maybe because of, the feline pupils. Her lips were full and pouting, her skin a smooth alabaster with a tinge of blue. The thick wavy hair hanging loose along the side of her face bore tiger stripes of black and blond. Her small ears swept up and back to points.

"We can no longer meet," Ka'in said in a pained whisper. "The rumors about us have put my credibility and honor in question. I cannot continue to hurt my wife like this nor you your husband. Twice he has sent assassins against me."

Bright anger flared in Fand's huge eyes, then darkened to sorrow. "Yes," she said at length, in a hushed, faraway voice. "You are right. The Danaan are no longer pleasing in the sight of men. The time of my race has passed, our science and boons forgotten. The belief in the power of the White Christ will soon sweep us all away into history.

"We have no choice but to stand aside and allow humanity to chart its own course, determine its own destiny. The Tuatha De Danaan will retreat into realms invisible, unseen by the eyes of man."

She spoke without heat, without bitterness, but a palpable sadness underscored her words. Ka'in's heart jerked in pain, to a tragic sense of loss, yet he knew she spoke truly. The old world and the ancient ways were in wane, entering a twilight time, and the mad love they shared could not arrest the tide of change.

A smile suddenly creased Fand's lips, as sudden as a shaft of brilliant sunlight bursting through dark cloud cover. "But still we have this night."

Her fingers undid the silver clasp at her throat and the cloak fell away, slithering down her slim body. As always, Ka'in's eyes drank in the feline grace and beauty of her form. Her legs were the longest in proportion to her body as he had ever seen in a woman.

Fand took his hands and placed them over her small but perfectly shaped breasts. The gem-hard nipples pressed against his callused palms. Her immense eyes focused on his, seeming to pour her own desires and passions into him.

Ka'in had often wondered if Fand had indeed seduced him with her powers, enchanted him with a love *geas* as others had accused. True, she was not completely human, but as he knew from delirious experience, she was more than human enough.

Sliding a leg between his thighs, she pressed her lips against his with such violence, Ka'in went down on the soft grass, half-smothered by a flurry of bruising kisses. He dredged up his last scrap of will to push her aside, but she had ever been a tigress in her passions, stronger than most men.

Fand put a hand between their bodies and beneath his kilt. Ka'in groaned as he felt her sharp-nailed fingers close tightly on his rigid shaft. She straddled him and moved backward along his body until she knelt between his legs. Swiftly, she lowered her head and took him into her mouth. Ka'in raised his pelvis and arched his back as her head rose and fell in an excruciating rhythm.

A roaring madness engulfed him, driving away all rational thoughts, all concerns for the future. Tearing off his clothes while Fand still suckled him, Ka'in struggled to his knees. As if she knew how close to climax he was, Fand released him and fell backward on the grass, arms upflung and legs open.

Cradling her buttocks, Ka'in placed the tip of his erect member at her moist and hot mound and fell forward, arching his back to drive fully into her. Fand gasped, squirmed and cried out sharply. She raised her pelvis to meet his deep plunges, her full lips peeled back over her perfect teeth in a half snarl, half grin of pleasure.

Ka'in maintained his steady, full-length thrusts as Fand levered herself up by her slender, muscular arms, locking her legs tightly around his hips. By arching her back and pushing, she rolled him over and sat astride him.

She bucked wildly above his body, her pants of exertion interspersed with little moaning cries. She rode with a wild, fierce intensity. Ka'in lifted his head and cupped her left breast, his tongue flicking over the nipple. He could feel the swelling tension in his shaft and so could Fand. She shifted position and rolled her hips in a frantic undulation.

With a hoarse savage cry of release, Ka'in writhed, clutched her around her narrow waist and shot a steady stream of his seed into her.

Fand cried out loudly, biting down on her lower lip. "Ka'in—!"

The word cut through his consciousness like a knife, forming a bridge between the dreaming Kane and the dream Ka'in.

KANE'S EYES SNAPPED wide and he came awake, breathing heavily, blinking back sweat sliding from his hairline. The bed quivered beneath him. Fand sat astride him, her head thrown back, her long hair hanging down behind her. Her white skin glistened with a sheen of perspiration, and her teeth were sunk into her lower lip. Her full breasts trembled, and even in the feeble lamplight Kane saw the flush spreading over them. The pulse throbbed wildly at the base of the slim column of her throat.

In a faint, aspirated whisper, she said, "Ah, you *did* remember. The souls of our past incarnations were at long last reunited to express their eternal love."

Kane was too numbed, too stupefied to say or do anything but pant for a long tick of time. His thoughts staggered in disorder, trying to reconcile his dream of Cuchulainn and Fand at the trysting place with the hard reality of Kane and Fand in a bed at the Ministry of Defense.

Fand fell forward over him, limp in postorgasmic weakness. She kissed the side of his neck, murmuring words in Gaelic. Kane's confusion finally gave to outrage. Gripping her by the long braid of hair, he pulled her head up and back. She yipped in pain, and then her face grew solemn when she saw the fury stamped on his face.

"You got into my mind again," he said between clenched teeth, voice so thick with rage it sounded like an animal's guttural growl. "You manipulated me, *forced* me—"

She stared at him, stricken and shocked. "No, Ka'in, it wasn't like that—"

He heaved her up and away from him, rolling her onto her side. Rising from the bed, still gripping her by the hair, he struggled to control the almost overwhelming urge to kill her. "*Kane,* goddammit! My name is Kane! Why did you do this? Why come to me like some kind of—" he paused to grope for a term "—succubus? If you know me as well as you claim you do, you should know force is the absolutely, positively *worst* approach to take."

Tears sprang to Fand's eyes, but they were of sorrow, not pain. "I would never force you. If the memories I raised to the surface were not of you, of *us,* this would not have happened. I stimulated your remembrances so you would understand how I feel."

He locked gazes with her, probing her huge golden eyes brimming with tears. He realized her distress was genuine and understood the source of his own fury. He was still angry over Lakesh's scheme to mate him with Beth-Li Rouch. The old man's plan to turn Cerberus into a colony and pass on Kane's superior genetic traits hadn't reached fruition because of Kane's unwavering resistance to it.

In Kane's mind, Lakesh's idea to breed only the best with the best was nothing but a continuation of the purity-control eugenics program practiced in the villes. The fact Beth-Li was a schemer herself, and her beautiful face masking a corrupt soul, hadn't contributed to his enthusiasm.

But he saw no such corruption in Fand's tear-streaked face, only guilt. Suddenly, he was so weary he could do nothing but shake his head at the absurdity of it all. He released his grip on her hair and sat down heavily on the edge of the bed.

Tentatively, Fand touched his bare back and whispered, "No matter what you think, I could not control your mind even had I cared to. Part of you desired to do this, part of you said yes. That is the part I asked. Consent was given. There is no need for shame."

Massaging his eyes with the heels of his hands, he said hoarsely, "Grant was right."

He shifted on the bed to look at her. "Let's talk about shame, Fand. What do you think I would feel if I return home and learn Brigid died while I was here with you, reliving an erotic encounter from a thousand years ago?"

He showed his teeth in a hard, humorless grin. "Shame wouldn't even begin to cover it."

"She has not died, Kane," Fand said in a hushed but confident voice.

"How the hell would you know?"

"*You* would know, not I. As it is, you have smothered the flame of your passion for her, for your *anamchara*. You fear if you fan it to life, it will consume you, blind you, make you a slave to it."

Kane knew his startlement was reflected in his eyes, for Fand smiled knowingly and a little triumphantly. "As courageous a warrior as you are, the prospect of expressing your deepest feelings for the woman Brigid terrifies you far more than any enemy you have ever faced."

Kane opened his mouth to voice an angry denial, but nothing came out. It was true. He had no choice but to acknowledge it.

Fand's smile broadened. "So brave, yet so fearful."

Annoyed, Kane demanded, "And what about you, what are your motivations?"

"Motivations?"

Remembering Ambika's self-important vow of chastity, Kane asked bluntly, "Did you figure it was time to lose your virginity?"

Fand surprised him by laughing. "That time came and went a number of years ago."

He stared at her, nonplussed. "Really?"

"Really. Did you think all those years I spent wandering the length and breadth of Erin I never came in contact with men? One of my duties—pleasures, actually—as the living embodiment of Ireland's spirit was to participate in fertility rituals."

"No wonder you were so popular."

She nodded. "Indeed. I also have three children, a boy and two girls, now living in the Priory's citadel. Phin's clan took care of them."

Kane's surprise grew. Haltingly, he said, "I had no... I guess I figured when we first met you were..." His words trailed off.

"That I was saving myself for the incarnation of Cuchulainn?" she supplied.

"Something like that."

She grinned. "Wonderfully romantic but hardly practical. I was mad, but I wasn't stupid. The Danaan Fand took many human lovers, though she loved her Ka'in the most intensely. Because her race was so long-lived, she knew her affairs with men were fleeting."

Kane studied her smooth, unlined features. Although she appeared to be barely twenty, he knew she had been born more than thirty years ago, after her mother's release from cryostasis. Strongbow claimed his mutagenic treatment had extended his longevity and so the Annunaki genes Fand carried doubtlessly slowed her own aging process, prolonging her life for God only knew how many years—or centuries.

With a touch of envy, he realized she would probably look exactly the same thirty years hence. He also finally accepted Fand didn't harbor sinister motives. She desired him, and as loath as he was to admit it, he desired her. He felt a trifle ridiculous when he realized how most, if not all, of his assumptions about her were wrong.

Repressing a sigh, Kane stood up, avoiding looking at Fand, almost unbearably lovely in her nudity. He glanced around for his clothes, saw them neatly folded over the back of a chair and wondered absently if Fand had taken them off or if he had. He decided it didn't matter.

She asked, "What did you mean when you said 'Grant was right'?"

Pulling on his pants, Kane answered, "There doesn't seem to be a good reason to have summoned me here unless it was for…for what we just did. The plan we came up with to board Northstar 40 would work—or not work—just as well even if I wasn't involved."

"Perhaps so," Fand admitted. "If anyone other than Quayle—Balor—were in command of it."

Kane's face twisted as if he suddenly tasted something extremely repugnant. "Another bit of unfinished business from the life of Cuchulainn?"

"In a way. Balor was ever the traitor, betraying his clan, his oaths, whenever the possibility of power beckoned. Always Cuchulainn was there to thwart him, to denounce him, to expose him."

"So you're saying only I can face off against the bastard and have any chance of winning?"

Fand pursed her lips. Choosing her words carefully, she replied, "Let us say your presence may tip the scales more in our favor and leave it at that."

Picking up his wrist chron and glancing at the LCD, Kane announced with a touch of surprise, "It's almost time to go."

Fand smiled impishly and toyed with her braid. "I *did* promise to wake you up, remember?"

# Chapter 23

*Hornblower's Wraith* pitched and bounced on the relentless chop, white spray flying from the cresting waves. The incessant rising and falling motion awoke nausea in stomachs all over the twenty-five-foot length of the boat.

The man at the wheel was named McCrae and he sang "I Wish I Was in Carrickfergus," completely oblivious to the discomfort his piloting caused. He paid no attention to how Fand, Phin, Grant and Kane swayed and stumbled on the deck of the little wheelhouse. Finally, Phin ordered him to ease off on the throttle with a stream of snarling Gaelic and a kick to the rump.

Even Grant, with his years of jockeying Deathbirds through all kinds of maneuvers and weather, looked relieved when the rocking became less violent.

*Hornblower's Wraith* was one of the few seaworthy vessels remaining in the imperial fleet. The frigates, the freighters and even the three-masted sloops had all been sunk. The twin-engine *Wraith* was more suited for hugging coastlines than the open ocean, but still she was a trim craft.

Grant had pointed out how the vessel was built a bit like the old PT boats of the twentieth century: long and slim in configuration, the wheelhouse and the cabin superstructure positioned forward, the long afterdeck covered with heavy cypress planking was fairly open, except for the tripod-mounted M-60 machine gun bolted to an upright stanchion.

The *Wraith* could cruise easily at twenty knots and was roomy enough to accommodate twelve men in the lower crew cabin. A dozen Celts and one frightened, motion-sick dragoon sat on the facing benches. The young man did not look out of place since almost all of the Irish warriors wore the red jackets and berets of the Imperium. They also carried H&K MP-5 subguns.

Only a handful of the Irish sitting on the low benches in the cabin possessed hard seamanship experience. They were landsmen; they didn't trust the ocean. More than one of them mumbled a prayer to the ancient sea god of Eire. Several of them were freshly shaved and closely cropped, and the forced shearing of their beards and manes hadn't improved their moods, either.

Although many of the uniforms bore bloodstains and bullet holes, Kane felt their appearance lent veracity to the story of battle-weary soldiers fleeing New London. He just hoped they wouldn't stain them further by throwing up. One hundred nautical miles was a long boat ride, especially one made in the dead of night in turbulent waters. McCrae had speculated it would require six or more hours to come within sight of the rig, but that estimation depended on how rough the seas were.

It worked both ways, Kane reflected. They would probably spy the oil platform at the same time the troopers aboard it spotted them. After studying the pix of Northstar 40, he knew it would be impossible to approach the structure unseen. They would be challenged, and that was why Harper, Quayle's orderly, would make the initial face-to-face contact.

A huge wave crashed over the prow of the *Wraith*, and McCrae wrestled with the wheel. He gunned the two diesel engines, and the boat shook with a stern-to-aft shiver. The wipers droned steadily, but they were unable to keep the windshield clear for more than an instant at a time. The bouncing, the engine roar, the pervasive diesel odor and the mumbled prayers—and occasional retching—from the Celts became an encapsulated world of its own, one both Kane and Grant were desperate to leave.

As it was, Kane was just as glad to be in the crowded, stuffy wheelhouse rather than down below. He felt awkward being alone with Fand and could not meet her eye. She wore the bulky combat vest and leather leggings again, her staff angled over a shoulder.

Earlier she had asked Kane how his shoulder felt and he mumbled it felt fine—which was true. Except for an occasional twinge, the pain and stiffness had vanished.

Grant, if he suspected anything had gone on between them, had the good taste to keep his suspicions to himself. As close as the two men were, both always respected matters of a personal nature.

"There she is," McCrae suddenly announced.

Kane and Grant looked out the windows on both sides of the wheelhouse, but saw nothing but miles of uninterrupted, heaving gray. The sky was the same pewter color, but a bit lighter in shade, heralding the approach of dawn.

Then, as *Hornblower's Wraith* rose on a swell, they saw off to starboard a vague outline. Kane guessed it was about a mile away and wouldn't have been visible at all except for the bright lights forming an irregular, glowing silhouette.

Kane leaned over and shouted into the open hatch, "Harper, front and center. It's nearly time for your performance."

The young man shakily climbed up the ladder, squinting at Kane with his one good eye. His other was swollen shut, his face bruised and puffy from the beating he had received the day before.

"Do you know your lines?" Grant asked.

Harper nodded, and as if by rote stated matter-of-factly, "New London has fallen into the hands of the savages. We're all that is left of its defenders. Sir, if it please you, we humbly ask permission to come aboard and join our fellows."

Phin shook his head in disgust. "Try to put a bit more feeling into it, lad. If you don't convince your captain, either he'll have you killed or I will."

Harper swallowed and repeated his lines, this time emphasizing certain key words and adding a wheedling note of humility. To Kane's ears, he sounded just dumb enough to be convincing.

Grant nodded as if satisfied. "At my word, get out on deck. And remember, there'll be at least three blasters aimed at your back."

"I'll remember." Screwing up his face, Harper clapped a hand over his mouth. Fand led him quickly to a window and slid it open just as Harper poked his head through. He vomited copiously, either due to fear or seasickness, or a combination of both. When only dry-heave shudders wracked his frame, he straightened up, wiping his mouth. His head and shoulders were drenched by salt spray. At least, Kane hoped it was salt spray.

Grant peered through a set of binoculars, focusing past the droplets of water sliding across the foreport. "Can't see much," he said with a grunt after a few moments. "The light is still too lousy."

He handed the binoculars over to Kane, who squinted through the eyepieces. The rolling swells hid all but the ninety-foot-tall derrick tower. Bleakly, he said, "Quayle could have left already."

Fand replied softly, "Let us hope not. Morrigan took the sole copy of the map with the isle's location. Without it, we have only a general idea of where it is, and that provided by the selkies. Their descriptions were hardly precise."

When a high wave lifted the *Wraith,* Kane received his first clear view of Northstar 40. Huge, dark tiers were outlined against the sky, and skeletal frameworks stretched between gargantuan metal storage tanks. The complex looked unfinished, like the bare bones of a structure someone intended to build one day. With mercury-vapor lamps flooding the platform with unearthly light, it took on the aspect of a forbidding, alien city.

He shifted his gaze and made out the long black knife-blade shape between two of the platform's massive legs. "The *Cromwell* is still there," he announced.

Fand sighed with relief. "Then so are Quayle and Morrigan."

As the boat heaved closer to the gargantuan Northstar 40 platform, the sun finally began to rise above the horizon, so that the world seemed to be a restless gray line layered with fire. Clouds of scarlet and gold formed a halo around the sun's ascent.

By the time the sun had climbed a finger's breadth above the ocean, the structure loomed over them like a mountain made of steel, its summit made of crisscrossed struts of metal, not stone, but wreathed in mist nevertheless.

Still staring through the binoculars, Kane caught fleeting glimpses of red jackets and bereted heads appearing on the upper tiers, peering over the railings, then darting this way and that.

"We've been announced," he said flatly.

Grant clapped Harper on the shoulder. "You're on, Private."

By force of habit, the young man squared his shoulders and responded crisply, "Aye, aye, sir."

Fand fetched her helmet from a shelf beneath an instrument panel. Phin climbed down to the crew quarters, putting on his own helmet and sliding his shield over his arm.

The prow of the craft cleaved a white froth through the sea slowly but steadily. As they drew closer to the arrangement of concrete quays and jetties extending over the water, they saw how thundering waves crashed and broke on the gargantuan support legs of the platform, foaming spray flying in all directions. The *Wraith* chugged past the *Cromwell,* and Kane eyed the gun emplacements and its curiously faceted contours. He saw no one on deck, but lights glowed through the ports of the elevated bridge housing.

McCrae steered the ship on a course parallel to a vertical stone slab, following it into a small, straight-walled artificial inlet protected on three sides from the open ocean. He headed the *Wraith*'s stern straight for a concrete jetty, extending out between two of the enormous ballast tanks. Turning the wheel, he ran expertly alongside it, so close that the hull scraped the pilings. Then he reversed the engines, backing water into a smother of foam.

"Go," Kane said to Harper.

Tugging on the hem of his jacket, making sure his beret was canted at the proper angle, the young man left the cabin and climbed down the short flight of stairs to the deck. The disguised Celts followed him, standing in the shadows cast by the overhang of the superstructure. The dim light was now to their advantage, making it difficult for the dragoons on the drilling platform to discern individual features. Since Harper stood in plain view and was easily recognizable, all eyes focused on him.

Harper stumbled a bit on the pitching, slippery deck boards. He knotted a rope hawser around a rusty cleat embedded in the concrete quay. A group of dragoons, blasters at their hips, clustered on a metal-railed catwalk above the jetty.

Harper waved to them, and a soldier shouted in surprise, "For God's sake—it's the orderly! What are you doing down there, lad?"

"Come all the way to fetch the captain's tea?" another man called.

A ripple of laughter passed among the assembled men, and blaster barrels lowered. Watching from the wheelhouse window, Kane felt a loosening of his anxiety.

Harper tried to grin good-naturedly, but to Kane it looked more like a rictus of stress, as if he were only seconds from throwing up again. "Where's Captain Quayle? I must speak to him."

A harsh voice boomed, "I'm here, Private."

The line of red jackets parted, and a huge figure, towering a full head over most of the men, appeared at the rail. Kane felt his flesh crawl at his first sight of the white-skinned, scar-faced cyclops. Standing beside him, Fand murmured a few words in Gaelic. The only one he understood was "Balor."

"I never expected to see you again, Private Harper," Quayle said loudly. "I was under the distinct impression you felt transferring my command here was the act of a poltroon."

Harper swallowed hard and launched immediately into his rehearsed speech. "New London has fallen into the hands of the savages. We're all that is left of its defenders—"

Quayle interrupted, "They took the ministry compound?"

Harper faltered, stammering, "Aye, sir. Around noon yesterday."

Quayle only grunted, but it was apparent to both Grant and Kane that the man's suspicions had been aroused. After a second or two of hesitation, Harper resumed his speech. "Sir, if it pleases you, we humbly ask permission to come aboard and join our fellows."

Quayle inclined his head in a nod. "You grovel almost as nicely as you dissemble, Private. Those qualities might do you some good at your hearing for desertion. You and your fellow deserters may indeed come aboard the platform—but first leave your weapons on deck, in plain sight."

A disconcerted murmuring broke out among the disguised Celts. They shifted from side to side, glancing back uncertainly over their shoulders where Phin stood out of sight in the gangway. He transferred that uncertain, questioning glance up to Grant and Kane in the wheelhouse.

Grant hissed out a disgusted breath between his teeth. "Shit."

The plan was to place a fully armed contingent of warriors aboard Northstar 40, where hopefully the element of surprise would result in a quick and relatively bloodless victory. No one had expected Captain Quayle to be so canny, making a connection between the records of the oil platform in Strongbow's files and the tale of the ministry being occupied by the enemy. Harper's spiel to the contrary and the surprise appearance of men who had elected to remain behind didn't earn his trust, either.

"He is as cunning as his other incarnation," breathed Fand tensely.

Kane's mind raced with alternate ideas, weighing half a dozen options inside of seconds. Then, to everyone's astonishment, Harper took the initiative. Marching across the deck, he gestured imperiously to the men grouped beneath the overhang. "Right, men. Do as the captain says."

He strode purposefully to the side, climbed over it and made his stiff-legged way up the slanting jetty.

"What's that little bastard doing?" Grant demanded in a growl.

Breaking into a sprint, Harper shouted at the top of his lungs, "Captain, it's a trap! They're Celts! It's a trap—"

A single shot cracked, like the snapping of a whip. Harper's beret floated away, surrounded by a mist of blood. Twisting in clumsy pirouette, he slammed down on the ramp and slid back toward the *Wraith,* leaving a wet trail of blood in his wake.

Quayle lowered his Beretta and bellowed, "Open fire!"

# Chapter 24

At least ten blaster bores lipped flame and thunder more or less simultaneously. Bullets poured down like hail, peeling up long splinters from the deck planking. Miniature waterspouts sprayed up just behind the *Wraith*'s stern, and sparks jumped from the metal-braced hull.

The Celts crowded back, shouting and swearing. The men in front whipped up their own MP-5s and returned the fire with hastily aimed bursts. A pair of dragoons swung their blasters toward the wheelhouse, and everyone dropped flat. Glass smashed in the pilot housing, sheet metal crumpled, boarding ripped away in long strips. Fand cried out in anger and fear as she lay beneath the stream of slugs.

McCrae cried out, too, doubling up, folding around a belly wound. He writhed and gasped, ''God save Ireland.''

''God save us, more like it,'' snarled Grant in frustration from his prone position on the deck.

In the crew compartment below, they heard Phin shouting over the jackhammering fusillade, ''Ah, well, back to the fuckin' war!''

Squirming around, brushing glass shards from his path, Grant kicked himself forward and slithered over the lip of the open hatch to the crew quarters.

The return fire from the Celts whiplashed up and

knocked a constellation of sparks from the railing behind which the dragoons hunkered. Phin pushed his way through his men. "Cover me, you walleyed bastards!"

Crouching behind his shield, Phin raced across the deck toward the machine-gun emplacement. Splinters of wood exploded at his heels as the dragoons tracked him with their MP-5s. Two bullets struck the brass disk on his arm, and the impact sent him staggering sideways. He slipped on the wet planking, but managed to turn his fall into a belly slide.

He stopped himself by grabbing the machine gun's support stanchion and, still crouching behind his shield, pulled himself up, leaning into the rifle stock. Slapping down the safety lever, he clutched the handle and depressed the trigger.

The tripod-mounted M-60 spit flickering spear points of flame. The gun trembled on its fastenings. Steel-jacketed bullets sped up and across the *Wraith*'s deck and the jetty as the cartridge belt writhed like the coilings of a gleaming serpent. The dragoons concentrated their field of fire on Phin. The bone-rattling chatter of the autoblasters joined the staccato hammering of the M-60.

Grant emerged from below, throwing a three-foot-long hollow tube ahead of him. It was a Miniman recoilless gun, a cross between a rocket launcher and a bazooka. The one-shot disposable weapon fired HESH—High Explosive Squash Head—rounds.

Kane pulled it toward him as Grant heaved himself up and out of the hatchway. He duck-walked to a bullet-shattered window, lifted his head to see over the frame and said, "Clear shot."

Kane toed the Miniman over to him, and Grant

lifted the lightweight fiberglass-and-plastic cylinder to his right shoulder. He jacked back the priming bolt and raised the sights.

Peering out of the window, Kane took a swift survey of the dragoons positioned on the catwalk. Even as he did, one pitched over the side, his torso stitched with a line of slugs fired from the M-60. The others were completely occupied with avoiding the 7.62 mm rounds ricocheting all around them.

"Clear," he announced.

Grant rose to his knees, inserted the mouth of the Miniman through the window and squeezed the wire trigger lever. "Watch your eyes. Fire in the hole."

Flame and smoke spewed from the hollow bore of the missile launcher. Propelled by a wavering ribbon of vapor and sparks, the HESH round leaped from the tube, accompanied by a ripping roar. Kane crouched over Fand, his head sunk between his shoulders as the backblast gouted a column of searing heat from the rear of the Miniman. It was so intense he felt it through his coat.

The projectile impacted on the ballast tanks' galvanized-metal hide exactly in the center. The HESH round vanished in an eruption of billowing orange-yellow flame and an eardrum-knocking concussion. The detonation drove razor-edged fragments of steel through the tanks.

From a gaping cavity cascaded a torrent of water, a high-pressure arc that resembled a horizontal waterfall. With a hissing rumble, the column of water curved up and smashed down upon the catwalk. The dragoons disappeared beneath the deluge. A second later, one of them reappeared, washed over the railing. He toppled straight down and struck the concrete quay, spread-eagled on his face.

As the pressure lessened and the foaming rooster tail drooped, Phin roared to his men, "Get aboard! Get aboard, damn you!"

Voicing cries of *"Erin go bragh,"* the Celtic assault force scrambled over the side of the boat and charged up the jetty. Kane noticed that one man carried a great battle-ax, like some beserker from the days of Cuchulainn. He figured he had borrowed it from Strongbow's military museum beneath the ministry compound.

Muzzle-flashes still stabbed down from the upper tiers of Northstar 40, but all of the Celts scrambled safely up the slanting slab of concrete. Grant, Kane and Fand made their way from the wheelhouse to the bullet-splintered deck. Phin sagged behind the machine gun, crimson gleaming dully on his upper right chest. Blood crawled between his fingers.

"I'm all right," he grated. "Just help me aboard so I can control my men. They'll be runnin' amok like blue-arsed baboons with no one to lead them."

He coughed, and pink foam frothed his lips. Fand said, "You've been hit in a lung. You're not going anywhere."

She slung one of Phin's arms over her slender shoulders, easily supporting his weight. To Kane and Grant, she said, "Quayle will make for the *Cromwell.* Once I attend to Phin, I'll make for that, see if I can disable it."

Both men nodded. Grant said, "The whole platform will be out of true once that ballast tank drains...and refills."

"Especially," Kane said with a cold smile, "if we decide to puncture a couple more."

Sin Eaters springing into their hands, Kane and Grant turned, raced across the deck and vaulted over the side of *Hornblower's Wraith*. They leaped over the crumpled bodies on the jetty and sprinted to the top of the ramp, inhaling the raw, brine-laden sea air.

"Good idea to blow the tank," Grant said, fitting the finger of his left hand into the trigger guard of the Copperhead.

"Thanks. Let's hope it does us some good."

As they entered the artificial canyon of steel girders and crisscrossed arches, the rattle of autofire and wild shouts reached them. More blasters blazed from above, and Kane tried to gauge how many dragoons were defending the platform's ramparts and how well armed they might be.

The air shivered with a crumping detonation, followed by a brief cessation of shots and agonized screams.

"Phin's people don't have grens," Grant said grimly, face locked in a tense teak mask.

Suddenly, the steel grating underfoot shivered with a prolonged vibration and tilted several degrees to the left, sending both men staggering against a pylon. Clattering creaks and groans of overstressed metal surrounded them.

"The ruptured tank has filled," Kane said. "I don't think this thing will capsize, but if we blow another one—"

Grant peered around, patted his remaining high-ex gren clipped to the combat harness beneath his coat. "I'll take care of that. You try to find Quayle."

Kane lifted his right index finger to his nose and snapped it away in the wry "one percent" salute. It was a gesture he and Grant had developed during their

Mag days and was reserved for undertakings with small chances of success.

Grant returned the salute gravely and moved away, sidling among a forest of I beams and struts. Kane followed the crash of gunfire, trotting along a narrow, curving promenade made of welded steel plates. When a man in a red jacket and beret stumbled around a bend, his Sin Eater snapped up, finger touching the trigger stud. Then he recognized one of Phin's warriors, a man named Ciernan.

Kane swore explosively. "Goddammit, you men better take off those imperial colors or you'll be chilling each other!"

Ciernan nodded glumly, cradling an apparently broken left wrist. "Thought about it. Decided not to. Confuses the snakes, it does. At least long enough for us to get the drop on 'em."

"What's going on?"

"Tryin' to find an unguarded way to the upper levels. Don't want any more bloody grenades dropped on us." His eyes narrowed at a sudden notion, and he craned his neck, peering beyond Kane. "Where's Phin and our lady?"

"Fand's taking care of him. He's hurt. My partner plans to blow another ballast tank, so keep alert. This thing may start to sink or tip over."

Ciernan nodded again and moved on.

Kane walked carefully along the promenade, alert for the appearance of any more Celts disguised as dragoons or the genuine article. The blasterfire tapered off to a distant, sporadic crackle. As he turned another bend, he saw, recessed into a shadowy cupola, a heavy wooden door reinforced with thick strips of iron. He tested the handle, then hit the door with his right shoulder. He grunted in pain and annoyance at his own stupidity, then backed away.

Plucking a high-ex gren from his harness, he pinched away the pin and rolled it against the bottom of the door, then whirled away. The detonation echoed like a thunderclap magnified a hundredfold. The door simply vanished in a blooming fireball of orange and white.

One instant there had been a wooden door braced with iron, and in the next there were empty hinges and charred splinters of wood. When the smoke subsided enough for him to see, Kane stepped cautiously through the doorway, leading with his Copperhead, the laser autotargeter casting a bright red kill-dot on the thinning planes of vapor. He saw nothing but a stairwell stretching upward.

Kane crept up the steps, the Copperhead in his left hand, the Sin Eater gripped in his right. His boots grated on the corrugated metal risers. The stairwell led to another tier. All around he saw giant pipes, huge fittings and girders. From beyond a pile of rust-streaked machine parts, he heard noises of activity— hurried footfalls, whispering voices, and the steady squeak-creak of wheels.

In a crouch, he glided toward the sounds. At least eight dragoons moved stealthily along the edge of the companionway, peering over the guardrail. Two men pushed a heavy L-37-AI machine gun mounted on a wheeled frame. Although the frame was poorly lubricated, the AI was a devastating weapon and could cut all the Celts to fish bait inside of ten seconds.

When the contingent of dragoons passed Kane's position and their backs were to him, he pulled his second and last concussion gren, tweaked out the pin and lobbed it underhanded toward the troopers. It struck the steel grating and bounced. Kane shielded his face, and they turned in the direction of the sound. The gren detonated with an eardrum-piercing bang. The eruption of white light turned the gray morning into triple high noon.

Kane poked up his head and saw two of the dragoons whimpering, writhing on the deck plates, hands over their eyes. With their mutagenically altered optic nerves, they were particularly sensitive to high light levels.

The others were stunned and dazzled, and stumbled and staggered about half-deaf and half-blind. Kane didn't hesitate. He charged forward, the Copperhead's killdot centering on the nearest chest. The silenced subgun whispered, and six rounds took the man in the torso, punching dark periods from groin to throat.

The man lurched backward, not knowing what hit him, wild with pain, dazed from the shock of the multiple impacts, tendrils of blood squirting from his chest. He howled and red-uniformed figures went in all directions. Only four stood their ground, leveling their weapons. Kane dropped into a crouch just in time to avoid a bullet that whistled over his head. He fired again, and saw one of the dragoons fall over the guardrail and plunge out of sight. Another burst from the Copperhead at close range chopped a soldier's head to pieces.

A shot from the Sin Eater took a man in the head, lifting the top of a dark blond scalp and flinging it and a beret twirling in the air. A second 280-grain blockbuster punched a dragoon in the side of the neck, sending him cartwheeling down the catwalk, leaving a red spray in his wake, like a liquid banner.

A dragoon frantically tried to swivel the barrel of the heavy machine gun toward him. Kane sprinted forward and launched himself over it. He collided with the soldier, and both of them went down, but Kane's knee was in the man's gut.

Due to his enhanced physique, the man beneath Kane was strong, perhaps even stronger than Grant, but his reflexes were hampered by fogged vision and impaired hearing. He closed one hand around the long barrel of the Copperhead and struggled to yank it away. His other hand closed on the Sin Eater.

For a very long moment, they were motionless, locked in straining combat, sweat breaking out on Kane's forehead, breath coming in harsh gasps from beneath the dragoon's lips.

The man jacked a knee up into Kane's left kidney, who ignored the pain and rammed his head downward, hearing and feeling the cartilage of the soldier's nose collapse beneath his forehead. Snarling, blowing a crimson spray, the man arched his back and bucked Kane off.

Kane threw himself backward, using the man's strength against him. But the dragoon didn't release his tenacious grip on the gun barrels. Planting a foot against the man's sternum, Kane levered him up and over. He had time for one high-pitched cry before he plunged over the guardrail and out of sight.

Kane pushed himself to his feet. Then he saw the naked woman.

# Chapter 25

Grant wended his way among the pylons and climbed over struts and cross braces. The damp sea air pulsed with the roar of heavy and continuous gunfire.

Sidling up to a girder, he hazarded a quick look around it. Three dragoons were directing subgun and pistol fire at two Celts crouched behind a stack of pipes. The bullet-riddled bodies of two other Celts lay in their own blood on the deck, scarlet spilling through the openings in the grate to the ocean below.

Grant announced his participation in the firefight with a prolonged burst from the Copperhead. The first three bullets hit a dragoon broadside, punching a deep, ugly cavity in his right rib cage. The other rounds spun the second man around like a top, blood spurting from mortal wounds in his head and upper back. He didn't fall. Instead, he swung his body and MP-5 toward Grant, snarling in silent rage. An autorifle burst from one of the Celts opened his skull in a spray of crimson.

Grant waved his Sin Eater in acknowledgment of the help and went on his way. Phin's men, howling like demons when they stormed Northstar 40, had achieved a measure of surprise, but they were now faced by a spirited and disciplined crew who fiercely defended the last bastion of the Imperium Britannia.

Grant continued to wriggle and climb through the jumble of rusty, corroded metal. He found his path to the portside ballast tank blocked by a gutter brawl of close-quarters slaughter. A churning mass of red-jacketed men fought, screamed and thrashed above the open area directly beneath the intersection of two companionways.

Because they were locked in hand-to-hand combat and all dressed identically, Grant couldn't tell the difference between Celt and dragoon or exactly how many men snarled and tore at each other. They were packed too closely together for firearms to be effective, so the participants used them as clubs. He saw the head of a broad-bladed ax, already stained with blood, rising and falling above the press of bodies.

Grant watched from the shelter of two I beams, appalled by the savagery. On land, either of the attackers would have retreated, but here there was no ground to give, so the wounded were trampled underfoot. He saw a man who had participated in the skirmish at the ministry compound spasming on the deck, his hands fluttering around the handle of a knife embedded in his groin. Over the hoarse yells and screams, he heard him calling for his mother.

Shuddering, Grant decided not to involve himself in the fray. He circled around the heaving mass of combatants, climbing along struts, swinging himself by using crossbars as stationary trapezes. From another area of Northstar 40, he heard the dull thump of an explosion and knew it was a high-ex gren.

After a minute of muscle-straining effort and clumsy gymnastics, Grant dropped down beside the pressure valve of the ballast tank. A dead dragoon lay beneath it, one hand crooked stiffly around the wheel. A long, horizontal gash bisected his lower back, completely severing the spine. The wound looked as if it had been made by an ax.

Grant figured that when the ruptured ballast tank threw Northstar 40 out of true, a group of dragoons had been dispatched to protect or equalize the balance in the other tanks. The dead man had crawled from the hand-to-hand battle and expired right as he reached the valve. Grant couldn't help but feel a twinge of admiration for the dragoons and a touch of compassion for this particular one. Mutated they might be, but they still knew how to fight and die like men.

The floor grille was suddenly shaken by a sharp concussion. Loose bits of metal fell clanging from overhead. He felt the air shiver from the shock wave. From the sound and feel of the explosion, Grant guessed Kane had used his last Alsatex gren.

As he removed the high-ex grenade from his harness, the crackle of renewed blasterfire reached him, but it didn't sound close. Jamming the gren into an elbow joint at the point where the feed pipe fitted into the tank itself, he set himself, tweaked away the pin and began a long-legged lope for the nearest cover, behind a pylon.

He was still loping when the grenade detonated with a hot flash, a ballooning fireball and a brutal wave of hot compressed air. Chunks of steel rang like wind chimes as they bounced against the pylon. The shock wave slammed into Grant and bowled him off his feet. He went with the kinetic force, throwing himself forward, catching himself on his hands and going into a somersault.

He fetched up hard against the support post and lay there at its base for a few moments. At a screeching, hissing rumble, he turned around just as a geyser of

seawater fountained up and out of the torn wall of the
ballast tank. The roaring torrent thundered at least
thirty feet in the air, drenching everything in the vicinity.

A few seconds later, the whole of Northstar 40 quivered violently. Rust sifted down from the overhead
catwalks. The deck lurched beneath him, rolling him
sideways. With a nerve-stinging groan, the oil platform listed to starboard. From beyond his range of
vision came the sound of glass shattering and the thudding of heavy objects toppling over.

Faintly, he heard a voice bellowing, "Pumps! Get
to the pumps!"

Grant recognized the voice as that of Quayle. He
also recognized the tremor of panic in it.

KANE RECOGNIZED the steel-gray hair and blank, blue-
white eyes of Morrigan instantly. His eyes took in her
pale, compact body and the purple patches marring it,
the angry red welts on her throat, her swollen lips and
bruised cheek.

She made her tottering way along the companionway, the red-stained knife in one hand tapping along
the guardrail, the other groping over a network of
pipes. From directly below, gunfire crashed. Several
bullets flattened themselves on the pipes right above
Morrigan's head. She seemed serenely oblivious to
them.

Kane bounded forward, catching her and falling
with her to the grille just as a stream of autofire burned
the air where she had been walking. The woman beneath him stared sightlessly upward, whipping up the
point of the knife, pressing it against the underside of
his chin. Then she smiled and touched his face, feeling

its contours. She tossed away the dagger. "Kane," she murmured.

Before he could respond, he heard the detonation of a high-ex gren. Another volley of shots stuttered from below, bullets whipsawing the air overhead, ricocheting away from steel with keening whines. Kane covered Morrigan with his body, shielding her with his coat. He felt a round tug at the tail.

When the blasterfire ceased, Kane began to help the woman to her feet. A racking shudder made the companionway flooring jump violently, and they both fell again. Northstar 40 squeaked, screeched and heeled over to starboard.

Her face only an inch away, Morrigan said between clenched teeth, "You must stop Quayle. You must rectify my madness."

"That's the general idea," he said gruffly, pushing himself to a crouch. He heard Quayle's voice roaring, "Pumps! Get to the pumps!"

"You mustn't let him escape," Morrigan said, voice tight with repressing a groan of pain.

"He has other problems right now...like putting what's left of his crew to work to keep this thing from sinking."

Helping her to her feet, he saw how her bare flesh was goose-pimpled from the raw wind. He shucked out of his coat, draping it over her like a cloak. She wasn't much taller than Domi, so the hem dragged on the floor grates. Gently, he fingered the red welts encircling her neck. "Did Quayle do this to you?"

Morrigan shook her head, tresses flying as if the question was annoyingly irrelevant. "The coordinates of Lyonesse are programmed into the *Cromwell*'s navigational computers. He doesn't need a crew to get there.''

"If we're lucky, Fand will have already disabled the ship.''

A line of consternation furrowed Morrigan's smooth forehead. "Fand? She is with you? I wouldn't have thought—''

The companionway tilted again, and both people nearly pitched over the rail. The wheeled machine gun rolled across the deck, the long barrel jamming between the crossbars. Kane tried to kick it free, but it was stuck fast. With an arm around her, he led her along the companionway.

The autofire from below resumed, and Kane hazarded a look over.

At least five dragoons were blazing away with MP-5s into the throat of a passageway. Kane couldn't see their target, but it didn't matter. They fought a retreating action, and they were almost directly below his position, their backs to him. Kane unslung the Copperhead, making sure his body was shielded by the guardrail, then depressed the trigger. He didn't have to aim. Every man below was a target.

Over the rattling roar and the clink of ejected cartridges, Kane heard cries of shock, pain and anger. Return fire raked upward, the short, hastily aimed fusillade of shots pockmarking the pipes, showering him with metal fragments. The dragoons turned and ran, out of Kane's field of vision and fire. They left two of their number leaking crimson on the floor plates. An instant later, a horde of howling Celts appeared, racing in pursuit.

Kane turned back to Morrigan. She seemed completely unperturbed by the crash of blasters and din of battle. In little panting gasps, she spoke quickly as if she were seeking to unburden herself. Kane only half listened as he led her toward a stairwell that pitched downward. He suspected she would have said the same thing to the first person she encountered.

"I thought it was a grand plan, a little daft perhaps, but to use the Imperium's fixation on power against them was so tempting—"

A dragoon appeared at the head of the stairs, stared at them and loosed a strafing burst toward them. Kane managed to slap himself and Morrigan against the wall, avoiding the swarm of lead. The slugs swept high, and by the time the man had his aim adjusted, blood was squirting from his chest where the last shot in the Copperhead's magazine hit him. The dragoon hurtled backward, his arms flailing, falling headfirst back down the steps.

Kane ejected the spent clip from the Copperhead, slamming in a fresh one detached from his combat harness. He cycled in a round and moved carefully forward again, Morrigan clinging to his arm.

She continued speaking as if she hadn't been interrupted by a near brush with death. "I underestimated Quayle, you see. I thought he was nothing but a jumped-up enlisted man with delusions of grandeur. He's as evil as Strongbow was. Worse. At least Strongbow never—"

Her words trailed off and her lower lip trembled, her eyes blinking repeatedly to hold back tears. In an aspirated whisper, she said, "The things he did to me. The things he made me do—me, a sister in the holy order of Awen. I was with him when the assault began. While his back was turned, I managed to stab him, but the wound wasn't mortal."

"He'll pay," Kane bit out. His tone carried a note of deadly conviction.

"'Twas my own arrogance that brought me to this pass. I believed I could trick Quayle into bringing a boatload of the orichalcum, the firestones, to Britain. I would give him false instructions on how to tap into their power. England and the Imperium would be laid waste within the blink of an eye."

"And so would a lot of your own people."

Morrigan nodded, a jerky spasm of her head. "I intended to send a secret signal to the Priory monastery that the *Cromwell* was returning to England, and they in turn would relay that information to our forces, telling them to pull out."

"What about your Scots allies?"

"In every war, particularly those for survival, sacrifices must be made."

Kane began to angrily tell her she had sacrificed her own dignity and honor, but as they began descending the stairs, his voice was drowned out by the jubilant shout of *"Erin go bragh!"* from many throats.

He peered through the banister railing and saw the victorious Celts disarming a group of dragoons. There were few unbloodied in either party. Kane led Morrigan around the heart-shot dragoon, lying facedown half on and half off the stairs. The tails of his coat dragged in the widening pool of blood.

He left her standing against the foot of the stairs and went to join the Irish. One dragoon wept bitterly, not because he was wounded but because of the shame of losing the fight and, in the process, the entire war.

Grant appeared on the far side of the group, coat beaded with moisture, and he snapped off the one-percent salute when he caught sight of Kane. The whoops of victory turned into cries of alarm as Northstar 40 gave another creaking jolt to starboard. A collection of bound-together pipes snapped cleanly away from their moorings and crashed down, rolling across the canted deck.

Everyone stumbled, Irish and Briton clasping each other to keep from falling. "Back to the ship!" a Celt yelled. He pushed the sobbing, wounded dragoon ahead of him, "You, too, weepy!"

"The *Cromwell* is closer," a dragoon protested.

Above the squealing of tortured metal, came the sound of big engines throbbing to life, the whine of turbines hitting a high-pitched note. Without hesitation, Kane bounded in the direction of the noise, gesturing first to Grant, then to Morrigan. "Take care of her," he shouted. "And my damn coat!"

If anyone was puzzled by Kane's exhortation to care for his coat, Grant wasn't. On the last trip to this area of the world, Kane had lost his Mag-issue coat and only recently found a replacement.

Kane ran, acutely aware of the great groaning shudders racking the forest of girders all around him, and jouncing the deck beneath his sprinting feet. Twice he was forced to take detours to avoid large pieces of machinery that slid down the tilted deck toward him. Dark water bubbled up through splits in the flooring, and by the time he glimpsed the *Cromwell*, he was sloshing ankle deep through the North Sea.

The black ship edged out into the open ocean. The concrete wharf was riven through with cracks, reinforcing bars poking up like gnarled fingers. Half of the ramp was already submerged.

As he ran down it, he saw a length of heavy rope trailing from a cleat at the *Cromwell*'s aft port side.

Measuring the distance, he slid his Sin Eater back into its holster, cast aside his Copperhead and hurled himself forward in a flat dive.

Although Kane knew the water would be cold, its icy temperature nearly made him cry out in shock. He stroked furiously through the boiling wake, hearing over his splashing progress the whine of turbines throttling up. He increased the speed of his arms, clawing water aside. His flailing left hand secured a grip on the end of the rope. Absently, he noticed it had been sliced cleanly through by a very sharp blade. He managed to close his other hand around it just as the *Cromwell* gave a great leaping surge, engines roaring.

Dragged along in the frothing backwash, Kane kept his mouth tightly closed to keep saltwater from filling it. As it was, the sea forced itself into his nostrils and he had to keep snorting his sinus passages clear in order to breathe.

He was rolled and tumbled by the turbulence, but he climbed hand over hand up the rope. His right shoulder socket burned with a bone-deep, gnawing pain.

Inch by agonizing inch, he hauled himself up and slapped one hand on the cleat. With a muscle-wrenching effort, Kane chinned himself up and twisted his body over the side and onto the deck.

Gasping, he raised himself to all fours, clothes heavy and sodden, his right arm once more feeling dead. Blinking against the stinging brine, raking his wet hair away from his face, he began to lever himself upright.

Then, over the engine throb and turbine whine, he heard Fand's shrill scream of pure terror. "Ka'in—!"

Adrenaline jolted through him, and he frantically palmed saltwater away from his eyes, regaining his vision just as the one-eyed giant slashed at him with a mirror-bright blade.

# Chapter 26

A bitter fire burned in Aubrey Quayle's brain, an extension of the hot wire that ran through his left hip. He panted as he ran, dodging among the trembling pipes, the shivering support pylons, the quaking girders. He had failed to maintain the Imperium. Worse, he'd been betrayed, sold out by that vicious vixen of an Irish slut—damn her delightful mouth—and then by one of his own kind, the hapless Harper. The pain of the stab wound inflicted by Morrigan was nothing compared to that scorching his soul. The cut in his hip was superficial, puncturing only a roll of flab, but it felt as if it went straight to his heart.

He made his way toward the concrete jetty, to the *Cromwell*'s berth, ducking his head against the bullets slicing the air overhead. The cutlass of Lord Nelson gleamed unscabbarded in his huge fist.

A few despairing dragoons still fought on behind him, but they had ignored his commands to man the pumps and save Northstar 40, so they had earned whatever fate befell them, either at the hands of the Celts or in the merciless bosom of the sea.

An Irish warrior, blasphemously decked out in the colors of the Imperium, lunged out of a wedge of shadow between two girders, swinging a broad-bladed ax. "Balor, you fat bastard!"

There wasn't room to swing the cutlass in a decapitating stroke, so Quayle stabbed it forward in a short, hard thrust. It sank deep into the man's midsection, and he rocked to a halt, eyes going wide. Quayle gave the long blade a twist, shearing through flesh, muscle and entrails, then whipped it loose. Blood drenched the handle of the cutlass, followed by an explosion of blue-and-red-sheened intestines.

The man fell to his knees, trying to raise his ax above his head to chop at Quayle's lower body. Quayle hammered down on the head of the weapon with the cutlass hilt, then drove the point through the Celt's eye and into his brain.

As the body fell forward, Quayle spit contemptuously, "A bloody ax! Who do you think you are, Brian fucking Boru?"

Wiping the blade clean on a sleeve, he continued on his way, clenching his teeth at the exultant shout from deep within the platform: *"Erin go bragh!"*

Quayle's hand tightened on the slippery cutlass handle, but he didn't look back. He had tried to rally a concerted resistance, but the Celts swarmed all over Northstar 40, scattering hither and yon like rats. They skulked and spied from bolt-holes, then sprang to the attack. His own men spread out in futile pursuit and offered easy targets.

The *Cromwell* heaved into view, and behind the window of the bridge housing, he glimpsed the shadowy outline of Dodd, his navigator. Only he and Morrigan knew he planned to set sail for Lyonesse that very morning. He had intended to take only a skeleton force of dragoons with him, but now he would have to settle for just beaky-nosed Dodd.

Quayle lumbered across the gangway from the berthing dock to the deck of the *Cromwell*, feeling it sag beneath his weight. From behind him, clashing, groaning shudders shook Northstar 40, causing the gangway to sway dangerously. Before it tipped over, he stepped down over the side and, rather than cast the mooring line loose, he slashed it in two with the cutlass. Swiftly, he moved along the deck and sliced through the other rope, then turned toward the staircase leading to the elevated bridge.

Quayle had envisioned himself moving regiments, ordering battalions and divisions, inspiring a fanatical devotion in all who served under his command. He wasn't quite ready to give up that vision. The Imperium was lost, but there was always an opportunity to build another one. He had the will to make that dream come true. There would be temporary setbacks, but in his mind his destiny was certain. He would extend a new empire beyond that of Strongbow's ambitions, to rule all of Europe and even the Mediterranean basin.

Quayle climbed the ladder one-handed, grunting in exertion, a little annoyed by how much effort it required. Opening the door, ducking his head, he announced sharply, "Power us up, Mr. Dodd—"

The remainder of his order clogged in his throat. It wasn't Dodd who whirled away from the control console but a tall, slender figure dressed outlandishly in brass helmet, combat vest and leather leggings.

Even with only one eye, Quayle discerned the female figure swelling beneath the unflattering ensemble, not to mention the smooth complexion and full lips. He also saw the long wooden staff topped by an egg-shaped knob leaning against the plot board. His eye flicked down its length and rested on Dodd, curled in a fetal position on the deck. A discolored welt showed on the side of his head.

In a clear, exceptionally strong tone, the woman declared, "I'm called Sister Fand. Your man here refused to follow my instructions." Dodd groaned, eyelids fluttering. "He's not dead," the woman added unnecessarily.

Quayle didn't waste any breath on demands. He lunged across the bridge room, like a flesh-and-blood typhoon, swinging the cutlass in a fast, flat arc. As fast as he was, Sister Fand moved with an eye-blurring, fluid grace, snatching up the staff and parrying the blade with the ovoid knob.

He wasn't sure from what material the egg-shape was fashioned, but the impact sounded like steel striking flint. The thought of nicking the four-hundred-year-old blade filled him with anger. Rather than take another chance with it, he dropped the cutlass to the deck and closed in on the helmeted woman, grabbing the staff and wresting it from her grasp.

At least, that was what he tried to do. To his astonishment, Quayle couldn't pull it from her hands. Muscles rippled up and down her slender bare arms, and Sister Fand's grip did not break.

Snarling wordlessly, Quayle pivoted at the waist, yanking the woman bodily off the floor. He released the staff and, carried by momentum, she slammed against the far bulkhead.

Without sparing her another glance, Quayle's big hands slapped at the controls, thumbing the ignition button, activating the turbines and keying on the main engines. He nudged up the throttle lever, and Sister Fand struck him on the back of the head with her knob-tipped staff, knocking off his beret. She barked, *"D'anam don diabhal!"*

Quayle spun around, not knowing what she said, but

he guessed it had something to do with the devil. He swung a keglike fist at her head, but she ducked and his knuckles banged painfully on the crest of her helmet, knocking it askew. Reflexively, she tried to adjust it and Quayle's massive hands closed around her throat. Savagely, he jerked her erect, holding her so her toes barely scrabbled on the floor plates.

Gagging, Sister Fand pried at his fingers with a startling strength. Accustomed to manhandling Morrigan like a child, he was dismayed by this woman's strength, which was little short of superhuman.

He bore down, tightening his stranglehold before she could pry loose any of his fingers and possibly break them. "Who are you, bitch?"

Hoarsely, she half gasped, "I am one with the hills, the winds and the gray seas of Erin. I am the spirit of the same land that has sent your empire into defeat!"

Enraged, Quayle shook her violently, as if she were a rag doll. The woman's helmet wobbled loosely on her head and fell to the deck with a dull bong. He stared at her. She was lovely, one of the most beautiful women he had ever seen, but her inhumanly huge eyes sent a chill stabbing through his heart—they reminded him of Strongbow's. He spit in her face.

Sister Fand's lips curled and she spit back, scoring a direct hit in his good eye. The fleeting notion of keeping the woman alive long enough to bugger her to death vanished in an inferno of homicidal fury. Teeth bared, Quayle dug both thumbs into her windpipe. She clawed for his face, but a sudden forward shift in the motion of the *Cromwell* sent them stumbling the length of the cabin.

Quayle cast a swift glance over his shoulder and saw Dodd upright, apparently groggy but able to handle the controls. "Good man!" he said. "Full speed ahead!"

"Aye, sir." Dodd pushed up the throttle lever, and the ship lunged into the open sea like a killer whale in pursuit of prey.

Quayle lowered Sister Fand to the floor. Her head lolled loosely on her neck, and her tongue protruded from her mouth. Her eyes, veiled by heavy lids, bore a glassy sheen. He wrestled her limp weight to the door, fumbling to turn the latch. He managed to get the door open. "Mr. Dodd, my sword, if you would be so kind."

Dodd stooped and picked up the cutlass as Quayle put his back to the doorway. He removed his right hand from the woman's throat. Dodd tossed the cutlass and he caught it smoothly by the handle. No sooner had his hand fitted into the basket guard than Sister Fand threw her full weight against his chest, back-heeling him with a foot in the same motion.

Caught off balance, Quayle toppled unceremoniously out the door and past the ladder, and landed on his back with a meaty thud. The back of his skull cracked sharply against the desk.

Air exploded from between his thick lips, and multicolored pinwheels spiraled before his eyes. Half-expecting Sister Fand to jump straight down onto his groin, Quayle elbowed himself to his left side, then used the rungs of the ladder to achieve a crouching posture. He dragged air into his laboring lungs, swung his head up, and saw the woman standing in the doorway with a stricken expression on her face.

She wasn't looking at him. Quayle followed her gaze and saw a soaking-wet, dark-haired man on his hands and knees port side aft. Rising to his feet,

Quayle ran toward him in a ponderous rush, cutlass held high for a decapitating stroke. He heard Sister Fand's shrill cry of pure terror. "Ka'in—!"

KANE HURLED HIS BODY into a sideways roll as the bright blade sliced down, chiming loudly against the black deck plates, a little burst of sparks flaring at the point of impact.

He rolled into a crouch and flexed the tendons in his right wrist—or tried to flex them. His arm was completely numb from the shoulder to the tips of his fingers.

Quayle hacked at him again, and Kane dodged the cutlass's razor-keen length by a fractional margin. After a half second of fumbling, he whipped his fourteen-inch, tungsten-steel, titanium-jacketed combat knife out of its scabbard.

The long sword in Quayle's hand swept toward him in a whistling backstroke. Kane parried, and the recoil of the meeting blades nearly sent him falling over the side.

Quayle lunged while the echo of the first clangorous strike still hung in the air. Kane leaned away from the polished blade, and the tip opened a rent in his shirt, only warming the flesh beneath.

Kane stepped back carefully, seeing Fand climbing down the ladder from the bridge housing but not interfering. She knew if she distracted Kane, Quayle could swiftly plunge his cutlass into his heart. As it was, both men's movements were cautious due to the rocking of the *Cromwell*.

Kane felt awkward holding his knife in his left hand, and though he wasn't ambidextrous, he was a veteran of dozens of vicious close-quarters melees. He constantly shifted position, sidestepped and circled in order to stay on Quayle's right side, his blind side. He noted the spreading bloodstain on the man's left hip.

He watched Quayle's one good eye. The man was immensely strong and far faster than a man of his bulk should have been. He let his weight soak up the attacks. The tip of the cutlass teased the combat knife, nudging it playfully to one side in preparation for a lunge.

Quayle said gutturally, "The point always beats the edge, sir."

He feinted with the sword, then lunged with it. Kane parried, steel clashing loudly against steel, twisted his knife over so the hilts of both weapons scraped and he lunged himself.

Quayle parried the lunge, point downward, and then turned his sword with such speed the tip missed Kane's throat by less than a quarter of an inch. The cutlass darted forward like the tongue of a steel snake, and Kane blocked it with a side sweep. Again the blades met, edge to edge, and the shock jarred Kane's arm, shook his body. He whipped his combat knife toward Quayle's good eye, and the man weaved to the left. He saw Quayle's face screw up at the pain in his hip as he was forced to balance all of his ponderous weight on his left leg.

The pain only made him angry. Quayle counterattacked with blinding speed, his cutlass crashing against the knife like a hammer against an anvil. Kane staggered, nearly driven completely around by the force of the strike. His misstep rescued him from a scything, skull-splitting back swing from the cutlass. Kane bounded to the side, and a vicious follow-up thrust of the cutlass missed his midsection by a finger's width, though he felt it slide against his upper right leg.

Kane didn't even realize he had been stabbed until he felt the sudden wet warmth flowing down his leg and saw bright blood bubbling out of the cut in the fabric. A bone-deep, boring pain spread over his upper thigh where the steel had sliced through flesh and muscle.

His leg buckled for just a fraction of an instant. That sliver of a second was all Quayle needed to press his attack. His cutlass hammered on the knife blade, twisted it with a scraping slither and tore it from Kane's hand.

Quayle lunged, aiming not for his heart but for his groin and the femoral artery. An accomplished duelist the man might be, but he was also an experienced down-and-dirty back-alley fighter.

Kane avoided being skewered only by a back-wrenching twisting leap, part broad jump, part cart-wheel. Falling heavily to the deck, he skidded across it on his left side. He heard Fand cry out in fear. He clenched his fingers to secure a grip on the welds and, to his overwhelming relief, the fingers of his right hand curled. The Sin Eater slapped solidly into his gloved palm.

With a snarl of bloodthirsty satisfaction, he flipped over, blaster leveled at the end of his extended arm, questing for target acquisition. He framed Quayle's bulky outline within the Sin Eater's sights and his finger curved toward the trigger stud—then froze.

Although Quayle stood before his gun, so did Fand—and the tip of the cutlass pricked her jugular vein. A thread of blood inched down the side of her long neck.

Panting heavily, Quayle said, "Always the point, remember that. I'm presuming your name is Kane. Very well, Mr. Kane. You will divest yourself of that rather unique firearm or I will take great pleasure in cutting this Irish mutie's throat. I don't care if you kill me immediately afterward. Putting this whore to death would be worth my death. I'll die knowing she can spread no more of her half-human spawn on the Earth."

Moving with deliberate caution, Kane rose to one knee, aiming at Quayle's round head squatting on his shoulders like a bloated albino toad. The man yanked roughly on Fand's braided hair, jerking her head to one side and dragging a short cry of pain from her lips. The point of the cutlass dug deeper into her soft flesh, and more bright blood spilled down her pale throat.

Quayle's pendulous lips twitched in a spasmodic imitation of a smile. "I know you're wondering if you can get me with one clean head shot before I kill her. Let me assure you that you cannot—kill me before I kill her, that is. Lower your weapon, Mr. Kane. You have three seconds. Three...two..."

Kane pushed the Sin Eater back into its holster and let his right arm drop to his side.

Quayle's smile broadened, the scar on his cheek acquiring a deep crease. "I have the strangest sensation we've met before, Mr. Kane. But that's hardly likely, is it?"

Kane shook his head. "I think I'd remember a slug like you, Captain."

Quayle inclined his head a fraction of an inch in a parody of a gracious nod, but he didn't remove the cutlass from Fand's throat. "True. I pride myself on leaving a lasting impression on those I meet. Now, sir, you will disarm and kick your weapon over here.''

Kane hesitated, looked at the gleefully malevolent smile on Quayle's face and began undoing the buckles and Velcro tabs of his holster.

# Chapter 27

Quayle easily worked out the intricacies of the Sin Eater's power holster. To Kane's disappointment, he unleathered the weapon without shooting himself in the foot. Once it was drawn and in his fist, he released Fand. She went to stand by Kane, wiping at the blood on her neck but maintaining a calm demeanor.

Quayle ordered them to turn around, to face astern. Kane expected to receive a bullet in the back of the head, but he then understood Quayle wanted to take a final look at the Northstar 40 drilling platform.

The entire three-tiered structure listed dangerously toward the surface of the Atlantic, barely kept afloat by the remaining ballast tanks. Flammable materials on board had ignited, and columns of black smoke corkscrewed into the morning sky.

In a lovely contralto voice, rich with mockery, Fand sang, "'Rule Britannia, Britannia rule the waves.'"

Even as they watched, the ninety-foot-tall derrick rig slowly bent at the midway point, folding in on itself like a jackknife. They saw pieces of it raining down.

"'Britannia needs no bulwarks,'" sang Fand, a cruel note of laughter twisting around her voice. "'No towers among the steep...her home is o'er the mountain waves, her home is on the deep.'"

Quayle didn't react to her taunting melody.

From the surf lashing at the giant support columns, a sharp-keeled boat appeared, turning in a wide, swinging curve then arrowing on a direct heading for the *Cromwell.*

"Your friends," Quayle intoned. "That boat doesn't have the legs to catch this ship."

He didn't sound absolutely certain, however. Over his shoulder, he bellowed, "Dodd! Mr. Dodd!"

Dodd leaned out of the bridge door. "Captain?"

"Deploy the fog. Rig for silent running."

"Aye, aye, sir."

Kane and Fand exchanged mystified glances. Although Kane had been aboard the *Cromwell* before, he hadn't been privy to the craft's full capabilities. From equidistant points around the deck, apertures opened. With a prolonged hissing as of faulty steam valves, wreaths of mist floated up and around the *Cromwell*'s hull.

Within seconds, the mist thickened to the consistency of a cloud, billowing and rolling across the deck, diffusing the sunlight. The steady throb of the diesel engines diminished to a mutter, replaced by a faint electric whine. There was only the foggiest outline of the ship's superstructure to be seen, brief glimpses of the gray water through the vapor shrouding the hull.

"Well-done," Quayle said in satisfaction. "You may turn around now, Mr. Kane and Sister Fand."

The two people did so, seeing Quayle as a looming shadow, his scarred features blurred by the fog. "Mr. Kane, I believe you've been on this vessel before, when you were in the employ of Lord Strongbow."

"I was never in his employ," Kane replied stolidly.

"Nevertheless, I recall your presence and that of your other American friends in New London. I know you set sail to Ireland under Strongbow's directive. I also know you apparently perished during the selkie attack. Was that all a ruse to gull Strongbow?''

"More like a beneficial accident, Captain."

Quayle grunted. "As this is, I suppose. I surmise you've been deeply involved in the insurrection against the Imperium for the past half year, plotting and scheming away all this time in Ireland. I always knew the Celts couldn't have managed military affairs on their own."

"They did," Kane shot back. "You're the one who couldn't handle Imperium affairs on your own, without Strongbow."

Quayle didn't seem angry, only mildly bemused. "There's a pawky irony in how Strongbow himself placed you among the Celts, thinking he was planting his own agents."

Without waiting for Kane to deny the observation, Quayle addressed Fand. "I know who you are, too. The much-debated Danaan sorceress, the Celtic goddess who so obsessed Strongbow. Most of us rank-and-file imperial soldiers believed you to be only a myth, a symbol concocted for the Irish to rally around."

"As Atlantis and Lyonesse are only myths?" Fand asked, voice purring with scorn.

"That is something we all shall learn in short order." Quayle stepped back, waggling the barrel of the Sin Eater. "Come with me."

Kane didn't move. Forcing a nonchalance into his voice, he said, "If you're going to kill us, why not do it here instead of making us walk someplace where it's convenient for you?"

"You think I intend to execute you?"

"I just want to know how to plan the rest of my day."

Quayle chuckled. "As tempting as the prospect is, I'm afraid I'm going to keep you alive a little longer. I intended to have a crew on this voyage, but as you can see, that is not the case. I'll need labor once we reach our destination, and since you two are all I have, you're the best I have. Besides, having the self-proclaimed spirit of Ireland in my hands may turn out to my advantage."

Doing his best to minimize his limp, Kane allowed Quayle to herd him and Fand across the mist-cloaked deck to an open gangway. It pitched downward into a dimly lit passage. They descended a short flight of stairs, and Quayle marched them beneath naked, wire-encased lightbulbs. He directed them into the brig, a small, sour-smelling cell with a pair of fold-down bunks chained to the bulkhead and a small stainless-steel toilet in the corner.

Kane kept alert for an opening, but Quayle maintained a safe distance behind them, and the passageway was so narrow he and Fand were jammed shoulder to shoulder. With his wounded leg slowing him up, he couldn't have made any sudden moves if he had been so inclined. Quayle could easily run him through with his sword or shoot him in the back with his own gun.

Quayle pulled the barred door closed on its floor and ceiling tracks, then flipped up a lever on the opposite bulkhead. The locks snapped shut with a blood-chilling click.

"I'll return when I can," Quayle said. "Once I'm certain we've eluded pursuit. I do hope you will both be reasonable and remain patient. If I were you, Mr.

Kane, and I were left alone with a woman of Sister Fand's obvious charms, I should certainly not let time hang heavy on my hands.''

He favored Fand with a one-eyed leer. ''And perhaps when I have some leisure time, you can help me while it away.''

Fand smiled coldly. ''Not in this or any other incarnation, Balor.''

Quayle snorted out a laugh and lumbered away. As soon as he was out of sight, Kane pulled down a bunk and plopped onto it, straightening out his stabbed leg. Although the flow of blood had ebbed, the wound ached as if he had been bitten by a shark.

Sitting down beside him, Fand ripped the rent in his trousers wider so she could examine the injury. The cutlass had slid in under a layer of flesh, and pierced a layer of muscle before Quayle had withdrawn it.

''Not too serious,'' she said. ''Provided it doesn't get infected.'' She saw him massaging his shoulder, wincing as he worked it up and down. She murmured sympathetically, ''You've really taken your blows on this trip, Kane. I'm sorry.''

He smiled wryly. ''I don't consider it a worthwhile month unless I get stabbed, shot or blown up at least once.''

Her golden eyes became troubled. ''You're joking, I hope.''

He started to assure her that he was, then considered all the injuries he had incurred over the past year and said, ''I wish I were.''

Fand opened her vest and ripped a strip of cloth from the hem of her shift. Taking it to the toilet she examined the water. ''It looks and smells clean,'' then dipped the roll of fabric into it. Returning to Kane, she dabbed at the cut, wiping most of the blood away.

From the pouch at her waist, she removed two little packets of powdered herbs. She poured heaps from both into her hand, squeezed water from the rag into it, and rubbed her palms together vigorously until the mixture acquired a pastelike consistency. Gently, she kneaded the substance into the sword wound on Kane's thigh, spreading it evenly over the edges. Almost immediately, the bleeding stopped.

"It's a natural coagulating agent," she said. "It'll nip infection, too. If I had my staff, I'd ease the pain, as well."

She wrapped the wet cloth around his thigh to keep the poultice moist. "Try to keep off your feet for a bit, let the herbs do their work."

"Thanks," Kane said. "I'll know better than to duel that fat bastard with just a knife next time."

Fand's lips turned down at the corners. "I failed to disable the *Cromwell.* I'm sorry. The role of warrior-queen is new to me. It doesn't come naturally."

Kane grinned crookedly. "You could have fooled me."

"I don't think I fooled Quayle."

"The day is still young. You might surprise him yet."

She stared at him reproachfully. "I sincerely hope not. Once Quayle is dealt with—"

"There'll be another like him," Kane interrupted bitterly. "Sooner or later, another megalomaniac will show up to make your life miserable. There's always some coldheart with the attitude that out of everyone on the planet he's the most important and anything he does to force the rest of the world to acknowledge it is justified. My land is divided up among nine of those kinds of egos.''

''And you contest with them?''

''Them and others like them.''

''Perhaps you could turn those ego-structures against one another, exploit that self-aggrandizement, destroy them from within, rather than without.''

Kane began to explain how difficult her suggestion would be, but the Cromwell suddenly changed direction, causing them both to sway against each other. The thud of the diesel engines began again, a distant rhythmic pounding which set up corresponding vibrations in the bulkheads.

''We're changing course,'' Fand said tensely. ''Heading for the open sea, probably around Land's End to avoid the blockades. Then to Lyonesse.''

''How long will it take?''

Fand shrugged. ''It all depends on our speed, the weather and the accuracy of Morrigan's coordinates. We could be talking as little as eight hours or as many as sixteen.''

''I found Morrigan,'' Kane told her. ''She'll be aboard the *Wraith,* so she'll provide the same coordinates she gave Quayle.''

Fand's eyes brightened with hope. ''Even if they lost us in the fog, they may be able to intercept us.''

''Let's hope they maintain a safe distance. The weapons systems on this tub are almost completely automated. Quayle could blow the *Wraith* to matchwood by pushing a few buttons.''

Fand shook her head in disgust, hope in her eyes replaced by a cold gleam. ''Technology. How did we ever get along without it?''

Kane laughed, but Fand didn't join in.

As the minutes they spent in the brig crept into an hour, Fand grew more agitated. She twined and untwined her fingers as she paced the cell from one bulkhead to the other. She stood at the door, peering past the bars down the featureless passageway, first in one direction then the other. She slapped the thick bars in angry frustration and resumed pacing.

"Try to relax," Kane suggested. "We're not going anywhere until Quayle decides we are."

Fand spun and threw him such a glare of molten fury he felt a jolt of unease. In her hot aureate eyes he saw a glint of the old Fand, mad and boiling with a regal wrath. Between clenched teeth, she bit out, "I've never been confined, imprisoned before. I don't think I can stand much more of this."

Kane reflected that since she had spent her entire life wandering through the open glades and dells of Ireland she was probably claustrophobic to the point of psychosis.

"Think of something else," he said gently, reaching for her hand. She evaded his touch and returned to the door, rattling the bars like an animal in a cage. She uttered a keening whimper of mounting panic.

Pitching his voice to a low, unemotional level, he said, "Don't go simple on me, Fand. I'm going to need you clearheaded and alert if we're to get out of this with a whole skin."

Her shoulders sagged in resignation, and she bowed her head, pressing her forehead against the bars. She murmured, *"A thuismitheoiri' Fad saol agat agus bhi' conai' air ansin go dti' go raibh."*

Kane didn't know if she was praying, cursing or lamenting so he said nothing. At length, Fand turned around to face him, tears glistening on her cheeks. "'Tis not an easy thing, Kane."

"Very few things in life are. Survival and sanity are probably two of the most difficult to achieve." He threw her an insouciant grin. "I guess I've spent my life focused on the one to the exclusion of the other."

She smiled at him wanly. "Which one?"

"If you take Brigid's word for it—" His grin faltered and his words trailed away. He cast his eyes to the deck.

"You miss her very much." Fand had not asked a question; she'd made a statement.

He inhaled sharply, then exhaled slowly, running a hand through his soggy, salt-stiff hair. Raising his gaze to Fand's face, he said levelly, "I miss her presence on an op like this. I miss her annoying-as-hell strict rationalizations. I miss the way she tries to keep me toeing the line. The way she keeps me honest."

Softly, Fand interjected, "And sane?"

In a rustling whisper, Kane replied, "Yes. And sane."

A sad, almost pitying smile ghosted over Fand's lips. "But you're not lovers?"

"Not in this life, anyway. Mebbe someday."

"Someday when?"

"When I can focus more on sanity than survival."

Fand regarded him inscrutably for a long moment, then nodded as if she understood completely. Kane doubted she did.

HE AWOKE INSTANTLY, upper body snapping erect and dislodging Fand's head from his shoulder. For a split second, he wasn't certain what had awakened him. Then he realized it wasn't a noise, but rather a sudden cessation of one. The steady throb of the diesel engines had faded completely. The disappearance of the sound had penetrated his sleeping mind and prodded his pointman's sense into raising an alarm.

Consulting his wrist chron, he saw by the glowing digits he had been sleeping for around three hours, which meant he and Fand had been in the brig nearly twelve.

Rubbing her eyes with the heels of her hands, Fand stifled a yawn and asked in a drowsy, little-girl voice, "What's going on?"

Kane didn't answer immediately. He cocked his head, listening intently, hearing the clanging rattle of what sounded like a chain, then a faint, distant splash. The *Cromwell* had dropped anchor. A moment later, he heard the clicking of a door latch and the scrape of metal on metal.

"I think we've arrived," he said quietly.

Heavy footfalls thumped down the passageway. Quayle appeared on the other side of the bars, smiling benignly, like a maimed Buddha. A Beretta M-92 was nestled in his huge hand, almost swallowed by it.

"I trust you did not let time hang heavy on your hands, Mr. Kane?"

"Not at all. I was more than ready for a little peace and quiet."

"Disappointed to hear that, Mr. Kane. Perhaps Sister Fand was, as well. I might be able to assuage her disappointment in a little while."

Fand made a spitting noise of contempt.

Quayle ignored her. "We're in sight of our destination, and your presence is required above." He nodded toward Fand. "I'm sure our spirit of Ireland here will have some fascinating observations to share with us.''

He reached out with one beamlike arm and pulled the lever on the bulkhead. Solenoids clicked open loudly, and Quayle slid back the brig's door. Not waiting for the man and woman to stir from the bunk, he walked carefully backward down the passage. ''Let's not dawdle,'' he said, an iron edge slipping into his oily voice.

Fand and Kane exchanged brief glances and left the cell. Kane's leg was stiff and each step sent little flares of pain through the thigh, but he managed to walk without limping.

By the time they reached the stairway, Quayle was already standing on the deck. ''Move along, now.''

They emerged under a sullen sky and a cloud-wreathed sun sinking to the horizon. The windless ocean swelled in long, slow waves that rocked the tangled kelp and sea grass up and down.

Quayle wordlessly pointed to starboard, and they turned in that direction. At first glance, they saw only dark crags rising from the languid surf. Upon second glance, Kane felt the prickling of dread at the nape of his neck.

The first thing he noticed was it wasn't an island at all, but more of a rocky atoll, projecting out of the ocean like the fist of a stone giant. The rim of the atoll rose straight up from the water. No shoreline was visible, nor any kind of beach at all. A deep, asymmetrical cleft climbed from the breakers between the rocks, and in the depression Kane saw a great flight of green-slimed stone steps.

They led up to a tumble of rock blocks, like the ruins of a huge wall, behind which loomed an edifice covered in dried mud. Barely visible behind the coating of mud, a huge bas-relief carving of a squid or an octopus waved its tentacles, as if in greeting.

All three people knew they looked upon antiquity given shape and form, a place so old that even whispers of its existence could only be measured in millennia.

# Chapter 28

The hoist lowered the small skiff over the side of the *Cromwell*. Under the watchful eye of Quayle—and the barrel of an MP-5 subgun—Fand and Kane scaled a rope ladder to the skiff. After they were seated, Quayle tossed Kane a big box-batteried xenon flashlight. It could project a beam of three million candlepower.

Quayle swung over the rail, and climbed down with surprising agility for one of his mammoth bulk. Hanging from his belt were three empty sacks, made of a dense black fabric. They were sealed with Velcro tabs. Also thrust through his belt was his cutlass. Still keeping the Fand and Kane in front of his blaster, he started the outboard motor clamped to the squared-off stern with a single yank of the pull cord. He gunned the throttle, the prow riding on a rush of foam.

The small craft was barely eight feet long, having contours similar to a bathtub, but it skimmed across the sea smoothly. The wind was biting and Fand rubbed her bare arms, but she made no complaint. She knew it wouldn't have done any good.

Quayle piloted the boat expertly over the breakers at the mouth of the stone stairs. Waves lapped over the sides, soaking their feet, the salt spray stinging their eyes. Quayle kept the small craft on course, seeming to know instinctively what swell could pile them up against a boulder.

He steered the skiff slowly to the foot of the stairs, between dark ramparts of rock. Then the hull grated on stone, and he cut the engine. He tossed a mooring line to Kane, who climbed out and looped it securely around a rock.

Fand and Kane preceded Quayle up the weather-eroded stairway, climbing between the black walls rearing above them like permanent thunderclouds. Not speaking, the three people scaled the crude, time-pitted stone slabs, picking their way carefully. In some places the steps were slippery with lichens and kelp. They made their way up the steep slant, boot soles slipping and sliding on the wet rock. It leveled off at the mouth of the paving-stone path that wound around a vista of ruins.

Massive stone blocks twice as high as Quayle lay in scattered profusion, many of them sheathed in verdigris-eaten bronze. Paving slabs were cracked and up-ended, all draped with strands of seaweed. They sniffed the dank sea smell and waded ankle deep through fetid ooze. Quayle seemed as awed as Fand and Kane, but he wasn't so entranced that he forgot to keep them before the barrel of the autoblaster. Inscribed on several monoliths, beneath the dried crustings of muck, they saw the squid motif.

"What's with the octopus symbol?" Kane asked, surprised by how hushed his voice sounded.

"It's a kraken," Quayle replied blithely. "A monster variety of squid. Extinct long ago, but there were allegedly sightings of them in historical times. Every Atlantean outpost had its own sigil, identifying it with the ocean—whales, sharks, sea horses."

Fand raised a questioningly eyebrow. "I had no idea you were such an expert, Captain."

"I'm full of surprises, Sister." He smiled with cruel triumph. "As your little slut-spy Morrigan learned. I daresay I've performed more research on the subject of Atlantis than anyone in the past two centuries."

The three of them walked to the silt-coated edifice they had seen from the ship. It was partly fallen in, but the portico, upheld by four marble columns, was still intact. Along the edge of the roof, a row of horn-headed stone gargoyles leered down—statues of monsters of bygone epochs, half human and half beast. The mixtures, thought Kane, of Atlantean legends.

There was no gate, no door. The portal stood open and empty. Quayle motioned to Kane. "If you would be so kind as to light our way, sir."

They went beneath the linteled arch into dimness and a brooding silence. The xenon cast an almost solid rod of white before them. Kane walked carefully on the bare, slimy stone floor, unconsciously slipping into the pointman's persona despite the circumstances. His eyes roamed from side to side, searching every nook and corner. He sensed nothing but ancient, bygone times, the shadows of long-gone presences.

The corridor was completely empty, even of debris. It was featureless, unbroken by either window or doorway. The passage ended after twenty yards, and an unrailed stairway plunged down into impenetrable darkness. Kane stood at its head, the incandescent beam of the flashlight illuminating only the first few steps.

Quayle prodded Fand hard in the small of the back with the bore of the subgun. She uttered a short cry of annoyed pain, and Kane took the first step down into the yawning blackness. He experienced the shuddery sensation of striding down the petrified tongue of a gargantuan sea monster, descending blithely into its gullet.

The light gleamed on a strange, sleek, glossy substance coating the walls, suggestive of ceramic or enamel. He assumed they were below sea level now and the composition of the walls kept out the water.

The stairs ended in an oval chamber, and by casting about the light, Kane saw the rubble of decayed furniture, scattered rags of tapestries, moldering heaps of trash and scatterings of rotten, soggy wood. Mixed in with the wood was a litter of oddly shaped metal bits, like the clasps and locks of jewelry or storage boxes.

At the far end of the chamber, rising on a pedestal, was a small statue of a kraken, tentacles curving up and over its cylindrical body. It appeared to be made of the same slightly reflective ceramic substance as on the walls. On closer inspection, the kraken and the pedestal itself seemed to be molded out of the wall that backed them, as if it were all one continuous piece.

Kane shone the xenon all around and with a cold sarcasm announced, "Congratulations, Quayle. You've discovered the city dump of Lyonesse."

He expected his voice to echo, but it didn't, as if the chamber had sound-absorbing qualities.

With his characteristic grunt, Quayle motioned Kane to move aside. "Keep your light on the statue," he ordered. "If you shine it in my eyes, I'll open fire very indiscriminately. Even if I can't see you, in these close quarters I'll kill at least one of you."

Kane didn't bother with a response, watching as Quayle carefully inspected the kraken, running his fingers all over the tentacles. After a few moments, he declared with a great deal of satisfaction, "Ah."

Quayle had the index finger of one hand inserted up to the first joint into a raised sucker ring of a tentacle. He threw a preening smile toward Kane and Fand as if he expected congratulations.

"So?" Kane demanded. "The arm is hollow."

Still smiling, Quayle removed from a jacket pocket a small sphere, holding it between thumb and forefinger. With a slight start, Kane recognized it from his jump-dream communication with Fand. He realized it bore the same glassy sheen as the walls of the chamber.

Quayle placed the bead of orichalcum into the sucker ring, fitting it perfectly on the molded rim. He tapped it and the orb disappeared. The sound of it clicking and rolling down the hollow tentacle was easily audible.

From the saucer-shaped eyes of the kraken beat a slow pulse of uncolored light. The wall to which the statue and pedestal were attached shivered, then began to rotate, turning a U curve on invisible pivots. Stale, fetid air gusted out, ruffling Kane's and Fand's hair and causing even Quayle to reflexively lift a hand to his nose. With the barrel of the MP-5, he gestured to the opening. "Ladies and prisoners first."

Squaring his shoulders, the short hairs at the back of his neck bristling, Kane stepped through the opening, the flashlight striking dull reflections on the glossy walls. The room was huge and long and filled with darkness. Dim shapes towered all around them in the gloom.

An immense statue loomed in the center of the chamber, rearing from a plinth of greenish-black stone. The effigy dwarfed everything else in the room, rising at least twenty feet high. It possessed humanoid legs and hips, but the upper body had the form of the kraken, with six tentacled arms, three on each side. The beaked head sported little nubbin horns, and the eyes in the blank face were fist-size gemstones.

"Belial, I presume," Quayle said with a quiet geniality. "Here is where his sons were made."

Kane followed the short sweep of the subgun's barrel and saw a dais of the same black-green stone, crafted into the likeness of many loopings of heavy chain, fantastically interwoven. The length of chain swarmed with monstrosities. The links were grotesque faces, deformed heads sporting stubby horns. A pair of chains crossed above the dais, and where the two strands intersected hung a face of horror, with fanged mouth agape in a demonic howl. Absently, Kane noted the dark, circular hollow behind the molded tongue.

The floor of the dais was a many-faceted convex disc of red-tinted crystalline stone, like semi-opaque quartz. He estimated it as at least five feet in diameter. Suspended above it by ceramic chains was an identical crystal disk, but this one was concave.

Fand murmured a few words in Gaelic, her tone full of loathing. Kane glanced toward her and saw she was not looking at the statue or the dais. Spreading out from a corner, piled high in a pyramid, were dozens, perhaps even scores of yellowed skulls. Almost all of them appeared to be malformed, with back-sloping foreheads and bony ridges jutting out over empty eye sockets. Twisted little knobs projected from the craniums—some of them blunt, others long and curved, like the horns of a ram.

"The birthing ward of the Firbolgs," Fand said in an unsteady whisper. "Unholy mixtures of animal and man."

Kane tried to control the nausea leapfrogging in his belly. He thought of Jacko, of the hybrids and even of Fand, who was herself a hybrid. The obsession to toy with the very essence of creation hadn't begun with the Totality Concept or even the Nazis.

Kane shifted the flashlight away from the stacked, grinning skulls and played it over a recess in the wall. A figure sat there, on a seat of the glassy stone roughly hewed into the likeness of a chair. It appeared to be the cadaver of a man wearing ornate armor, the flesh-less head tilted back with the mouth hanging open. The helmet and metal corslet had a waxy sheen, as if they were lacquered with the same substance as coated the walls.

He didn't devote any time to wondering who the man might have been or why he was sitting there. His eyes were drawn to the naked broadsword lying at the corpse's feet. Though the metal was dulled, the blade was well over three feet in length. Kane didn't linger over it. He swept the xenon beam around, pretending to be fascinated by the friezes and geometric forms carved on the walls.

"I don't see your balls, Captain," Kane dead-panned.

The big man boomed out a laugh, but not in appreciation of Kane's wit. "That's because you look, but you do not see."

Quayle's gaze was fixed upon the monstrous effigy of Belial, smiling up at it beatifically. Kane followed his cyclopean stare, casting the flashlight onto it. The brilliant beam struck little twinkles of incandescence on the swarm of tentacles. Embedded in each one of the sucker rings gleamed orbs of orichalcum.

"What are you going to do now, Balor?" Fand demanded. "Pry them out and ship them back to England—and blow your entire country to atoms?"

Quayle threw her a mocking glance. "Hardly *my* country."

Fand waved to the sphere-studded tentacles. "The beads of orichalcum are highly unstable. Without the proper machinery, you'd be far safer transporting a boatload of plutonium."

Quayle patted one of the black bags at his belt. "As long the beads aren't exposed directly to the sun and don't absorb solar rays, the safety factor is acceptable."

Fand snorted disdainfully. "That's what Morrigan wanted you to believe."

"I've done my own research."

"Not nearly enough of it. Otherwise, you'd know it takes only one bead of orichalcum to trigger a chain reaction."

Quayle frowned, but he said nothing.

Fand went on in a rush, "If one bead detonates, it will touch off all the others in the vicinity, regardless of whether you have them in a sunless and airtight container or not. It'll be a firestorm of the likes not seen since the cataclysm that tore the world asunder and sank Atlantis and all her colonies millennia ago."

Quayle squinted with his good eye, gesturing to orbs on the statue's six arms. "Why didn't those ignite during the cataclysm?"

"Several reasons," Kane spoke up. "First of all, the stuff this vault is made out of probably acts as shielding, like vanadium alloy or lead. Not only can light not penetrate, but neither can whatever radiation the orichalcum emits."

"Not to mention," said Fand, picking up Kane's

thread of theory, "there is a million square miles of ocean between here and where the Atlantean homeland was supposedly located, near the Mid-Atlantic Ridge. Lyonesse wasn't spared the tsunamis or earth changes, but its supply of orichalcum was protected."

Quayle shifted his feet uncertainly. "Morrigan wanted me to take the beads back to England so I'd destroy it?"

"Exactly," Fand said decisively. "She was willing to sacrifice herself if it meant turning Britain into a cinder."

"And you don't want that to happen?"

"No. I am a protector of life, a creator of it, not a destroyer." Fand softened her tone, trying to smooth out the edges, substituting compassion for arrogance. "Even if the orichalcum could be restricted only to England, I would still try to prevent such a catastrophe. Now that Strongbow no longer rules England, now that the Imperium is no more, our two nations with their intertwined histories should become one people. The divisions should end between us. Don't you see that's the only logical course to take, Aubrey?"

Kane watched Quayle's face during Fand's brief appeal to reason, and saw indecision registered on it. But with her use of his name, his head swiveled swiftly toward her. Both of his eyes glinted gimlet hard.

"Aubrey," he echoed, stretching out the syllables, *Awww-braaay.* "And Morrigan called me 'my captain.'" He glared at Kane. "And what do you call me? Evil-eye? Balor? The fat bastard?"

Kane kept his own suggestions to himself. Still staring into his face, Quayle took a quick sidestep and slammed the frame of the MP-5 against the side of

Fand's head. She went staggering across the chamber and fell, long arms and legs asprawl.

Kane made a blind, instinctive lunge for Quayle, and the man pounded the butt of the subgun into the pit of his belly. As he folded over in the direction of the sickening blow, Quayle jacked up a knee against his chin. It was like being kicked by a redwood.

Kane fell onto his side, dropping the xenon flashlight as he did so. It fell over, the beam glancing in sparkling pinpoints from the gemstones in the idol's eyes.

"Get up!" Quayle roared, kicking him on his injured thigh. "Get the fuck up! Get up and start pulling the orichalcum out of those fucking arms!"

Fiery agony spread up and down Kane's leg as he forced himself to his elbows, teeth clamped tight on a cry of pain. He grated, "Pull your own fucking arms, Aubrey."

A full-throated shriek filled the chamber, reverberating like the echoes of a gong. Blood streaming down her face, Fand bounded toward Quayle, the broadsword held in a two-fisted grip. Her golden eyes seethed with the wild fury of the Fand who was one with the hills, the winds and the gray seas of Erin.

The mad Fand.

# Chapter 29

She screamed a torrent of enraged Gaelic, and swung the huge sword like a cleaver. All Kane could think of to do was scramble out of her way.

The point of the sword snagged in the loose folds of Quayle's throat, but it only pierced the outer flesh, drawing a fine thread of blood, bright against the stark pallor of his complexion.

He backpedaled as fast as his bulk would allow, bringing up his MP-5. He squeezed off only a single round before the sword swept across and clanged loudly against the barrel of the blaster, ripping it from his hands and sending it flying. It clattered end over end onto the crystal-floored dais.

The one shot took Fand high in the chest. Kane saw a scrap of the combat vest fly away, exposing the metal mesh beneath. The piledriving impact rocked her back on her heels and drove most of the air from her lungs. As she staggered, leather-shod feet rasping for purchase on the floor, she hurled the broadsword straight up, point first.

Kane shot out an arm and his hand closed around the hilt. He spun around to face Quayle, whose white face was twisted in fury as he drew his cutlass. Kane hefted the broadsword with one hand. Although the weapon seemed as heavy as lead, he gave two short strokes to loosen his wrist.

As he stared at Quayle, for just an instant, a fleeting microsecond, the man's bleached flesh and uniform rippled away, like water sluicing over a pane of dusty glass. He saw Balor facing him, his gray beard plaited into two thick braids upon his chest.

The image faded almost immediately, but Kane growled, "This was a long time in coming between you and me, Evil-eye."

Quayle's eye flickered in momentary confusion. His chalk-colored lips twitched and whispered, almost to himself, "Kane? Ka'in?"

Kane lunged. Quayle met the attack by hacking wildly, his blade gleaming brightly in the illumination shed by the xenon. The cutlass engaged the broadsword with bold cross strokes and furious thrusts.

Kane kept his sword from being knocked out of line as the two men circled each other, the blades ringing together with an almost continuous clangor. He made use of the heavier broadsword to drive Quayle backward.

The huge man didn't care for a forced retreat. He closed in on his opponent, body to body, blades crossed and locked. For a long second, they stood eye-to-eye with each other. Quayle drove his head forward between the edges of the two swords, trying to butt Kane in the face. He sliced open his left cheek in the attempt.

Pushing off from Quayle, using his enormous body as a springboard, Kane slammed back against the plinth supporting the idol of Belial. Quayle pressed his advantage, hammering away with his cutlass as if to beat Kane to his knees. Kane blocked and parried. It was all he could do to hold on to the broadsword handle while the giant albino smashed and battered at him.

Kane's right arm began to lose all feeling, the strength seeping away. A fireball of agony burned in his shoulder socket. He placed both hands beneath the cross guard and tried to knock the cutlass aside long enough for him to get away from the statue.

He pressed himself to one of the huge legs and eased around it. Quayle's blade was a constant flicker of light. It lashed past Kane's guard, and its keen edge hissed along his collarbone before a beat of the broadsword knocked it clear. Kane felt the slow spread of blood beneath his shirt.

He slashed swiftly in return, a half cut, half thrust with the point, directed at Quayle's groin, ripping a straight slash in his trousers. Quayle's parry was frantic, barely in time. He sprang back, crimson oozing from a cut just above his pelvic bone.

"Always the point," Kane said breathlessly. "Remember that."

Quayle's lips drew back from his discolored teeth in a silent snarl, and he lunged, whipping the cutlass toward Kane's chest. He had no choice but to leap backward to avoid the razored blade. The back of his head bumped smartly against the curve of a curling tentacle, and he stumbled.

Quayle moved in to deliver a killing stroke. Anticipating the swing, Kane ducked aside at the last microsecond. The cutlass bit deeply into the tentacle, shearing through it, but the four-hundred-year-old blade broke on impact. The top half of the sword splintered and fell chiming to the floor, beside the sliced-off piece of statuary. The little sphere of orichalcum rolled away from the tentacle.

Quayle bleated his disbelief and grief. Eye bulging in its socket, he gaped at the jagged stump of his pre-

cious cutlass as if trying to convince himself that a
trick of the light gave it only the illusion of being
snapped in half.

Then, with a sobbing, bestial roar, he flung down
the hilt and lumbered in an elephantine charge to retrieve the MP-5. Kane knew trying to tackle the be-
hemoth would have the same effect as body-blocking
a mountain. Quayle would just carry him piggyback
to the dais. His toe nudged the orb of orichalcum and
it rolled across the floor.

Glancing up, Kane focused on the open hole in the
carved, demonic face above the dais. He dropped the
sword, bent over, snatched up the little sphere and
raced after Quayle. The big man had a three-yard head
start, but Kane didn't have Quayle's extra two hun-
dred-plus pounds of weight slowing him up. He could
have easily caught or passed him, but Kane stayed at
his heels.

Reaching the edge of the dais, Quayle half jumped,
half crawled onto the crystal disk, grunting with the
effort. He stooped, fumbling to pick up the subgun.
As he bent over, Kane leaped up, slapped the orichalcum bead precisely into the mouth of the lasciviously
grinning demon face and threw himself to the right.

Quayle whirled around, teeth bared in a grimace of
homicidal fury. He worked the MP-5's trigger, spray-
ing a wild storm of lead in Kane's general direction.
Kane performed a frantic somersault, trying to roll
ahead of the deadly, copper-jacketed stream. The slugs
slashed long trenches in the chamber floor, showering
him with rock chips. The walls threw back and magnified the rattling, stuttering roar.

The facets of the crystals above and below Quayle
winked with the strobing muzzle-flash of the subgun.

They danced with inner sparks, seeming to gather the flickering light into themselves until they glowed with a throbbing flame. A nimbus of luminescence spilled from above and crept up from below, swiftly encasing Quayle's body in a shimmering skein of witch-fire.

At first the maddened man was oblivious to the phenomenon. Only when he was completely veiled by the wavering cocoon did he stop firing. He looked around wildly and made a convulsive lurch to leave the dais.

The convulsion turned into a spasm, one rippling shudder following the other until his entire body quaked, as if vibrating violently from within. He writhed, his eye wide and staring, saliva spilling from his slack lips. He dropped the MP-5.

His hairless scalp squirmed in half a dozen different places, as if tiny worms wriggled and burrowed just beneath the flesh. The white skin stretched and split amid little spurting geysers of blood. Rising to a crouch, Kane saw blunt-tipped horns sprouting from his skull, punching through the flesh.

Quayle screamed, a high-pitched ululating wail of agony ripped from pain centers Kane never knew existed in the human organism. The man clutched both sides of his head, his tongue protruding from his mouth. It was black and wet, then red as a gush of scarlet spewed from between his gaping jaws. The fabric of his sleeves over his elbows stretched out, then ripped as scarlet-coated spurs of bone erupted in a vermilion mist.

Quayle's body sagged as if bowed beneath his own ponderous weight. The right side of his face hung slackly from the bone, like wax exposed to great heat. With a wet, mucky pop, the flesh fell away and lay in a quivering lump of protoplasm on the disk.

Quayle turned his head, one entire side of it nothing but reddened bone. Gurgling around the blood bubbling from his mouth, he said, "You were right. I should've done more research."

His body fell flat on the crystal, and after a few twitches of feet and fingers, he moved no more.

Head spinning, Kane climbed to his feet, not able to tear his eyes away from the transformation Quayle's body was still undergoing. He didn't understand any of it except he had instinctively known that the dais was somehow involved in the creation of the mixtures.

Fand made her slow, stiff way over to him, face crimson streaked, the braid in her hair loosened. He put an arm around her, and she leaned into him, wincing. "You all right?" he asked.

"Aside from a desperate headache, I think I may have a cracked clavicle. But our skins are whole, more or less."

Kane indicated Quayle's light-sheathed body. "Which is more than can be said for him."

She kissed him on the cheek. "I knew only you would be able to best Balor, Ka'in."

"Kane," he corrected automatically.

"How did you know how to activate the machine with the orichalcum if you are only Kane?" she challenged.

He swept his gaze over the statue of Belial, about to tell her how he, Kane, not Ka'in, reasoned out the process due to his own experiences over the past year. Then he saw Belial's tentacles exuding a gibbous glow, like captured moonbeams. All of the beads embedded in the swirl of arms gleamed.

Fand saw it, too, and a gasp of fright tore from her

throat. "You did more than activate the machine—you triggered a chain reaction!"

"How?" Kane snarled out the word. "The beads weren't exposed to solar radiation!"

"How do I know?" Fand shot back, voice high and trembling. "These devices haven't been used in thousands and thousands of years. They're probably as unstable as the energy that powers them."

"Shit!" Even as Kane hissed the word, he pivoted on a heel and dragged Fand in a sprint across the chamber. She shook loose and, long legs pumping, outdistanced him within seconds.

When they pushed through the opening, Fand grasped the carved image of the kraken. "Give me a hand. If we seal up the chamber, it might contain the—"

Kane didn't need to hear the rest. Clutching the tentacles, he hurled his entire weight into a muscle-cracking shove, the toes of his boots digging into the floor. For a long, heart-stopping second, nothing happened. It was like trying to uproot the temple itself. Then their combined strength prevailed, and with a prolonged screech of ancient gears and pulleys, the curved section of the wall slowly shifted. It joined seamlessly with the stone blocks, thudding solidly into place.

Body quivering with exertion, Kane followed the loping Fand up the dark staircase and then in a crazed, gasping dash down the long corridor and out of the building.

Fand still maintained the lead when they reached the stone steps leading to the sea. She leaped down them four at a time. Kane followed her closely, not daring to look behind him. A single misstep could pitch him headlong into a neck-breaking fall.

They piled aboard the skiff, casting off the line. It started immediately and Kane piloted it in a reckless swerve, the hull scraping on half-submerged rocks. The boat roared across the water, bouncing as violently as a stone skimming the surface of a pond.

When they had covered a little more than half the distance to where the *Cromwell* lay at anchor, Kane dared to cast a glance over his shoulder. The craggy atoll looked exactly the same as when they'd first seen it.

Shouting in order to be heard over the rush of the wind and the steady growl of the engine, Kane demanded, "If something was going to happen, shouldn't it have by now?"

The world staggered. An intolerable white glare filled his eyes. The sea heaved and the boat catapulted forward, riding mountainous ridges of flying foam. The skiff rose high on a rolling torrent, turning sideways, then flipping upside down.

Kane tried to cling to something, sought to reach Fand, but he plunged into a maelstrom of such force that he felt his bones compress. Even as the sea buffeted him, tossed him like a cork, he was aware of the thundering vibration of destruction. The orichalcum's detonating energy, pent-up in the vault below sea level, had burst forth in an apocalyptic torrent.

He rolled helplessly, seeing nothing, not knowing in which direction lay the surface or the bottom. There was nothing for him to do but somehow stay alive.

His lungs ached and blood roared in his head as he was swept and tumbled along by wave after wave of concussive force. He felt a pounding as of immense hammers upon his brain, then a vast numbness. Water seeped into his mouth, and he struggled to keep from inhaling it, clamping his lips tight.

Then a hand took one of his. His eyes, squeezed shut against the unholy glare, opened and he saw cool, greenish light, not the incandescent ball of hellfire that had scorched across the sky. Fand floated above him, her long unbound hair flowing around her head like a luminous veil.

Her golden eyes were blank, lost in shock. Dark red clouds puffed from around her ears. Slowly, Kane kicked his leaden legs and moved them both toward the surface. Her own legs began to stir, sluggishly at first, then with more determination.

Their heads broke the surface together. They dog-paddled in the shallow troughs between the rough waves, gasping and retching, vomiting out the water they had swallowed. When she was able to speak, Fand said in a strangulated voice, "I'm deaf."

"Your eardrums have ruptured," Kane told her. "You'll recover."

She gave him an angry glare. "I can't hear you!"

Kane turned in the direction of the atoll and saw only a great, bubbling froth from which shifting rays of smoky pink light shone, like the aurora borealis as seen through several layers of cloud cover.

Fand coughed, splashed and said, "Look."

Kane turned around and saw the *Cromwell* still at anchor, bobbing up and down in the last of the giant ripples. She was less than twenty yards away. With a bit of surprise, Kane realized they had been pushed for nearly half a mile by the shock wave.

Cutting a white wake off the *Cromwell*'s port side chugged *Hornblower's Wraith*. He was able to see

Grant and Phin standing on the deck in front of the wheelhouse. Fand began to stroke toward the black ship. "Dodd can still fire on them."

Even as Kane swam after her, gritting his teeth at the acidic burn of brine on his cuts, the door to the *Cromwell*'s bridge opened. Dodd appeared, frantically waving a square of white cloth at the *Wraith*.

Fand released her breath in a deep sigh. She turned her beautiful, bruised face to Kane, her eyes alight with exuberance. She clutched at him, grabbing handfuls of his sodden shirt.

"It's all over now," she said, her voice scratchy and raw but holding a thrill of happiness. "The Imperium is defeated, and hell rose and sank again!"

Kane managed to muster a weak smile. Now that it was done, he was too exhausted to care. All he could think about was Brigid Baptiste, and what she might be thinking—or dreaming.

# Epilogue

After turning Trillium over to the stable hand, Brigid started to return to the house, but on impulse turned up the path to the formal gardens. Still in glorious bloom this fall, the garden with its huge rhododendron hedges and winding paths had always drawn her like a magnet from the time she was a small child. The winding path she now walked had aromatic herbs growing in its crevices. The mint in particular released a fragrance that always lifted her spirits. But today, not even the garden could calm all the disturbing thoughts that swirled through her mind. She had a sense of great events building in the distance, and she knew somehow Captain Kane was involved with them.

When she entered the house through the solarium doors, she was surprised and not at all happy to find Paul Delmas waiting for her. He was wearing a beautifully tailored riding habit and he swished the crop through the air in annoyance. In a voice ragged with asperity, he demanded, "Where have you been? I thought we were to ride together."

Brigid let him wait for a reply. Something of a dandy, Paul was amazingly handsome and tailored to a fault. Brigid could picture him spending hours before a glass, his patient valet in attendance, turning first this way, then that, posing first with one outfit, then another, searching the flaxen-haired reflection for that elusive perfect look.

With his charm, dandified good looks and money, he'd seemed at first to be the perfect match for Brigid. Temperamentally, they were extremely unsuited for each other.

"I'm waiting, Brigid." Paul's eyebrows drew down over the bridge of his aquiline nose.

"Oh, do be quiet, Paul. It simply slipped my mind." Brigid's quick retort surprised him with its note of defiance.

Paul gazed at her for one second with an emotion that bordered on shock, but quickly transmuted into patronizing amusement. "Why, Brigid, we're unusually wasp-tongued today. Is something the matter? May I be of assistance?"

He stepped close to her and, firmly grasping her elbows, drew her close to him. His gaze traveled from her head to her toes. She tried to withdraw from his grasp without seeming repulsed, which she most definitely was.

"Brigid!" he said sharply. "You must tell me what this is all about! Tell me everything at once, you silly goose."

She didn't know what to tell him about anything, much less everything. She felt herself withdrawing, not just from him but from her entire life as if it were unreal, taking on the quality of a dream.

Bernard, the butler, cleared his throat peremptorily from the foyer. Paul swiftly released Brigid, stepping away. The old white-haired servant proffered a silver salver to Brigid upon which lay a small white calling card, facedown.

Lips pursed in a moue of distaste, Bernard said,

"You have a visitor, Mam'selle. A gentleman." He spoke the word as if he found the taste and texture of it extremely repugnant. "He awaits you in the garden."

Brigid glanced through the glass-paneled door and saw the figure of a man pacing impatiently back and forth between the rose bed and grape arbor. She couldn't understand why she hadn't seen him when she walked past them just moments before. His face was in shadow, but the sun glinted from the silver knob and ferrule of his cane.

Cane...

Brigid picked up the card and read the handwritten inscription on the obverse side. In flowing cursive script she read, "I'm waiting for you. Come back to me, *anam-chara.*"

Turning away from Paul, Brigid hurried toward the door. He called after her, a strident, angry question. "Who is this so-called gentleman? I demand you tell me his name immediately!"

She paid him no heed, turning the brass door handles and stepping out into a white antiseptic world.

Instead of the perfume of flowers, she smelled the scent of sterilizing fluids, of starched and laundered sheets. Instead of the sun, she saw neon strips shedding an artificial glow. She felt a light, warm pressure on her right hand. Everything was fuzzy, blurred around the edges so she blinked them into focus.

Kane sat beside her in a chair, head bowed, eyes closed as if he were sleeping. He looked exhausted to the point of being ill, his face pale and drawn tight over the facial bones, his hair in disarray. Her hand was nestled in his palm.

Brigid stirred, clearing a throat dry as dust, trying

to move her tongue, which felt like a shriveled strip of shoe leather. Kane's head snapped up, eyes widening. They were weary eyes, worried eyes, red-netted and wet. He leaned over her urgently, tightening his grip on her hand. "Brigid?"

She noted absently how he addressed her by her first name, not as Baptiste. With effort, she raised her left hand and ran her fingers through his tousled hair.

In a strained whisper so faint she barely heard herself, Brigid said, "I got your message."

Kane regarded her inscrutably for a long moment, then nodded as if he understood completely. Brigid knew he did.

# James Axler

# OUTLANDERS®

# DOOM DYNASTY

Kane, once a keeper of law and order in the new America, is part of the driving machine to return power to the true inheritors of the earth. California is the opening salvo in one baron's savage quest for immortality—and a fateful act of defiance against earth's dangerous oppressors. Yet their sanctity is grimly uncertain as an unseen force arrives for a final confrontation with those who seek to rule, or reclaim, planet Earth.